HAWKMISTRESS!

"Sunstar, too, seemed flooded with the restlessness of the four moons and their light . . . now she was deep in rapport with the stallion . . . this was not new to her, she had somehow sensed this before in bygone summers, but never with the full strength of her awakened laran, her suddenly wakeful body . . . the scent of the grass, the flooding of life through her veins till she was all one great aching tension . . . sweet scents with a tang of what seemed to her shared and doubled senses a tang of musk and summer flowers and something she did not even recognize, so deeply was it part of herself, profoundly sexual, sweeping away barriers of thought and understanding . . . at one and the same time she was with the great stallion, and she was Romilly. . . ."

HAWKMISTRESS!

Marion Zimmer Bradley

ARROW BOOKS

ACKNOWLEDGEMENTS

The soldier's drinking song in Part III was suggested by the *Ballad of Arilinn Tower*, a "filk song" written by Bettina Helms and copyright 1979. The song *Aldones Bless the Human Elbow* was suggested by a folk song by that most prolific of authors, *Anonymous;* with a bow to the Berkeley-based folk-song trio OAK, ASH AND THORN and their manager Sharon Green.

Although *Hawkmistress!*, like most of the Darkover novels, is complete in itself, requiring no knowledge of the other books in the series, those who follow the chronicles of Darkover may wish to know that it comes during the time of the Hundred Kingdoms, between *Stormqueen* and *Two to Conquer*.

—M.Z.B.

Book One:

FALCONSWARD,
in the Kilghard Hills

CHAPTER ONE

Romilly was so weary that she could hardly stand on her feet.

It was dark in the mews, with no light but a carefully shielded lantern hanging from one rafter; but the eyes of the hawk were as bright, as untamed and filled with rage as ever. No, Romilly reminded herself; not rage alone, but terror.

She is afraid. She does not hate me; she is only afraid.

She could feel it all inside herself, that terror which pounded behind the rage, until she hardly knew which was herself—weary, her eyes burning, ready to fall into the dirty straw in an exhausted heap—and what was flooding into her mind from the brain of the hawk; hatred, fear, a wild frenzy of hunger for blood and for freedom.

Even as Romilly pulled the small sharp knife from her belt, and carefully cut a piece from the carcass placed conveniently near, she was shaking with the effort not to strike out, to pull away in a frenzy from the strap that held her—*no, not her, held the hawk*—to the falcon-block; *merciless leathers, cutting her feet*—

The hawk bated, wings flapping and thrashing, and Romilly jerked, with a convulsive reflex action, and the strip of raw meat fell into the straw. Romilly felt the struggle inside herself, the fury and frenzy of terror, as if the leather lines

5

holding the big bird to the block were tying her too, cutting into her feet in agony . . . she tried to bend, to search for the meat calmly, but the emotions of the hawk, flooding into her mind, were too much for her. She flung her hands over her eyes and moaned aloud, letting it all become part of her, the crashing frenzy of wings, beating, beating . . . once, the first time this had happened to her, more than a year ago, she had run out of the mews in panic, running and running until she stumbled and skidded and fell, a hand's-breadth from the edges of the crags that tumbled down from Castle Falconsward to the very rocks of the Kadarin far below.

She must not let it go so deep into her mind, she must remember that she was human, was Romilly MacAran . . . she forced her breathing back to calm, remembering the words of the young *leronis* who had talked with her, briefly and in secret, before returning to Tramontana Tower.

You have a rare gift, child—one of the rarest of the gifts called laran. *I do not know why your father is so bitter, why he will not let you and your sister and brothers be tested and trained to the use of these gifts—surely he must know that an untrained telepath is a menace to herself and to everyone around her; he himself has the gift in full measure!*

Romilly knew; and she suspected the *leronis* knew, too, but out of loyalty to her father she would not speak of it outside the family, and the *leronis* was a stranger, after all; The MacAran had given her hospitality, as with any guest, but had coldly refused the purpose of the woman's visit, to test the children of Falconsward for *laran* gifts.

"You are my guest, *Domna* Marelie, but I have lost one son to the accursed Towers which blight our land and lure the sons of honest men—aye, and their daughters too—from home and family loyalties! You may shelter beneath this roof while the storm lasts, and have all that belongs to a guest in honor; but keep your prying hands from the minds of my children!"

Lost one son to the accursed Towers, Romilly thought, remembering her brother Ruyven who had fled to Neskaya Tower, across the Kadarin, four years ago. *And like to lose another, for even I can see that Darren is more fit for the Tower or the monastery of Nevarsin, than for the Heirship to Falconsward.* Darren would have been still in Nevarsin, as custom demanded of a nobleman's son in the hill country, and had wished to remain; but, obedient to their father's will, returned to his duties as the Heir.

How could Ruyven desert his brother that way? Darren

cannot be Heir to Falconsward without his brother at his side. There was less than a year between the brothers, and they had always clung together as if they were twin-born; but they had gone together to Nevarsin, and only Darren had returned; Ruyven, he told their father, had gone to the Tower. Ruyven had sent a message, which only their father had read; but then he had flung it into the midden and from that moment he had never spoken Ruyven's name, and forbidden any other to speak it.

"I have but two sons," he said, his face like stone. "And one is in the monastery and the other at his mother's knee."

The *leronis* Marelie had frowned as she remembered, and said to Romilly, "I did my best, child, but he would not hear of it; so you must do the best you can to master your gift, or it will master you. And I can help you but little in what time I have; and I am sure that if he knew I had spoken to you like this, he would not shelter me this night. But I dare not leave you without some protection when your *laran* wakens. You are alone with it, and it will not be easy to master it alone, but it is not impossible, for I know of a few who have done it, your brother among them."

"You know my brother!" Romilly whispered.

"I know him, child—who, think you, sent me here to speak with you? You must not think he deserted you without cause," Marelie added gently, as Romilly's lips tightened, "He loves you well; he loves your father, too. But a cagebird cannot be a falcon, and a falcon cannot be a *kyorebni*. To return hither, to live his life without full use of his *laran*—that would be death for him, Romilly; can you understand? It would be like being made deaf and blind, without the company of his own kind."

"But what can this *laran* be, that he would forsake us all for it?" Romilly had cried, and Marelie had only looked sad.

"You will know that when your own *laran* wakens, my child."

And Romilly had cried out, "I hate *laran*! And I hate the Towers! They stole Ruyven from us!" and she had turned away, refusing to speak again to Marelie; and the *leronis* had sighed and said, "I cannot fault you for loyalty to your father, my child," and gone away to the room assigned to her, and departed the next morning, without further speech with Romilly.

That had been two years ago, and Romilly had tried to put it from her mind; but in this last year she had begun to realize that she had the Gift of the MacArans in fullest

7

measure—that strangeness in her mind which could enter into the mind of hawk, or hound, or horse, or any animal, and had begun to wish that she could have spoken with the *leronis* about it. . . .

But that was not even to be thought about. *I may have laran*, she told herself again and again, *but never would I abandon home and family for something of that sort!*

So she had struggled to master it alone; and now she forced herself to be calm, to breathe quietly, and felt the calming effect of the breathing composing her mind as well and even soothing, a little, the raging fury of the hawk; the chained bird was motionless, and the waiting girl knew that she was Romilly again, not a chained thing struggling in a frenzy to be free of the biting jesses. . . .

Slowly she picked that one bit of information out of the madness of fear and frenzy. *The jesses are too tight. They hurt her.* She bent, trying to send out soothing waves of calm all around her, into the mind of the hawk—*but she is too mad with hunger and terror to understand, or she would be quiet and know I mean her no harm.* She bent and tugged at the slitted straps which were wound about the hawk's legs. At the very back of her mind, carefully blanked out behind the soothing thoughts she was trying to send out to the hawk, Romilly's own fear struggled against what she was doing—once she had seen a young hawker lose an eye by getting too close to a frightened bird's beak—but she commanded the fear to be quiet and not interfere with what she had to do—if the hawk was in pain, the frenzy and fear would be worse, too.

She fumbled one-handed in the semidarkness, and blessed the persevering practice which had taught her all the falconer's knots, blindfolded and one-handed; old Davin had emphasized that, again and again, *most of the time you will be in a dark mews, and one hand will be busy about your hawk.* And so, hour after hour, she had tightened and loosened, tied and untied these same knots on twig after twig before ever she was let near the thin legs of any bird. The leather was damp with the sweat of her fingers, but she managed to loosen it slightly—not too much or the bird would be out of the jesses and would fly free, perhaps breaking her wings inside the walls of the mews, but loose enough so that it was no longer cutting into the leathery skin of the upper leg. Then she bent again and fumbled in the straw for the strip of meat, brushing the dirt from it. She knew it did not matter too much—birds, she knew, had to swallow dirt and stones to grind up their food inside their crops—but the dirty

8

bits of straw clinging to the meat revolted her and she picked them fastidiously free and, once again, held out her gloved hand to the hawk on the block. Would the bird ever feed from her hand? Well, she must simply stay here until hunger overcame fear and the bird took the meat, or they would lose this hawk, too. And Romilly had resolved this would not happen.

She was glad, now, that she had let the other bird go. At first she had it in her mind, when she had found old Davin tossing and moaning with the summer fever, that she could save both of the hawks he had taken three days before. He had told her to let them both go, or they would starve, for they would not yet take food from any human hand. When he had captured them, he had promised Romilly that she should have the training of one of them while he was busied with the other. But then the fever had come to Falconsward, and when he had taken the sickness, he had told her to release them both—there would be other seasons, other hawks.

But they were valuable birds, the finest *verrin* hawks he had taken for many seasons. Loosing the larger of the two, Romilly had known Davin was right. A hawk like this was all but priceless—King Carolin in Carcosa has no finer birds, Davin had said, and he should know; Romilly's grandfather had been hawkmaster to the exiled King Carolin before the rebellion which had sent Carolin into the Hellers and probably to death, and the usurper Rakhal had sent most of Carolin's men to their own estates, surrounding himself with men he could trust.

It had been his own loss; Romilly's grandfather was known from the Kadarin to the Sea of Dalereuth as the finest man with hawks in the Kilghard Hills, and he had taught all his arts to Mikhail, now The MacAran, and to his commoner cousin Davin Hawkmaster. *Verrin* hawks, taken full-grown in the wild, were more stubborn than hatchlings reared to handling; a bird caught wild might let itself starve before it would take food from the hand, and better it should fly free to hatch others of the same fine breed, than die of fear and hunger in the mews, untamed.

So Romilly, with regret, had taken the larger of the birds from the mews, and slipped the jesses from the leathery skin of the leg; and, behind the stables, had climbed to a high rock and let her fly free. Her eyes had blurred with tears as she watched the falcon climb out of sight, and deep within her, something had flown with the hawk, in the wild ecstasy of rising, spiraling, free, *free* . . . for an instant Romilly had seen the dizzying panorama of Castle Falconsward lying below, deep ravines filled to the brim with forest, and far away a white shape, glimmering, that she knew to be Hali Tower on the shores of the Lake . . . *was her brother there, even now?* . . . and then she was alone again, shivering with the cold on the high rock, and her eyes were dazzled from staring into the light, and the hawk was gone.

She had returned to the mews, and her hand was already outstretched to take the other one and free it as well, but then the hawk's eyes had met her own for a moment, and there had been an instant when she knew, a strong and dizzying knowledge within her, *I can tame this one, I need not let her go, I can master her.*

The fever which had come to the castle and struck down Davin was almost her friend. On any ordinary day, Romilly would have had duties and lessons; but the governess she shared with her younger sister Mallina had a touch of the fever, too, and was shivering beside the fire in the schoolroom, having given Romilly permission to go to the stables and ride, or take her lesson-book or her needlework to the conservatory high in the castle, and study there among the leaves and flowers—the light still hurt *Domna* Calinda's eyes. Old Gwennis, who had been Romilly's nurse when she and her sister were little children, was busy with Mallina, who had a touch of fever, though she was not dangerously ill. And the Lady Luciella, their stepmother, would not stir from the side of nine-year-old Rael, for he had the fever in its most dangerous form, the debilitating sweats and inability to swallow.

So Romilly had promised herself a delicious day of freedom in stables and hawk-house—was *Domna* Calinda really enough of a fool to think she would spend a day free of lessons over her stupid lesson-book or needlework? But she had found Davin, too, sick of the fever, and he had welcomed her coming—his apprentice was not yet skilled enough to go near the untrained birds, though he was good enough to feed the others and clean the mews—and so he had ordered Romilly to release them both. And she had started to obey—

But this hawk was *hers!* Never mind that it sat on its block, angry and sullen, red eyes veiled with rage and terror, bating wildly at the slightest movement near her, the wings exploding in the wild frenzy of flapping and thrashing; it was hers, and soon or late, it would know of the bond between them.

But she had known it would be neither quick nor easy. She had reared eyasses—young birds hatched in the mews or captured still helpless, accustomed before they were feathered to feed from a hand or glove. But this hawk had learned to fly, to hunt and feed itself in the wild; they were better hunters than hawks reared in captivity, but harder to tame; two out of five such birds, more or less, would let themselves die of hunger before they would feed. The thought that this could happen to *her* hawk was a dread Romilly refused to face. Somehow, she would, she *must* bridge the gulf between them.

The falcon bated again, thrashing furious wings, and Romilly struggled to maintain the sense of *herself*, not merging into the terror and fury of the angry bird, at the same time trying to send out waves of calm. *I will not hurt you, lovely one. See, here is food.* But it ignored the signal, flapping angrily, and Romilly struggled hard not to shrink back in terror, not to be overcome with the flooding, surging waves of rage and terror she could feel radiating from the chained bird.

Surely, this time, the beating wings had flapped into quiet sooner than before? The falcon was tiring. Was it growing weaker, would it fight its way down into death and exhaustion before it was ready to surrender and feed from the gauntlet? Romilly had lost track of time, but as the hawk quieted and her brain cleared, so that she knew again that she was Romilly and not the frenzied bird, her breathing quieted again and she let the gauntlet slip for a moment from her hand. Her wrist and shoulder felt as if they were going to drop off, but she was not sure whether it was because the gauntlet was too heavy for her, (she had spent hours holding it at arm's length, enduring the pain of cramped muscles and tension, to accustom herself to its weight) or whether it had something to do with the frenzied beating of her wings . . . no. No, she must remember which was herself, which the hawk. She leaned back against the rough wall behind her, half-closing her eyes. She was almost asleep on her feet. But she must not sleep, nor move.

You don't leave a hawk at this stage, Davin had told her. Not for a moment. She remembered asking, when she was small, not even to eat? And he had snorted, "If it comes to that, you can go without food and water longer than a hawk can; if you can't out-wait a hawk you're taming, you have no business around one."

But he had been speaking of himself. It had not occurred to him, then, that a girl could tame a hawk or wish to. He had indulged her wish to learn all the arts of the falconer—after all, the birds might one day be hers, even though she had two older brothers; it would not be the first time Falcon-

11

sward had passed down through the female line, from a strong husband to the woman heir. Nor was it unknown for a woman to ride out, with a docile and well-trained bird; even Romilly's stepmother had been known to ride forth, a delicately trained bird, no larger than a pigeon, adorning her wrist like a rare jewel. Although Luciella would never have touched one of the *verrin* hawks, and the thought that her stepdaughter would wish to do so had never entered her mind.

But why not? Romilly asked herself in a rage. *I was born with the MacAran Gift; the laran which would give me mastery over hawk or horse or hound. Not laran, I will never admit that I have that evil curse of the Hastur-kinfolk; but the ancient Gift of the MacArans . . . I have a right to that, it is not laran, not really. . . . I may be a woman, but I am as much a MacAran as my brothers!*

Again she stepped toward the hawk, the meat extended on the gauntlet, but the hawk thrust up its head and the beady eyes stared coldly at Romilly; it moved away, with a little hop, as far away as the dimensions of the block allowed. She could sense that the jesses were no longer giving it pain. She murmured small sounds of reassurance, and her own hunger came surging up inside her. She should have brought some food in her pocket for herself, she had seen Davin, often enough, thrust cold meats and bread into his pouch so that he could munch on something while he waited out the long stay with a hawk. If only she could sneak away for a moment to the kitchen or pantry—and to the privy, too; her bladder ached with tension. Her father or brothers could have stepped away, turned aside for a moment, undone breeches and relieved themselves against the wall, but Romilly, though she contemplated it for a moment, would have had too many strings and fastenings to undo, even though she was wearing a pair of Ruyven's old breeches. But she sighed, staying where she was.

If you can't wait out a hawk, Davin had said, *you have no business around one.* That was the only real disadvantage she could think of for a girl, around the stables, and this was the first time it had been any real disadvantage for her.

You're hungry too, she said silently to the hawk, *come on, here's food, just because I'm hungry doesn't mean you can't eat, you stubborn thing, you!* But the hawk made no move to touch the food. It moved a little, and for a moment Romilly feared it would explode into another of those wild bursts of

12

bating. But it stayed still, and after a moment she relaxed into the motionless quiet of her vigil.

When my brothers were my age, it was taken for granted—a MacAran son should train his own hound, his own horse, his own hawk. Even Rael, he is only nine, but already Father insists he shall teach his dogs manners. When she had been younger—before Ruyven had left them, before Darren was sent to Nevarsin—her father had been proud to let Romilly work with horses and hounds.

He used to say; Romilly's a MacAran, she has the Gift; there's no horse she can't ride, no dog she can't make friends with, the very bitches come and whelp in her lap. He was proud of me. He used to tell Ruyven and Darren that I would be a better MacAran than either of them, tell them to watch my way with a horse.

But now—now it makes him angry.

Since Ruyven had gone, Romilly had been sternly turned over to her stepmother, expected to stay indoors, to "behave like a lady." She was now almost fifteen; her younger sister Mallina had already begun dressing her hair with a woman's butterfly-clasp, Mallina was content to sit and learn embroidery stitches, to ride decorously in a lady's saddle, to play with little stupid lap-dogs instead of the sensible herding-dogs and working-dogs around the pastures and stables. Mallina had grown into a fool, and the dreadful thing was that their father preferred her as a fool and wished audibly that Romilly would emulate her.

Never. I'd rather be dead than stay inside the house all the time and stitch like a lady. Mallina used to ride well, and now she's like Luciella, soft and flabby, she startles away when a horse moves its head near her, she couldn't ride for half an hour at a good gallop without falling off gasping like a fish in a tree, and now, like Luciella, she simpers and twitters, and the worst thing is, Father likes them that way!

There was a little stir at the far end of the hawk-house, and one of the eyasses there screamed, the wild screaming sound of an untrained fledgling that scents food. The sound sent Romilly's hawk into a wild explosion of bating, and Romilly, one with the mad flapping of wings, the fierce hunger gripping like claws in her belly, knew that the hawkmaster's boy had come into the hawk-house to feed the other birds. He went from one to another, slowly, muttering to them, and Romilly knew it was near sunset; she had been there since mid-morning. He finished his work and raised his head to see her.

13

"Mistress Romilly! What are you doing here, *damisela?*"

At his voice the hawk bated again, and Romilly felt again the dreadful ache, as if her hands and arms would drop off into the straw. She struggled to keep herself free of frenzy, fear, anger, blood-lust—*blood bursting forth, exploding into her mouth under tearing beak and talons . . .* and forced herself to the low tone that would not further terrify the frenzied bird.

"I am manning this hawk. Go away, Ker, your work is finished and you will frighten her."

"But I heard Davin say the hawk's to be released, and The MacAran's in a rage about it," Ker mumbled. "He didna' want to lose the *verrin* birds, and he's threatened Davin wi' being turned off, old man that he is, if he loses them—"

"Well, Father's not going to lose this one, unless you frighten her out of her senses," Romilly said crisply, "Go away, Ker, before she bates again—" for she could feel the trembling build in the bird's body and mind, she felt if that flapping frenzy exploded again she would collapse with exhaustion, scream herself in fury and frustration. It made her voice sharp. "Go away!"

Her own agitation communicated itself to the bird; it burst into the frenzied flapping of wings again, surges of hatred and terror coming and going, threatening to drown all her own awareness and identity. She fought it, silently, trying to cling to calm, to send out calm to the terrified bird. *There, there, lovely one, no one shall harm you, see, here is food* . . . and when she knew who or where she was again, the boy had gone.

He had left the door open, and there was a draught of cold air from the evening mists; and soon the night's rain or snow would start to fall—damn the wretch! She stole for a few seconds on tiptoe away from the block to draw the door closed—it would avail her nothing to tame this hawk if all the birds died with the cold! Once away from the bird's side, she began to wonder what she was doing here and why. How was it that she thought that she, a young woman, could accomplish something at which even the skilled Davin failed two out of five times? She should have told the boy that the bird was at the end of exhaustion, have him come and take over . . . she had seen what he could do with a wild, raging, exhausted stallion from the wild herds of the ravines and outer hills. An hour, maybe two, with her father at one end of a lunge line and the stallion at the other, and he would come to the bridle, lower his big head and rub it against The

14

MacAran's chest . . . surely he could still save this bird, too. She was weary and cold and exhausted, she longed for the old days when she could climb into her father's lap and tell him all her troubles. . . .

Then the voice struck through to her, angry and cold—but there was tenderness in it too; the voice of Mikhail, lord of Falconsward, The MacAran.

"Romilly!" he said, shocked but compassionate, "Daughter, what do you think you are doing? This is no task for a maiden, manning a *verrin* hawk! I gave orders to that wretch Davin and he lies slack in bed while one hawk is mishandled by a child, and the other, I doubt not, starved on its block. . . ."

Romilly could hardly speak through the tears threatening to surge up inside her and break her control.

"The other hawk flies free to hatch more of her kind," she said, "I released her myself at dawn. And this one has not been mishandled, Father—"

At the words and movement the hawk bated again, more fiercely than before, and Romilly gasped, struggling to keep her sense of self against the fury of thrashing wings, the hunger, the blood-lust, the frenzy to break free, fly free, dash itself to death against the dark enclosing beams . . . but it subsided, and Romilly, crooning to the bird, sensed another mind touching hers, sending out waves of calm . . . *so that's how Father does it,* she thought with a corner of her mind, brushed a dripping lock of hair out of her eyes and stepped toward the hawk again.

Here is food, come and eat . . . nausea rushed through her stomach at the smell and sight of the dead meat on the gauntlet. *Yes, hawks feed on fresh-caught food, they must be tamed by starvation into feeding on carrion. . . .*

Abruptly the touching of minds, girl, man, hawk, broke, and Mikhail of MacAran said harshly, "Romilly, what am I to do with you, girl? You have no business here in the hawk-house; it is no work for a lady." His voice softened. "No doubt Davin put you up to this; and I'll deal with him. Leave the meat and go, Romilly. Sometimes a hawk will feed from an empty block when she's hungry enough, and if she does we can keep her; if not, Davin can release her tomorrow, or that boy of his can do something for once to earn his porridge! It's too late tonight for her to fly. She won't die, and if she does, it won't be the first hawk we've lost. Go in, Romilly, get a bath and go to your bed. Leave the hawks to the hawkmaster and his boy—that's why they're here, love, my

15

little girl doesn't need to do this. Go in the house, Romi, child."

She swallowed hard, feeling tears break through.

"Father, please," she begged, "I'm sure I can tame her. Let me stay, I beg of you."

"Zandru's hells," the MacAran swore, "If but one of your brothers had your strength and skill, girl! But I'll not have it said that my daughters must work in mews and stable! Get you inside, Romilly, and not another word from you!"

His face was angry and implacable; the hawk bated again, at his anger, and Romilly felt it surging through her too, an explosion of fury, frustration, anger, terror. She dropped the gauntlet and ran, sobbing with rage, and behind her, her father strode out of the mews and locked it behind him.

Romilly went to her room, where she emptied her aching bladder, ate a little bread and honey and drank a cup of milk from the tray one of the serving-women brought her; but her mind was still with the chained, suffering, starving hawk in the mews.

It would not eat, and soon it would die. It had begun, just a little, to trust Romilly . . . surely, the last two or three times it had bated, before her father had disturbed them, it had quieted sooner, feeling her soothing touch. But now it would surely die.

Romilly began to draw off her shoes. The MacAran was not to be disobeyed, certainly not by his daughter. Even Ruyven, six feet tall and almost a man, had never dared open disobedience until the final break. Romilly, Darren, Mallina—all of them obeyed his word and seldom dared even a look of defiance; only the youngest, spoilt little Rael, would sometimes tease and wheedle and coax in the face of his father's edicts.

In the next room, past the glass doors separating their chambers, Mallina already slept in her cot, her pale-red hair and lacy nightgown pale against the pillow. Lady Calinda had long gone to her bed, and old Gwennis drowsed in a chair beside the sleeping Mallina; and although Romilly was not glad of her sister's illness, she was glad that the old nurse was busy about her sister; if she had seen Romilly in her current state—ruefully, Romilly surveyed her filthy and sweat-soaked clothes—there would have been an argument, a lecture, trouble.

She was exhausted, and thought longingly of clean clothes, a bath, her own soft bed. She had surely done all she could

16

to save the hawk. Perhaps she should abandon the effort.
It might feed from the block; but once it had done that,
though it would not die, it could never be tamed enough to
feed from the hawker's hand or gauntlet, and must be released. Well, let it go then. And if, in its state of exhaustion
and terror, it would not feed from the block, and died . . .
well, hawks had died before this at Falconsward.

*But never one with whom I had gone so deeply into rap-
port. . . .*

And once again, as if she were still standing, exhausted
and tense, in the hawk-house, she felt that furious frenzy
building up again . . . even safely tied to the block, the hawk
in her terrified threshing could break her wings . . . never to
fly again, to sit dumb and broken on a perch, or to die . . .
*like me inside a house, wearing women's clothes and stitching
at foolish embroideries. . . .*

And then she knew she would not let it happen that way.

Her father, she thought with detachment, would be very
angry. This time he might even give her the beating he had
threatened last time she disobeyed him. He had never, yet,
laid a hand on her; her governess had spanked her a time or
two when she was very small, but mostly she had been pun-
ished with confinement, with being forbidden to ride, with
harsh words or loss of some promised treat or outing.

This time he will surely beat me, she thought, and the un-
fairness surged within her; *I will be beaten because I cannot
resign myself to let the poor thing die or thrash itself to death
in terror. . . .*

*Well, I shall be beaten then. No one ever died of a beating,
I suppose.* Romilly knew already that she was going to defy
her father. She shrank from the thought of his rage, even
more than from the imagined blows, but she knew she would
never be able to face herself again if she sat quietly in her
chamber and let the hawk die.

She should have released them both yesterday at dawn, as
Davin said. Perhaps she deserved a beating for that disobedience; but having begun, it would be too cruel to stop now. At
least, Romilly thought, she could understand why she was
being beaten; the hawk would not understand the reasons for
the long ordeal till it was finished. Her father himself had always told her that a good animal handler never began
anything, with hawk or hound or horse, that he could not finish; it was not fair to a dumb creature who knew nothing of
reason.

If, he had told them once, *you break faith with a human*

being for some reason which seems good to you, you can at least explain to him or her. But if you break faith with a dumb creature, you have hurt that creature in a way which is unforgivable, because you can never make it understand. Never in her life had Romilly heard her father speak of faith in any religion, or speak of any God except in a curse; but that time, even as he spoke, she had sensed the depths of his belief and knew that he spoke from the very depths of his being. She was disobeying him, yes; but in a deeper sense she was doing what he had taught her to think right; and so, even if he should beat her for it, he would one day know that what she had done was both right and necessary.

Romilly took another swallow of water—she could face hunger, if she must, but thirst was the real torture; Davin usually kept a water pail within reach when he was working a hawk, and Romilly had forgotten to set a pail and dipper within reach. Then she slipped quietly out of the room. With luck, the hawk would "break" before dawn—would feed from the gauntlet, and sleep. This interruption might lose the hawk, she knew—if it did not soon feed, it would die—but at least she would know that she, who had confined it there, had not been the one to break faith and abandon it to death.

She had already left the chamber when she turned and went back for her flint-and-steel lighter; doubtless, her father or the hawkmaster's boy would have extinguished the lantern and she would have to relight it. Gwennis, in the room beyond the glass doors, stirred and yawned, and Romilly froze, but the nurse only bent to feel Mallina's forehead to see if her fever had broken, sighed, and settled back in her chair without a glance in Romilly's direction.

On noiseless feet, she crept down the stairs.

Even the dogs were sleeping. Two of the great grey-brown hounds called Rousers were asleep right across the doorway; they were not fierce dogs, and would not bite or attack even an intruder unless he offered to hurt them, but they were noisy creatures, and in their friendly, noisy barking, their function was to rouse the household against intruder or friend. But Romilly had known both dogs since they were whelped, had given them their first solid tidbits when they left off sucking their dam; she shoved them slightly away from the door, and the dogs, feeling a familiar and beloved hand, only snuffled a little in their sleep and let her pass.

The light in the hawk-house had indeed been extinguished. As she stepped across the doorsill she thought of an old ballad her own mother had sung in her childhood, of how, at

18

night, the birds talked among themselves when no human creature was near. She found she was walking tip-toe, half expecting to overhear what they might be saying. But the birds in the mews where the tame ones were kept were only hunched forms on the blocks, fast asleep, and she felt from them only a confused silence.

I wonder if they are telepathic among themselves, she wondered, if they are aware of one another's fear or pain? Even the *leronis* had not been able to tell her this. Now, she supposed, most of the birds, at least, were head-blind, without telepathic awareness or *laran*, or they would all be awake and restless now; for Romilly could still feel, beating up at her in waves of dread and fury, of hunger and rage, the emotions of the great *verrin* hawk.

She lighted the lamp, with hands that shook. Father had never believed, then, that it would feed from the block; he certainly knew that no hawk would feed in darkness. How could he have done that? Even if he was angry with her, Romilly, he need not have deprived her hawk of its last chance at life.

Now it was all to do again. She saw the dead meat lying on the block; unpecked, untouched. The hawk had not fed. The meat was beginning to smell rancid, and Romilly had to overcome her own revulsion as she handled the dead thing— *ugh, if I were a hawk I wouldn't touch this carrion either.*

The hawk bated again in its frenzy and Romilly stepped closer, crooning, murmuring calm. And after a few seconds the thrashing wings quieted. Could it be that the hawk remembered her? Perhaps the interruption had not wholly wrecked her chances. She slid her hand into the gauntlet, cut a fresh strip of meat from the carcass and held it out to the bird, but again it seemed that the disgust of the dead smell was more sickening and overpowering than it had been.

Was she feeling, then, what the hawk felt? For a moment, in a dizzy wave of sickness, Romilly met the great yellow-green eyes of the bird, and it seemed to her that she was badly balanced on some narrow space without any proper place to stand, unfamiliar leather chafing her ankles, and that some strange and hateful *presence* was there, trying to force her to swallow some revolting filthy mess, absolutely unfit to eat . . . for a split second Romilly was again a child too young to speak, tied into her high chair and her nurse was spooning some horrid nasty stuff down her throat and she could only struggle and scream. . . .

Shaken and sick, she stepped back, letting the dead carcass

19

fall to the floor. Was *that* how the hawk regarded her? She should have let the hawk fly, she could never live with such hatred . . . *do all the animals we master hate us like that? Why, then, a trainer of horses and hounds is more evil than a molester of children . . . and he who takes a hawk from the sky, to chain it on a block, he is no better than a rapist, a violator of women. . . .* But the bating, struggling hawk was off her perch this time, and Romilly moved forward, patiently adjusting the block so that the hawk could find a secure place to stand, until it found its feet and balanced securely again.

Then she stood silent, trying not to trouble the hawk even with breath, while the battle went on inside her mind. Part of her fought with the chained hawk, terror and rage contending for place, but Romilly, in her own struggle for interior calm, filled her mind with the memory of the last time she had hunted with her own favorite falcon . . . soaring upward with it, striking, and something inside her remembered clearly that sudden feeling, which in herself would have been pride and pleasure, as the hawk fed from her glove . . . and she knew it would have been stronger still if she herself had trained the hawk; that pleasure in accomplishment, that sense of sudden union with the bird, would have been deeper still.

And she had shared the delight, inarticulate, impossible to frame in words, but a joy deep and swelling, when her favorite bitch brought her puppies to her; the animal's pleasure at the caress was something like the love she felt for her own father, her joy and pride at his rare praise. And even though she had felt the real pain and fear when a young horse struggled against bridle and saddle, she had shared in the communion and trust between horse and rider, and known it for real love, too; so that she loved to ride breakneck, knowing she could come to no harm while the horse carried her, and she let the horse go at her own pace and pleasure, sharing the delight in the running. . . .

No, she thought, it is not a violation to teach or train an animal, no more than when nurse taught me to eat porridge, even though I thought it nasty at first and wanted nothing but milk; because if she had fed me upon milk and babies' pap after my teeth were grown, I would have been sickly and weak, and needed solid food to grow strong. I had to learn even to eat what was good for me, and to wear clothes even though, no doubt, I would sooner, then, have been wrapped in my blankets like a swaddled baby! And later I had to learn to cut my meat with knife and fork instead of gnawing at it

20

with fingers and teeth as an animal would do. And now I am glad to know all these things.

When the hawk bated again, Romilly did not withdraw from the fear and terror, but let herself share it, whispering half aloud, "Trust me, lovely one, you will fly free again and we will hunt together, you and I, as friends, not as master and slave, I promise you. . . ."

She filled her mind with images of soaring free above the trees in sunlight, trying to open her mind to the memory of the last time she had hunted; seeing the bird come spiraling down with its prey, of tearing apart the freshly killed meat so she could give the bird its share of the kill . . . and again, with an urgency that made her feel sick, she felt the maddening hunger, the hawk's mind-picture of striking, fresh blood flowing into her mouth . . . her own human revulsion, the hawk's hunger, so mingled in her that she hardly knew which was which. Sensing that hunger, she held out the strip of rabbithorn meat, but now the smell revolted her as much as the hawk; she felt that she would vomit.

But you must eat and grow strong, *preciosa*, she sent out the thought again and again, feeling the hawk's hunger, her weakening struggles. *Preciosa; that is your name, that is what I will call you, and I want you to eat and grow strong, Preciosa, so we can hunt together, but first you must trust me and eat . . . I want you to eat because I love you and I want to share this with you, but first you must learn to eat from my hand . . . eat, Preciosa, my lovely one, my darling, my beauty, won't you eat this? I don't want you to die. . . .*

Hours, she felt, must have crawled by while she stood there, tensed into the endless struggle with the weakening hawk. Every time the frenzied bating was weaker, the surges of hunger so intense that Romilly's own body cramped with pain. The hawk's eyes were as bright as ever, as filled with terror, and from those eyes it all flooded into Romilly, too, in growing despair.

The hawk was weakening, surely; if she did not feed soon, after all this struggle, she would die; she had taken no food since she was captured four days ago. Would she die, still fighting?

Maybe her father had been right, maybe no woman had the strength for this. . . .

And then she remembered the moment when she had looked out from the hawk's eyes and she, Romilly MacAran, had not even been a memory, and she had been something other than human. Fear and despair flooded her; she saw her-

21

self ripping off the gauntlet, beaten to take up her needlework, letting walls close round her forever. A prisoner, more a prisoner than the chained hawk, who, at least, would now and then have a chance to fly, and to feel again the soaring ecstasy of flight and freedom. . . .

No. Rather than live like that, prisoner, she too would let herself die. . . .

No; there must be a way, if only I can find it.

She would not surrender, never admit that the hawk had beaten her. She was Romilly MacAran, born with the Mac-Aran Gift, and she was stronger than any hawk. She would not let the hawk die . . . no, it was not "the hawk" any more, it was Preciosa, whom she loved, and she would fight for her life even if she must stand here till they dropped together and died. One more time she reached out, moving fearlessly into the bird-mind, this time aware fully of herself as a shadowy and now familiar torture in Preciosa's mind, and the sickening, rank smell of the meat on the gauntlet . . . for a moment she thought Preciosa would go into another frenzy of bating, but this time the bird bent its head toward the meat on the glove.

Romilly held her breath. *Yes, yes, eat and grow stronger* . . . and then Romilly was overcome by sickness, feeling that she would vomit where she stood from the sickening rotten smell of the meat.

Now she wants to eat, she would trust me, but she cannot eat this now; perhaps if she had taken it before she was so weak, but not now . . . she is no carrion feeder. . . .

Romilly was overcome by despair. She had brought the freshest food she could find in the kitchens, but now it was not fresh enough; the hawk was beginning to trust her, might perhaps have taken food from her gauntlet, if she had brought something she could actually have managed to swallow without sickness . . . a rat scurried in the straw, and she discovered that she was looking out from the bird's eyes with real hunger at the little animal. . . .

Dawn was near. In the garden outside she heard the chirp of a sleepy wraithbird, and from the cotes the half-wakened chirp of the caged pigeons who were sometimes roasted for special guests or for the sick. Even before the thought was clear in her mind she was moving, and at the back of her thoughts she heard herself say, *the fowl-keeper will be very angry with me, I am not allowed to touch the pigeons without leave*, but the hunger flooding through her mind, the bird-mind, would not be denied. Romilly flung away the piece

22

of dead rabbithorn meat, flinging it on the midden; it would rot there, or some scavenger would find it, or one of the dogs who was less fastidious in feeding. There was a fluttering, flapping stir as she thrust her hand into the pigeon-cote and brought out one, flapping its wings and squawking; its fear filled her with something that was half pain and half excitement, adrenalin running through her body and cramping her legs and buttocks with familiar dread; but Romilly had been farm-bred and was not squeamish; fowl were for the pot in return for safe cotes and lifelong grain. She held the struggling bird for an instant of brief regret between her hands, then fought one-handed to hold it while she got the gauntlet on again. She thrust into the hawk-mind, without words, a swift sharp awareness of hunger and fresh food . . . then, with one decisive movement, wrung the pigeon's neck and thrust the still-warm corpse toward Preciosa.

For an instant, one more time, it seemed that the bird was about to explode into a last frenzy of bating, and Romilly felt the sickness of failure . . . but this time the hawk bent her head and with a thrust so swift that Romilly could not follow it with her eyes, stabbed with the strong beak, so hard that Romilly staggered under the killing thrust. Blood spurted; the hawk pecked one more time and began to eat.

Romilly sobbed aloud through the flooding ecstasy of strength filling her as she felt the bird tear, swallow, tear again at the fresh meat. "Oh, you beauty," she whispered, "You beauty, you precious, you wonder!"

When the hawk had fed . . . she could feel the dulling of hunger, and even her own thirst receded . . . she set it on the block again, and slipped a hood over Preciosa's head. Now it would sleep, and wake remembering where its food came from. She must leave orders that food for this hawk must be very fresh; she would have birds or mice killed freshly for it until Preciosa could hunt for herself. It would not be long. It was an intelligent bird, or it would not have struggled so long; Romilly, still lightly in link with the bird, knew that now Preciosa would recognize her as the source of food, and that one day they would hunt together.

Her arm felt as if it would fall off; she slipped off the heavy gauntlet, and wiped her forehead with a sweaty arm. She could clearly see light outside the hawk-house; she had stood there all night. And as she took conscious note of the light—soon the household would be stirring—she saw her father and Davin standing in the doorway.

"Mistress Romilly! Have you been here all night?" Davin asked, shocked and concerned.

But her father's temples were swollen with rage.

"You wretched girl, I ordered you back to the house! Do you think I am going to let you defy me like this? Come out of there and leave the hawk—"

"The hawk has fed," said Romilly, "I saved her for you. Doesn't that mean anything?" And then all her fury flooded through her again, and like a bating hawk, she exploded. "Beat me if you want to—if it's more important to you that I should act like a lady and let a harmless bird die! If that is being a lady, I hope I shall never be one! I have the *laran*—" in her anger she used the word without thinking, "and I don't think the gods make mistakes; it must mean that I am meant to use it! It isn't my fault that I have the MacAran Gift when my brother doesn't, but it was given to me so that now I didn't have to stand by and let Preciosa die. . . ." and she stopped, swallowing back sobs that threatened to choke her voice entirely.

"She's right, sir," said old Davin slowly. "She's not the first lady of MacAran to have the Gift, and, be the gods willing, she won't be the last."

The MacAran glared; but he stepped forward, took up a feather, and gently stroked the breast of the drowsing hawk. "A beautiful bird," he said, at last. "What did you call her? Preciosa? A good name, too. You have done well, daughter." It was wrenched out of him, unwilling; then he scowled, and it was like the flood of fury flooding through the hawk.

"Get you gone from here, inside the house, and have a bath and fresh clothes—I will not have you filthy as a stable wench! Go and call your maid, and don't let me see you beyond the house door again!" And as she slipped past him she could feel that blow he started to give her, then held back—he could not bring himself to strike anything, and she *had* saved the life of the hawk. But out of his rage of frustration he shouted after her at the top of his lungs, "You haven't heard the last of this, damn you, Romilly!"

CHAPTER TWO

Romilly stared out the window, her head in her hands. The great red sun was angling downward from noon; two of the small moons stood, pale dayshine reflections, in the sky, and the distant line of the Kilghard Hills lured her mind out there in the sky, with the clouds and the birds flying. A page of finished sums, put aside, lay before her on the wooden desk, and a still-damp page of neatly copied maxims from the *cristoforo* Book of Burdens; but she did not see them, nor did she hear the voice of her governess; Calinda was fussing at Mallina for her badly blotted pages.

This afternoon, when I have done flying Preciosa to the lure, I will have Windracer saddled, and carry Preciosa before me on my saddle, hooded, to accustom her to the horse's smell and motion. I cannot trust her yet to fly free, but it will not be long. . . .

Across the room her brother Rael scuffled his feet noisily, and Calinda rebuked him with a silent shake of her head. Rael, Romilly thought, was dreadfully spoiled now—he had been so dangerously ill, and this was his first day back in the schoolroom. Silence fell over the children, except for the noisy scratching of Mallina's pen, and the almost-noiseless click of Calinda's knotting-pins; she was making a woolly undervest for Rael, and when it was finished, Romilly thought, not without malice, then she would only face the problem of getting Rael to wear it!

Her eyes glazed in a drowse of perfect boredom, Romilly

25

stared out the window, until the quiet was interrupted by a noisy wail from Mallina.

"Curse this pen! It sheds blots like nuts in autumn! Now I have blotted another sheet!"

"Hush, Mallina," said the governess severely. "Romilly, read to your sister the last of the maxims I set you to copy from the Book of Burdens."

Sighing, recalled against her will to the schoolroom, Romilly read sullenly aloud. "A poor worker blames only the tool in his hand."

"It is not the fault of the pen if you cannot write without blots," Calinda reproved, and came to guide the pen in her pupil's hand. "See, hold your hand so—"

"My fingers ache," Mallina grumbled, "Why must I learn to write anyway, spoiling my eyes and making my hands hurt? None of the daughters of High Crags can write, or read either, and they are none the worse for it; they are already betrothed, and it is no loss to them!"

"You should think yourself lucky," said the governess sternly, "Your father does not wish his daughters to grow up in ignorance, able only to sew and spin and embroider, without enough learning even to write 'Apple and nut conserve' on your jars at harvest time! When I was a girl, I had to fight for even so much learning as that! Your father is a man of sense, who knows that his daughters will need learning as much as do his sons! So you will sit there until you have filled another sheet without a single blot. Romilly, let me see your work. Yes, that is very neat. While I check your sums, will you hear your brother read from his book?"

Romilly rose with alacrity, to join Rael at his seat; anything was better than sitting motionless at her desk! Calinda bent to guide Mallina's hand on her pen, and Rael leaned against Romilly's shoulder; she gave the child a surreptitious hug, then dutifully pointed her finger at the first hand-lettered line of the primer. It was very old; she had been taught to read from this same book, and so, she thought, had Ruyven and Darren before her—the book had been made, and sewn, by her own grandmother when her father had first learned to read; and written in the front were the crudely sprawled letters that said *Mikhail MacAran, his own book*. The ink was beginning to fade a little, but it was still perfectly legible.

"The horse is in the stable," Rael spelled out slowly, "The fowl is in the nest. The bird is in the air. The tree is in the wood. The boat is on the water. The nut is on the tree. The boy is in the—" he scowled at the word and guessed. "Barn?"

26

Romilly chuckled softly. "I am sure he wishes he were, as you do," she whispered, "but that's not right, Rael. Look, what is that first letter? Spell it out—"

"The boy is in the kitchen," he read glumly. "The bread is in the—pan?"

"Rael, you're guessing again," she said. "Look at the letters. You know better than that."

"The bread is in the oven."

"That's right. Try the next page, now."

"The cook bakes the bread. The farmer—" he hesitated, moving his lips, scowling at the page. "Gathers?"

"That's right, go on."

"The farmer gathers the nuts. The soldier rides the horse. The groom puts the saddle on the horse. Romy, when can I read something that makes sense?"

Romilly chuckled again. "When you know your letters a bit better," she said. "Let me see your copybook. Yes, your letters are written there, but look, they sprawl all over the line like ducks waddling, when they should march along neatly like soldiers—see where Calinda ruled the line for you?" She put the primer aside. "But I will tell Calinda you know your lesson, shall I?"

"Then perhaps we can go out to the stables," whispered Rael. "Romy, did father beat you for taming the hawk? I heard Mother say he should."

I doubt that not at all, Romilly thought, but the Lady Luciella was Rael's mother and she would not speak evil of her to the child. And Luciella had never been really unkind to her. She said "No, I was not beaten; father said I did well—he would have lost the hawk otherwise, and *verrin* hawks are costly and rare. And this one was near to starving on its block—"

"How did you do it? Can I tame a hawk some day? I would be afraid, they are so fierce—"

But he had raised his voice, and Calinda looked up and frowned at them. "Rael, Romilly, are you minding the lesson?"

"No, *mestra*," said Romilly politely, "he has finished, he read two pages in the primer with only one mistake. May we go now?"

"You know you are not supposed to whisper and chatter when you are working," said the governess, but she looked tired, too. "Rael, bring me your sheet of letters. Oh, this is disgraceful," she said, frowning, "Why, they are all over the

27

page! A big boy like you should write better than this! Sit down, now, and take your pen!"

"I don't want to," Rael sulked, "My head hurts."

"If your head hurts, I shall tell your mother you are not well enough to ride after your lesson," said Calinda, hiding the smile that sprang to her lips, and Rael glumly sat down, curled his fist around the pen and began to print another series of tipsy letters along the line, his tongue just protruding between his teeth, scowling over the page.

"Mallina, go and wash the ink from your fingers. Romilly, bring your embroidery-work, and you may as well bring Mallina's too," said the governess, bending over Rael's desk. Romilly, frowning, went to the cupboard and pulled out her workbasket and her sister's. She was quick enough with her pen, but, she thought angrily, *put a needle in my hand and I might as well have a hoof instead of fingers!*

"I will show you one more time how to do the knot-stitch neatly," said Calinda, taking the grubby, wrinkled linen in her own hands, trying to smooth it, while Romilly pricked her finger threading the needle and yelped like a puppy. "This is a disgrace, Romilly; why, Rael could do better if he tried, I do believe!"

"Then why not let Rael do it?" Romilly scowled.

"For shame, a big girl, almost fifteen, old enough to be married," Calinda said, glancing over Rael's shoulder. "Why, what have you written here?"

Startled by the tone in the woman's voice, Romilly looked over her small brother's shoulder. In uneven printing, he had lettered *I wish my brother Ruyven come home.*

"Well, I do," said Rael, blinking his eyes hard and digging his fists into them.

"Tear it up, quickly," said Calinda, taking the paper and suiting the action to the word. "If your father saw it—you know he has ordered that your brother's name is not to be mentioned in this house!"

"I didn't mention it, I only printed it," said Rael angrily, "and he's *my* brother and I'll talk about him if I want to! Ruyven Ruyven, Ruyven—so *there!*"

"Hush, hush, Rael," said Calinda, "We all—" she broke off, thinking better of what she had begun to say, but Romilly heard it with her new senses, as clearly as if Calinda had said, *We all miss Ruyven.* More gently, Calinda said, "Put your book away, and run along to your riding-lesson, Rael."

Rael slammed his primer into his desk and raced for the door. Romilly watched her brother enviously, scowling at the wrinkled stitchery in her hand. After a minute Calinda sighed and said, "It is hard for a child to understand. Your brother Darren will be home at Midsummer, and I am glad—Rael needs his brother, I think. Here, Romilly, watch my fingers—wrap the thread *so*, three times around the needle, and pull it through—see, you can do it neatly enough when you try."

"A knot-stitch is easy," said Mallina complacently, looking up from her smooth panel of bleached linen, where a brilliant flower bloomed under her needle.

"Aren't you ashamed, Romilly? Why, Mallina has already embroidered a dozen cushion-covers for her marriage-chest, and now she is working on her wedding sheets—"

"Well," said Romilly, driven to the wall, "What do I need of embroidered cushion-covers? A cushion is to sit on, not to show fancy stitching. And I hope, if I have a husband, he will be looking at me, and not the embroidered flowers on our wedding sheets!"

Mallina giggled and blushed, and Calinda said, "Oh, hush, Romilly, what a thing to say!" But she was smiling. "When you have your own house, you will be proud to have beautiful things to adorn it."

I doubt that very much, Romilly thought, but she picked up the stitchery-piece with resignation and thrust the needle through it. Mallina bent over the quilt she was making, delicately appliqued with white starflowers on blue, and began to set tiny stitches into the frame.

Yes, it was pretty, Romilly thought, but why did it matter so much? A plain one would keep her just as warm at night, and so would a saddle-blanket! She would not have minded, if she could have made something sensible, like a riding-cloak, or a hood for a hawk, but this stupid flower-pattern, designed to show off the fancy stitching she hated! Grimly she bent over her work, needle clutched awkwardly in her fist, as the governess looked over the paper of sums she had done that morning.

"You have gone past my teaching in this, Romilly," the governess said at last, "I will speak to *Dom* Mikhail, and ask if the steward can give you lessons in keeping account-books and ciphering. It would be a pity to waste an intelligence as keen as yours."

"Lessons from the steward?" said a voice from the doorway. "Nonsense, *mestra*; Romilly is too old to have lessons from a man, it would be scandalous. And what need has a lady, to keep account-books?" Romilly raised her head from the tangle of threads, to see her stepmother Luciella coming into the room.

"If I could keep my own accounts, foster-mother," Romilly said, "I need never be afraid I would be cheated by a dishonest steward."

Luciella smiled kindly. She was a small plump woman, her hair carefully curled, as meticulously dressed as if she were about to entertain the Queen at a garden-party. She said, "I think we can find you a husband good enough that he will see to all that for you, foster-daughter." She bent to kiss Mallina on the cheek, patted Romilly's head. "Has Rael gone already to his riding-lesson? I hope the sun will not be too strong for him, he is still not entirely recovered." She frowned at the tangled threads and drunken line of colored stitching. "Oh, dear, dear, this will never do! Give me the needle, child, you hold it as if it were a currycomb! Look, hold it like this. See? Now the knot is neat—isn't that easier, when you hold it so?"

Grudgingly, Romilly nodded. *Domna* Luciella had never been anything but kind to her; it was only that she could not imagine why Romilly was not exactly like Mallina, only more so, being older.

"Let me see you make another one, as I showed you," Luciella said. "See, that is much better, my dear. I knew you could do it, you are clever enough with your fingers—your handwriting is much neater than Mallina's, only you will not try. Calinda, I came to ask you to give the children a holiday—Rael has already run off to the stables? Well enough—I only need the girls, I want them to come and be fitted for their new riding-habits; they must be ready when the guests come at Midsummer."

Predictably, Mallina squealed.

"Am I to have a new riding-habit, foster-mother? What color is it? Is it made of velvet like a lady's?"

"No, my dear, yours is made of gabardine, for hard wear and more growing," said Luciella, and Mallina grumbled "I am tired of wearing dresses all clumsy in the seams so they can be let out when I grow half a dozen times, and all faded so everyone can see where they have been let out and the hem let down—"

"You must just hurry and finish growing, then," said Luciella kindly, "There is no sense making a dress to your measure when you will have outgrown it in six months wear, and you have not even a younger sister to pass it on to. You are lucky you are to have a new habit at all, you know," she added smiling, "You should wear Romilly's old ones, but we all know that Romilly gives her riding-clothes such hard wear that after half a year there is nothing at all left of them—they are hardly fit to pass on to the dairy-woman."

"Well, I *ride* a horse," Romilly said, "I don't sit on its back and simper at the stableboy!"

"Bitch," said Mallina, giving her a surreptitious kick on the ankle, "You would, fast enough, if he'd look at you, but nobody ever will—you're like a broom-handle dressed up in a gown!"

"And you're a fat pig," retorted Romilly, "You couldn't wear my cast-off gowns anyway, because you're so fat from all the honey-cakes you gobble whenever you can sneak into the kitchen!"

"Girls! Girls!" Luciella entreated, "Must you always squabble like this? I came to ask a holiday for you—do you want to sit all day in the schoolroom and hem dishtowels instead?"

"No, indeed, foster-mother, forgive me," said Romilly quickly, and Mallina said sullenly, "Am I supposed to let her insult me?"

"No, nor should you insult her in turn," said Luciella, sighing. "Come, come, the sewing-women are waiting for you."

"Do you need me, *vai domna?*" Calinda asked.

"No, go and rest, *mestra*—I am sure you need it, after a morning with my brood. Send the groom first to look for Rael, he must have his new jacket fitted today, but I can wait till he has finished his riding-lesson."

Romilly had been apprehensive, as she followed her stepmother into the room where the sewing-women worked, light and airy with broad windows and green growing plants in the sunny light; not flowers, for Luciella was a practical woman, but growing pots of kitchen herbs and medicinals which smelled sweet in the sun through the glass. Luciella's taste ran heavily to ruffles and flounces, and, from some battles when she was a young girl, Romilly feared that if Luciella had ordered her riding-clothes they would be some disgustingly frilly style. But when she saw the dark-green velvet, cut deftly to accentuate her slenderness, but plainly, with no trim but a single white band at her throat, the whole dress of a green which caught the color of her green eyes and made her coppery hair shine, she flushed with pleasure.

"It is beautiful, foster-mother," she said, standing as still as she could while the sewing-women fitted it with pins to her body, "It is almost too fine for me!"

"Well, you will need a good one, for hawking and hunting

31

when the people from High Crags come for the Midsummer feasting and parties," said Luciella, "It is well to show off what a fine horse-woman you are, though I think you need a horse better suited to a lady than old Windracer. I have spoken to Mikhail about a good horse for you—was there not one you trained yourself?"

Romilly's delighted gasp made her stepmother smile. She had been allowed to help her father in training three of the fine blacks from the Lanart estates, and they were all among the finest horses to grace the stables at Falconsward. If her father agreed that she might have one of *those* horses—she thought with delight and pleasure of racing over the hills on one of the spirited blacks, with Preciosa on her arm, and gave Luciella a spontaneous hug that startled the older woman. "Oh, thank you, thank you, stepmother!"

"It is a pleasure to see you looking so much like a lady," Luciella said, smiling at the pretty picture Romilly made in the green habit. "Take it off now, my dear, so it can be stitched. No, Dara," she added to the sewing-woman who was fitting Mallina's habit over her full young breasts, "Not so tight in the tunic there, it is unseemly for so young a girl."

Mallina sulked, "Why must all my dresses be cut like a child's tunic? I have already more of a woman's figure than Romilly!"

"You certainly have," Romilly said, "If you grow much more in the tits, you can hire out for a wet-nurse." She looked critically at Mallina's swelling body, and the younger girl snarled, "A woman's habit is wasted on you, you could wear a pair of Darren's old britches! You'd rather run around looking like a stableboy, in a man's old leathers, like one of the Sisterhood of the Sword—"

"Come, come," said Luciella peacefully, "Don't make fun of your sister's figure, Romilly, she is growing faster than you, that is all. And you be quiet too, Mallina; Romilly is grown, now, and your father has given strict orders that she is not to ride astride in boots and breeches any more, but is to have a proper lady's habit and a lady's saddle for Midsummer, when the people from High Crags will be coming here for hawking and hunting, and perhaps Aldaran of Scathfell with his sons and daughters, and some of the people from Storn Heights."

Mallina squealed with pleasure—the twin daughters of Scathfell were her closest friends, and during the winter, heavy snowfalls had separated Falconsward from Scathfell or from High Crags. Romilly felt no such pleasure—Jessamy and Jeralda were about her own age, but they were like Mallina, plump and soft, an insult to any horse that carried them, much more concerned with the fit of their riding-habits and the ornaments of saddle and reins than in the well-being of the horses they rode, or their own riding-skill. The oldest son at High Crags was about Ruyven's age and had been his dearest friend; he treated Romilly and even Darren as silly children. And the folk from Storn were all grown, and most of them married some with children.

Well, perhaps she would have a chance to ride with her father, and with Darren who would be home from Nevarsin, and to fly Preciosa; it would not be too bad, even if, while there were guests, she must wear a lady's riding-habit and use a lady's saddle instead of the boots and breeches more suitable for hunting; the guests would only be here for a few days and then she could go back to her sensible boy's clothes for riding; she was willing to dress up properly to meet her parents' guests. She had learned, as a matter of course, to manage proper riding-skirts and a lady's saddle when there were guests, and to please her stepmother.

She was humming when she returned to her room to change her dress for riding; perhaps she would take Rael with her when she went to exercise Preciosa to the lure, the long line whirled around her head with scraps of meat and feathers to train and exercise a hawk. But when she searched behind her door for the old boots and breeches she always wore for riding—they were an ancient pair of Ruyven's— they could not be found.

She clapped her hands to summon the maid who waited on the children, but it was old Gwennis who came.

"What is this, Nurse? Where are my riding-breeches?"

"Your father has given strict orders," Gwennis said, "Lady Luciella made me throw them out—they're hardly fit for the hawkmaster's boy now, those old things. Your new habit's being made, and you can wear your old one till it's ready, my pet." She pointed to the riding-skirt and tunic laid out on Romilly's bed. "Here, my lamb, I'll help you lace it up."

"You threw them out?" Romilly exploded, "How dared you?"

"Oh, come, don't talk like that, my little love, we all have to do what Lady Luciella says, don't we? That habit still fits you fine, even if it's a little tight at the waist—see, I let it out for you yesterday, when Lady Luciella told me."

"I can't ride Windracer in this!" Romilly wadded up the offending skirts and flung them across the room. "He's not

33

used to a lady's saddle, and I hate it, and there aren't guests or anything like that! Get me some riding breeches," she stormed, but Gwennis shook her head sternly.

"I can't do that, lovey, your father's given orders, you're not to ride in breeches any more, and it's about time, you'll be fifteen ten days before Midsummer, and we must think now about getting you married, and what man will want to marry a hoyden who races around in breeches like some camp-follower, or one of those scandalous women of the Sisterhood, with sword and ears pierced? Really, Romy, you should be ashamed. A big girl like you, running off to the hawk-house and staying out all night like that—it's time you were tamed down into a lady! Now put on your riding-skirts, if you want to ride, and let's not have any more of this nonsense."

Romilly stared in horror at her nurse. So this was to be her father's punishment. Worse, far worse than a beating, and she knew that from her father's orders there would be no appeal.

I wish he had beaten me. At least he would have been dealing with me, directly, with Romilly, with a person. But to turn me over to Luciella, to let her make me into her image of a lady. . . .

"It's an insult to a decent horse," Romilly stormed, "I won't do it!"

She aimed a savage kick at the offending habit on the floor.

"Well, then, lovey, you can just stay inside the house like a lady, you don't need to ride," said Gwennis complacently, "You spend too much time in the stables as it is, it's time you stayed more in the house, and left the hawks and horses to your brothers as you should."

Appalled, Romilly swallowed down a lump in her throat, looking from the habit on the floor to her beaming nurse. "I expected this of Luciella," she said, "she hates me, doesn't she? It's the sort of spiteful thing Mallina might do, just because she can't ride a decent horse. But I didn't think you'd join with them against me, Nurse!"

"Come, you mustn't talk like that," Gwennis said, clucking ruefully, "How can you say that about your kind stepmother? I tell you, not many stepmothers with grown daughters are as good to them as Lady Luciella is to you and Mallina, dressing them up in beautiful things when you're both prettier than she is, knowing Darren's to be Lord here and her own son only a younger son, not much better than a *nedestro!* Why, your own mother would have had you out of breeches

34

three years ago, she'd never have let you run around all these years like a hoyden! How can you say that she hates you?"

Romilly looked at the floor, her eyes stinging. It was true; no one could have been kinder to her than Luciella. It would have been easier if Luciella had ever showed her the slightest unkindness. *I could fight against her, if she was cruel to me. What can I do now?*

And Preciosa would be waiting for her; did Gwennis really think she would leave her own hawk to the hawkmaster's boy, or even to Davin himself? Her hands shook with fury as she pulled on the detested habit, threadbare blue gabardine and in spite of Gwennis's alterations, still too tight in the waist, so that the lacings gaped wide over her under-tunic. Better to ride in skirts than not to ride at all, she supposed, but if they thought they had beaten her this easily, they could think again!

Will she even know me in this stupid girl's outfit?

Fuming, she strode toward the stables and hawk-house, tripping once or twice over the annoying skirts, slowing her step perforce to a proper ladylike pace. So Luciella would bribe her with a pretty habit, to soften the blow? Just like a woman, that silly devious trick, not even telling her outright that she must put aside her riding-breeches!

Inside the hawk-house, she went directly to the block, slipping on her old gauntlet and taking Preciosa up on her arm. With her free hand she stroked the hawk's breast with the feather kept for that purpose—the touch of a hand on the hawk's feathers would take the coating from the feathers and damage them. Preciosa sensed her agitation and moved uneasily on her wrist, and Romilly made an effort to calm herself, taking down the hanging lure of feathers and signalling to the boy Ker.

"Have you fresh meat for Preciosa?"

"Yes, *damisela*, I had a pigeon just killed for the table and I kept all the innards for her, they haven't been out of the bird more than ten minutes," Ker said, and she sniffed suspiciously at the fresh meat, then threaded it on to the lure. Preciosa smelled the fresh food and jerked uneasily and fluttered; Romilly spoke soothingly to her, and walked on, kicking the skirt out of her way. She went into the stableyard and loosed the jesses, whirling the lure high over her head; Preciosa flung herself upward, the recoil thrusting Romilly's hand down, and wheeled high into the sky over the stableyard, stooping down swiftly on the lure, striking almost before it hit the ground. Romilly let her feed in peace for a moment before calling her with the little falconer's whistle, which the bird must learn to associate with her food, and slipping the hood over her head again. She handed the lure to Ker and said, "You whirl it; I want to watch her fly."

Obediently the hawkmaster's boy took the lure and began to whirl it over his head; again Romilly loosed the hawk, watched her fly high, and descend to Romilly's whistle to the flying bait. Twice more the maneuver was repeated, then Romilly let the hawk finish her meal in peace, before hooding her and setting her back on the block. She stroked her again and again tenderly with the feather, crooning nonsense words of love to her, feeling the sense of closeness and satisfaction from the fed hawk. She was learning. Soon she would fly free and catch her own prey, and return to the wrist. . . .

"Go and saddle Windracer," she said, glumly adding, "I suppose you must use my sidesaddle."

The groom would not look at her.

"I am sorry, *damisela*—The MacAran gave strict orders. Very angry, he was."

So this, then, was her punishment. More subtle than a beating, and not her father's way—the delicate stitches set by Luciella's hand could be clearly seen in this. She could almost hear in her imagination the words her stepmother must have used; see, a big girl like Romilly, and you let her run about the stables, why are you surprised at anything she might do? But leave her to me, and I will make a lady of her. . . .

Romilly was about to fling at the groom, angrily, to forget it, a sidesaddle was an insult to any self-respecting horse . . . but on her arm Preciosa bated in agitation, and she knew the bird was picking up her own rage—she struggled for calm and said quietly, "Very well, put a lady's saddle on her, then." Anger or no, sidesaddle or no, Preciosa must be habituated to the motion of the horse; and a ride on a lady's saddle was better than no ride at all.

But she thought about it, long and hard, as she rode that day. Appeal to her father would be useless: evidently he had turned responsibility over to Luciella, the new riding-habit had been only a signal showing which way the wind now blew. No doubt, a day would come when she would be forbidden to ride at all—no, for Luciella had told her of his plans to give her a good horse. But she would ride as a lady, decorously because no horse could do anything better than a ladylike trot with a lady's sidesaddle; ride cumbered in skirts, unable even to school her hawk properly; there was no proper room for a hawk as there was on a man's saddle where she could carry the block before her. And soon, no doubt, she would be forbidden the stables and hawk-house except for such ladylike rides as this. And what could she do about it? She was not yet of age—she would be fifteen at Midsummer, and had no recourse except to do as her father and guardians bade her. It seemed that the walls were closing about her.

Why, then, had she been given this *laran*, since it seemed that only a man had the freedom to use it? Romilly could have wept. Why had she not, then, been born a man? She knew the answer that would be given her, if she asked Luciella what she would do with her Gift; it is, the woman would say, so that your sons will have it.

And was she nothing but a vehicle for giving some unknown husband sons? She had often thought she would like to have children—she remembered Rael as a baby, little and cunning and as soft and lovable as an unweaned puppy. But to give up everything, to stay in the house and grow soft and flabby like Luciella, her own life at an end, living only through her children? It was too high a price to pay, even for babies as adorable as that. Furiously, Romilly blinked back tears, knowing that the emotion would come through to hawk and horse, and disciplined herself to quiet.

She must wait. Perhaps, when her father's first anger had cooled, he could be made to see reason. And then she remembered; before Midsummer, Darren would be home, and perhaps he, as her father's sole remaining heir, could intercede for her with her father. She stroked the hawk with its feather to quiet her, and rode back toward Falconsward with a glimmer of hope in her heart.

CHAPTER THREE

Ten days before Midsummer, on Romilly's fifteenth birthday, her brother Darren came home.

It was Rael who saw the riders first, as the family sat at breakfast on the terrace; the weather was so fine that Luciella had given orders for breakfast to be served on that outdoor balcony overlooking the valley of the Kadarin. Rael had taken his second piece of bread and honey to the railing, despite Luciella's gentle reprimand that he should sit down nicely and finish his food, and was hanging over the edge, throwing crumbs of bread at the broad leaves of the ivy that crawled up the sides of the castle toward the high balcony.

"Look, Mother," he called, "there are riders, coming up the path—are they coming here, do you think? Father, do you see?"

The MacAran frowned at the child, raising his cup to his lips. "Hush. Rael, I am talking to your mother—" but Romilly abruptly knew who the riders were.

"It is Darren," she cried, and flew to the railing. "I know his horse—I am going down to meet him!"

"Romilly! Sit down and finish your food," Luciella scolded, but Romilly was already out the door, her braids flapping against her shoulderblades, and flying down the long stairway. Behind her she heard the clattering of Rael's boots, and laughed at the thought of Luciella's disquiet—the peaceful meal had been disrupted for good, this time. She licked her fingers, which were sticky with honey, and went out into the courtyard, Rael behind her; the boy was hanging on the big gates, calling to the yard-men to come and open them.

"It is my brother Darren—he is coming!"

Good-naturedly, the men came and began to tug on the doors, even before the sound of the horses' hooves reached them; Rael was a favorite, spoiled by everyone. He clung to the gates, laughing, as the men shoved them under him, and waved his arm excitedly at the riders.

"It is Darren, and there is someone with him, Romilly, come and see, come and meet him!"

But Romilly hung back a little, suddenly shy, conscious of her hastily-braided, crooked hair, her smeared fingers and mouth, the bread and honey still in her hand; she flung it quickly to the yard-dog and rubbed her kerchief over the sticky smears on her mouth. Why did she feel like this? It was only Darren and some friend he had made at the monastery. Darren slid from his horse and Rael was clambering all over him, hugging him, talking so fast he could hardly be understood. Darren laughed, set Rael down and came to take Romilly into his arms.

"You have grown, sister, you are almost a woman."

"It's her birthday, Darren, what did you bring her?" Rael demanded, and Darren chuckled. He was tall and thin, his red hair clustered in thick curls over his eyes, his face had the indoor pallor of a winter spent among the snows of Nevarsin.

"I had forgotten your birthday, sister—will you forgive me? I will have a gift for you at Midsummer," he said.

"It is gift enough that you have come today, Darren," she said, and pain struck through her; she loved Darren, but Ruyven was the brother to whom she had always been closest, while Mallina and Darren had always shared everything. And Ruyven would not come home, would never come home. Hatred for the Towers who had taken her brother from her surged within her, and she swallowed hard, flicking away angry tears.

"Father and Luciella are at breakfast," she said, "Come up to the terrace, Darren; tell the *coridom* to have your saddle-bags taken to your room." She caught his hand and would have drawn him along, but he turned back to the stranger who had given his horse to the groom.

"First I want you to know my friend," he said, and pulled the young man forward. "Alderic of Castamir; my oldest sister Romilly."

Alderic was even taller than Darren, his hair glinting with

39

faint copper through gold; his eyes were steel-grey, set deep beneath a high forehead. He was shabbily dressed, an odd contrast to the richness of Darren's garments—Darren, as the eldest son of Falconsward, was richly clad in rust-colored velveteen trimmed with dark fur, but the cloak the Castamir youngster wore was threadbare, as if he had had it from his father or even his grandfather, and the mean edging of rabbithorn wool was coming away in places.

So he has made a friend of a youth poorer than himself, no doubt brought him here because his friend had not the means to journey to his home for the holidays. Darren is always kind. She put kind welcome, too, and a trace of condescension, into her voice, as she said, "You are welcome, *dom* Alderic. Come up and join my parents at breakfast, will you not? Garin—" she beckoned to the steward, "Take my brother's bags to his room, and put dom Alderic's things in the red chamber for the moment; unless the Lady Luciella gives other orders, it will be good to have him close to my brother's quarters."

"Yes, come along." Darren linked arms with Romilly, drew Alderic with them up the stairs. "I cannot walk if you hang on me like that, Rael—go ahead of us, do!"

"He has been missing you," Romilly said, "And—" she had started to speak of their other brother, but this was to bring family matters out before a stranger; she and Darren would have time enough for confidences. They reached the terrace, and Darren was enfolded in Mallina's arms, and Romilly was left to present Alderic of Castamir to her father.

The MacAran said with grave courtesy, "You are welcome to our home, lad. A friend of my son has a friend's welcome here. Are you akin to Valdrin Castamir of Highgarth? He and I were in the guard of King Rafael before the king was most foully murdered."

"Only distantly, sir," said Alderic. "Knew you not that Lord Valdrin was dead, and his castle burnt about his ears with *clingfire* because he sheltered Carolin in his road to exile?"

The MacAran swallowed visibly. "Valdrin dead? We were playfellows and *bredin*," he said, "but Valdrin was always a fool, as any man is a fool who meddles in the affairs of the great folk of the land."

Alderic said stiffly, "I honor the memory of the Lord Valdrin for his loyalty to our rightful king in exile, sir."

"Honor," The MacAran said bitterly, "Honor is of no use to the dead, and to all of his folk whom he entangled in the

40

quarrel of the great ones; great honor to his wife and little children, I doubt it not, to die with the flesh burnt from their very bones? As if it mattered to me, or to any reasonable man, which great donkey kept the throne warm with his royal backsides while better men went about their business?"

Romilly could see that Alderic was ready with a sharp answer, but he bowed and said nothing; he would not offend his host. Mallina was introduced to Alderic and simpered up at him, while Romilly watched in disdain—anything in breeches, she thought, and Mallina willingly practices her silly womanish wiles on him, even this shabby political refugee Darren picked up at Nevarsin and brought home, no doubt to give the boy a few good meals—he looked thin as a rake, and no doubt, at Nevarsin, they feed them on porridge of acorns and cold water!

Mallina was still chattering to the young men.

"And the folk from Storn Heights are coming, and the sons and daughters of Aldaran of Scathfell, and all during the Midsummer-festival there will be parties and hawkings and hunts, and a great Midsummer-dance—" and she slanted her long-lashed eyes at Alderic and said, "Are you fond of dancing, *dom* Alderic?"

"I have done but little dancing since I was a child," said Alderic, "I have danced only the clodhopper-dances of the monks and novices when they dance together at midwinter—but I shall expect you to teach them to me, *damisela*." He bowed to her and to Romilly, but Mallina said, "Oh, Romilly will not dance with men—she is more at home in the stables, and would rather show you her hawks and hounds!"

"Mallina, go to your lessons," said Luciella, in a voice that clearly said, *I'll deal with you later, young lady*. "You must forgive her, *dom* Alderic, she is only a spiteful child."

Mallina burst into tears and ran out of the room, but Alderic smiled at Romilly and said, "I too feel more at ease in the company of hawks and horses than that of women. I believe one of the horses we brought from Nevarsin is yours?"

"It belonged to—" Darren caught his father's scowl and amended, "a relative of ours; he left it in Nevarsin to be returned to us." But Romilly intercepted the glance that passed between Darren and Alderic and knew that her brother had confided the whole story to his friend. How far, she wondered, had that scandal spread, that the son of The MacAran had quarreled with his family and fled to a Tower?

"Romilly," said her father, "should you not be in the schoolroom with Mistress Calinda?"

"You promised me a holiday on my birthday," Romilly reminded her stepmother, and Luciella said with an ill grace, "Well, as I have promised—I suppose you want to spend the time with your brother. Go, then, if you wish."

She smiled at her brother and said, "I would like to show you my new *verrin* hawk—"

"Romilly trained it herself," Rael burst out, while her father frowned. "When Davin was sick. She waited up all night until it would feed, and the hawkmaster said that father could not have done better himself—"

"Aye," The MacAran said roughly, "your sister has done what you would not do, boy—you should take lessons from her in skill and courage! Would that she had been the boy, and you the maiden, so that you might put skirts about your knees and spend the day in scribbling and embroidering within the house—"

Darren flushed to the roots of his hair. He said, "Do not mock me before my friend, Father. I will do as well as I am able, I pledge to you. But I am as the Gods made me, and no other. A rabbithorn cannot be a war-horse and will only become a laughing-stock if he should try."

"Is that what they have taught you among the damned monks?"

"They taught me that what I am, I am," said Darren, and Romilly saw the glint of tears in his eyes, "and yet, Father, I am here at your will, to do my poor best for you." Romilly could hear, as plain as if the forbidden name had been spoken, *it is not my fault that I am not Ruyven, nor was it my doing that he went from here.*

The MacAran set his massive jaw, and Romilly knew that he, too, heard the forbidden words. He said, scowling, "Take your brother to the hawk-house, Romy, and show him your hawk; perhaps it will shame him into striving to equal what a girl can do."

Darren opened his mouth to speak, but Romilly nudged him in the ribs, as if to say, *Let us go while we can, before he says worse.* Darren said, muffled, "Come along, Alderic, unless hawks weary you," and Alderic, saying something courteous and noncommittal, bowed to The MacAran and to Lady Luciella and went with them down the stairs.

For the last few days Preciosa had been placed on her block among the already-trained hawks; moving quietly, Romilly slid gauntlet on wrist and took up the bird, then returned to the two young men.

"This is Preciosa," she said, pride swelling her voice, and

42

asked Darren, "Would you like to hold her for a moment while I fetch the lures and lines? She must learn to tolerate another's hand and voice—"

But as she moved toward him, he flinched away, in a startled movement, and Romilly, sensing how the fear in him reverberated in the bird-mind, turned her attention to soothing Preciosa, stroking her with a feather. She said, not reproving, but so intent on what she was doing that she did not stop to think how her words would sound to another, "Never move so quickly around a hawk—you should know that! You will frighten her—one would think you were afraid of her!"

"It is only—I am not used to be so close to anything so large and so fierce," Darren said, biting his lip.

"Fierce? Preciosa? Why, she is gentle as a puppy dog," Romilly said, disbelieving. She beckoned to the hawkmaster's boy. "Fetch the lures, Ker—" and when he brought them, she examined the bait, frowning and wrinkling up her nose.

"Is this what you have for the other hawks? Do you think they are carrion feeders? Why, a dog would turn away from this in disgust! I have orders that Preciosa was to have fresh-killed meat, mice if nothing better was available from the kitchens, but nothing as old and rank as this."

"It's what Davin had set aside for the birds, Mistress Romilly."

Romilly opened her mouth to give him the tongue-lashing he deserved, but even before a sound was out, the hawk on her wrist bated furiously, and she knew her own anger was reaching Preciosa's mind. She drew a long breath and said quietly, "I will have a word with Davin. I would ask no decent hawk to feed on this garbage. For now, go and fetch me something fresh-killed for my bird; if not a pigeon, take one of the dogs and find mice or a rat, and at once."

Darren had drawn back from the frenzied flapping of wings, but as Ker scuttled away to obey orders, he said, "I see that working with the hawk has at least given you some command of that temper and tongue, Romy—it has been good for you!"

"I wish Father would agree to that," Romilly said, still stroking Preciosa with the feather, trying to calm her. "But birds are like babies, they pick up the emotions of those who tend them, I really do not think it is more than that. Have you forgotten when Rael was a babe, that nurse Luciella had for him—no, I cannot bring her name to mind just now—Marja, Moyra, something of that sort—Luciella had to send her away because the woman's older son drowned, and she wept when she saw Rael, and it gave him colic, so that was when Gwennis came to us——"

"No, it is more than that," said Alderic, as they moved out of the darkness of the hawk-house into the tiled courtyard, "There is a well-known *laran*, and it appeared first, I am told, among the Delleray and MacAran folk; empathy with hawk and horse and sentry-bird . . . it was for *that* they trained it, in warfare in the days of King Felix. Among the Delleray folk, it was tied to some lethal genes and so died away, but MacArans have had the Gift for generations."

Darren said with an uneasy smile, "I beg you, my friend, speak not of *laran* so freely when my father is by to hear."

"Why, is he one who would speak of sweetnut-blossom because snowflakes are too cold for him?" Alderic asked with a grin. "All my life I have heard of the horses trained by The MacAran as the finest in the world, and *Dom* Mikhail is one of the more notable of MacAran lords. Surely he knows well the Gifts and *laran* of his house and his lady's."

"Still, he will not hear the word spoken," said Darren, "Not since Ruyven fled to the Tower, and I blame him not, though some would say I am the gainer by what Ruyven has done . . . Romilly, now while Father is not by, I will say this to you and you may tell Mallina secretly; I think Rael is too young to keep it to himself, but use your own judgment. At the monastery, I had a letter from Ruyven; he is well, and loves the work he does, and is happy. He sends his love and a kiss to all of you, and bids me speak of him again to Father when I judge the time is right."

"Which will be when apples and blackfruit grow on the ice cliffs of Nevarsin," said Romilly, "You were there, you know what he feels——"

Darren shook his head. "Ah, no, sister, I am not so much a telepath as you, though I knew that he was angry——"

Romilly turned on him, blinking in disbelief. "Can you not hear a thing unless it is spoken aloud?" she demanded, "Are you head blind like the witless donkey you ride?"

Slow color, the red of shame, suffused Darren's face as he lowered his eyes. "Even so, sister," he said, and Romilly shut her eyes as if to avoid looking on some gross deformity. She had never known or guessed this, she had always taken it for granted that all her siblings shared the Gift she had come to take for granted even before she knew what it was.

She turned with relief to Davin, who was coming through the courtyard. "Was it you, old friend, gave orders to feed

44

the hawks on the offal of the kitchens, and not even fresh at that?" She pointed at the pan of offending refuse; Davin picked it up, sniffed disdainfully at it, and put it aside.

"That lazybones of a lad brought *this?* He'll make no hawker! I sent him for fresher food from the kitchens, but Lady Luciella says there are to be no more fresh birds killed for hawk-bait; I doubt not Ker was too lazy to catch mice, but I'll find something fresher to exercise your hawk, Mistress Romilly."

Alderic asked, "May I touch her?" and took the feather from Romilly's hand, stroking the hawk's sleek feathers. "She is indeed beautiful; *verrin* hawks are not easy to keep, though I have tried it. Not with success, unless they were yard-hatched. And this was a haggard? Who trained her?"

"I did, and am still working with her; she has not yet flown free," Romilly said, and smiled shyly at his look of amazement.

"You trained her? A girl? But why not, you are a Mac-Aran. In the Tower where I dwelt for a time, some of the woman tamed and flew *verrin* hawks taken in the wild, and we are apt to say there, to one who has notable success with a hawk, *Why, you have the hand of a MacAran with a bird. . . ."*

"Are there MacArans in the Towers, then, that they should say so?" Romilly asked, "I knew not that there were any Mac-Arans within their walls, until my brother went thither—"

Alderic said, "The saying was known in my father's time and in his father's—the Gift of a MacAran." The word he used was not the ordinary word in the Kilghard Hills, *laran,* but the old casta word *donas.* "But your father is not pleased, then, to have a son in the Tower? Most hill-folk would be proud."

Darren's smile was bitter. "I have no gift for working with animals—and small gift for anything else, save learning; but while Ruyven was my father's Heir it did not matter; I was destined for the monastery, and I was happy with the Brotherhood. Now he will even try to hammer this bent nail into the place laid out for my brother—"

"Have you not a third brother?" Alderic asked, "Is the little lad who greeted you *nedestro,* or feebleminded, that your father cannot give a son to St.-Valentine-of-the-Snows and rear Rafael, Rael, whatever you called him, to the lordship of Falconsward? Or, seeing what Mistress Romilly can do—" his smile was generous, and Romilly blushed. But Darren said bitterly, "You do not know my father—" and broke

45

off while Romilly was still pondering this; did it seem reasonable to Alderic, then, that she might even take Ruyven's place at Falconsward?

"I've brought fresh-killed meat for your hawk, Mistress Romilly," Davin said, coming into the stableyard, "One of the cooks had just killed a fowl for roasting at dinner; she let me have the innards for your bird, and I gave orders for the freshest offal of every day to be put aside for you in the morning; that garbage Ker brought was from the day before, because one of the cooks put it aside for the dogs, and he was too busy eyeing the wenches in the kitchen to ask for the fresh meat. He'll never make a hawker, that one! I swear, I'd turn him off for a *sekal*, and start teaching little Master Rael the handling!"

Romilly chuckled. "Luciella would have much to say about that," she told him, "but put Ker to feeding the pigs or tending the kennels, and surely there must be someone on the estate who has some hawk-sense!"

Darren grinned mirthlessly. He said, "Try Nelda's boy Garris; he was festival-got, and rumor speaks wide about who had his fathering. If he's good with the beasts, it will bring him under my father's eye, which Nelda was too proud to do. Once I suggested he should be put to share lessons with Rael, and our great Lady and Mistress Luciella had fits—one would think I'd suggested bringing the pig-boy in to dine at the high table."

"You should know that Luciella hears only what she wants to hear," said Romilly. "Perhaps she thought that bastardy is like fleas, catching. . . ." She fumbled for the lures and lines, cumbered with Preciosa's weight on her wrist. "Damnation, Darren, can't you hold her for me a moment? If not, for charity's sake, at least thread the meat on the lure—she smells it and will go wild in a moment!"

"I will take her, if you will trust me with your hawk," said Alderic, and held out his arm. "So, will you come to me, pretty one?" Carefully, he lifted the nervous hawk from Romilly's wrist to his own. "What is it you call her, Preciosa? And so she is, are you not, precious one?"

Romilly watched jealously as the hooded hawk settled down comfortably on Alderic's wrist; but Preciosa seemed content and she turned to tying the line around the meat, so that Preciosa could not snap it away too swiftly, and must bring it down to the ground to eat, as a good hunting-hawk must learn to do; badly tamed hawks tended to snatch food from a lure in midair, which taught them little about hunting

46

practice. They must be taught to bring the prey down to their master, and to wait until the meat was given to them from the hand.

"Give me the line and lure," said Darren. "If I can do nothing else, I can at least throw out the lure—"

Romilly handed it to him with relief. "Thank you—you are taller than I, you can whirl it higher," she said, and took Preciosa again on her wrist. One handed, she slipped the hood from the hawk's head, raising her arm to let it fly. Trailing its lines, the hawk rose higher, higher—coming to the end of the line, Romilly saw it turn its head, see the flying, whistling lure—swiftly, dropping with suddenly folded wings, it descended on the lure, seizing it with beak and talons, and dropped swiftly to Romilly's feet. Romilly gave the sharp whistle which the hawk was being taught to associate with food, and scooped Preciosa up on her glove, tearing the food from the lure.

Preciosa was bending so swiftly to the food that she hopped sidewise on Romilly's arm, her claws contracting painfully in the girl's thinly-clad forearm above the gauntlet. Blood burst out, staining her dress; Romilly set her mouth and did not cry out, but as the crimson spread across the blue fabric, Darren cried out sharply.

"Oh, sister—!"

Preciosa, startled by the cry, lost her balance and fell, bated awkwardly, her wings beating into Darren's face; Romilly reached for her, but Darren cried out in panic and flung up his hands to ward away the beak and talons which were dangerously close to his face. At his scream, Preciosa tottered again and flew upward, checking with a shrill scream of rage at the end of her lines.

Her jaws set, Romilly hissed in a whisper "Damn you, Darren, she could have broken a flight-feather! Don't you know better than to move that fast around a hawk? Get back before you frighten her worse than that!"

Darren stammered "You—you—you're bleeding—"

"So what?" Romilly demanded harshly, shoved him back with a rough hand, and whistled softly, coaxingly to Preciosa. "I might better bring Rael into the hawk-house, you lackwit! Get out of here!"

"And this is what I have for a son and heir," said The MacAran bitterly. He was standing in the door of the hawk-house, watching the three young people unseen. His voice, even in his anger, was low—he knew better than to raise his voice near a frightened bird. He stood silent, staring

47

with his brows knitted in a scowl, as Romilly coaxed the hawk down to her wrist and untangled the lines. "Are you not ashamed, Darren, to stand by while a little girl bests you at what should come by instinct to any son of mine? But that I knew your mother so well, I would swear you had been fathered by some chance-come beggar of the roads. . . . Bearer of Burdens, why have you weighted my life with a son so unfit for his place?" He grabbed Darren's arm and jerked him inside the hawk-house; Romilly heard Darren cry out and her teeth met in her lip as if the blow had landed on her own shoulders.

"Get out there, now, and try to behave like a man for once! Take this hawk—no, not like that, damnation take you, you have hands like great hams for all your writing and scribbling! Take the hawk out there and exercise her on a lure, and if I see you ducking away from it like that, I swear I'll have you beaten and sent to bed with bread and water as if you were Rael's age!"

Alderic's face was dead white and his jaw set, but he bent his eyes on the backs of his hands and did not speak. Romilly, fighting for calm—there was no sense in upsetting Preciosa again—threaded meat on the lure again. Without words, Alderic reached for the line and began to swing it high, and Romilly watched Preciosa wing off, both of them trying to ignore Darren, his face red and swollen, clumsily trying to unhood a strange hawk at the far end of the stableyard. It was all they could do for Darren now.

She thought; *at least, he is trying. Perhaps that is braver than what I did, defying Father; I had the Gift, I was only doing what is natural for me, and Darren, obeying, is going against everything which is natural to him. . . .* and her throat swelled as if she would cry, but she fought the tears back. It would not help Darren. Nothing would help him except trying to conquer his own nervousness. And, somewhere inside her, she could not help feeling a tiny sting of contempt . . . *how could he bungle anything which was so easy and simple?*

CHAPTER FOUR

Romilly did not see the first of the guests arrive for the
Midsummer-feast; the day had dawned clear and brilliant, the
red sun rising over just a hint of cloud at the horizon. For
three days there had been neither snow nor rain, and everywhere in the courtyard flowers were bursting into bloom. She
sat up in her bed, drawing a breath of excitement; today she
was to fly Preciosa free for the very first time.

This was the final excruciating test for hawk and trainer.
All too often, when first freed, the hawk would rise into the
sky, wing away into the violet clouds—and never return. She
faced that knowledge; she could not bear to lose Preciosa
now, and it was all the more likely with a haggard who had
hunted and fed for herself in the wild.

But Preciosa would return, Romilly was confident of that.
She flung off her nightgown and dressed for the hunt; her
stepmother had had her new green-velvet habit laid enticingly
ready, but she put on an old tunic and shirt, and a pair of
Darren's old breeches. If her father was angry, then he must
be angry as he would; she would not spoil Preciosa's first
hunt by worrying about whether or not she spotted her new
velvet clothing.

As she slipped out into the corridor she stumbled over a
basket set in her door; the traditional Midsummer-gift from
the men of the family to mothers, sisters, daughters. Her father was always generous; she set the basket inside,
rummaged through it for a handy apple and a few of the
sweets that always appeared there too, and thrust them into

49

her pockets—just what she wanted for hunting, and after a moment she pocketed a few more for Darren and Alderic. There was a second basket there too; Darren's? And a tiny one clumsily pasted of paper strips, which she had seen Rael trying to hide in the schoolroom; she smiled indulgently, for it was filled with a handful of nuts which she knew he had saved from his own desserts. What a darling he was, her little brother! For a moment she was tempted to ask him, too, on this special ride, but after a minute of reflection she sighed and decided not to risk her stepmother's anger. She would arrange some special treat for him later.

She went silently down the hallway and joined Darren and Alderic, who were waiting at the doorway, having let the dogs outside—it was, after all, well after daylight. The three young people went toward the stable.

Darren said, "I told father we were going hawking at dawn. He gave you leave to fly his racer if you would, Alderic."

"He is generous," said Alderic, and went quietly toward the hawk.

"Which one will you take, Darren?" asked Romilly, slipping Preciosa on to her wrist. Darren, raising his eyes to her with a smile, said, "I think you know, sister, that I take no pleasure in hawks. If father had bidden me to exercise one of his birds, I would obey him; but in honor of the holiday, perhaps, he forbore to lay any such command on me."

His tone was so bitter that Alderic looked up and said, "I think he means to be kind, *bredu*."

"Aye. No doubt." But Darren did not raise his head as they went across to the stable, where the horses were ready.

Romilly set Preciosa on the perch as she saddled her own horse. She would not command any man to disobey her father against his conscience; but she would not ride sidesaddle on this holiday ride, either. If her father chose to punish her, she would accept whatever he chose to do.

It was sheer ecstasy to be on a horse again in proper riding clothes, feeling the cool morning wind against her face, and Preciosa before her on the saddle, hooded but alert. She could feel a trickle of awareness from the bird which was blended of emotions Romilly herself could not identify . . . not quite fear as she had come to know it, not quite excitement, but to her great relief it was wholly unmixed with the terrifying rage she had felt when she began training the hawk. The clouds melted away as they rode into the hills, and under their horses' hooves there was only the tiniest crackling of frost.

"Where shall we go, Darren? You know these hills," Alderic asked, and Darren laughed at them.

"Ask Romilly, not me, my—" he broke off sharply and Romilly, raising her eyes suddenly from her bird, intercepted the sharp, almost warning look Alderic gave the younger man. Darren said quickly, "My sister knows more of the hills and of the hawks than I do, Lord 'Deric."

"This way, I think," she said, "To the far horse-pasture; we can fly the birds there and none will disturb us. And there are always small birds and small animals in the coverts."

As they topped the rise they looked down on the pasture, a wide stretch of hillside grassland, dotted here and there with clumps of berry-briars, small bushes and underbrush. A few horses were cropping the bunchy grass, green with summer, and the fields and bushes were coated with clusters of blue and yellow wildflowers. Insects buzzed in the grass; the horses raised their heads in alert inquiry, but seeing nothing to disturb them, went on nibbling grass. One small filly flung up her head and came trotting, on spindly legs, toward them; Romilly laughed, slid from her horse and went to nuzzle the baby horse; she came not much higher than Romilly's shoulder.

"This is Angel," she said to the young men, "She was born last winter, and I used to feed her with apple scraps—no, Angel, that's *my* breakfast," she added, slapping the soft muzzle away from the pocket where the horse was trying to rummage. But she relented and pulled her knife, cutting a small slice of apple for the filly.

"No more, now, it will give you a bellyache," she said, and the little animal, evidently taking her word for it, trotted off on her long spindly legs.

"Let us go on, or old Windy will be on us," she said laughing, "He is out to pasture in this field. He is too old a gelding for the mares to take any notice of him, and his teeth are almost too old to chew grass; Father would have him put down this spring, but, he said he should have one last summer and before winter comes. He will send him quietly to his rest; he should not have to endure another winter of cold with his old joints."

"I will grieve when that is my task," said Darren, "We all learned to ride on him, he was like an old rocking-chair to sit on." He looked with a distant sadness at the aged, half-blind pony chomping at soft grass in a corner of the field. "I think Father spared him because he was Ruyven's first horse. . . ."

"He had a good life, and will make a good end," said Alderic, "Unlike men, horses are not allowed to live till they are senile and half mad . . . if they gave men such mercy as that, I should not—there would not now be a usurper king on the throne in Hali and—and the king would not now be wandering in his exile."

"I do not understand," said Romilly. Darren frowned, but Alderic said, "You are not old enough to remember when King Felix died? He was more than a hundred and fifty, an *emmasca*, very old and without sons; and he had long outlived sense and wit, so he sought to put the eldest son of his youngest brother on the throne, rather than his next brother's elder son, who was rightfully Heir. And so the Lord Rakhal, who flattered and cozened an old and senile king and got the Regents all in his hand with bribes and lies, an aged lecher from whom no woman is safe, nor, 'tis said, the young son of any courtier who would like to curry favor, sits on the throne of the Hasturs at Hali. And Carolin and his sons wander across the Kadarin, at the mercy of any bandit or robber who would like the bounty set on their heads by our most gracious Lord Rakhal . . . for I will never give him the name of king."

"Do you know the—the exiled king?"

Darren said, "The young prince was at Nevarsin among the monks for a time; but he fled when word came that Lord Rakhal sought him there."

"And you support the young prince and the—the king in exile?" Romilly asked.

"Aye. That I do. And if some kindly courtier had relieved the ancient Felix of his life before 'twas a burden to him, Carolin would now rule in Hali as a just king, rather than turning the holy city of the Hasturs into a—a cesspool of filth and indecencies, where no man dares come for justice without a bribe in hand, and upstart lordlings and outlanders wrangle and divide our land among them!"

Romilly did not answer; she knew nothing of courts and kings, and had never been even so far as the foothill city of Neskaya, far less into the lowlands, or near to the Lake of Hali. She reached for Preciosa's hood, and then hesitated, showing Alderic the courtesy due a guest.

"Will you fly first, sir?"

He smiled and shook his head. "I think we are all as eager as you to see how Preciosa has come through her training."

52

With shaking hands, Romilly slipped the hood from Preciosa's head, watching the hawk mantling her feathers. Now. Now was the test, not only of her mastery of the hawk, but of the hawk's acceptance of her training, the hawk's tie to her. She felt she could not bear to see this hawk she had loved, over whom she had spent so many anxious and painful hours, fly from her and never return. It flashed through her mind, *is this how Father feels now that Ruyven has gone?* Yet she must try the hawk in free flight. Otherwise, she was no more than a tame cagebird, sitting dull on a block, not a wild hawk at all. But she felt tears blurring her sight as she raised her fist and felt the hawk balance a moment, then, with a single long wing-stroke, fly free.

She rose on a long, slanting arch into the sunlight, and Romilly, her mind full of anxious thoughts—will she fly well, has this long period of inactivity dulled her flight?—watched her rise. And something in her rose with the hawk, feeling the wordless joy of the morning sun on her wings, the light dazzling her eyes as she winged upward, rose, hovered, soared—wheeled and winged strongly away.

Romilly let out a long breath. She was gone, she would not return—

"You have lost her, I fear," said Alderic at last. "I am sorry, *damisela.*"

Loss and pain, and a sharing of ecstasy, battled in Romilly. Free flight, something of her soaring with the hawk . . . and then fading away in the distance. She shook her head. If she had lost the hawk, then she had never really possessed her. She thought, *I would rather lose her than tie her to me against her will. . . .*

Why cannot Father see that? She knew the thought was Darren's, because of the bitterness. Then he was not head-blind? Or was his telepathy erratic, as hers had once been, coming only rarely and when she was deeply moved . . . her own had strengthened when she had begun working with the animals, but Darren had none of that gift. . . .

So Preciosa was free, and it was all an illusion. She might as well sit quietly in the house and mind her stitchery for all it would profit her to hang about the hawk-house, trying like a man to work with the birds. . . .

And then it seemed that her heart would stop. For through the infinite pain of loss, a thread of awareness stole, high flight, the world laid out beneath her like one of the maps in her schoolbooks, only colored and curiously sharp, with a sight stronger than her own, and little flickers of life coming

53

from here, from there, small birds in flight, small animals in the grass. . . .

Preciosa! The hawk was still in rapport, the hawk had not flown wild! Darren said something; she did not hear. She heard Alderic saying, "Don't waste your voice, *bredu,* she cannot hear you. She is with the hawk. . . ."

Romilly sat, with automatic habit, in the saddle, upright, silent, but the real part of her soared over the high pasture, keen with hunger, in the ecstasy of the flight. Supernaturally keen, her sight and senses, aware of the life of small birds, so that she felt she was smacking her lips and almost giggled and broke out of the rapport with the absurdity of it, sudden burning hunger and a desire almost sexual in its ferocity . . . down. Down on long soaring wings, the beak striking, blood bursting into her mouth, the sudden fierceness of bursting life and death. . . .

Down. Wavering down. She had just enough of her self-hood left to hold out her fist rock-steady, under the sudden jarring stop of a heavy hawk laden with her kill. She felt tears streaming down her face, but there was no time for emotion; her knife was in her free hand as she cut the head away, thrust her portion, headless rabbit, into her wallet with the free hand; all her own awareness was feeding with the greedy hawk on her portion. Alderic had loosed his own hawk, but she did not know; she was weeping outright with love and relief as she slipped the hood on Preciosa's head.

Preciosa had come back. She had returned of her free will, out of freedom into bondage and the hood. She choked back her tears as she stroked the hawk with the feather, and knew her hands were shaking.

What have I done to deserve this? How can I possibly be worthy of it? That a wild thing should give up her freedom for me . . . what can I possibly do to make me worthy enough for that gift?

Later they ate the apples and sweets that Romilly had brought, before riding back, through the growing light, to Falconsward. As the young people came through the courtyard they saw strange horses being unsaddled there, one with the banners of Aldaran of Scathfell, and knew that the highest-born of the guests had arrived.

Alderic asked, anxiously, "Is it old lord Gareth still Lord of Scathfell?"

"He is not, my lord; Gareth of Scathfell is not more than forty-nine," said Romilly. Alderic looked relieved, and Romilly intercepted a questioning look between Darren and

Alderic. Alderic said shortly, "He might well know me by sight."

"Do you not trust to the laws of—" Darren began, frowned in Romilly's direction, and broke off, and Romilly, bending her head over her hawk, thought; *what kind of fool do they think me? I would need be deaf, blind, dumb and head-blind as well, not to know he is allied in partisanship to Carolin in exile, perhaps the young prince himself. And I know as well as he why my father must get no word of it.*

"True; Old Gareth died three winters gone, sir," Darren said, "and was half-blind at that. Will all of the folk of Scathfell be here, Romilly?"

Romilly, relieved that the tension had passed, began to recite the grown sons and daughters of the middle-aged lord of Scathfell; his Heir, yet another Gareth ("But they call him Garris, in lowland fashion," she added), "*Dom* Garris is not wed, he has buried three wives; I think he is only in his thirtieth year, but looks older, and is lame with a wasting disease of one leg."

"And you dislike him," said Alderic, and she grinned, her impish smile. "Why, how could you possibly know that, Lord Alderic? But it is true; he is always fumbling the maidens in corners, he was not above pawing at Mallina last year, when she had not even put up her hair. . . ."

"Lecherous old goat!" Darren said, "Did Father know?"

"None of us wanted a quarrel with neighbors; Luciella only told Mallina and me to keep away from him if we could do so without being uncivil. Then there is *Dom* Edric, who is blind, and his wife Ruanna, who keeps the estate books as well as any man. And there are the young twins, Cathal and Cinhil, they are not so young either—they are Ruyven's age; twenty-two. And Cathal's wife, who was one of my childhood friends—Darissa Storn. Cinhil is not wed, and Father once spoke of betrothing us, but nothing came of it, which gladdened my heart—I would not want to live at Scathfell, it is like a bandit's hold! Though I would not mind being close to Darissa, and Cinhil is a nice enough boy."

"It seems to me you are over young to be wedded," said Alderic, and Darren laughed. "Women marry young in these hills, and Romilly is fifteen. And, I doubt not, she thinks it long till she is in a home of her own, and out from Luciella's guidance—what's the ancient saying, *where two women rule a hearthfire, the thatch may burn with the sparks flying . . .* yet I think Father could do better for Romilly than a younger son, a fourth son at that. Better lady in a cottage than serving-woman in a castle, and when *Dom* Garris weds again—or if old Scathfell should take a wife—Cinhil's wife would be lowest of all, not much better than waiting-women to all the rest. Darissa was pretty and bright when she was wedded, and now she looks ten years older than Cathal, and all out of shape with bearing children."

"I am in no haste to marry," Romilly said, "And there are men enough, I suppose, in these hills; Manfred Storn is Heir to Storn Heights, and he is about Darren's age, so it's likely, when I am old enough to marry, Father will speak to old Lord Storn. The folk of High Crags will be coming too, and they have a couple of unmarried sons and daughters, it's likely that they will marry Rael into that kindred, or me." She shrugged. "What does it matter, after all? Men are all alike."

Alderic chuckled. "By those words I know how young you are, Mistress Romilly—I hope your father does not seek to have you married till you are old enough to distinguish between one man or another, or you may awaken some day and discover you are married to the very last man on earth you would have sought for husband. Shall we go in the house? The sun is high, and your stepmother said something of a festival breakfast—and I smelled the cooks making spicebread as we passed the kitchens!"

Romilly only hoped, now, that she could get up to her room unobserved, to change her clothing and bathe before the festal meal. But, coming around a corridor, she almost bumped into a tall, pale, fattish man with fair hair, coming from the big bathing-room with hot pools, fed by volcanic springs. He was wrapped in a loose robe and his hair was damp and mussed; he had evidently gone to soak away the fatigue of riding. Romilly curtseyed politely as she had been taught, then remembered that she was wearing breeches—curse it! If she had gone on about her business he might simply have taken her for an out-of-place servant boy on some errand. Instead his pale flabby face tightened in a dimply creased smile.

"Mistress Romilly," he said, his eyes sliding up and down her long legs, "An unexpected pleasure. Why, what a pair of legs you have, girl! And you have—grown," he added, the pallid china-blue eyes resting on the straining laces of the old tunic pulled over her full breasts, "It will be a pleasure to dance with you tonight, now I have had the delights of seeing

56

what so many women so carefully conceal from their admirers. ..."

Romilly flushed, feeling heat in her face, ducked her head and escaped. Through the scalding heat flooding to her ears, she thought, wretchedly, *Now do I know what Luciella meant, that I was too big to run about in breeches—I might as well be naked, the way he looked at me.* All her life she had run about in her brother's clothes, as free of self-consciousness or shame as if she were another lad; now, under the man's lustful eyes, she felt as if her body had actually been rudely handled; her breasts prickled and there was a curious crawling sensation lower down in her belly.

She took refuge in her room, her heart pounding, and went swiftly to the washstand, splashing her hot face with cold water to cool it.

"Luciella was right. Oh, why didn't she tell me?" she wondered wretchedly, then realized that there was no way to speak of it, and if she had been told, without this experience, she would only have laughed it away. Her hands were still shaking as she undid the laces of the boy's tunic, dropped the breeches to the floor, and for the first time in her life, looked clearly in the mirror and saw her body as a woman's. She was still slender, her breasts scarcely rounded, the hips scarcely more flared than a boy's, and the long legs were really boyish. *But*, she thought, *if ever I wear boy's clothes again, I shall be sure they fit me loosely enough that I truly look like a male.*

Through the glass connecting doors to Mallina's room she saw her sister exploring her Midsummer-baskets; like Romilly herself, she had three, which made Romilly turn back to her father's generous basket, with more fruits and sweets than flowers—The MacAran had quite a realistic view of little girls' appetites, which were just as greedy as those of young boys—and the smaller basket she thought was from Darren. Now, examining it closely, she realized that it was filled with garden and hothouse flowers, exquisitely arranged, and with one or two exotic fruits which he must have gotten in Nevarsin, since they did not grow near Falconsward. Then she saw the card, and read in surprise;

> I have neither sister or mother to receive
> Midsummer-Gifts; accept these with my
> homage, *Alderic, student.*

Mallina burst into her room.

"Romy, aren't you dressed yet? We mustn't be late for Festival breakfast! Are you going to wear your holiday gown?

Calinda is with Mother, will you button the back of my dress for me? What beautiful flowers, Romy! Mine are all garden flowers, though there is a beautiful bunch of ice-grapes, as sweet as honey—you know, they leave them on the trees in Nevarsin till they freeze, like redfruit, and then they lose their sourness and grow sweet . . . Romy, who do you think he is? He looks so romantic—do you think *Dom* Alderic is trying to court one of us. I would be happy indeed to be betrothed to him, he is so handsome and gallant, like the hero of some fairy-tale—"

"What a silly chatterbox you are, Mally," said Romilly, but she smiled, "I think he is a thoughtful guest, no more; no doubt he has sent to mother a basket as fine as this."

"*Domna* Luciella will not appreciate it," Mallina said, "Still she thinks Festival Night is a heathen observance not worthy of a good *cristoforo;* she scolded Calinda because she had Rael making Festival baskets, but Father said everyone deserved a holiday and one excuse was as good as another for giving the farm workers a day of leisure and some well-deserved bonus gifts, and he should let Rael enjoy the Festival while he was still a child—he would be as good a *cristoforo* as he need, if he was a good boy and minded the Book of Burdens."

Romilly smiled. "Father has said much the same every Festival since I can remember," she said, "And I doubt not he likes spicebread and sweetbaked saffron cakes and fruits as well as anyone else. He quoted from the Book of Burdens that the beast should not be grudged his grain, nor the worker his wage, nor his holiday, and Father may be a harsh man, but he is always just to his workmen." She did up the last button on the gown and spun her sister around. "How fine you are, Mally! But it is fortunate you do not wear this dress on a work day—it needs a maid to do it up for you! That is why I had my festival gown made with laces, so I could do it up for myself." She finished fastening the embroidered cuffs of her under-tunic, slipped the long loose surplice, rust-red and embroidered with butterflies, over her head, and turned for Mallina to pin up her braid at her neck with the butterfly-clasp that modestly hid the neck of her frock.

Mallina turned to choose a flower for her hair from the baskets. "Does this rose-plant suit me? It is pink like my dress . . . oh, Romy, look!" she said, with a scandalized half-breath, "Saw you not, he has put golden-flower, *dorilys*, into your basket!"

"And so what, silly?" asked Romy, choosing the blue *kire-seth* blossom for her knotted braid, but Mallina caught her hand.

"No, indeed, you must not, Romilly—what, don't you know the flower-language? The gift of golden-flower is—well, the flower is an aphrodisiac, you know as well as I do what it means, when a man offers a maiden *dorilys.* . . ."

Romilly blushed, again feeling the lustful eyes on her. She swallowed hard—Alderic, was he too looking at her with this kind of greed? Then common sense came back. She said crisply, "Nonsense; he is a stranger to these hills, that is all. But if that kind of talk is commonplace among silly girls, I will not wear the flower—shame to them, for it is the prettiest of all the flowers, but do you choose me a flower, then, for my braids."

The sisters went down in their finery to the family feast, bearing with them, as custom dictated, the fruits from their festival baskets to be shared with father and brothers. The family was gathered in the great dining-hall rather than the small room used for family meals, and *Domna* Luciella was there, welcoming her guests. Rael was there in his best suit, and Calinda in a new gown too, dark and decent as suited her station, but well-made and new, not a shabby or outworn family castoff; Luciella was a kind woman, Romilly thought, even to poor relations. Darren wore his best clothing too, and Alderic, though his best was sombre as befitted a student at Nevarsin, and bore no trace of family colors or badges. She wondered who he was, and kept to herself the thought that had come to her, that he might well be one of the king's men, exiled, or even the young prince . . . no, she would say nothing; but she wished that Darren had trusted her with his secret.

The middle-aged Gareth of Scathfell, as the man of highest rank in the assembly, had been given the high seat usually assigned to The MacAran at his own table; her father had taken a lower place. The young couples and single men and women were at a separate table; Romilly saw Darissa seated beside Cathal and would have joined her friend, but her stepmother gestured to an empty seat left beside *Dom* Garris; Romilly blushed, but would not incite a confrontation here; she took her seat, biting her lip and hoping that in the very presence of her parents he would say nothing to her.

"Now, clothed as befits your beauty, you are even more lovely, *damisela,*" he said, and that was all; the words were perfectly polite, but she looked at his pale slab of face with dislike and did not answer. But after all, he had done nothing, the words had been polite enough, what could she say, there was no way she could complain of him.

There were delicacies of every kind, for this was breakfast and mid-day meal in one; the feasting went on for some time, and before the dishes were cleared, the musicians had come in and begun to play. The curtains had been drawn back to their furthest to let in the midsummer sun, and the doors flung open; the furniture in the lower hall had been moved away to clear it for dancing. As Darren led his sister out for the first dance, as custom demanded, she heard them discussing, at the high table, the men that had been sent out to seek the exiled Carolin.

"It's nothing to me," The MacAran said, "I care not who sits on the throne; but I'll not have my men bribed to be thief-takers, either. There was a time when MacArans ruled this as a kingdom; but then, we had little to do but keep it by force of arms, and I've no wish to make my lands an armed camp, and the Hasturs are welcome to rule as they will; but I curse their brotherslaying wars!"

"I had heard word that Carolin and his older son had crossed the Kadarin," Lord Scathfell said, "No doubt to seek refuge with my cousin of Aldaran—there is old hatred between the Hastur-kin and the Aldarans."

Her father drew up his mouth in a one-sided grin. "None so keen at the hunting of wolves as the dog with wolf blood," he said, "Were not the Aldarans, long ago, come from that same Hastur-blood?"

"So they say," Lord Scathfell said with a grim nod, "I put no stock in all those tales of the children of Gods . . . though, the Gods know, there is *laran* in the Aldaran line, even among my own sons and daughters, as among yours; have you not one son in a Tower, *Dom* Mikhail?"

Her father's brow clouded. "Not by my will or wish, nor by my leave," he spat out, "I give no name of son to him who dwells among the *Hali'imyn!*" On his lips the harmless word was an obscenity; he calmed himself with an effort and added, "But this is no talk for a festal board. Will it please you to dance, my Lord?"

"I will leave that for younger folk," said Lord Scathfell, "But lead your lady out to dance if you will," he added, and The MacAran turned dutifully to Lady Luciella and led her on to the dance floor.

After the first ceremonious dance, the younger folk gathered for a ring-dance, all the young men in the outer

60

ring, all the girls and women in the inner one; the dancing grew riotous after a bit, and Romilly saw Darissa drop out of the dancers, her hand pressed to her side; she went to fetch her friend a drink, and sat beside her, chatting. Darissa wore the loose ungirdled gown of a pregnant woman, but even so she loosed the clasps on her tunic, and fanned herself—she was red and panting.

"I shall dance no more till this one is born," she said, pressing her long fingers against her swollen body, "He holds his own dance, I think, and will dance from now till harvest-time, mostly when I am trying to sleep!" Cathal came and bent solicitously over his wife, but she gestured him back to the dancing. "Go and dance with the men, my husband, I will sit here for a little and talk with my old playmate—what have you been doing with yourself, Romilly? Are you not betrothed yet? You are fifteen now, are you not?"

Romilly nodded. She was shocked at her friend, who had been so pretty and graceful but three years ago; now she had grown heavy-footed, her small breasts swollen and thick beneath the laces of her gown, her waist clumsy. In three years, Darissa had had two children and now she was bearing another already! As if reading her thoughts, Darissa said with a bitter twist of her lips, "Oh, I know well, I am not so pretty as I was when I was a maiden—enjoy your last year of dancing, Romilly, 'tis likely that next year you too will be on the sidelines, swelling with your first; my husband's father spoke of wedding you to Cinhil, or perhaps Mallina; he thinks her more docile and lady-like."

Romilly said in shock, "But need you have another so soon? I should think two in three years was enough—"

Darissa shrugged and smiled. "Oh, well, it is the way of things—this one I think I will feed at my own breast and not put out to nurse, and perhaps I will not get with child again this year. I love my little ones, but I think three is enough for a time—"

"It would be more than enough for me for a lifetime," said Romilly vigorously, and Darissa laughed. "So say we all when we are young girls. Lord Scathfell is pleased with me because I have already given them two sons, and I hope this one is a daughter; I would like a little girl—later I will take you to see my babies; they are pretty children, little Gareth has red hair; maybe he will have *laran*, a magician for the Towers—"

"Would you want him to—?" Romilly murmured, and Darissa laughed. "Oh, yes, Tramontana Tower would be ready to take him, the Aldarans are Hastur-kin from away back before the Hundred Kingdoms, and they have old ties with Tramontana." She lowered her voice. "Have you truly no news of Ruyven? Did your father really disown him?"

Romilly nodded, and Darissa's eyes widened; she and Ruyven had played together as children, too.

"I remember, one year at Midsummer, he sent me a Festival-basket," she said, "and I wore the sprig of golden-flower he sent me; but at the end of that Festival, Father betrothed me to Cathal, and we have been happy enough, and now there are our children—but I think kindly of Ruyven, and I would gladly have been your sister, Romilly. Do you think The MacAran will give you to Cinhil if he should ask? Then should we be sisters indeed—"

"I do not dislike Cinhil," Romilly said, but inwardly she shrank away; three years from now, then, would she be like Darissa, grown fat and short of breath, her skin blotched and her body misshapen from breeding? "The one good thing about such a marriage would be, it would bring me close to you," she said truthfully, "but I see no haste to marry; and Luciella says, fifteen is too young to settle down; she would as soon not have us betrothed till we are seventeen or more. One does not breed a good bitch in her first heat."

"Oh, Romilly," Darissa said, blushing, and they giggled together like children.

"Well, enjoy the dancing while you can, for your dancing days will be over soon," Darissa said. "Look, there is Darren's friend from the monastery—he looks like a monk in his dark suit; is he one of the brethren, then?"

Romilly shook her head. "I know not who he is, only that he is a friend of Darren's and of the Castamir clan," she said, and kept her suspicions to herself. Darissa said, "Castamir is a Hastur clan! I wonder he will come here freely—they held by the old king, I heard. Does your father hold to Carolin, or support the new king?"

"I do not think Father knows or cares, one king or another," said Romilly, but before she could say more, Alderic stood beside them.

"Mistress Romilly? It is a set dance—will you partner me?"

"Do you mind being left alone, Darissa?"

"No, there is Cathal; I will ask him to fetch me a glass of wine," Darissa said, and Romilly let Alderic draw her into the forming set, six couples—although one of them was Rael and Jessamy Storn who was eleven, and half a head taller than her partner. They faced one another, and Darren and Jeralda Storn, at the head of the line, led off, taking hands, circling each couple in the complex figures of the dance. When it came Alderic's turn she reached confidently for his hands; they were square, hard and warm, not the soft hands of a scholar at all, but calloused and strong like a swordsman's. An unlikely monk, indeed, she thought, and put her mind to the intricacies of the dance, which at the end of the figure put her opposite Darren, and then opposite her brother Rael. When the set brought her briefly into partnership, crossing hands and circling with Cinhil, he squeezed her hand and smiled, but she cast her eyes down and did not return the smile. So Lord Scathfell thought to marry her to Cinhil this year, so she could be fat and swollen with baby after baby like Darissa? Not likely! Some day, she supposed, she would have to be married, but not to this raw boy, if she could help it! Her father was not so much in awe of the Aldaran Lords as that, and besides, it was only Aldaran of Scathfell, not Aldaran of Castle Aldaran. Scathfell was the richest and most influential of their neighbors, but The MacAran had been an independent landholder since, she had heard, before the raising of Caer Donn city!

Now the set brought her face to face with *Dom* Garris again. He smiled at her and pressed her hand too, and she blushed, holding her own hands cold and stiff against his, just touching as the dance required. She was relieved when the set brought them back to their original places, with Alderic facing her. The musicians swung into a couple-dance, and she saw *Dom* Garris start toward her purposefully; she grabbed at Alderic's sleeve and whispered, "Will you ask me to dance, *Dom* Alderic?"

"To be sure," he said, smiling, and led her out. She said after a moment, returning his smile as they left Garris staring after them, "You are not a clodhopper at all."

"No?" He laughed. "It has been long since I danced, save with the monks—"

"You dance in the monastery?"

"Sometimes. To keep warm. And there is a sacred dance at some of the services. And some of the students who are not to be of the brethren go into the village and dance at Festival, though I—" it seemed to her that he hesitated a moment, "I had small leisure for that."

"They keep you so hard at your studies? *Domna* Luciella said that Darren looks thin and pale—do they give you enough to eat, and warm clothes?"

He nodded. "I am used enough to hardships," he said, and fell silent, while Romilly enjoyed the dance, the music. He said, as they separated at the end of the music, "You wear my flowers—I hope they pleased you?"

"Very much," she said, then felt shy again; had he put the *dorilys* into her basket as the invitation Mallina said it was, or was it simply a stranger's unfamiliarity with the country-side? She would have liked to ask, but was too bashful. But again it was as if he read her thoughts; he said abruptly, "Darren told me—I meant nothing improper, believe me, Mistress Romilly. In my country—I am a lowlander—the starflower, *dorilys*, it is the gift of the lord Hastur to the Blessed Cassilda, and I meant a courteous compliment in honor of the day, no more."

She said, smiling up at him, "I do not think anyone would believe you capable of any improper innuendo, *Dom* Alderic."

"I am your brother's friend; you need not say *Dom* to me," said Alderic. "After all, we have hunted and flown hawks together—"

"Nor need you call me *damisela*," she said, "My brothers and sister call me Romy—"

"Good; we shall be even as kinfolk, as I am to Darren," said Alderic. "Will you have some wine?" They had moved close to the refreshment-table. She shook her head and said ingenuously, "I am not allowed to drink wine in company."

"*Shallan*, then?" He dipped her up some of the sweet fruit-drink. She sipped it thirstily. After the romping dance she knew that her hair was beginning to come down, but she did not want to withdraw to the giggling girls in the corner and pin it up.

"You are fond of hawking?" she asked him.

"I am; the women of our family train sentry-birds. Have you ever flown one, *dami*—Romy?"

She shook her head. She had seen the great fierce birds, but said, "I knew not that they could be tamed! Why, they can bring down a rabbithorn! I should think they were no great sport—"

"They are not flown for sport," Alderic said, "but trained for war, or for fire-watch; it is done with *laran*. A sentry-bird in flight can spy out intruders into a peaceful countryside, or bandits, or a forest-fire. But it is no task for sport, and in truth the birds are fierce, and not easy to handle. Yet I think you could do it, Romilly, if your *laran* was trained."

"It is not, nor likely to be," she said, "and doubtless you

64

know why, if Darren has told you so much. Sentry-birds!"
She felt a little shiver, half pleasant, trickle down her spine at
the thought of handling the great fierce birds of prey. "I
think it would be no harder to train a banshee!"

Alderic chuckled. "I have even heard of that in the far
hills," he said, "And banshee-birds are very stupid; it takes
little craft to handle them, only to rear them from hatchlings
and feed them on warm food; and they will do what you will,
spying out game-tracks with the warmth left in the ground,
and they make fine watch-birds, for they will scream terribly
at any strange smell—"

Now she did shiver; the thought of the great, blind,
flightless carnivores trained for watchman-duty. She said,
"Who needs a banshee for that when a good Rouser hound is
as useful, and much nicer to have around the house?"

"I'll not argue that," said Alderic, "and I would sooner
climb High Kimbi in my bare feet than try to train a
banshee; but it can be done. I cannot handle even sentry-
birds; I have not the gift, but some of the women of our
family do so, and I have seen it done in the Tower, where
they use them for fire-watch; their eyes see further than any
human's." Soft strains of music began again and he asked,
"Would you like to dance this one?"

She shook her head. "Not yet, thanks—it is warm, the sun
coming in like this."

Alderic bowed to someone behind her, and Romilly turned
to see Luciella standing there. She said, "Romilly, you have
not yet danced with *Dom* Garris!"

She said scornfully, "It is like him to complain to my
stepmother instead of coming like a man to ask me himself."

"Romilly! He is heir to Scathfell!"

"I don't care if he is heir to Cloudland Staircase or to Zandru's ninth hell, if he wants to dance—" she began, but *Dom*
Garris appeared behind Luciella and said, with his plump
smile, "Will you honor me with a dance. Mistress Romilly?"

There was, after all, no way to refuse without being really
rude. He was her parents' guest, even though she felt he
should dance with the women his own age and not hang
around gawking at the young girls. She accepted his hand on
her wrist to lead her out to dance. After all, he could not say
or do anything rude in the full view of her father and her
brothers, and half the countryside round. His hand on hers
was unpleasantly damp, but she supposed that was not anything he could help.

"Why, you are light as a feather on your feet, *damisela*—

quite the young lady! Who would have thought it this morning, seeing you in your boots and breeches like a boy—I suppose all the young lads in the countryside are hanging around you, heh?"

Romilly shook her head silently. She detested this kind of talk, though she knew it would have made Mallina giggle and blush. When they had finished the dance he asked her for another, but she declined politely, saying she had a stitch in her side. He wanted to fetch her wine or a glass of *shallan*, but when she said she only wished to sit down by Darissa for a little he sat beside them and insisted on fanning her. Fortunately, by the time that dance was over, the musicians had struck up another ring-dance and all the young folks were gathering into circles, laughing and kicking up their heels in the rowdy figure. *Dom* Garris finally went away, sulking, and Romilly released her breath.

"You have made another conquest," Darissa teased.

"Not likely; dancing with me is like grabbing at a scullery-girl, something he can do without committing himself to anything," Romilly said. "The Aldarans of Scathfell are too high to marry into our clan, except for their younger sons. Father spoke once of marrying me to Manfred Storn, but he's not fifteen yet, and there's no hurry. Yet, though I am not high enough to marry, I am too well-born for him to seduce without reprisal, and I do not like him well enough for that." She smiled and added, "The worst thing about wedding with Cinhil, should he offer for me, would be having to call that great fat slug *brother*. Yet kinship's dues, I dare say, would at least make it unseemly for him to pay me more than the attention due a brother's wife."

"I would not count on that," said Darissa in an undertone, "When I was pregnant with little Rafael, last year, he came and sought me out—he said that since I was already with child I need fear no unseemly consequences, and when I chided him, he said he looked backward to the old days in the hills, when brothers and sisters held all their wives in common . . . and surely, he said, Cathal would pay him a brother's kindness and not care if I shared his bed now and again, since his wife was also big with breeding—I kicked his shins and told him to find a servant-girl for his bed if he could pay one to overlook his ugliness; and so I wounded his pride and he has not come near me again. To tell the truth he is not so bad-looking, only he whines and his hands are always flabby and damp. And—" she added, showing the dimples which were almost the only thing unchanged from

66

the time when she and Romilly had been girls together, "I love Cathal too well to seek any other bed."

Romilly blushed, and looked away; reared among animals, she knew perfectly well what Darissa was talking about, but Luciella was a strictly-observing *cristoforo* and did not think it seemly to speak of such things among young girls. Darissa mistook her blush. She said, almost defensively, "Well, I bear children without much trouble—I am not like Garris's wife; she left no living children, and died in childbirth just before Midwinter. He has worn out three wives, *Dom* Garris, trying to get him an Heir, and I have marked that all his children die at birth—I have no wish to get myself with child by *him* or I should follow his wives into death, no doubt.

"My older sister went for a time to Tramontana Tower when she was a girl, and she said she had heard there about the days of the old breeding-program, when the Aldarans had some strange gifts of *laran*, but they were bound, in their line, to lethal genes—do you know what those are? Yes, of course, your father breeds his own horses, does he not? And Cathal has them not, but I think *Dom* Garris will leave no heir, so one day my sons by Cathal will inherit Scathfell—" Darissa rattled on.

"And you will rule the roost as their mother," said Romilly, laughing, but then Rael came up and pulled them into the set-dance, saying they had not enough women to make up a second set, and she dropped that line of thought.

The dancing and feasting went on all day, and before midnight The MacAran and Lord Scathfell and the rest of the older people, with their ladies, retired to rest, leaving the young people to their dancing and merry-making. Rael was taken away by the governess, also the protesting Mallina, who was comforted only by seeing that her friends Jessamy and Jeralda were also being sent to bed. Romilly was tired, and almost ready to go with the children—she had, after all, been awake before daylight. But Alderic and her brother Darren were still dancing, and she would not admit that her brother could stay awake longer than she could. But she saw, with a little sinking awareness, that Darissa was leaving the hall— pregnant as she was, she said, she needed her sleep.

I will stay close to Darren. In my brother's presence Dom *Garris cannot come too near for comfort . . .* and then she wondered why she was worrying; he had, after all, offered her no word out of the way, and how could she complain, after all, of a mere look? Nevertheless, the memory of his eyes on her made her squirm; and now she thought about it, she realized that all this day and evening she had been somehow, in the back of her mind, aware of his eyes on her.

Is this, then, laran?

I would rather not dance at all, I would rather sit here and talk about hawks and horses with my brother and his friends. . . .

But Cinhil claimed her for a dance, and then she could not in courtesy refuse *Dom* Garris. The dancing was a little wilder, the music faster, now that the elderly and more staid people had left the hall. He whirled her about till she was dizzy, and she was conscious that his hands were no longer decorously on her sleeve but that he was holding her somewhat closer than was comfortable, and when she tried self-consciously to squirm away from them he only chuckled and eased her closer still.

"No, now, you cannot tell me you are so shy as that," he said, and she could tell from the flushed look of his face and the slight slurring of his words that he had drunk over long of the stronger wine at the high table, "Not when you run about with those lovely long legs showing in breeches, and your breasts showing through a tunic three sizes too small, you cannot play Lady Modesty with me now!" He pulled her close and his lips nuzzled her cheek, but she twisted indignantly away.

"Don't!" And then she said, crossly, "I do not like the stink of too much wine on your breath, and you are drunk, *Dom* Garris. Let me go."

"Well, you should have been drinking more," he said easily, and guided them in the dance into one of the long galleries that led away from the hall. "Here, give me a kiss, Romy—"

"I am not *Romy* to you," she said, and pulled her head away from him, "and if you had not been spying about where you had no right to be, you would not have seen me in my brother's clothes, which I wear only in the sight of my little brothers. If you think I was showing myself to you, you are very much mistaken."

"No, only to that haughty young sprig of the *Hali'imyn* who was squiring you to the hunt and hawking?" he asked, and laughed. She said, twisting her rumpled hair free, "I want to go back to the hall. I did not come out here with you of my own will, I just did not want to make a scene on the dance floor. Take me back to the hall, or I will shout to my brother now! And then my father will horsewhip you!"

He laughed, holding her close. "Ah, on a night like this, what do you think your brother will be doing, then? He would not thank you for calling him away from what every young man will be about, on Midsummer-Night. Must I alone be refused? You are not such a child as all that. Come, give me a kiss then—"

"No!" Romilly struggled away from his intruding hands, crying now, and he let her go.

"I am sorry," he said gently, "I was testing you; I see now that you are a good girl, and all the Gods forbid I should interfere with you." He bent and dropped a suddenly respectful kiss on her wrist. She swallowed hard, blinked back her tears and fled from the gallery, back through the hall and upstairs, where she bundled off her festival gown and hid beneath her warm quilts, sobbing.

How she hated him!

CHAPTER FIVE

Every year The MacAran held his great Midsummer-feast as preliminary to a great market in hawks, trained dogs and horses. On the morning after the Festival, Romilly wakened to the great bustle in the courtyard, and men and women thronging, while on the field beyond the enclosed yard, horses were neighing as men put them through their paces, and men and women were coming and going. Romilly dressed quickly in an old gown—there were still guests, so there could be no thought of borrowing a pair of Darren's breeches—and ran down. Calinda, meeting her on the stairs, gave a rueful laugh.

"I knew I should get no work out of Rael this day—he is

beyond me, his father must send him soon to Nevarsin for teaching by men who can handle him," she said, "But must you, too, hang about the market, Romilly? Ah well—" she smiled kindly at her charge, "Go if you will, I shall have the whole day to work with Mallina on her penmanship—she takes guidance better when you and Rael are not there to hear. And I suppose you would not mind your book if your heart and thoughts were all out in the courtyard. But you must work all the harder tomorrow," she said firmly, and Romilly hugged the older woman with a vehemence that left her breathless.

"Thank you, Calinda, thank you!"

She picked her way carefully through the trampled mud of the courtyard and into the field. Davin was displaying the flight to a lure of one of the best-trained hawks, a great bird in whose training Romilly had played no small part; she stood watching in excitement till Davin spotted her.

"And this hawk is fierce and strong, but so gentle that even a young maiden could fly her," Davin said, "Mistress Romilly, will you take the bird?"

She slid the gauntlet over her arm and held out her wrist; he set the bird on it, and swirled the lure, and the bird took off, quickly climbing the sky, then, as the whirling leather thong with the meat and feathers came swooping down, striking so quickly that eyes could hardly follow the swift strike. Romilly picked up bird and lure and stood feeding the hawk from her free hand, to the accompaniment of little cries of amazement and delight.

"I shall have that hawk, then, for my lady," said Cathal Aldaran of Scathfell, "She has not had enough exercise since her children were born, and so fine a hawk will encourage her to be out and about, and to ride—"

"No," said the elderly *Dom* Gareth firmly, "No woman shall fly such a hawk as that under my roof; but your training methods are excellent, *messire*, and I will take one of the smaller hawks for Lady Darissa—have you a good lady's hawk? Mistress Romilly, can you advise me, perhaps, as to what hawk my daughter-in-law could best fly?"

She said, lowering her eyes modestly, "I fly a *verrin* hawk, *vai dom*, but either of these—" she indicated three of the smaller birds, with wing-spans not much longer than her arm, "are well-trained and I think Darissa would have no trouble in handling them. But I give you my word, sir, that if you want to buy the larger bird for her, she is so well trained that Darissa could fly her, and the larger birds are better for hunting for the kitchens; the smaller hawks can bring down nothing bigger than a field-shrew."

He snorted. "The women of my household have no need to hunt for meat for the pot; if they fly hawks, they do so only to have a reason to take air and exercise. And The MacAran still lets a great girl like you hunt with a *verrin* hawk? Disgraceful!"

Romilly bit back the protest on her lip—*Aldaran might not approve of women flying hawks, but perhaps other men were not so stuffy and narrow-minded as he was himself*—realizing that a saucy answer would only alienate a valued neighbor and customer of her father's. While they produced most of what they needed on the estate at Falconsward, still coined money was always in short supply, and most of her father's ready money came from this sale every year. She curtseyed to Lord Scathfell and withdrew, handing back the hawk to Davin. While he haggled with the man, she cast a quick frightened glance around the field—her father might have decided to punish her by putting Preciosa up for sale—but Preciosa was not there, but still safe within the mews. At the far end, her father was putting one or two of his best horses through their paces, while the kennel-man was displaying working dogs trained to obedience to word or gesture. The high nobility who had danced last night at their feast rubbed elbows with small-holders and farmers who had come to pick up dogs for their herding, or perhaps to trade for a horse rejected by the nobles. Darren was stationed at the far end, writing down all the details of the transactions for the steward; Rael was running in and out of the crowd, playing catch-the-monkey with a group of small boys his own age, his face and hands already grubby and his jacket torn.

"Can you take me to see your father's horses?" Alderic said at her elbow, "I would like to trade my nag for a somewhat better one; I have not much money, but perhaps I could work some time for him in return for the difference—do you think he would be interested in a deal like that? I have marked that your *coridom* is old and feeble—perhaps I could work for him for forty days or so while he finds himself a man better suited to the needs of his business, and the old man could be retired to an indoor steward."

She blinked in surprise—she had begun to be sure that he was, in fact, the Hastur prince in disguise, and here he was offering to hire himself, a paid worker, to The MacAran in return for a horse-trade! But she said politely, "About the deal, you must ask him yourself; but we have some good horses

71

which are not good-looking enough to attract the attention of the highly-born, and must be sold at a lower cost; perhaps one of them would suit you, if it was well-trained. That one, for instance—" she pointed out a great ungainly horse, an ugly color of brown, spotted unevenly with black, his mane and tail growing somewhat askew, "He is an ugly raw-boned brute, but if you look carefully at his gait, and the way he carries his tail, you will see that he is a fine strong horse, and spirited too. But he is no ride for a lady, nor for any soft-handed fellow who wants his horse to plod along at a gentle pace; he wants firm hands and good handling. His sire was our best stallion, but the dam was only a cull, so though his blood is not bad, he is an ugly brute and not good-colored."

"His haunches look strong, indeed," said Alderic, "But I would like to look at his teeth for myself. I suppose he is broken to the saddle?"

"Yes, though father was at first intending to make a draft-horse of him; he is too big for most riders," she said, "But you are tall, you would need a large horse. Ruyven broke him to the bridle, but I myself have ridden him—although," she said, with a mischievous smile, "Father does not know it, and you need not tell him."

"And you can handle him, *damisela?*" Alderic looked incredulous.

"I will not ride him before all these people to prove it," she said, "but I would not stoop to lie about it to you, and—" she met his eyes briefly, "I think perhaps you would know if I did."

"That I would, Romilly," he said gravely.

"I give you my word, the horse is good-tempered enough, but he wants firm handling," she said, "I think perhaps he has a sense of humor—if a horse can laugh, I would swear I have seen him laugh at people who think they need only clamber on a horse and let him do all the work, and he had Darren off in two minutes; but my father can ride him without even a bridle, only a saddle and halter; because The MacAran knows how to make him, or any horse, behave."

"Aye, and I am told you have the same gift," he said. "Well, I will make your father an offer for him; would he take my horse in trade, do you think?"

"Oh, yes, he has always need of cheaply-priced horseflesh, to sell to farmers and such," she said, "Men who will use their horses well, but cannot afford much in the way of stables. One of our old mares, no longer young enough to carry active young folk who would be in the saddle all day,

72

he gave for almost nothing to an elderly man who lives nearby, who was too poor to buy a good horse, just so that the old horse might live out her life in a good home and have only light work. No doubt he would do the same for your horse—is she very old?"

"No," Alderic said, "but I must be into the Hellers when summer comes, and even in summertime it takes a strong horse to ride such trails."

"Into the far Hellers?" She wondered what would take him into the almost-impassable mountain ranges in the summer, but he turned the subject deftly before she could ask.

"I had not expected to find a young woman such a judge of horseflesh—how came you to know so much?"

"I am a MacAran, sir; I have worked at my father's side since I was old enough to follow him about the stables, and when Ruyven left—" she broke off, unable to say to anyone outside the family that her oldest brother's defection had left her father with no one but paid help to share his love of the animals he bred and trained. Yet she sensed that he understood her, for he smiled in sympathy.

"I like your father," Alderic said, "He is harsh, yes, but he is just, and he speaks freely to his children."

"Does not your father?"

Alderic shook his head. "I have hardly had speech with my father half a dozen times since I was out of short dresses. My mother was wedded to him in a dynastic marriage, and there was little love to lose between them; I doubt they have said a civil word to one another since my sister was conceived, and now they dwell in separate houses and meet formally a few times a year, no more. My father is a kindly man, I suppose, but I think he cannot look on my face without seeing my mother's features, and so he has always been ill at ease with me. Even as a babe I called him *sir*, and have hardly spoken with him since I was grown to man's size."

"That cannot have been so long ago," Romilly teased, but he said, with a poignancy that stopped her teasing cold, "Still, I envy you; I have seen Rael climb without fear into his father's lap—I cannot remember that I ever did so with my father, but you can go to your father, speak with him freely, he treats you almost as a friend and listens when you speak. Even though my father is high in—" Alderic stopped himself short, and there was a moment of awkward silence before he finished weakly, "High in station and honor, I wish I need not always address him as *My Lord*. I swear I would trade fathers with you at any moment."

"He might think it a bargain," said Romilly bitterly, but she knew she was not quite truthful; her father loved her, harsh as he was, and she knew it. She said, "Look, there he stands and for the moment he has no customer, go now and ask for such a trade for Redwing."

"I thank you," he said, and went; then Davin called to her to show the paces of one of the dogs she had trained, and she forgot Alderic again. She worked all day on the sale fields, displaying the obedience of the dogs, explaining bloodlines and stud-books, exhibiting the hawks; her noon-meal was a mouthful of bread and cheese and a few nuts, swallowed in the enclosure behind the stables among The MacAran's men, and by the time the trading was called to a halt by the evening rain and the guests began to depart, she was famished and filthy, ready for a bath and to be dressed in a comfortable worn tunic and skirt for the family's dinner. A good smell of roasting meat and fresh-baked bread came as she passed the hall, and she went in and took her seat. Rael was still chattering to anyone who would listen about his day spent among the animals, and Luciella finally silenced him with a weary "Hush, Rael, or you shall have supper in the nursery; there are others in this family who would like to speak a word or two without being drowned out! How did it go today, my dear?" she asked The MacAran as he took his seat and picked up his mug. He took a long drink before answering.

"Well enough; I made a good trade for Redwing, who is a fine horse for anyone who has wit to see what lies beneath that ugly coat of his. *Dom* Alderic told me you recommended that sale, Romilly," he said, with a kind glance at his elder daughter.

"Did I well, father? I did not want to interfere, but it seemed to me that he would be a good ride for *Dom* Alderic," she said shyly, "and——" she looked around to see if Alderic had come in, but Darren's place was still empty and his friend was not at table either, "He told me he was short of ready money, so I knew that one of the blacks would be beyond his purse."

"I am grateful to you; I wanted Redwing in good hands," said her father, "and most people could not handle him; but with young Castamir, he was gentle as a child's cagebird. So I thank you, daughter,"

"But still," Luciella complained, "this must be the last year she goes out into the fields with the men, showing off hawks and horses—she is a grown woman, Mikhail!"

74

"No fear of that," said The MacAran, smiling, "Other news I have too. Romilly, my dear, you know you are of an age to be married; I had not thought I would have such a good offer for you, but *Dom* Garris of Scathfell has asked me for your hand in marriage, and I have answered him; yes."

Romilly felt as if an ice-cold hand was closing about her throat.

"Father!" she protested, while Luciella beamed and Mallina squeaked with excitement, "Not *Dom* Garris!"

"Come, come," her father said with a genial smile, "Surely you have not set your heart on someone else? Manfred Storn is not yet ready to marry, and I thought you loved Darissa well, and would welcome marrying into that family, so you might be near your best friend."

"I had thought—perhaps Cinhil—"

"If that young man has trifled with your affections," said The MacAran, "I'll turn him over my knee and dust his breeches for him—he's too much a child to be worth calling challenge! Why marry the younger son when you can marry the Heir, my dear?"

Her heart sank as she remembered the moment in the galleries. *I was only testing you. Now I see you are a good girl.* So, she thought, if she had liked *Dom* Garris well enough to kiss him she would have been deprived of marriage, as if it were a prize for good conduct! But since she had showed her loathing, she was then worthy of his attentions? Her eyes burned, but she would not cry here before her father.

"Father, I hate him," she said, pleading, "Please, don't make me marry him!"

"Romilly," said Mallina, "You will be Lady Scathfell! Why, he's Heir to Scathfell, and perhaps even to Aldaran itself some day! Why, the folk of Aldaran were of the Hastur-kinfolk!"

The MacAran gestured the younger girl to silence.

"Romy," he said gravely, "Marriage is not a matter of whim. I have chosen a good young man for you—"

"So young he is not," she flared, "he has buried three wives, and all of them have died in childbirth!"

"That is because he married into Aldaran kindred," her father said, "Any horse-breeder will tell you it is unwise to cross close kindred so often. You have no Aldaran blood and can probably give him healthy children."

She thought of Darissa, not much older than herself, swollen and shapeless with bearing children. Would she be like that, and would those children have been fathered by *Dom*

Garris, with his whining voice and damp flabby hands? The thought made her flesh crawl.

"No more talk," said her father firmly, "All silly girls think they know what man they want, but older heads must make the decision as it is best for their lives. I would not have you married before harvest time—I will not have my daughter hustled to marriage—but at the harvest you will marry *Dom* Garris, and that is all I have to say."

"So while I thought you were having a sale of horses and hawks," she said bitterly, "You were also making a sale of your daughters! Tell me, Father, did *Dom* Garris give a good price?"

She knew by the unlovely flush that spread over her father's face that she had caught him on the raw. He said, "I'll hear none of your impertinence, my pert young mistress!"

"I doubt it not," she flung back at him, "You would rather trade in hawks and horses because they cannot talk back—and you can give them what fate you will!"

He opened his mouth to reply; then gave her a heavy glance.

"My lady," he said to Luciella, "It is your task to bring my daughters under control; see to it, will you? I will dine with the steward; I'll not have this brangling at my family table." He rose and strode out of the room.

"Oh, Mother," Romilly wailed, crumpling and throwing her head into Luciella's lap, "Do I have to marry that—that—" words almost failed her, but finally she came out with, "that great *slug*? He is like something with a dozen legs that crawled out from under a piece of rotten wood!"

Luciella stroked her hair gently, puzzled. "There, there, child," she murmured, "It will not be so bad as you think; why, didn't you tell *Dom* Alderic that a horse should not be judged by his ugly coat? *Dom* Garris is a good and honorable man. Why, at your age, I had already my first child, and so had your own dear mother, Romy. There, there, don't cry," she added helplessly, and Romilly knew there was no help for it; Luciella would never defy her father. Nor could she. She was only a girl and there was no escape.

Alone in her room, or riding alone over the hills with Preciosa on her saddle, Romilly pondered what she could do. It seemed that she was trapped. She had never known her father to alter a judgment given—he would not hear of forgiveness for Ruyven, for instance—or to change his mind, once made up. He would not break his agreement with *Dom* Garris—or had it been made with Gareth of Scathfell himself?—though the heavens should fall. Her governess, her stepmother even, could sometimes be teased or argued out of a punishment or a judgment; in all the years of her life, her father had never been known to go back on what he had said, even when he knew it was wrong. Far and wide in the Kilghard Hills, the word of a MacAran was like the word of Hastur; as good as another man's signed bond or sworn oath.

What if she should defy him? It would not be the first time. Something inside her quailed at the thought of his rage. But when she countered her father's rage with the thought of the alternative, confronting *Dom* Garris and the memory of lust in his eyes, she realized that she would rather that her father beat her every day for a year than that he should deliver her over to *Dom* Garris. Didn't he *know* what the man was like? And then, with her heart sinking, she realized that The MacAran was a man and would never have seen that side of Garris of Aldaran; *that*, *Dom* Garris showed only to a woman he desired.

If he touches me, I will vomit, she thought, and then she knew that whatever her father's anger, she must make a final appeal to him.

She found him in the stable, supervising a stableboy in poulticing the knees of a black pony who had fallen in the yard. She knew it was not an auspicious moment, for he looked cross and abstracted.

"Keep up the poulticing," he directed the boy, "Hot and cold, for at least two hours, and then treat the knees with *karalla* powder and bandage them well. And see he doesn't lie down in the muck—make sure he has fresh straw every few hours. Even with all we can do, he will be scarred and I'll have to sell him at a loss, or keep him for light work on the farm; if his knees get infected, we may lose him altogether. I'm putting you in charge—if anything goes wrong, I'll have it out of your hide, you young rascal, since it was your careless riding let him fall!" The stableboy opened his mouth to protest, but The MacAran gestured him to silence. "And don't give me any back-talk—I saw you running him on the stones! Damned young fool, I ought to put you to mucking-out and not let you exercise any of them for forty days!" He turned his head irritably and saw Romilly.

"What do you want in the stables, girl?"

"I came to find you, father," she said, trying to steady her voice, "I would like a word with you, if you can spare the time."

"Time? I have none this morning, with this pony hurt and

77

perhaps spoilt," he said, but he stepped out of the stable and leaned against one of the rail fences. "What is it, child?"

But she could not speak for a moment, her throat swelling as she looked at the panorama behind her, the mountains that rose across the valley, the green paddock with the brood mares near their time, placidly grazing, the house-folk washing clothes in the yard, over a steaming cauldron poised on the smouldering fire of little sticks . . . this was all so dear to her, and now, whatever came of this, she must leave it . . . Falconsward was as dear to her as to any of her father's sons, yet she must leave her home to be married away, and any of her father's sons, even Ruyven who had abandoned it, could stay here forever, with the horses and the home hills. She swallowed hard and felt tears starting from her eyes. Why could she not be her father's Heir in Ruyven's place, since he cared nothing for it, and bring her husband here, rather than marrying someone she must hate, and living in a strange place.

"What is it, daughter?" he asked gently, and she knew he had seen her tears.

She swallowed hard, trying to control her voice. She said "Father, I have always known I must marry, and I would gladly do your will, but—but—Father, why must it be *Dom* Garris? I hate him! I cannot bear him! The man is like a toad!" Her voice rose, and her father frowned, but quickly smoothed his face into the forced calm she dreaded.

He said reasonably, "I tried to make you the best marriage I could, Romy. He is nearest Heir to Scathfell, and not far from the lordship of Aldaran of Aldaran, should the old man die without children, which now looks likely. I am not a rich man, and I cannot pay much of a marriage-portion for you; and Scathfell is rich enough not to care what you can bring. *Dom* Garris is in need of a wife—"

"And he has worn out three," said Romilly, desperately, "And goes again to marry another girl of fifteen. . . ."

"One reason he asked me for you," her father said, "was that his other wives have been weaklings and too near akin to him; he wanted new blood for the house. If you bear him a healthy son, you will have great honor, and everything you could possibly wish for—"

"And if I do not I will be dead and no one will have to care whether I am happy or not," she cried, her tears starting forth again. "Father, I cannot, I will not marry that—that loathsome man! Oh, Father, I am not trying to defy you, I would willingly marry almost anyone else—Cinhil, or—or *Dom* Alderic—"

"Alderic, hey?" Her father took her chin in his big hand and tipped up her face to look at it. "Tell me the truth, now, child. Have you been playing about in a way you should not? *Dom* Garris will expect to find you chaste; will he be disappointed? Has that arrogant young Castamir sprig been trifling with your feelings, girl? A guest under this roof—"

"*Dom* Alderic has never spoken a word to me, or done anything, which he could not have done in full view of you and Mother," she flared indignantly, "I named him only because I would not find him loathsome, nor Cinhil, nor any healthy kind young man somewhere near my own age! But that—that slimy—" words failed her, and she bit her lip hard so she would not cry.

"Romilly," said her father gently, still holding her face between his hands, "*Dom* Garris is not so old as *that*: it is not, after all, as if I had tried to give you to Lord Gareth, or to any man I knew to be evil-tempered, or a drunkard, or a gambler, or one who was a wastrel of substance. I have known Garris all his life; he is a good, honorable and well-born young man, and you should not hold his face against him, since he did not make it. A handsome face will soon be worn away, but honor and good birth and a kindly temper are the things I want for my daughter's husband. You are only a silly young girl, and you can see no further than a man's handsome face and grace at dancing; which is why fathers and mothers make marriages for young girls, so that they can see a man's true worth."

She swallowed, and felt shame overcoming her, to speak of this to her father, but the alternative was worse. She said, "He—he looks at me in such a way—as if I were naked—and when we were dancing, he put his hands on me—"

Her father frowned and looked aside and she knew he was embarrassed too. At last he sighed and said, "The man is wanting a wife, that is all; when he is wedded he will not need to do so. And at least you know that he is not a—" he coughed nervously, "he is not a lover of men, and will not desert you to hold hands with one of his paxmen or a pretty young page-boy or Guardsman. I think he will make you a good husband, Romy. He may be awkward and not know how to make himself known to you, but I think he means you well and you will be happy together."

Romilly felt the tears breaking and spilling. She said, feeling her voice break in sobs, "Father—oh, Father, *please*

. . . anyone, anyone else, I swear I will obey you without question, but not—not *Dom* Garris—"

The MacAran scowled, biting his lip. He said, "Romilly, this matter has gone so far I cannot honorably draw back. The folk of Scathfell are neighbors, and I am dependent on their good will; to break my word at this point, would be an affront to their honor which I could not recover in a lifetime. If I had had any idea you felt like this, I would never have given my word; but done is done, and I have pledged it in honor. There's no more to be said, child. You are young; you will soon grow used to him, and it will be well, I promise you. Now cheer up, don't cry; I promised you a pair of fine blacks, broken with my own hand, for a wedding-present, and I am going to make over the small farm at Greyrock to you, so you will always have something, a place of your own. And I have told Luciella to send to the markets in Caer Donn for fine stuff for a wedding-dress, so you need not be married in homespun. So cheer up, dry your eyes, and decide for yourself which of the blacks you want for a wedding-present, and you may ask Luciella to have new dresses made for you, three—no, four new outfits and everything to go with them, all kinds of petticoats and feathers and bonnets and gewgaws such as girls like, no girl in the hills will be better outfitted for her wedding."

She bent her head, swallowing hard. She had known it was hopeless, and he had given his word to *Dom* Garris and to Lord Scathfell. He would never draw back now, and it would be useless, no matter what she should say. He mistook her silence for agreement and patted her cheek.

"There's my fine, good girl," he said awkwardly, "I am proud of you, child—would that any of your brothers had your strength and spirit."

"I wish I had been your son," she blurted out, "and that I could stay at home with you always—"

Her father took her gently into his arms. "So do I, girl," he said against her hair, "So do I. But it's for man to wish and the Gods to Give, and the Bearer of Burdens alone knows why he gifted only my daughter with those things a man wants from his sons. The world will go as it will and not as you or I would have it, Romy." He patted her, gently, and she cried, holding on to him, cried hopelessly, as if she would never stop.

In a way, she thought desperately later, his sympathy made it worse. If he had stormed and shouted at her, raged and threatened her with a beating, she could at least have felt that she had a right to rebel. Before his kindness she could only see his point of view——that she was a young girl, that her good parents and guardians were doing what they thought best for her, and that she was silly and thoughtless to speak out against their caution for her.

So she tried to seem interested in the preparations for her wedding which, so The MacAran said, would be at the harvest. Luciella sent to Caer Donn for spider-silk for her wedding-gown and fine dyed stuff, crimson and blue and violet, for her new dresses, and had ordered so many petticoats and camisoles and fine underthings that Mallina was openly jealous and sulked while the sewing was being done.

One morning, a rider came from Scathfell, and when he was welcomed in the courtyard, uncovered a cage before him on the saddle.

"A message from *Dom* Garris, sir," he said to The MacAran, "and a gift for Mistress Romilly."

The MacAran took the letter, scowling slightly, and tore it open. "Your eyes are better than mine, Darren," he said to his son, "Read it for me."

Romilly thought, annoyed, that if the letter concerned *her*, she should have been the one to read it. But perhaps The MacAran did not want it known that his daughter was so much a better scholar than his Nevarsin-educated son. Darren glanced through the letter and frowned, then read aloud.

"To The MacAran of Falconsward and to my affianced wife Romilly, greeting from Gareth-Regis Aldaran at Scathfell. Your daughter informed me that she flies a *verrin* hawk, which is understandable in the daughter of the finest hawk-trainer in these hills, but would be unseemly for the wife of Aldaran's Heir. Therefore I take the liberty of sending her two fine ladybirds which will fittingly adorn the most beautiful wrist in all of the Kilghard Hills, so that she need not fly a man's hawk. I beg her acceptance of these fine birds, and I send them now so that she may be accustomed to their flight. Kindly convey my compliments and respectful wishes to my promised wife, and to you my most respectful greetings, sir." Darren looked up, saying, "It has Scathfell's own seal affixed."

The MacAran raised his eyebrows, but said, "A courteous letter indeed. Uncover the cage, man."

The cover lifted, two beautiful little hawks were revealed; their hoods were of fine scarlet-dyed leather with an Aldaran crest worked in gold thread, and the jesses glimmered with gold threads too. They were tiny brilliant birds, gleaming with gloss and health, and Romilly caught her breath at the sight of them.

"A beautiful gift," she said, "and most thoughtful. Tell my—my promised husband," she said, and stumbled over the words, "That I am most grateful to him and I shall fly them with all kind thoughts of him." She held out her wrist, and lifted one of the hawks on to her glove. It sat so quietly that she could tell it was perfectly trained. Never mind that such hawks were no good for anything but flying at field-mice, they were exquisite little birds and for *Dom* Garris to pay so much heed to her known interests was a good sign. For a little while she thought better of her promised husband; but later she began to think it over; was this simply his way of telling her that when she was his wife she would not be allowed to work with a proper hawk at all? From what Gareth of Scathfell—the old man—had said, she was inclined to think so. *It would be unseemly for the wife of Scathfell's Heir.* She made up her mind, firmly, whatever they said, she would never be argued or bullied into giving up Preciosa! The bond between them was too strong for that.

While she was first flying the little hawks—with a guilty thought that she was being disloyal to her beloved Preciosa—she reached out for contact, the strong bond between hawk and flyer. But the tiny birds gave only a faint sense of confusion, exhilaration; there was no close emotion, no sense of rapport and union—the smaller hawks were too lowly-organized to have the capacity for *laran*. She knew the cagebirds had no such abilities—she had once or twice tried to communicate with them—in fact, "the mind of a cage-bird" was a byword for a stupid woman! Flying the small hawks was dull; she could watch them fly, and they were beautiful indeed, but there was none of the excitement, the sense of rapport and completion, she felt with Preciosa. She flew them dutifully every day for exercise, but it was always with relief that she hooded them again with the beautifully-worked hoods and cast off Preciosa into the sky, climbing the sky with her in an ecstasy of flight and soaring freedom.

She rode mostly with Darren, now, and Rael; Alderic had been put to the *coridom*'s work and was always busy about the place with accounts, arranging the stud-books, supervising the many men about court and stables. She seldom saw him, except now and again for a decorous word as he sat by the fire in the evening, or played a game of *castles* or cards with Darren or her father, or sometimes whittled wooden toys to amuse Rael in the long evenings.

82

Her days, too, were filled; her father had said she need do no more lessons, and the plan for her to study ciphering with the old steward had of course been put aside, since she was to be married so soon, so Calinda filled her days with stitching, and taught her how to oversee the kitchen-women and the sewing-women and even the dairies . . . not that there would be so much need for her to do any of these things, but, Calinda said, she must know how to do these things so that she could know whether her servants did them well or not; Lord Scathfell was a widower and she would be the first lady in authority at Scathfell; she must not let them think that Falconsward was a poorly run household, so that the daughter of Falconsward could not fitly supervise her women. Romilly thought she would rather muck out barns and milk dairy-animals and make the butter herself than have to oversee other women doing it; while as for the sewing-women, she was grimly certain that the youngest and least skilled of them would be better than she, so how could she ever presume to supervise or oversee, far less chide or correct? Luciella, too, hunted up one of Mallina's old dolls, and dressed it in Rael's cast-off babyclothes and taught both Mallina and Romilly how to bathe a young baby, how to hold it and support its floppy little head, how to change its napkins and what to do to keep it from having rashes and skin disorders; Romilly could not imagine why, if there were skilled nurses and midwives there, and Darissa with two—no, three children by now—she should have to know how to do all this herself, even before she had any children, but Luciella insisted that it was part of a young wife's proper knowledge. Romilly had no particular objection to having children—Rael as a baby had been adorable—but when she thought of having children, she thought first of Darissa, soft and flabby and fat and sick, and then of the inevitable process by which those children would be gotten. She was farmbred and healthy, and had often thought, with secret pleasure, of the time when she would have a lover, a husband, but when she sought to put *Dom* Garris's face into that place, which (to do her credit) she virtuously tried to do, she only felt sick, and now even when she thought of any man, the very idea made her feel queasy and faint. No, but she *could* not, she would run away, she would join the Sisterhood of the Sword and wear weapons and fight as a mercenary soldier for one of the kings contending for this land, she would cut her hair and pierce her ears—and when she got to this point she realized how foolish she was, for if she ran away they would only follow her and drag her back. And then she would make wild plans, a final appeal to her father, to her stepmother, to Lord Scathfell himself—when they put the bracelets on her she would scream "No" and tear them off, when they tried to lead her to the bedding she would fall on *Dom* Garris with a knife. . . . Surely then he would put her away, he would not want her . . . she would tell him how much she loathed him, and he would refuse to have her. . . .

But she knew in her heart that all this was useless. She must marry . . . and she could not!

The summer drew on; the evening snow was only a brief trickle of rain, and the hills were bright with flowers and budding trees; the nut-bushes were covered with little green lumps which would ripen into nuts, and almost every day she and Mallina could cut fresh mushrooms from the sides of the old trees which had been implanted with fungus-roots. She picked berries dutifully and helped to stem them for conserves, helped churn butter in the dairies, and seldom had leisure even for a ride, let alone to give Preciosa proper exercise; but every day she visited her hawk in the mews, and begged Darren or Alderic to take her out and fly her. Darren was afraid of hawks, and still avoided them when he could, but when Alderic had leisure he would take out Preciosa on his saddle.

"But she does not fly well for me," he told her one evening, "I think she is pining for you, Romilly."

"And I am neglecting her," Romilly said, with a pang of guilt. She had herself formed the tie with this wild thing; now she could not betray it. She resolved that tomorrow, no matter what duties Luciella laid on her, she would find some time for a ride, and to take out the hawk.

She flew through her work the next morning with such speed and willingness that Luciella stared, and said, "Why, what you can do when you are willing, child!"

"Since I have finished, foster-mother, may I take my hawk out for a little while?"

Luciella hesitated, then said, "Why yes; you must not neglect *Dom* Garris's gift. Go then, Romilly, enjoy yourself in the fresh air."

Released, she fled to put on her riding-habit and boots, to order her horse saddled—she supposed it would have to be a lady's saddle, but riding sidesaddle was better than not riding at all—and was swiftly off to the mews. Darren was in the yard, glumly exercising one or two of the hawks; she noted his clumsy movements, and told him she was going hawking—would he come? He went, with relief, and had his own horse saddled. She was taking Preciosa from her block, holding her familiar weight on the gauntlet with pleasure, extending her senses toward the hawk to set up the old contact, when her father stepped into the mews.

"Romilly," he said sharply, "Take your own hawks, not that one. You know what your promised husband said; it is unseemly to fly a *verrin* hawk, and you have hawks of your own. Put her back."

"Father!" she protested, in a sudden flood of anger, "Preciosa is my own hawk, I trained her myself! She is mine, mine! No one else shall fly her! How can it be unseemly for me to fly a hawk I trained? Are you going to let *Dom* Garris tell you what it is right for your own daughter to do, in your own stable-yard?"

She saw conflict and dismay on his face; but he said sharply, "I told you, put that hawk back on the block and take out your own! I will not have you defy me, girl!" He strode toward her; Preciosa sensed Romilly's agitation and bated wildly, threshing furiously on her wrist, whirling up to the length of the fastened jesses, then settling restively back.

"Father—" she pleaded, lowering her voice not to disturb the easily-frightened birds, "Don't say this—"

The MacAran thrust out his hand and firmly gripped Preciosa's feet. He set her back on the block and said, "I will be obeyed, and that is all there is to it."

"She's not getting enough exercise," Romilly pleaded, "she needs to be flown!"

The MacAran paused. "That's right," he said, and beckoned to Darren.

"Here," he jerked his head to indicate Preciosa on her block, "Take her; I give her to you. You need a good hawk to work with, and this is the best we have. Take her out today, and start getting used to her."

Romilly's mouth fell open in indignant surprise. He could not do *that* to her—nor to Preciosa! The MacAran grasped the bird again, held it firmly until the bating quieted, then set her on Darren's wrist; he jerked back, startled, and Preciosa, even hooded, thrust her head about, trying to peck, beating her wings; Darren ducked away, his wrist twisting so that she overbalanced and fell, hanging from her jesses. He stood holding the wildly bating hawk, and The MacAran said in a harsh whisper, "Pick her up! Quiet her, damn you, if she breaks a wing-feather I'll break your neck, boy!"

Darren made ineffectual movements to quiet the bird, finally getting her to something like quiet on his glove. But his voice broke into falsetto as he said, "It's not—not fair, sir. Father, I beg you—Romilly trained that hawk herself, and with her own *laran*—"

"Silence, young man! Don't you dare speak that word in my presence!"

"Refusing to hear it won't make it less true, sir. It's Romilly's hawk, she trained it, she *earned* it, and I don't want it—I won't take it from her!"

"But you will take it from *me*," said The MacAran, his jaw thrusting forth, his jutting chin hard with fury, "How dare you say a hawk trained at Falconsward in my own mews is not mine to give? Romilly has been given hawks by her promised husband. She needs not this one, and you will take it or—" he leaned toward Darren, his eyes blazing, his breath coming and going in rough harsh noises, "Or I will wring its neck here before you both! I will not be defied here in my own mews!" He made a threatening gesture as if to carry out his threat here and now, and Romilly cried out.

"No! No, Father—no, please! Darren, don't let him—take the hawk, it's better for you to have it—"

Darren drew a long, shaking breath. He wet his lips with his tongue, and settled the hawk on his arm. He said shakily, "Only because you ask me, Romilly. Only for that, I promise you."

Her eyes burning, Romilly turned aside to take up one of the tiny, useless hawks that had been *Dom* Garris' gift. At that moment she hated them, the little half-brained, stupid things. Beautiful as they were, elegantly trapped, they were only ornaments, pretty meaningless jewels, not real hawks at all, no more than one of Rael's carven toys! But it was not their fault, poor silly little things, that they were not Preciosa. Her heart yearned over Preciosa, perched unsteadily on Darren's awkward wrist.

My hawk. Mine. And now that fool of a Darren will spoil her . . . ah, Preciosa, Preciosa, why did this have to happen to us? She felt that she hated her father too, and Darren, clumsily transferring Preciosa from his glove to the block on the saddle. Tears blurred her eyes as she mounted. Her father had called for his great rawboned grey; he would ride with them, he said wrathfully, to make sure Darren used the hawk well, and if he did not, he would learn it as he had learned his alphabet, beaten into him with The MacAran's own riding-crop!

They were all silent, miserable, as they rode down the

pathway from the peaks of Falconsward. Romilly rode last, staring in open hatred at her father, at Darren's saddle where Preciosa perched restlessly. She sent out her consciousness, her *laran*—since the word had been used—toward Preciosa, but the hawk was too agitated; she felt only a blur of confusion and hatred, a reddish-tinged rage that blurred her mind, too, till she had all she could do to sit in the saddle.

All too soon they reached the great open meadow where they had flown their hawks that day—only then it had been Alderic with them, a friendly face and helping hands, not their furious father. Awkwardly, pinching her in his haste, Darren took the hood from Preciosa's head, raised her on his fist and cast her off; Romilly, reaching out her senses to merge with the rising hawk, felt how fury dropped away as Preciosa climbed the sky, and she thought, in despair, *Let her go free. She will never be mine again, and I cannot bear to see her mishandled by Darren. He means well, but he has no hands or heart for hawks.* As she sank into the hawk's mind and heart, her whole soul seemed to go into the cry.

Go, Preciosa! Fly away, fly free—one of us at least should be free! Higher—higher—now, turn and go—

"Romilly, what ails you?" Her father's voice was filled with asperity, "Get your bird out, girl!"

She brought herself painfully back to the moment, her practiced hands loosing the embroidered hood. The little hawk, shining like a jewel in the red sunlight, angled off, high on the wind, and Romilly watched, not seeing—her eyes were blurred with tears, her whole awareness with Preciosa.

Higher, higher . . . now, down the wind, and away, away . . . free on the wind, flying free and away. . . . a last quick sight of the country, spread out below her like a colored picture in one of Rael's schoolbooks, then the frail link snapped asunder and she was alone again, alone in her own mind, her hands and heart empty, and only the shrill tiny screaming of the small hawk striking at some little rodent in the long grass, lifting—the bird lighted on her saddle. With automatic hands she tore at the small carcass, letting the hawk feed from her glove, but her heart was empty.

Preciosa. She is gone. Gone. Never again. . . .

Her father's head was thrown back, scanning the sky where Preciosa had vanished. "She has gone long," he said, "Romilly, do you usually let her fly out of sight?"

Romilly shook her head. The MacAran waited, frozen, and Darren's head was thrown back, his mouth a round 'O' of dread. They waited. At last The MacAran said in a fury,

"You have lost her, damn your clumsiness! The best hawk in the mews, and the very first time you fly her, you have lost her, worthless son that you are, worthless brat good for nothing but scribbling. . . ." he raised his riding-crop and the whip came down over Darren's shoulders. He yelped, more from startlement than pain, but the sound galvanized Romilly; she flung herself headlong from her horse and scrambled toward the men, throwing herself between her father and Darren so that the blows fell on her.

"Beat me instead," she cried, "It's not Darren's fault! I lost her, I let her go—I cannot be free, I must be chained inside a house and robbed of my hawk, you damned tyrant, but I will not have Preciosa chained too! I bade her go with my *laran*—with my *laran*—you have driven Ruyven away with your tyranny, you have made Darren afraid of you, but I am not afraid of you, and at least you will never mistreat my hawk again, *my hawk, mine*—" and she burst into wild crying. Her father checked a moment as the first blow fell on her shoulders, but as he heard the flood of abuse, as the forbidden words *Ruyven* and *laran* fell on his ears, his face turned furious black, congested with wrath, and he raised the riding-crop and struck her hard. He raised it again and again; Romilly shuddered with the pain, and shrieked at him, incoherently, harder than ever; her father slid from his horse and stood over her, beating her about the back and shoulders with the crop until finally Darren flung his arms around his father, shouting and yelling, and then another voice; *Dom* Alderic, restraining her father with his strong arms.

"Here, here, sir—I'm sorry, but you mustn't beat a girl like that—good God, Romilly, your back is all bloody—look, sir, you've torn her dress!" He wrenched the crop from her father's hands. The man made no protest, letting his arms fall dazed to his sides. Romilly swayed, feeling bloody wetness on her back, numb and smarting, and Alderic shoved her father into Darren's arms, coming to support her with his arm. The MacAran looked dazed, his wrath giving way to numbness; he looked hastily, in dismay, at Romilly's torn dress where the crop had cut the stiff material into ribbons, and then away again.

He said numbly, "I—I did not know what I was doing—I am in your debt, *Dom* Alderic. I—I—" and his voice failed him. He swayed where he stood and would have fallen, but Darren held him upright. The MacAran stared at Romilly, and said harshly, "I lost my temper. I shall not forgive you, girl, that you caused me to forget myself so shamefully! Had you been a boy, I would still beat you senseless! But soon enough your husband will have charge of you, and if you speak to him like that, I doubt it not he will break your head in two! Get out of my sight!"

Romilly stumbled; Alderic pushed her toward her horse. "Can you ride?" he asked in an undertone.

She nodded, numb, tears bursting out again.

"You had better get back to the house," he muttered, "while he is still in shock at what he has done."

The MacAran stood, still shaking his head in dismay and wrath. "In all the years of my life," he said, "Never have I laid hand on a woman or girl! I shall not forgive myself, nor Romilly for provoking me!" He stared up into the sky where the hawk had vanished, and muttered something, but Romilly, under a push from Alderic, rode away blindly toward Falconsward.

When she stumbled into the house, and into her rooms, her old nurse met her with dismay. "Oh, my lamb, my little one, what has happened to you? Your back—your riding-dress—"

"Father beat me," she mumbled, breaking out into terrible crying, "He beat me because Darren lost my hawk. . . ."

Gwennis soaked the remains of the dress from her back, dressed the broken skin and bruised flesh with oil and herb-salve, put her into an old robe of soft cloth, and brought her hot soup in her bed. Romilly had begun to shiver and felt sick and feverish. Gwennis was grumbling, but she shook her head and demanded, "How did you come to anger your father so much? He is such a gentle man, he must have been beside himself to do something like this!" Romilly could not speak; her teeth were chattering and she kept crying, even though she tried and tried to stop. Gwennis, alarmed, went to fetch Luciella, who cried herself over Romilly's bruises and cuts and her ruined habit, and nevertheless repeated what Gwennis had said—"How in the world came you to anger your father like *this*? He would *never* have done a thing like this unless you provoked him beyond bearing!"

They blame me, Romilly thought, *they all blame me because I was beaten. . . .*

And now there is no hope for me. Preciosa is gone. My father cares more to be on good terms with Aldaran than he cares for me. He will beat Darren ruthlessly into shape because Darren does not have my gifts, but he will not let me be what I am, nor Darren what he is; he cares nothing for what we are, but only for what he would have us be. She would not listen to Luciella's kind words, not to Gwennis's cosseting. She could not stop crying; she cried until her eyes were sore and her head ached and her nose was reddened and dripping. And at last she cried herself to sleep.

She woke late, when the whole of Falconsward was silent, and the great violet face of Kyrrdis hung full and shining in her window. Her head still ached terribly, and her back stung and smarted despite the healing salves Gwennis had put on it. She was hungry; she decided to slip downstairs and find some bread and cold meat in the kitchen.

My father hates me. He drove Ruyven away with his tyranny, but Ruyven at least is free, learning to be what he must be, in a Tower. Ruyven was right; at least, out of range of my father's iron will, he can be what he is, not what Father would have him be. And suddenly Romilly knew that she, too, must be free, as Preciosa was free in the wild to be what she was.

Shaking, she pulled an old knitted vest over her sore back, and put on the old tunic and breeches she had worn. She slipped quietly along the corridor, her boots in her hand. They were women's boots; a woman, she had heard all of her life, was not safe alone on the roads, and after the way *Dom* Garris had looked at her at Midsummer, she knew why. Ruyven's room was shut up, all his things as he had left them; noiselessly she slipped inside, took from a chest one of his plainer shirts and an old pair of leather breeches, a little too large for her, shucked off Darren's too-tight ones and dressed in Ruyven's ample ones; she took a cloak too, and a leather over-tunic, slipped into her room again for her own hawking-glove. Remembering that Preciosa was gone, she almost left it behind, but she thought, *some day I will have a hawk again, and I will remember Preciosa by this.* At the last, before she slid her old dagger into its sheath, she cut her hair short to the nape of her neck, and as she stole outside, thrust the braid deep into the midden, so they would not find it. She had locked Ruyven's door again, and they would never think to look among his old clothes and count the shirts. She would carry her habit with her, so they would be looking for a girl with long hair in a green riding-habit, not a nondescript young boy in plain old clothes. Slipping into the stable, she put an old saddle, dustcovered and hidden behind other discarded bits of harness, on her own horse, then thought better of it and left him in the stall. A black horse, a fine well-bred one, would betray her anywhere as a MacAran. She carried the saddle carefully outside and made a small bundle of it with her tack and her girl's clothes. She left it there and slipped quietly into the kitchen—in the summer, all the kitchen work was done in an outer building so the building would not be too hot—and found herself meat and a cut loaf of bread, a handful of nuts and some flat cakes of coarse grain which the cook baked every day for the best of the dogs, the breeding bitches and those who were nursing pups . . . they were palatable enough and would not be missed as other breads might be, since they were baked by the dozen, almost by the hundred . . . a handful would never be counted. She rolled them in a kitchen towel and tied the neck of the improvised bag, then put her boots on, went outside and carried bag and saddle to the outer pasture, where old horses and culls were left to grass. She scanned them for a horse who would not be missed for some days—let them think she had gone afoot. Finally she decided on an elderly hack who was used only once in a great while, when the old *coridom*, now retired and seldom out of doors at all, visited the far pastures. She clucked softly—all the horses knew her—and he came cantering quietly to the fence. She murmured to him, fed him a handful of coarse vegetables, then put the saddle on his back, and led him softly away down the path, not mounting till she was well out of earshot of the walls. Once a dog began to bark inside the castle and she held her breath and fiercely *willed* the animal to be silent.

At the foot of the hill, she clambered into the saddle, wincing as her fresh bruises were jolted, but setting her teeth against the pain and wrapping herself in her cloak against the midnight chill. Once she looked up at Falconsward on its crag, high above her.

Bearer of Burdens! I cannot, I cannot—Father is sorry he beat me, this is madness, I should go back before I am missed. . . .

But then the memory of Darren's face as she gave him the hawk, of her father's rage, of Ruyven's set, despairing eyes the last time she had seen him, before he ran away from Nevarsin. . . . *No, Father will have us what he wishes, not what we are.* The memory of *Dom* Garris handling her rudely at Midsummer, the thought of how he would behave when she was turned over to him, his wife, *his property to do with as he would*—

She set her face like iron. Had there been anyone to see, at that moment, they would have marked; she was very like her father. She rode away from Falconsward without once looking back.

Book Two:

THE FUGITIVE

CHAPTER ONE

———— •◦• ◄—► •◦• ————

On the third day it began to snow. Romilly, who had lived all her life in the foothills of the Hellers, knew that she must find shelter quickly; nothing alive could survive a storm, even at this season, except under cover. The wind whipped like a knife, and howled along the trees lining the path like the voices of ten thousand devils. Briefly she considered retracing her steps to the little hill-farm she had passed early that morning, and asking shelter there . . . but no. The farmers there might have been among those who came, now and again, to Falconsward, and even in her boy's dress might know her for The MacAran's daughter. She did not know them; but she had never been this far from her home, and was not sure where she was.

She knew vaguely that if she followed this trail, keeping to the north, she would come at last to Nevarsin, where she could take the road to Tramontana Tower. There she would find her brother Ruyven—or if he had been sent elsewhere by the *leroni* who ruled in the Towers, she could find news of him. It was in her mind that she might seek the training of her *laran* within the Towers, as the *leronis* Marelie had invited her to do some years ago. Alternatively, she might remain in Nevarsin for the winter—she had lived in the Hellers long enough to know that travelling in the winter, by the roads she must take to Nevarsin, was a dangerous enterprise, undertaken only by the mad or the desperate. Surely in Nevarsin she could seek to find work somewhere as a hawkmaster's apprentice, or with some blacksmith or horse-keeper as a stableboy—for she had no intention of revealing herself as a girl. She had seldom been away from her own home, where even the kitchen-girls and washerwomen were treated kindly and properly supervised by *Domna* Luciella, but the very way they reacted to this treatment told her how rare it was, and one of the women, who had worked as a tavern wench for years, had told many stories of the treatment she was apt to receive. Romilly did not doubt her own ability to care for herself and to keep unwelcome hands off her; but even the lowest stable boy was paid more than any cook-woman or tavern maid, and Romilly had few skills to lift her above the lowest scullery-maid's tasks. All she knew was horses and hawks, and the supervision of servants. Dressmakers and children's nurses, she knew, could earn higher wages, but even the thought of working as a sewing-woman made her smile, remembering the botchery she made of her sewing, and for a child's nurse they would want to know much more about her than she would be willing to tell. No, if she chose to stay in Nevarsin for the winter she would remain a boy to all appearances, and seek work in stables or mews.

And that way, at least, she would be around horses and hawks. She thought with a bitter pang of the lost Preciosa.

But I am glad it happened, she thought fiercely, hunching against the slashing wind and drawing her cloak high over her face, almost to covering her eyes. *Otherwise, I would never have had the courage to break away! I would have remained obedient, perhaps even married* Dom *Garris* . . . and a shiver of revulsion went through her. No, she was well out of that, even if she must spend the rest of her life working as a boy in some stranger's stables!

The snow was beginning to turn to a wet, soggy rain; the horse's feet slipped and slithered on the steep trail, and Romilly, sliding into rapport, felt the chill of the wind, the uneasy way the horse shivered and set down his feet with uncertain care on the slippery road. The rain was freezing as it fell; her cloak was stiffening with ice. They must find shelter soon, indeed.

They came to a steep turn in the road, where it forked, one path leading upward through thick trees that lined the trail, the other broader, but steeply downward. Romilly slid off the horse's back and went, craning her neck to stare through the thick misty rain. Downward she could see nothing except a small runnel of water cascading out of sight over the rocks beside the road; but upward, it seemed to her, she could make out the walls of some kind of building, a herder's hut or shelter for animals. The broadening road might lead down to a village or a cluster of valley farms, but she had no assurance, nor did she see any lights in the valley, and the rains were coming ever faster.

Upward, then, it must be, to the shelter, no matter how crude; it would at least be out of the wind or rain. She did not mount again—on a trail as steep as this upward path, the horse would fare better without her weight. She took her horse's bridle, speaking soothingly to the animal as it jerked its head away. She wished she could have had her own horse; this one was a stranger. Yet it was docile enough and even friendly.

The darkness through snow and rain grew darker; it was some building, indeed; not large, but it appeared weather-tight. The door was sagging, half off its hinges, and gave a loud protesting noise when she shoved it and went in.

"Who's there?" a quavering voice cried out, and Romilly felt her heart race and her throat tighten with fear. Dark as it looked, dilapidated, it was not deserted after all.

She said quickly, "I mean you no harm, ma'am—I was lost in the storm and the rain is freezing. May I come in?"

"Honor to the Bearer of Burdens, and thanks be that you have come," the voice said; a trembling, old voice. "My grandson went to the town and I make no doubt, in this storm he has had to shelter somewhere, I heard your horse's steps and thought for a moment it was Rory comin' back, but he rides a stag-pony and I see you have a horse. I canna' leave my bed; can ye throw a branch on the fire, boy?"

Now her face was beginning to thaw a little she could smell the smoke; groping in the darkness, she went toward the dull embers. The fire was almost out. Romilly stirred the embers, coaxed it alive with small sticks, and when they caught, built it up again with a bigger branch and then with a log. She stood warming her hands, in the growing light, her eyes made out a few sticks of decrepit furniture, a bench or two, an ancient chest, a box-bed built into the wall, in which lay an old, old woman, propped up against the back of the bed.

As the firelight grew, she said, "Come here, boy. Let me look at you."

"My horse—" Romilly hesitated.

"You can lead him round into the stable," said the old voice. "Do that first, then come back."

She had to force herself to wrap the cloak over her face and go into the bitter cold. The stable was deserted, except for a couple of scrawny cats, who whined and rubbed against her legs, and after she had unsaddled her horse and given it a couple of pieces of the dog's bread—the grain would be enough to feed it for tonight—they followed her through the door into the warmth of the now-blazing fire.

"Good, good," said the old woman, in her shaky voice, "I thought of them out in the cold, but I could not get up to let them in. Come here and let me look at you, then, lad." And as Romilly went and stood by the box-bed, she hitched herself up a little further, peering with her face wrinkled up at Romilly's face. "How come ye out in such weather, boy?"

"I am travelling to Nevarsin, *mestra*," said Romilly.

"All alone? In such a storm?"

"I set out three days ago when the weather was fine."

"Are ye from south of the Kadarin? Red hair—ye have a look of the *Hali'imyn* about ye," the old woman said. She was wrapped in several layers of ragged shawls, and three or four threadbare blankets, not much better than horse-blankets, were piled on her bed. She looked gaunt, emaciated, exhausted.

The old woman let out her breath in a trembling sigh. She said, "I hoped he would be back from Nevarsin early this day, but no doubt the snow is worse to the North— well, with you to mend the fire, I will not freeze here alone in the storm. My old bones cannot stand the cold the way I could before, and before he left he built up the fire to last three days, saying he would surely be back before then. . . ."

"Can I do anything else for you, *mestra?*"

"If you can cook a pot of porridge, ye can have a share of it," said the old woman, indicating an empty pot, bowl and spoon at her side, "But get out of your wet things first, lad."

Romilly drew breath; the old woman apparently accepted her as a farm boy. She took off cloak and boots, hanging the cloak near the warmth of the fire to dry; there was a barrel of water near the fire, and she took the empty porridge-pot, rinsed it, and, as the old woman directed her, found a half-empty sack of coarse meal, more ground nuts than grain, and salt, and hung the mixture in the kettle from the long hook over the fireplace. The old woman beckoned her back, then.

"Where are you off to at this bitter time of the year, my lad?"

At that offhand "my lad" Romilly felt a bursting sigh of relief; at least the old woman had accepted her for what she seemed to be, a young boy and not a girl at the edge of being a woman. Then it occurred to her that the deception of an old woman, half-blind, was not so great a matter after all, and people with younger eyes and quicker wits might see through her more easily. And then she realized that the old woman in the box-bed was still peering out at her through those wrinkled eyelids, waiting for her answer.

"I am travelling to Nevarsin," she said at last, "My brother is there."

"In the monastery? Why, you are far off your road for that, youngster—you should have taken the left-hand fork at the bottom of the mountain. But too late now, you must stay till the storm is over, and when Rory is back he will set you on your proper path."

"I thank you, *mestra*."

"What is your name, lad?"

"Rom—" Romilly hesitated, swallowing back her name, realizing she had not thought of this for a moment. She pondered saying "Ruyven," but then she might not remember to answer to that but would look about for her brother. She swallowed, pretended to have choked for a moment on the smoke of the fire, and said "Rumal."

"And why are you going to Nevarsin all on your own? Are you to become a monk, or being sent there to be taught by the brothers, as they do with the sons of the gentry? You have a look of gentry about you, at that, as if you'd been born in a Great House—and your hands are finer than a stable-boy's."

Romilly almost laughed, thinking of the time when Gwennis, scowling at her calloused hands, worn by reins and claws, had said, reproving, "You will have the hands of a stable-boy if you do not take care!" But once again the old woman was waiting for an answer, and she thought swiftly of Nelda's son Loran—everyone at Falconsward knew him to be the MacAran's *nedestro* son, though Luciella liked to pretend she did not know, and refused to admit the boy existed. She said, "I was brought up in a Great House; but my mother was too proud to bring me under my father's eye, since I was festival-got; so she said I could make more of myself in a city, and I hope to find work in Nevarsin—I was apprentice to the hawk-master." *And that, at least, was true; she was more Davin's apprentice than that worthless Ker.*

"Well, Rumal, you are welcome," the old woman said. "I live here alone with my grandson—my daughter died when he was born, and his father's away in the lowlands in the service of King Rafael, across the Kadarin to the south. My name is Mhari, and I have dwelt here in this hut most of my life; we make a kind of living from the nut-farming, or we did until I grew too old for it; it's hard for Rory to look after the trees at all seasons, and care for me too, but he's a good lad, and he went to sell our nuts in the market at Nevarsin, and bring home flour for porridge, and herb-medicines for my old bones. When he's a wee bit older, perhaps, he can find him a wife and they can make a living here, for it's all I have to leave him."

"I think the porridge is boiling over," said Romilly, and hurried to the fire, to move the kettle a little further from the flame. When it was done, she dipped up a bowl for the old woman, and propped her up to eat it, then shook out Mhari's pillows and soothed her bedcovers and settled her down for the night.

"You are neat-handed as a girl," said Mhari, and Romilly's heart stopped till she went on, "I suppose that comes from handling birds; I never had the hands for that, nor the patience, either. But your porridge will be cold, child; go and eat it, and you can sleep there in Rory's pallet by the fire, since it's not likely he'll be home in this storm."

Romilly settled down by the banked fire to eat her bowlful, then rinsed the bowl in the barrel of water, set it near the fire to dry and stretched out, wrapped in her cloak, by the hearth. It was a hard bed, but on the trail she had slept in worse places, and she lay awake for a time, drowsily listening to the beating storm outside, and to the occasional drop of water which made its way down the chimney to sizzle briefly in the fire. Twice she woke during the night to make certain the fire was still alive. Toward morning the noise of the storm died away a little, and she slept heavily, to be wakened by a great pounding on the door. Mhari sat upright in her bed.

"It is Rory's voice," she said, "Did you draw the bolt, then?"

Romilly felt like a fool. The last thing she had done before settling down to sleep was to lock the inside door—which of course the crippled old woman could never have done. No wonder the voice outside sounded loud and agitated! She hurried to the door and drew the bolt.

She looked into the face of a huge burly young man, be-whiskered and clad in threadbare sacking and a cloak of a fashion which had not been worn in the Hellers since her father was a child. He had his dagger out, and would have rushed at her with it, but he heard old Mhari's cry.

"No, Rory—the boy meant no harm—he cared for me and cooked my supper hot—I bade him sleep here!"

The rough-looking young man let the dagger fall and hurried to the box-bed. "You are really all right, Granny? When I felt the door locked, and then when I saw a stranger within, I was only afraid someone had come, forced his way in and done you some harm—"

"Now, now, now," old Mhari said, "I am safe and sound, and it was well for me that he came, for the fire was near out, and I could have frozen in the night!"

"I am grateful to you, whoever you are, fellow," said the big young man, sliding his dagger into its sheath and bending to kiss his grandmother on the forehead. "The storm was so bad, and all night I could think only of Granny, alone here with the fire burnt out and no way to feed herself. My hearth is yours while you have need of it," he added, in the ancient mountain phrase of hospitality given a stranger. "I left my shelter the moment the rain died, and came home, though my hosts bade me stay till sunrise. And you are well and warm, that's the important thing, Granny dear." He looked tenderly on the old woman. Then, flinging off his cloak on to a bench, he went to the porridge-pot still hanging by the fire, dipped up some with the ladle, thick and stiff after the night by the hearth, and began to munch on the heavy stuff from his fingers. "Ah, warm food is good—it's cold as Zandru's breath out there still, and all the rain has frozen on the trees and the road—I feared old Horny would slip and break a leg. But I traded for some grain, Granny, so you shall have bread as well as porridge, and I have dried blackfruits as well in my bag; the miller's wife sent them for you, saying you would like the change." He turned to Romilly and asked, "Could I trouble you to get the saddlebags from my beast? My hands are so cold they are all but frozen, and I could not unfasten the tack till they are warm again; and you have spent the night in the warm."

"Gladly," said Romilly, "I must go out and see to my horse, in any case."

"You have a horse?" A look almost of greed lighted Rory's face. "I have always wanted a horse; but they are not for the

98

likes of me! You must indeed have been brought up in a Great House."

Romilly went outside, flinging her cloak over her shoulders, and unfastened the heavy saddlebags lying across the heavy-boned stag-like chervine Rory had ridden. She took the sack of coarse grain into the byre, and brought the saddlebags into the cottage, dumping them on the floor near the fire.

Rory was bending over his grandmother, talking in low tones; she was sure he had not heard her, so she slipped out again into the byre, went into her own bags and fed her horse one or two cakes of the dog-bread, stroking its muzzle and talking to it. There was an old-fashioned outhouse inside the byre, and she went into it; as she was readjusting her clothing, she paused, dismayed, at the bloodstains lining her underwear; because of the storm she had lost track of the days. *When I thought to pass myself off as a man*, she said to herself wryly, *I had forgotten certain very important points which I must remember.* She had never thought it would be simple, to remember to pitch her voice at its deepest level and to remember to move with the free stride for which Luciella and her governess had always reproved her, but she had forgotten the inexorable rhythms of female biology which could have betrayed her more than any of this.

As she was tearing up one of the old petticoats in her pack—she could wash it privately by night, perhaps—she took stock of what she should do now. The old woman had promised that Rory would set her on her road to Nevarsin. Would it be ungracious, she wondered, to insist that she must leave at once? She should have invented someone who was waiting for her in that city and would come to look for her if she did not appear at the appointed time. She made certain that there were no telltale bulges in her clothing, fed the horse and led Rory's stag-pony inside, spreading fresh straw and fodder for it—she did not like the looks of that heavy-set young roughneck, but the riding-animal was certainly not to blame and should not suffer for her dislike of his master's face.

Then she stepped back through the door—and paused, hearing the old woman's voice.

"The youngster was kind to me, Rory. This is an evil thing you do, and a breach of hospitality, which the Gods hate."

Rory's voice was sullen. "You know how long I have wished for a horse, and while I dwell here at the world's end, I shall never have a better chance. If this is a runaway bastard from somewhere, he'll never be missed. Why, did you see his cloak—in all my years I have never even had a chance at such a cloak, and the brooch in it alone would pay a healer to come all the way from Nevarsin to cure your joint-aches! As for your debt to him, well, he had lodging and fire the night—it was not all kindliness on his part. And I can cut his throat quick as a puff of wind, and he'll never have the time to be afeared."

Romilly caught, terrified, at her throat. He meant to kill her! Never had she for a moment thought, even in the poverty of the hut, that her horse and cloak, let alone the copper brooch in its fastening and the money in her small purse, might endanger her very life. She would have turned, noiselessly, to flee; but without cloak or horse, without food, she would die quickly in the bitter cold! She gripped her fingers on the dagger in its sheath at her side. At least, he would find no unaware or easy victim; she would sell her life as dearly as she could. But she must not allow them to know that she knew of their plans, but pretend to suspect nothing till she had her cloak and her pack, and could make a run for the horse. She turned quietly about and went noiselessly back to the byre, where she put her saddle on her horse, and turned him about, ready to flee. Now she must have her cloak, or she would freeze in the hills.

Keeping her hand unobtrusively near the dagger's hilt, she came back to the door, careful to make some noise as she opened it. When she came in, Rory was sitting on the bench fiddling with his boots, and old Mhari had laid her head back on the pillow and was asleep, or pretending to be. As Romilly came in, Rory said, "Would you give me a hand wi' my boots, young fellow?"

"Gladly," Romilly said, thinking fast. If he had his boots off, at least he could not pursue her too quickly. She knelt before him, putting both hands to the boot, and hauled it free of his foot; bent forward to the other. She had both hands on it, and was tugging hard, when Rory bent forward, and she saw the glint of the knife in his hand.

Romilly acted without thought; she pushed hard on the leg with the boot, sending it up so that Rory's knee slammed into his chin, with a loud crack. The bench went over backward, with Rory tangled in it, and she scrambled to her feet and ran for the door, snatching up her cloak as she ran. She fumbled at the latch-string, her heart pounding, hearing Rory curse and shout behind her. A quick glance told her; his mouth was bleeding, either the blow had knocked out a tooth or cut his lip. She was swiftly through the door and tried to thrust it shut with her shoulder, but he wrestled it open behind her and then he was on her. She did not see the knife; perhaps he had dropped it, perhaps he meant to use only his huge hands. Her tunic ripped all the way down as he grabbed her; he pulled her close, his hands closing around her throat; then his eyes widened as he saw the ripped tunic and he tore it all the way down.

"By the Burden! Tits like a very cow! A girl, huh?" He grabbed Romilly's hand, which was clawing at his eyes, and held her immobile; then whirled her about and marched her back into the little kitchen.

"Hey, there! Granny! Look what I found, after all? Hell's own waste to hurt her——haven't I been after a wife these four years, and not a copper for a bride-price, and now one comes to my very door!" He laughed, jubilantly. "Don't be frightened, wench, I wouldn't hurt a hair of your little head now! I've something better to do, hey, Granny? And she can stay with you and wait on you while I'm out at the farming, or away to the mill or the town!" Laughing, the big man squeezed her tight in his arms and mashed a kiss against her mouth. "Runaway servant girl to the gentry, are you, then? Well, pretty thing, here you'll have your own kitchen and hearthfire, what do you say to that?"

Paralyzed by this torrent of words, Romilly was silent, filled with terror, but thinking faster than she had ever thought in her life.

He wanted her. He would not hurt her, at least for a little while, while he still hoped to have her. His mouth against hers filled her with revulsion, but she concealed the crawling sense of sickness and forced herself to smile up at him.

"At least you are no worse than the man they would have had me marry," she said, and realized as she said it that she was telling the absolute truth. "Old, more than twice my age, and always pawing at helpless girls, while you, at least, are young and clean."

He said, contented, "I think we will suit well enough when we are used to each other; and we need only share a bed, a meal and a fireside, and we will be as lawful wedded as if Lord Storn himself had locked the *catenas* on our arms like gentlefolk! I will build up the fire in the inner room where there is a bed, and you can get about cooking a meal for us to share. There is flour in the sacks, and can you make a loaf with blackfruit? I do like a good fruity bread, and I've had nothing but nut-porridge for forty days and more!"

"I will——try my best," Romilly said, forcing her voice to

calm, "and if I am not sure what to do, no doubt *mestra* Mhari will tell me."

"Ah, you think yourself my old Granny's betters, do you?" Rory demanded truculently, "You will say *Dame Mhari* till *she* gives you leave to say *Granny*, do you hear?"

Romilly realized, abruptly, that she had automatically used the form of a noblewoman speaking to an inferior. She hung her head, pretending to be ashamed, and murmured, "I meant no harm—"

"And since you're a girl, it's more suitable for you to wash Granny's face and put her into a clean bedgown, get her ready for the day," Rory said, "D'you think you could sit in the hearth for a little today, Granny? If our fine lady here gets you fresh and ready?"

"Aye, I'll sit in the hearth for your wedding meal, Rory," said the old woman, and Romilly, biting her lip, said meekly that she would be glad to do whatever she could for Dame Mhari.

"I knew she was too fine-handed for a lad," said Mhari, as Romilly bent to lift her, and went to dip hot water from the barrel. As she washed the old woman's face and hands, and brought a clean but threadbare gown from the ancient clothes-press in the corner, she was thinking harder than she had ever done. How could she escape? They would watch her moment by moment until the marriage was consummated; *by which time* she thought grimly, *they would think her too beaten to try and get away*. It made her sick at her stomach to think of that great unwashed lout taking her to bed, but she supposed it wouldn't kill her, and since she was actually in the bleeding part of her woman's cycles, at least he was unlikely to make her pregnant. And then she stopped short in what she was doing, remembering gleefully something Darissa had whispered to her a few months after her marriage. At the time, Romilly had only been embarrassed and giggled about it—what great sillies men were, to be superstitious about such a thing! But now she could make it serve her.

"I am cold, wet and bare like this," the old woman complained, "Wrap me in my gown, girl—what am I to call you?"

Romilly started to tell the woman her name—after all, now they knew she was a girl what did it matter?—but then she thought; her father might seek her even as far as this. She said the first name that came into her head.

"Calinda."

"Wrap me in my gown, Calinda, I am shivering!"

"I am sorry, Mother Mhari," she said, using the meek term of respect for any aging woman, "I had a heavy thought—" and she bent close to the old woman as she wrapped her in gown and woolly shawl and then laid her on her pillows, drying her hands with a towel. "I—I—I will gladly wed your grandson—" and she thought the words would choke her.

"And well you should," said the old woman, "He is a good kind man, and he will use you well and never beat you unless you really deserve it."

Romilly gulped; at least *that* she would never have had to fear from *Dom* Garris. "B-but," she said, pretending to be embarrassed, which was not difficult, "He will be angry with me if he tries to share my bed *this* night, for my—my cycles are on me, and I am bleeding. . . ."

"Ah, well," said the old lady, "You did well to tell me; men are funny that way, he might well have beaten you for it; my man used to thump me well if I did not tell him well before the time, so he could keep away or sleep with the dairy-maid—ah, yes, once I was well off, I had a dairy-maid and a cook-wench at one time, and now look at me. But with a woman's care, I will grow better soon, and Rory will not have to cook porridge and bake bread, which is no work for a man. Look what a fine man you are getting, he never scorned to wash and turn his old Granny in her bed, or bring her food, or even empty my chamberpot. And speaking of a chamberpot—" She gestured, and Romilly fetched the utensil and supported the old woman.

She thinks this life will make me well off; so long as I have a man for husband, I need ask no better than to drudge about barn and byre and kitchen, waiting hand and foot on a bedridden old woman, so long as I have the name of wife. She shivered as she thought, *perhaps some women would truly think themselves well off—a home of their own and a hardworking man, one who was kind to his old grandmother.* She settled the woman in the bed again and went to empty the chamberpot. She was used to working with her hands about animals, and the work itself did not disgust her, but she was frightened of Rory.

I did not refuse Dom *Garris to be married by force to a woodsman, however honest or good. And now I have won myself a few days time. I will pretend to be meek and mild and biddable, and soon or late, they must let me out of their sight.*

When the old woman was washed and dressed in a fresh gown, Romilly went to the pump in the yard to draw water, placing the great kettle over the fire to heat for the washing of linens, then, guided by directions from Dame Mhari, set about mixing and baking a loaf of bread with small lumps of sliced blackfruit in the dough. When the bread was baking in the covered pot in the ashes by the hearth, and Dame Mhari dozing in her box-bed, she sat down on one of the benches to rest for a moment, and think.

She had gained time. A swift visit to the outhouse showed her that her horse had been unsaddled again and tied with hard knots; well, if a moment served to escape, she must somehow have her dagger ready to cut the knots and flee; choose a moment, perhaps, when Rory had his boots off, and hopefully his breeches too. Her pack she could abandon if she must—the food was gone and she could live without the other things—but her warm cloak she must have, her boots and her saddle . . . though she could ride bareback better than many women could ride saddled. Food, too, she must somehow have; it would not be stealing, she had worked hard and cared for the old woman well, it was but her just due.

Perhaps tonight, when they were all asleep, she thought, and, hauling her weary body up from the bench, set about washing the musty linens from the old woman's bed, and the sheets from the bed in the inner room, which had been long unused—Dame Mhari said that when the weather was warm, Rory slept in there, and only in chilly weather did he sleep on the pallet before the fire. Well, that was something—if she must bed that wretched animal of a man, at least it would not be under the peering eyes of the old grandmother, as it might have been in a poorer cottage with only one room. She shuddered suddenly—was this how folk lived, away from the Great Houses?

Should I give up, flee back to my family, exchange my freedom then for the protected life I would live as the wife of Dom Garris? And for a moment, shivering at the thought of what must lie before her, even if she escaped from Rory and his grandmother, she was halfway tempted.

Like a hawk on a block, chained, hooded and dumb, in exchange for being fed and cherished, guarded preciously as a prize possession. . . .

Oh, Preciosa, and that was what I would have brought to you. . . . she thought, and was fiercely glad she had freed the hawk. At least she would never be Darren's possession. She could have kept it clear with her conscience to keep Preciosa herself—the hawk had returned to her of its free will, out of love, after being allowed to fly free. She would never return to Darren.

She is free, she belongs to no man. Nor shall I. Rory might take her—once—as the price of making him think her beaten and submissive. But she would never belong to him; he could not enslave her. Like a hawk badly trained, the moment she was tested in free flight, she would be away into the sky. . . .

She sighed, ferociously sousing the sheets in the harsh soap. Her hands were sore, and ached, but the sheets were clean—at least she would not be taken in that man's dirty bed!

She hung the sheets on a rack near the fire to dry, took the bread from the oven, and hunted in the rickety shelves of the kitchen; she found dried beans and herbs, and put them in the empty kettle to make soup. Rory, stamping in snow-covered from outside, saw her doing this and beamed, flinging down a sack of mushrooms on the table.

"Here; for the soup, girl. For our wedding supper," he said, and stooped to enfold her in an awkward embrace, landing a damp kiss on the back of her neck. She gritted her teeth and did not draw away, and he took her quiet endurance for consent, pulled her round and mashed another kiss against her mouth.

"Tomorrow you will not be so shy, heh, my fine lady—well, Granny, has she taken care of you properly? If she hasn't, I'll teach her." He flung off his own rough cloak and took up hers, slinging it around his shoulders with strutting pride.

"I'll have this; you'll have no need to further out of doors than the outhouse, not till the spring-thaw, and then you'll not need it," he said, and went out again. Romilly swallowed her rage at seeing her brother's well-made, fur-lined cape over his shoulders. Well, if she found a chance to escape, then, she must snatch up Rory's cape; coarse as it was, it was warm enough to shelter her. The few coins in the purse tied at her waist, those she must have too, few as they were, for when she reached Nevarsin. Pitifully small the hoard was—The MacAran was generous with his daughters and his wife, buying them whatever they wished, but he felt they could have small need for ready money, and gave them only a few small silver bits now and again to spend at a fair. But to Rory, she knew, they would seem more; so she found a moment to conceal herself from Dame Mhari's eyes behind the clothes-press and transfer the little hoard of coins from the pocket tied at her waist, into a folded cloth hidden between her breasts; surely, soon or late, he would take the pocket from her, and she left one or two small pieces in it to satisfy his greed—maybe he would seek no further.

As dark closed down from the short gloomy day, she sat with them at the crude table to eat the soup she had made and the bread she had baked. Rory grumbled—the bread was not very good—was this all the skill she had at cooking? But Dame Mhari said peaceably that the girl was young, she would learn, and the bread, however heavy, was at least a good change from nut-porridge! When bedtime came he said sharply, looking away from her, that tonight she might sleep in the box-bed with Dame Mhari, and that he would wait four days, no more, for her return to health.

Now she knew the limits of her time. But if she had had any idea that she might escape while they slept, it vanished when Dame Mhari said, "Let you sleep on the inside of the bed, my girl; do you think I don't know you would run away if you could? You don't know when you are well off; but when you are Rory's wife you will not wish to run away."

Oh, won't I? Romilly thought, gritting her teeth, and lay down fully resolved to try for an escape as soon as the old woman slept. But she was weary from a day of heavy and unaccustomed work, and fell asleep the moment she laid her head on the pillow; and when she woke in the night, whenever she stirred, she saw by firelight the old woman's eyes, wide awake and beady as a hawk's, watching her.

Three days passed in much the same way. She cooked coarse meals, washed the old woman's sheets and gowns, found a little time to wash her own clothes, including the torn-up petticoat she had put to use . . . fortunately she was not too closely observed at the wash-kettle, so she had a chance to dry the cloths and fold them and hide them under her tunic.

If she was ever to pass herself off as a boy—and she was more resolved than ever that she would not travel as a woman in these mountains—she must find some better way of concealing this personal necessity. She had heard gossip about the woman soldiers, the Sisterhood of the Sword, who were pledged never to wear women's gowns nor to let their hair grow. She had never seen one, only heard gossip, but it was rumored that they knew of a herb which would keep women from bleeding at their cycles, and she wished she knew their secret! She had learned something of herb-lore for doctoring animals, and she knew of herb-medicines which would bring a cow or bitch—or, for that matter—a woman *into* the fertile cycles, but none to suppress it, though there was a drug which would keep a bitch, briefly, from going into heat when it was inconvenient to breed her. Was that what they used? Maybe she could try it, but she was not a dog, and a dog's cycle of heat was very different from the female human's. It was all theoretical speculation at the moment anyhow, for she had no access to the herb, and would not know how to recognize it in the wild state anyhow, but only when prepared for use by a beast-healer.

On the fourth day, when he rose, Rory said, smirking, "Tonight you shall sleep with me in the inner room. We have shared meal and fireside; it needs only now to bed you, to make the marriage legal in all ways."

And in the mountains, she had heard, *a law would return a runaway wife to her husband.* No matter that she had been wedded without her consent, a woman had small recourse in law; so if she escaped *after* Rory had bedded her, there would be *two* people seeking her, her father and her husband; would a Tower even take her in under those circumstances?

Well, she would ride that colt when it was grown to bear a saddle. But she would try very hard to find a way of escape today.

All day, as she went about the drudgery of the household, she pondered a variety of options. It was possible that she could wait till he had taken her . . . then slip away when he slept afterward, as she had heard that men were likely to do. Certainly the old woman could not follow her—but she might rouse Rory from sleep. Somehow, one way or other, she must manage to prevent Rory from following her. . . .

And if she did that, she might as well have let him take her on that first night. Her throat closed in revulsion at the thought of being a passive victim, letting him take her unchallenged.

Possibly, when they undressed for bed, she might somehow contrive to hide his boots and his leather breeches, so that he could not at once follow her; barefoot and unbreeched, would even he manage to chase her, afoot—for she would also cut loose his riding-chervine and drive it into the woods. By the time he found boots and breeches, and rounded up his chervine, she and her horse would be well on the way to Nevarsin.

But she would have to submit to him first. . . .

And then she thought; when we are undressed for bed, a well-placed knee in the groin would cripple him long enough to evade pursuit, certainly. Only she must have the courage to kick hard, and hit her target at the first touch; otherwise, he would certainly half kill her when he caught her, and would never trust her again. She remembered what her own mother had taught her when she and Ruyven were very small, that she must never hit or kick him there even in play, because a relatively light blow to that area would cause serious and possibly permanent damage; if the parts were ruptured, even death. And that made her stop and think.

Was she prepared to kill, if she must, to prevent him from taking her?

After all, he had first tried to kill her; if she had truly been a boy, or if her tunic had not torn, revealing her as a woman, he would have cut her throat for her horse and her cloak. Yes, he had been kind to her after his own fashion when he discovered she was a woman, but that was because he thought that rather than a corpse, he would prefer to have a slave . . . for surely that was what her life with him would be, drudging daylong at heavy work and waiting on the whims of the old woman; he could get more from her, that way, and have horse and fine cloak too! No, she would not scruple.

In early afternoon, Rory came in where she was listlessly kneading bread, and dumped the carcass of a rabbithorn on the table.

"I have it cleaned and skinned," he said. "Roast a haunch of it for dinner tonight—I have not tasted meat this tenday—and tomorrow we will salt the rest; for tonight, hang it in the stables, well out of reach of vermin."

"As you wish, Rory," she said, and inwardly she gloated. The meat, frozen as it would certainly be, would keep her for some time if she could manage to take it with her on her way out. She would be careful to hang it near to her own saddle.

The roast meat soon began to fill the hut with a good smell; Romilly was hungry; but even after she had fed the old woman, wiped her chin and settled her for the night, she found that she could not chew and swallow without choking.

I must be ready. I must be ready. It is tonight or never. She lingered at the table, sipping nervously at a hot cup of bark-tea, until Rory came and wound his arms around her from behind.

"I have built a fire on the hearth in the inner room, so we will not be cold, come, Calinda." She supposed the old woman had told him her assumed name. Certainly she had not. Well, it was upon her; she could delay no longer. Her knees felt weak and wobbly, and for a minute she wondered if she could ever have the courage to carry out her resolve.

She let him lead her into the inner room and close the door and fasten it with a hook from inside. Not good. If she was to make her escape at all, she must have a clear way outside. "Must you lock the door?" she asked. "Certainly Gran—Dame Mhari cannot enter our room at any awkward time, for she cannot walk at all."

"I thought we would be more private this way," he said, smirking again, and she said "But suppose—suppose—" she fumbled a moment, then said, "But suppose Dame Mhari has need of me in the night, and I do not hear her? Leave the door part way open so she can call me if she has a pain or wants me to shift her to her other side."

"You have a good heart, girl," Rory said, and pushed the door open a crack, then sat heavily on the edge of the bed and began to draw off his boots.

"Here, let me help you," she said, and came to draw them off, then deliberately wrinkled her nose.

"Faugh, how they stink, you must have stepped in the manure pile! Give them to me, my husband," she used the word deliberately, "and I will clean them before you rise in the morning. You might as well give me your leather breeches too." and she stopped, had she gone too far? But Rory suspected nothing.

"Aye, and I will have a clean shirt for the morning if you have one cleaned and dried," he said, and piled his clothes into her arms. "Take them out to the washpot to wait for morning, if they smell of manure they will be better there than in our bridal chamber."

Better and better! But he could still be after her in a flash if he suspected; lingering by the wash pot, half ready to make a dash for freedom then—naked, he could not chase her very far—she heard his suspicious call.

"Calinda! I am waiting for you! Get in here!"

"I am coming," she called, raising her voice, and went back to him. Fate had decided it for her, then. She went back into the bedroom and drew off her own shoes and stockings, her outer tunic and breeches.

He turned back the covers of the bed and got into it. He reached for her as she came and sat on the edge of the bed, and his hand closed on her breast in what was meant, she supposed, for a caress, but his hand was so heavy that she cried out in pain. He twisted his mouth down over hers and wrestled her own on the bed.

"You like to fight, do you? Well, if that's what you want, girl, I'll give it to you that way—" he panted, covering her with his naked body; his breath was hot and sour.

Romilly's qualms were gone. She managed to draw away just a little, then shot out her foot in the hardest kick she had ever given. It landed directly on target, and Rory, with a howl of pain, rolled off the bed, shrieking with fury and outrage, his hands clutched spasmodically between his legs.

"Augh! Augh! Hellcat, tiger, bitch! Augh!"

She heard Dame Mhari's voice anxiously crying out in question; but Romilly scrambled from the bed, clutching her cloak about her, pulling on her tunic with hasty fingers as she fled. She shoved the door open and was in the kitchen, snatching up the remnants of the loaf and the roast meat, grabbing Rory's boots and breeches and her own in an untidy armful, hastily fumbling at the lock of the byre. Behind her Rory was still howling, wordless screams of agony and wrath; they beat out at her, almost immobilizing her, but she fought for breath, thrusting her way into the byre. With her dagger she slashed through the knots which tied Rory's riding-cherv- ine and slapped the animal hard on the rump, driving it with a yell into the courtyard; slashed at her horse's reins and fumbled to thrust on the bridle. Rory's howls and Dame Mhari's voice raised in querulous complaint—she did not know what had happened and Rory was not yet able to be articulate—blended in a terrifying duet, it seemed that Rory's agony throbbed painfully in her own body, but that was *laran*, she thought dimly that it was a small price to pay for that avenging blow.

He would have killed me, he would have ravished me—I need feel no guilt for him!

She was about to fling his boots and breeches out in the snow; she fastened her tunic carefully against the cold, bent to pick up Rory's boots, then had a better thought. She flung open the door of the small outhouse and thrust them, with a savage movement, down into the privy, thrust the breeches down on top of them. Now let him find them and clean them before he can follow me, she thought, flung herself on her horse, snatched up the hastily bundled provisions, and dug her heels, with a yell, into her horse's side. The horse plunged away into the woods and she took the steep path downward, giving her horse his head in her haste to get away. She had to cling to the horse's neck, so steep was the road, but there was no horse alive to whose back she could not stick if she must, and she knew she would not fall. She remembered Dame Mhari's words, *you should have taken the left-hand fork at the bottom of the mountain.* Her heart was pounding so hard she could hardly hear the sharp clatter of her horse on the path under her feet.

She was free, and for a little time at least, Rory could not pursue her. No matter that she was abroad on a dark night, with rain falling underfoot, and with scant provision and no money except for the few coins in ·a cloth between her breasts; she was at least out of the hands of Rory and the old woman.

Now I am free. Now I must decide what to do with my freedom. She pondered, briefly, returning to Falconsward— but that would be taken, by her father, as a sign of abject surrender. *Dom* Garris might give her a slavery more comfortable that she would find with Rory in the woods; but she had not used all her ingenuity to get free of them, to go back to imprisonment.

No; she would seek the Tower, and training of her *laran*. She told herself, all the old tales of heroism and quests always begin with the hero having to overcome many trials. *Now I am the hero—why is a hero always a man?—of my own quest, and I have passed the first trial.*

And she shivered at the thought that this might be, not a road to freedom, but only the first of the main trials on her quest.

CHAPTER TWO

———•◆•———

Romilly did not slacken her speed till the moon had set; riding in the dark, letting her horse have his head, she finally eased off the reins and let him slow to a walk. She was not sure herself quite where she was; she knew she had not taken the left-hand fork she should have taken at the bottom of the hill, to set her on the way to Nevarsin—it would have been all too easy for Rory to trace her that way. And now she knew that she was lost; she would not even be sure what direction she was riding until the sun should rise and she could get her bearings.

She found an overhanging clump of trees, unsaddled her horse and tied him at the foot of one tree, then wrapped herself in the cloak and the rough blanket she had caught up in her flight, digging into a little hollow at the foot of the tree. She was cold and cramped, but she slept, even though she kept starting out of sleep with nightmares in which a faceless man who was both Rory and *Dom* Garris—no, but he had a look of her father too—came down at her with inexorable slowness, while she could not move hand or foot. It was certain that if Rory ever set eyes on her again, she had better have her dagger ready. But someone had thrown her dagger down into the privy pit, and she could not look for it because her only clothing was one of her blood-stained rags, and somehow or other they were holding the Festival dance in the meadow where her father had his horse-fair. . . . She was wakened by the horse, restlessly snorting and nuzzling; the sun was up and the ice melting from the trees.

She had been lucky, in her breakneck flight last night, in the dark, that her horse had not broken a leg on the frosty road. Now, soberly, she took stock.

Among the things she had snatched up last night were a frozen quarter of rabbithorn meat, which she could cook and smoke—she had no salt for it, but in this weather it was not likely to spoil. At worst she could slice thin slivers away from the frozen haunch and eat them raw, though she had little liking for raw meat. She had lost flint and steel for firemaking . . . no, what a fool she was, she had her dagger and could search for a flint when the ice was thawed off the road. She had Rory's coarse cloak instead of her own fur-lined one, but that was all to the good; it would keep her warm without exciting the same greed as her finely woven and embroidered one, lined with rich fur. She had boots and heavy leather breeches, her dagger, a few small hoarded coins in their hiding-place between her breasts—she had abandoned the pocket with its few bits; perhaps that and the good cloak would satisfy Rory's greed and he would not pursue her. But she would take no chances, and press on. In her saddle-pack she had still a few pieces of the dog-bread on which she could feed her horse; she got out one of them, and gave it to the horse, letting him chew on the coarse grain while she arranged her clothing properly—she had fled the cottage half-dressed and all put together anyhow—and combed her short, ragged hair with her fingers. Certainly she must look disreputable enough to be a runaway hawkmaster's apprentice! Now the sun was high; it would be a fine day, for already the trees were casting off their snow-pods and beginning to bud again. She shaved a few thin slices of frozen rabbithorn and chewed on them; the meat was tough and unsavory, but she had been taught that anything a bird could eat, a human could digest, and since the hawks were fed on such fare it would certainly not harm her, even if she really preferred cooked food.

She got her bearings by the climbing sun, and set off again toward the north. Sooner or later she must meet with someone who would give her the right road for Nevarsin City, and from there she could inquire the way to Tramontana Tower.

She rode all that day without setting eyes on a single person or a single dwelling. She was not afraid, for she could find food in this country and while the weather kept fine, she would be safe and well. But before there was another storm, she must find shelter. Perhaps she could sell the horse in Nevarsin, bartering him for a stag-pony and enough in ready money to provide herself with food and a few items of clothing she should have in this weather. She had thrust her feet into her boots in such haste, she had left her warm stockings.

She sighed, put her knife away, and swallowed the last of the tough meat. A few withered winter apples clung to a bush; she pocketed them. They were small and sour, but the horse would like them. High above in the sky she heard the cry of a hawk; as she watched it, circling, she thought of Preciosa. It seemed to her for a moment—but surely it was only memory or imagination?—that she could feel that faint tenuous touch she had felt with Preciosa, as if the world lay spread below her, she saw herself and her horse as tiny specks . . . *Oh, Preciosa, you were mine and I loved you, but now you are free and I too am seeking freedom.*

She slept that night in a long-abandoned travel-shelter, which had not been kept up since the Aldarans declared their independence of the Six Domains of the lowlands; there was not much coming and going across the Kadarin between Thendara and Nevarsin these days. But it kept the rain off, and was better than sleeping under a tree. She managed to make a fire, too, so she slept warm, and roasted some of the rabbithorn. She hoped she would find some nuts—she was tired of meat—but while she was fed, however coarsely, she could not complain. Even the dog-bread she could eat, if she must, but the horse would get more good of it than she would.

So she travelled alone for three more days. By now, she supposed, they must have abandoned the search for her at home. She wondered if her father grieved, if he thought her dead.

When I come to Nevarsin, I will leave a message for him, I will get word to him somehow that I am safe. But no doubt it will be with me as it was with Ruyven, he will cast me off and say I am not his daughter. She felt a tightness in her throat, but she could not cry. She had cried too much already, and had gained nothing from her tears except an aching head and aching eyes, till she left off crying and acted to help herself.

Women think tears will help them. I think men have the right idea when they say tears are womanish; yes, women cry and so they are helpless, but men act on their anger and so they are never without power, not wasting time or anger in tears. . . .

She finished the last of the rabbithorn, and was not sorry—toward the end, she supposed even a dog would have to be fiercely hungry to eat it, and certainly any hawk would have turned up its beak at the stuff. On the fifth night she had only some nuts, found on an abandoned tree, and some woody mushrooms, for her supper. Perhaps tomorrow she could snare some birds, or she would meet with someone who could tell her if she was again on the road to Nevarsin—but she thought not, for this road grew ever poorer and worse-kept, and if she were nearing the biggest city in these hills, she would certainly have come to some travelled roads and inhabited parts before this!

The dog-bread was gone too, and so she stopped several hours before sunset, to let her horse graze for a while. Fortunately the weather kept fine, and she could sleep in the open. She was very tired of travelling, but reflected that she could not now return to her home even if she wished—she had no idea of the road to Falconsward. Well, so much the better; now she could cut all ties with her home.

She slept poorly, hungry and cold, and waked early. The road was so poor . . . perhaps she should retrace her steps for a distance and see if she could come to more travelled parts? She tore some rags and bound her feet with them to ease the chafing of her boots . . . heels and toe were raw and sore. High in the sky, a single hawk circled—why was there never more than one in sight at a single time? Did they keep territories like some other animals for their hunting? And again that strange flash, as if she saw through the hawk's eyes—was it her *laran* again?—and thought of Preciosa. Prediosa, gone, free, lost. *It is strange, I miss her more than father or brothers or home. . . .*

The time for fruiting was past, but she found a few small fruits still clinging to a bush, and ate them, wishing there were more. There was a tree which she knew she could strip the outer bark and eat the soft inner part, but she was not that hungry, not yet. She saddled her horse, weary in spite of her long sleep. Slowly it was beginning to come over her that she could lose herself and even die in these lonely and utterly uninhabited forests. But perhaps today she would meet with someone and begin to find her way to Nevarsin, or some to some little village where she could buy food.

After an hour of riding she came to a fork in the road, and paused there, indecisive, aching with hunger, exhausted. Well, she would let her horse graze for a bit while she climbed to the top of a little knoll nearby and looked about, to see if she could spy out any human habitation, the smoke of a woodcutter's fire, a herder's hut even. She had never felt so alone in her life. *Of course not. I have never* been *so alone in all my life,* she thought, with wry humor, and clambered up the knoll, her knees aching.

I have not eaten well for days. I must somehow find food and fire this night, whatever comes of it. She was almost wishing she had stayed with Rory and his abominable old grandmother; at least there she had been warm and fed . . . would it really have been so bad, to marry that oaf?

I would rather die in the wilderness, she told herself fiercely, but she was frightened and hungry, and from the top of the knoll she could see only what looked like a wilderness of trees. Far away, at the furthest edge of her sight, a high mountain loomed, to the Northwest, and pale shadows around it which she knew to be snowcapped peaks . . . there lay the Hellers themselves, to which these foothills were only little lumps in the land, and beyond them, the Wall Around the World, which was, as far as she knew from traveller's tales, impassable; at least no one she had ever known had gone beyond it, and on every map she had ever seen, it delimited the very edge of known country. Once she had asked her governess what lay beyond it.

"The frozen waste," her governess told her, "No man knows. . . ." The thought had intrigued Romilly, then. Now she had had enough of wandering in unknown country, and felt that some human company would be welcome.

Although what she had seen already did not make her feel very hopeful about what she would meet with from men on the roads. . . .

Well, she had been unlucky, that was all. She sighed, and pulled her belt tighter. It would not hurt her to go on fasting another day, though tonight she must find some food, whatever happened. She looked around again, carefully taking the bearings of the great peak—it seemed to her that there was something near the top, a white building, some kind of manmade structure; she wondered if it was castle, Great House or, perhaps, one of the Towers. Northwest; she must be careful to keep track of the angle of the sun and the passage of time so that she would not begin walking in circles. But if she followed where the road led, she would be unlikely to do that.

She should get back to her horse. She glanced up again. Strange. The hawk still hovered. She wondered, on wild surmise, if it could be the same hawk . . . no. It was just that hawks were plentiful in these hills and wherever you cast your eyes on the sky, there was sure to be some kind of bird

116

of prey within sight. For an instant it seemed as if she hovered, seeing the white pinnacle of the Tower and a faint blue lightning that struck from within . . . she felt faint and dizzy, not knowing whether it was the hawk or herself that saw . . . she shook herself and pulled out of the rapport. It would be all too easy to lose herself in that communion with sky and wind and cloud. . . .

She went back to her horse and painstakingly saddled him again. At least the animal was fed. She said aloud, "I almost wish I could eat grass as you do, old fellow," and was startled at the sound of her own voice.

It was answered by another sound; the high, shrill crying of a striking hawk—yes, the hawk had found some prey, for she could feel, somewhere in her mind, the flow of warm blood, a sensation that made her mouth tickle and flood with saliva, reawakening fierce hunger. The horse startled nervously away, and she pulled on the reins, speaking softly—and then dark pinions swooped across her vision. Without thought she thrust out her arm, felt the cruel grip of talons, and fell blindly into the familiar rapport.

"Preciosa!" She was sobbing as she spoke the name. How, why the hawk had followed her through her wandering, she would never know. The shrill cry and the flapping wings roused her from her tears and she was aware that there was a good-sized bird, still warm, gripped in the bird's claws. With one hand she gripped the bird's legs, lifting the claw away from her wrist—it was bleeding a little where the claws had cut, it was her own fault, for she had no proper glove. She set the bird on the saddle, her heart pounding, and pulled out her dagger; gave head and wings to Preciosa, and while the hawk fed—praise to the Bearer of Burdens, the horse knew enough to stand quietly when his saddle was made into an impromptu perch—she plucked what was left of the carcass, struck flint and steel and made a small fire where she roasted the carcass.

She came to me when I was hungry. She knew. She brought me food, giving up her own freedom. The jesses were still clinging to Preciosa's legs. Romilly cut them free with her dagger.

If she wants to stay with me now it shall be of her free will. Never again will I bind her with any mark of ownership. She belongs to herself. But her eyes were still flooding with tears. She met the hawk's eyes, and suddenly awareness leaped between hawk and girl, a strange, fierce emotion flooding her—not love as she knew it, but pure emotion, almost jealousy. *She is not my hawk. I am her girl*, Romilly thought, *she has adopted me, not the other way round!*

The hawk did not stir when she moved toward it; balancing a little by shifting her weight from foot to foot, she stared motionless into Romilly's eyes; then gave a little upward hop and alighted on her shoulder. Romilly caught her breath with the pain as the talons tightened on her flesh, even through tunic and cloak, and immediately the grip slackened, so that Preciosa was holding her just tightly enough to keep her balance.

"You beauty, you wonder, you marvel," Romilly whispered, while the hawk craned her neck and preened the set of her feathers.

Never have I known of such a thing as this, that a hawk once set free should return. . . . and Romilly supposed it was the mark of her *laran* which had brought her close to the hawk.

She stayed quiet, in that wordless communion, for what seemed a long time, while Romilly finished the roasted meat, covered the fire and resaddled the horse; her hands moved automatically about her tasks, but her eyes kept coming back and her mind dropping into silent closeness to the bird.

Will she stay with me now? Or fly away again? It no longer matters. We are together.

At last she cut a branch and trimmed it, fastening it to her saddle behind, as a perch for Preciosa if she chose to stay there, and mounted, setting Preciosa on the improvised perch. Preciosa stayed quiet for a moment, then flapped her wings and rose high, wheeling just at the height of the treetop, hovering near. Romilly drew a long breath. Preciosa would not leave her entirely.

Then she drew on the horse's reins, for she heard voices; a rough man's voice proclaiming, "I tell you, it was smoke I saw," and another one protesting something. There were horse's hooves, too, and somewhere a sharp barking.

Romilly was off her horse, sliding down, leading him into the thickest part of the trees at the edge of the road. She had no wish to meet with any travellers before she could get a look at them and see what they were up to and what they looked like.

Another voice spoke, rough and male, but this time in the cultivated accents of an educated man—a lowlander, Romilly thought; he spoke like Alderic. "If anyone else travels on this road, Orain, he is no doubt in our own case, and will be as glad as we are to see another human face." The riders came

118

into sight now, a tall man with flame-red hair, wearing ragged clothing but with a certain look of elegance—this one was no yokel like Rory. Somehow he reminded her of Lord Storn, or the elderly Lord Scathfell, though his dress was as rough as her own, his beard and hair untrimmed. The man at his side was tall too, almost gaunt, wearing a shirtcloak of antique fashion and boots that looked hand-botched together from untanned leather. On a block before him, on his saddle, a huge hooded bird, which did not look like any hawk Romilly had ever seen before, moved uneasily from foot to foot, and Romilly, still partly in rapport with Preciosa at treetop-height, felt a little shudder of anger and something like fear. She did not know what sort of bird it was, but she knew instinctively that she did not like to be around it.

Behind the two men in the lead, five or six others rode. Only the two in the vanguard had horses; the others rode an assortment of *chervines*, none of them very large or very good, their coats ill-cared-for and their horns ragged and rough; one or two of the stag-beasts had been crudely dehorned with a lack of skill that made Romilly wince. Her father would have turned away any hired man who kept his riding-animals in any such condition, and as for the dehorning, she could almost have done better herself! She liked the look of the two men who rode ahead, but she thought she had never seen such ruffians as the men behind them!

The gaunt, bearded man in the lead, riding at the side of the red-haired aristocrat (so she immediately styled him in her mind) got off his horse and said, "Here's trace of fire; and horse-droppings, too; there's been a rider here."

"And with a horse, in the wild?" the red-haired man inquired with a lift of his eyebrows. He glanced around, but it was the gaunt, crudely dressed man whose eyes lighted on Romilly where she stood by the horse in the thickest part of the trees.

"Come out, boy. We mean ye' no harm," he said, beckoning, and the red-haired man slid from his horse and stood by the remains of her fire. He poked about the carefully covered coals—like everyone brought up in the Hellers, Romilly was over-cautious about fire in the woods—and finally extracted a few live sparks; threw in a twig or two.

"You have saved us the trouble of making fire," he said in his quiet, educated voice, "Come and share it with us, no one will hurt you."

And indeed Romilly felt no sense of menace from any of

them. She led the horse from the concealed thicket and stood with her hand on the bridle.

"Well, lad, who are ye' and whereaway bound?" asked the gaunt man, and his voice was kind. He was, she thought, not quite as old as her father, but older than any of her brothers. She repeated the tale she had thought of.

"I am a hawkmaster's apprentice—I was brought up in a Great House, but my mother was too proud to claim me a nobleman's son, and I thought I could better myself in Nevarsin; so I took the road there, but I am lost."

"But you have horse and cloak, dagger and—if I make no mistake—a hawk too," said the redhead, his grey eyes lighting on the improvised perch, to which Romilly had tied the cut-away jesses—her whole training had taught her never to throw away a scrap of leather, it could always be used for something. "Did you steal the hawk? Or what is an apprentice doing with a bird—and where is she?"

Romilly raised her arm; Preciosa swooped down and caught her lifted forearm. She said fiercely, "She is mine; no other can claim her, for I trained her with my own hand."

"I doubt you not," said the aristocrat, "for in this wild, without even jesses, she could fly away if she would, and in that sense at least, you own her as much as anything human can own a wild thing."

He understands that! Romilly felt a sudden extreme sense of kinship with this man, as if he were a brother, a kinsman. She smiled up at him, and he returned the smile. Then he looked around at the men ringing the grove, and said, "We too are on our way to Nevarsin, though the route we travel is somewhat circuitous—for reasons of caution. Ride with us, if you will."

"What *Dom* Carlo means," said the gaunt man at his side, "is that if we rode the main roads, there are those who'd have the hangman on us, quick!"

Were they outlaws, bandits? Romilly wondered whether she had not, in escaping Rory and taking up with these rough-looking men, walked from the trap to the cookpot! But the redhead smiled, a look of pure affection and love, at the other man and said, "You make us sound like a crew of murderers, Orain. We are landless men who lost the estates of our fathers, and some of us lost our kin, too, because we supported the rightful king instead of yonder rascal who thinks to claim the throne of the Hasturs. He assured he would have supporters enough by poison, rope or knife for all those who would not support him, and had enough lands to reward his

120

followers, by murdering, or sending into exile, anyone who looked at him cross-eyed and did not bend the knee fast enough. So we are bound for Nevarsin, to raise an army there—Rakhal shall not have the Crystal Palace unchallenged! Him a Hastur?" The man laughed shortly. "I'll shall his head rest in that crown while any of us are alive! I am Carlo of Blue Lake; and this is my paxman and friend Orain."

The word he had used for "friend" was one which could also mean *cousin* or *foster-brother;* and Romilly saw that the gaunt Orain looked on *Dom* Carlo with a devotion like that of a good hound for his master.

"But if the lad is a hawk-trainer," Orain said, "I doubt not he could tell ye what ails our sentry-birds, *Dom* Carlo."

Carlo looked sharply at Romilly. "What's your name, boy?"

"Rumal."

"And from your accent I can tell you were reared north of the Kadarin," said he. "Well, Rumal, have you knowledge of hawks?"

Romilly nodded. "I have, sir."

"Show him the birds, Orain."

Orain went to his horse, and took the great bird from the saddle. He beckoned to two of the other men, who were carrying similar birds on their saddles; warily, Orain drew the hood from the head of the bird, being careful to stay out of reach; it jerked its head around, making pecking movements, but was too listless to peck. There was a long feathered crest over the eye-sockets, but the head was naked and ugly, the feathers unkempt and unpreened, even the creature's talons scaly and dirty-looking. She thought she had never seen such ugly fierce-looking birds; but if in good health they might have had the beauty of any wild creature. Now they just looked hunched and miserable. One of them cocked its neck and let out a long scream, then drooped its head between its wings and looked disreputable again.

Romilly said, "I have never seen birds of this kind." Though she thought they looked more like *kyorebni,* the savage scavenger-birds of the high hills, than any proper hunting-bird of prey.

"Still, a bird is a bird," said Carlo, "We got these from a well-wisher and we would take them as a gift to Carolin's armies, in Nevarsin, but they are failing fast and may not live till we get there—we cannot make out what ails them, though some of us have trained and flown hawks—but none of us

121

know how to treat them when they ail. Have you knowledge of their ills, Master Rumal?"

"A little," Romilly said, trying desperately to muster her small knowledge of curing sick animals. These were sick indeed; any bird, from cagebird to *verrin* hawk, who will not preen its feathers and keep its feet in trim is a sick bird. She had been taught to mend a broken flight feather, but she knew little of medicining sick birds, and if they had molt-rot or something of the sort, she had not the faintest idea what to do about it.

Nevertheless she went up to the strange, fierce-looking birds, and held out her hand to the one Orain held, looking it into the eye and reaching out with that instinctive rapport. A dullness spread through her, a sickness and pain that made her want to retch. She pulled out of the rapport, feeling nauseated, and said, "What have you been feeding them?"

That was a good guess; she remembered Preciosa, sickened by insufficiently fresh food.

"Only the best and freshest food," said one of the men behind Orain, defensively, "I lived in a Great House where there were hawks kept, and knew them meat-eaters; when our hunting was poor, all of us went short to give the damned birds fresh meat, for all the good it did us," he added, looking distressedly at the drooping bird on his saddleblock.

"Only fresh meat?" said Romilly, "There is your trouble, sir. Look at their beak and claws, and then look at my hawk's. That's a scavenger-bird, sir; she should be freed to hunt food for herself. She can't tear apart fresh meat, her beak's not strong enough, and if you've been carrying her on your saddle and not let her free, she's not been able to peck gravel and stones for her crop. She feeds on half-rotted meat, and she must have fur or feathers too—the muscle meat alone, and skinned as well—wasn't it?"

"We thought that was the way to do it," said Orain, and Romilly shook her head. "If you *must* feed them on killed meat, leave feather and fur on it, and make sure she gets a chance to peck up stones and twigs and even a bit of green stuff now and then. These birds, though I am sure you've tried to feed them on the best, are starving because they can't digest what you've given them. They should be allowed to hunt for themselves, even if you have to fly them on a lure-line."

"Zandru's hells, it makes good sense, Orain," said *Dom* Carlo, blinking, "I should have seen it . . . well, now we know. What can we do?"

122

Romilly thought about it, quickly. Preciosa had wheeled up into the sky, and hovered there; Romilly went quickly into rapport with the bird, seeing for a moment through her eyes; then said, "There is something dead in the thicket over there. I'm not familiar with your—what do you call them—sentry-birds; are they territorial, or will they feed together?"

"We daren't let them too near each other," said Orain, "for they fight; this one I carry near pecked out the eyes of that one on Gawin's saddle there."

Romilly said, "Then there's no help for it; you'll have to feed them separately. There—" she pointed, "is something dead for at least a couple of days—you'll have to fetch it and cut it up for them."

The men hesitated.

"Well," said *Dom* Carlo sharply, "What are you waiting for? Carolin needs these birds, and no doubt at Tramontana they'll have a *leronis* who can fly them, but we've got to get them there alive!"

"Ye squeamish, lily-gutted, cack-handed incompetents," Orain swore, "Afraid to get yer hands dirty, are ye? I'll set an example, then! Where's this dead thing ye spied, lad?"

Romilly began to walk toward the thicket; Orain followed and *Dom* Carlo said with asperity, "Go and help him, you men, as many as he needs! Will you let one man and a child drag carrion for three birds?"

Reluctantly, a couple of the men followed. Whatever animal lay dead in the thicket—she suspected it was one of the small multicolored woods chervines—it announced its presence very soon by the smell, and Romilly wrinkled her nose.

Orain said incredulously, "We're to feed *that* to those fine birds?" He bent down and hauled gingerly at the smelly carcass; a stream of small insects were parading in and out of the empty eye-holes, but it was not yet disintegrated enough to come apart in their hands, and Romilly took one end of the carcass and hoisted, trying to breathe through her mouth so she would not have to breathe in much of the foul smell.

"A *kyorebni* would think it fine fare," Romilly said, "I have never kept a scavenger-bird, but their bellies are not like those of hawks, and how would you like to be fed on grass?"

"I doubt not that y're right," said Orain glumly, "But I never thought to be handling stinking carrion even for the king's men!" The other men came and lent a hand in the hauling; Romilly was glad when it was over, but some of the men gagged and retched as they handled the stuff. Orain, however, drew a formidable knife and began hacking it into three parts; even before he was finished the hooded bird on his saddle set up a screaming. Romilly drew a long breath of relief. She did not like to think what would have happened if she had been wrong, but evidently she had been right. She took up a small handful of fine pebbly dirt and strewed it over the cut hunk of the carcass, then, hesitating—but remembering the moment of rapport with the sick bird—went and unfastened the hood.

Orain shouted, "Hey! Look out there, lad, she'll pick out yer eyes—"

But the bird, under her light hands, seemed gentle and submissive. *Poor hungry thing,* Romilly thought, and lifted the heavy weight—it took all her strength—to set it on the ground beside the hacked carcass. With a scream, the bird plunged its beak into the carcass and tore hard, gulping down fur, pebbles, the smelly half-decomposed meat.

"You see?" said Romilly simply, and went to lift down the other bird. Orain came to help her, but the strange bird thrust angry beak at him, and he drew back, letting Romilly handle it.

When all of the birds had fed and were preening their feathers, making little croaking sounds of satisfaction, *Dom* Carlo lifted his eyebrow at Orain, and Orain said, "Ride with us to Nevarsin, lad, and then to Tramontana to deliver these birds to Carolin's men; and keep them healthy on the way. We'll feed you and your horse, and give you three silver bits for every tenday ye're with us while the birds stay healthy. Your hawk," he added with a droll grin, "Can no doubt hunt for himself."

"Herself," Romilly corrected, and Orain chuckled.

"Be a bird male or female, none cares except another bird of its own kind," he said. "Otherwise with humankind, aye, *Dom* Carlo?" And he laughed, though Romilly could not quite see the joke. "Well, what about it, boy, will ye' have along of us and the sentry-birds?"

Romilly had already made up her mind. She herself was bound, first to Nevarsin and then to Tramontana to seek her brother or news of him. This would give her protection and keep her fed. She said, "Gladly, *Dom* Carlo and Master Orain."

"Bargain, then," said Orain, and stuck out his calloused hand with a grin. "Now the birds have fed, shall we move out of range of the smell of their feeding, and have a bait of vittles for ourselves?"

"Sounds good," Romilly said, and went to unsaddle her horse.

The food was heavy dough, baked by the simple method of thrusting twists of the dough on to sticks and baking over the fire; and a few thick tubers roasted in the ashes. Romilly sat beside Orain, who offered her salt from a little pouch drawn from his pocket. When the meal was done, the birds hooded and taken on their saddles again—Orain asked Romilly for help with getting the hoods back on the birds—she heard one or two of the men grumbling.

"That lad rides a horse when we make do wi' a stag-pony each? What about it—shall we have it from him?"

"Try it," said Orain, turning, "and ye' can ride alone in these woods, Alaric—there are no thieves and bandits in our company, and if ye' lay one finger on the boy's horse, it'll be for *Dom* Carlo to deal with ye'!"

Romilly felt a surge of gratitude; it seemed she had found a protector in Orain, and for the moment, facing the ragged crew, she was a little frightened.

Soon or late, though, she might have to face them on her own, without a protector. . . .

"What are the birds' names?" she asked Orain. He grinned at her. "Does anyone name uglies like these, as if they were a child's cagebird or the old wife's pet cow?"

"I do," Romilly said, "You must give any animal with which you wish to work closely, a name, so that he will read it in your mind and know it is of him—or her—that you speak, and to her you are directing your attention."

"Is it so?" Orain asked, chuckling, "I suppose you could call them Ugly-mug One, Ugly-mug Two, and Ugly-mug Three!"

"By no means," said Romilly with indignation. The bird on her first fluttered restlessly, and she added, "Birds are very sensitive! If you are ever to work with them, you must love them—" before the open derision in the men's eyes she knew she was blushing, but went on nevertheless, "You must *respect* them, and care for them, and feel a real kindness for them. Do you think they do not know that you dislike them and are afraid of them?"

"And you don't?" *Dom* Carlo asked. He sounded genuinely interested, and she turned to him with relief. She said, "Would you mock your best hunting-dog if you wanted to have a good hunt, with him working to your word or gesture? Don't you think he would know?"

"I have not hunted since I was a young lad," *Dom* Carlo

said, "but certainly I would not treat any beast I sought to tame to my service, with anything but respect. Listen to what the lad says, men; he's got the right of it. I heard the same from my own hawkmaster once. And surely—" he patted the neck of the superb black mare he rode, "we all have love and respect for our beasts, horse or chervine, who carry us so faithfully."

"Well," said Orain, again with that droll curl of his lip, looking down at the great gross body of the sentry-bird, "We could call this one Beauty, that one Lovely, and that one over there we might call Gorgeous. I doubt not they're beautiful enough to one another—lovesome's as lovesome does, or so my old Ma used to say."

Romilly giggled. "I think that would be overdoing," she said. "Beauty they may not have, but—let me think—I shall call them after the Virtues," she added after a moment. "This one—" she lifted the heavy bird on to its block on Orain's saddle, "Shall be Prudence. This one—" she went, frowned at the dirty perch and thrust the hooded bird on to Orain's gloved fist while she dug out her knife and scraped off a disgusting accumulation of filth and droppings. "This one shall be Temperance, and this one—" turning to the third, "Diligence."

"How are we to tell them apart?" demanded one of the men, and she said seriously, "Why, they are nothing alike. Diligence is the big one with the blue tips on her wings—see? And Temperance—you can't see it now, it's under the hood, but her crest is big and white-speckled. And Prudence is the little one with the extra toe on her feet—see?" She pointed out the features one by one, and Orain stared in amazement.

"Why, so they are different—I never thought to notice."

Romilly climbed into her saddle. She said seriously, "The first thing you have to learn about birds is to think of each one as an individual. In their manners and their habits, too, they are no more alike than you and *Dom* Carlo." She turned in her saddle to the redhaired man and said, "Forgive me, sir, perhaps I should have consulted you before naming your birds—"

He shook his head. "I never thought of it. They seem good names, indeed . . . are you a *cristoforo*, my lad?"

She nodded. "I was reared as one. And you, sir?"

"I serve the Lord of Light," he said briefly. Romilly said nothing, but was a little startled—the *Hali'imyn* did not come all that often into these hills. But of course, if they were Carolin's men in exile, they would serve the Gods of the

126

Hastur-kindred. And if Carolin's armies were massing at Nevarsin—excitement caught in her throat. No doubt this was the reason Alderic was in these hills, to join the king when the time was ripe. She speculated again, briefly, about Alderic's real identity. If these were Carolin's men, perhaps they knew him and were his friends. But that was not her business and the last thing she should do was to entangle herself in any man's cause. Her father had said it, and it was true, why should it matter which rascal sat on the throne, so long as they left honest folk alone to do their own business?

She rode in the line of men, keeping rather nervously close to Orain and *Dom* Carlo—she did not like the way the man Alaric stared at her, and, no doubt, like the villainous Rory, he coveted her horse. At least he did not know she was a female and so he did not covet her body; and she could protect her horse, at least while she had *Dom* Carlo's protection.

Come to think of it, she hadn't done such a bad job of protecting her body, at that.

They rode all day, stopping at noon for some porridge made by stirring cold well-water into finely-ground porridge powder. This, with a handful of nuts, made a hearty meal. After the meal they rested for a time, but Romilly busied herself with her knife, trimming and balancing proper perches—the sentry-birds were, she could see, in considerable distress from the poorly-balanced saddle-blocks. She checked the knots in the jesses, too, and found that one of the birds had a festered place in its leg from too-tight knots, which she treated with cold water and a poultice of healing leaves. The other men were lying around in the clearing, enjoying the sun, but when Romilly came back from checking the birds, she saw that *Dom* Carlo was awake and watching her. Nevertheless she went on with her work. One of the men's stag-ponies was poorly dehorned and the horn-bud trickling blood at the base; she trimmed it and scraped it clean, drying it with a bit of rag and packing it with absorbent moss, then went from stag-pony to stag-pony, checking one which had been limping, and picking, with her knife-point, a little stone from between the hoof-segments.

"So," said *Dom* Carlo at last, lazily, opening his eyes, "You go about your self-appointed tasks well—you are not lazy, Rumal. Where got you your knowledge of beasts? You have the skill of a MacAran with them—" and he sat up and looked at her, "and I would say you had a touch of their *laran* as well. And now I think of it, you've a look of that clan, too." His grey eyes met hers, and Romilly felt a curious sense that he looked at her inside and out, and she quailed—could he tell, if he was one of the Gifted Hastur-kinfolk, that she was a girl? But he seemed not to be aware of her dismay, only went on looking at her—it was, she thought, as if it never occurred to him that anyone would refuse to answer him when he asked.

She said, her words stumbling over themselves, "I was—I said—brought up—I know some of them—"

"Born the wrong side of the bed? Aye, it's an old enough story in these hills, and elsewhere too," said *Dom* Carlo, "Which is why that ruffian Rakhal sits on the throne and Carolin—awaits us in Nevarsin."

"You know the king well, sir? You seem one of the *Hali'imyn*—"

"Why, so I am," *Dom* Carlo said easily, "No, Orain, don't look like that, the word's not the insult in these mountains that it would be South of the Kadarin. The boy means no harm. Know the King? I have—not seen him often," *Dom* Carlo said, "but he is kin to me, and I hold by him. As I said, a few too many bastards with ambitions put Carolin in this difficulty—his father was too tender-hearted with his ambitious kinsmen, and only a tyrant assures his throne by murdering all others with the shadow of a claim to it. So I have sympathy with your plight, boy—if the usurper Rakhal laid hands on me, for instance, or any of Carolin's sons, their heads would soon be decorating the walls of his castle. I suppose you have some of the MacAran *donas,* though, or you could not handle beasts as you do. There is a MacAran *laranzu* in Tramontana—it is to him and his fellow workers that we mean these birds to go, in the end. Know you anything of sentry-birds, then, my boy?"

Romilly shook her head. "Not until today did I ever set eyes on one, though I have heard they are used for spying—"

"True," said *Dom* Carlo, "One who has the *laran* of your family or something like to it, must work with them, stay in rapport as they fly where you wish to see. If there is an army on the road, you can spy out their numbers and report their movements. The side with the best-trained spy-birds is often the side that wins the battle, for they can take the other by surprise."

"And these are to be trained for this?"

"They must be trained so that they can be handled easily," said Carlo. "A royal gift this was, from one of Carolin's supporters in these hills; but my men knew little of them, which

128

is why it is as if the very Gods sent you to us, who can keep them in health and perhaps gentle them a little to working."

"The one who will fly them at last should do that," Romilly said, "but I will try hard to accustom them to human hands and human voices, and keep them healthy and properly fed." And she wondered; for Ruyven was at Tramontana, so she had heard, and perhaps he was the *laranzu* for whose hands these birds were destined. How strangely Fate turned . . . perhaps, if she could make her way to Tramontana, her gifts could be trained to the handling of such birds. "If your men have any hunting skills, it would be well if they could bring down some medium-small game and feed it to the birds, but not too fresh, unless they can cut it up very fine and feed them skin and feathers with it. . . ."

"I'll leave their diet to you," *Dom* Carlo said, "And if you have any trouble with them, tell me. These are valuable creatures and I'll not have them mishandled." He looked up into the sky, crimsoning as the great sun began to decline somewhat from noon, where, just at the very edge of sight, Romilly could see Preciosa, a tiny dark speck hovering near. "Your hawk stays near even when she flies free? How did you train her to that? What is her name?"

"Preciosa, sir."

"*Preciosa*," jeered the man Alaric, coming to saddle *Dom* Carlo's horse, "Like a wee girl naming her doll!"

"Don't mock the lad," *Dom* Carlo said gently, "Till you can better his way with the birds, we need his skills. And you should take better care of your own beast—a chervine can be well-kept, even if he is not a horse. You should thank Rumal for finding the stone in Greywalker's hoof!"

"Oh, an' indeed I do," said Alaric with a surly scowl, and turned away. Romilly watched with a faint frown of distaste. It seemed she already had an enemy among these men, which she had done nothing to deserve. But perhaps she had been tactless in caring for the chervine's hoof—perhaps she should simply have warned Alaric that his beast was going lame. But couldn't he *see*, or feel the poor thing limping? She supposed that was what it was to be head-blind. He could not communicate with any dumb brute. And with the intolerance of the very young, she thought, *if he does not understand animals better than that, he should not try to ride one!*

Soon after, they mounted and rode on through the afternoon. The trails were steeper now, and Romilly began to lag behind somewhat—on these paths and roads, a mountain-bred chervine was better than a horse, and there were places on the narrow mountain paths where Romilly, Orain and *Dom* Carlo had to dismount and lead their horses by the bridle while the men on the sure-footed stag-like riding-beasts stayed in their saddles, secure as ever. She had lived in the hills all her life and was in general not afraid of anything, but some of the steep edges and sheer cliffs over abysses of empty space and clouds made her gasp and catch her breath, biting her lip against showing her fear. Up they went, and upward still, climbing through cold layers of mist and cloud, and her ears began to ache and her breath grew shorter while her heart pounded so loudly in her ears that she could hardly hear the hooves of the horses and stag-ponies on the rocky path. Once she dislodged a stone with her foot and saw it bouncing down the cliffside, rebounding every ten or fifteen feet until it disappeared into the clouds below.

They paused and drew close together in the throat of the pass, and Orain pointed to a cluster of lights against the dusk of the next mountain. His voice was very low, but Romilly, lagging with the other horses, heard him.

"There it lies. Nevarsin, The City of Snows, *vai dom*. Two or at the most, three more days on the road, and you will be safe behind the walls of St.-Valentine-of-the-Snows."

"And your faithful heart can rest without fear, *bredu*? But all these men are loyal, and even if they knew—"

"Don't even whisper it aloud, my lord—*Dom* Carlo," Orain said urgently.

Dom Carlo reached out and gave the other man's thin shoulder an affectionate touch.

"You have sheltered me with your care since we were children—who but you should be at my side then, foster-brother?"

"Ah, you'll have dozens and hundreds then to care for you, my—" again he paused, *"vai dom."*

"But none with your faithfulness," said *Dom* Carlo gently. "You'll have all the rewards I can give—"

"Reward enough to see you where you belong again—Carlo," said Orain, and turned back to oversee the descent of the others down through the narrow defile which led away toward the bottom of the ravine.

They camped in the open that night, under a crude tent pitched beneath a tree, just a slanting sheet to keep the worst of the rain from them. As befitted a paxman, Orain kept close to *Dom* Carlo, but as they were spreading their blankets, and Romilly checking the birds and feeding them the

130

last of the carrion—the men grumbled and snarled about the smell, but no one would gainsay *Dom* Carlo—Orain said briefly, "Rumal, you'd better spread your blankets near to us—you haven't much in the way of blankets and even wi' your cloak you'll freeze, lad."

Romilly thanked them meekly and crawled in between the two men. She had taken off only her boots—she did not want to be seen in fewer clothes than this—but even with cloak and blanket she felt chilled, and was grateful for shared blankets and warmth. She was vaguely aware, at the edge of sleep, when Preciosa swooped down and roosted within the circle of the fires; and beyond that, something else . . . a faint awareness, the touch of *laran*—*Dom* Carlo's thoughts, stirring, circling about the camp to make sure that all was well with men, riding-beasts and birds.

Then she slept.

CHAPTER THREE

In the clear dawnlight, moving around the clearing to fetch water for the birds, and taking stock—one of the men should hunt today, to kill something for the sentry-birds, although already they looked better and were preening their feathers and cleaning their feet—Romilly could see the walls of Nevarsin, clear in the light as if they were made of snow or salt. An ancient city, built into the side of the mountain, just below the level of the eternal snow; and above them, like the very bones of the mountain projecting through the never-ending snow, the grey walls of the monastery, carved from living rock.

One of the men whose name she did not know was fetching water for porridge; another was doling out grain for the horses and *chervines*. The one called Alaric, a heavy glowering man, roughly clad, was the one she feared most, but she could not avoid him completely, and in any case, he must have some feeling for the sentry-birds, he had carried one of them on that crude perch before his saddle.

"Excuse me," said Romilly politely, "but you must go out and kill something for the sentry-birds; if it is killed this morning, by night it will be beginning to decay, and be right for them to eat."

"Oh, so," snarled the man, "So after one night with our good leader you now think yourself free to give orders to men who've been with him this whole hungry year? Which of them had you, or did they take turns at you, little catamite?"

Shocked by the crudeness of the insult, Romilly recoiled, her face flaming. "You've no right to say that to me; *Dom* Carlo put me in charge of the birds and bade me see they were properly fed, and I obey the *vai dom* as you do yourself!"

"Aye, I may say so," the man sneered, "Maybe you'd like to put that pretty girl-face and those little ladylike hands to—" and the rest of the words were so foul that Romilly literally did not understand what he meant by them, and was perfectly sure she did not want to know. Clinging to what dignity she could—she honestly did not know how one of her brothers would have reacted to such foulness except, perhaps, by drawing a knife, and she was not big enough to fight on even terms with the giant Alaric—she said, "Perhaps if the *vai dom* himself gives you his orders you will take them," and moved away, clenching her teeth and her whole face tightly against the tears that threatened to explode through her taut mouth and eyes. *Damn him. Damn him! I must not cry, I must not. . . .*

"Here, here, what a face like a thundercloud, my lad?" said Orain, his lean face twisted with amusement, "Hurt? What ails ye—"

She clutched at the remnants of self-possession and said the first thing that came into her head.

"Have you a spare glove I can borrow, Uncle?" She used the informal term for any friend of a father's generation. "I cannot handle the sentry-birds with my bare fist, though I can manage a hawk; their talons are too long, and my hand is bleeding still from yesterday. I think I must fly them on a

132

line to try and let them hunt for small animals or find carrion—"

"A glove you shall have," said *Dom* Carlo behind them, "Give him your old one, Orain; shabby it may be, but it will protect his hand. There are bits of leather in the baggage, you can fashion one for yourself tonight. But why must you fly them? Why not give orders to one of the men to catch fresh food for them? We have hunting-snares enough, and we need meat for ourselves too. Send any of the men to fetch fresh food—" and as he looked on Romilly, his reddish eyebrows went up.

"Oh, is that the way of it?" he asked softly, "Which of them was it—Rumal?"

Romilly looked at the ground. She said almost inaudibly "I don't wish to make trouble, *vai dom.* Indeed, I can fly them, and they should have exercise in any case."

"No doubt they should," Carlo said, "So fly them for exercise, if you will. But I'll not have my orders disobeyed, either. Give her a glove, Orain, and then I'll have a word with Alaric."

Romilly saw the flash of his eyes, like greyish steel striking fire from flint; she took the glove and, head down, went to take down Temperance from her block, attach the lure-lines and set them up to fly. She found a cast feather and used it to stroke the bird's breast, at which the great wicked head bent and dipped with something like pleasure; she was making a good beginning at accustoming the large, savage birds to human touch and presence. When she had flown Temperance and watched her pounce on some small dead thing in the grass, she stood and watched the sentry-bird feed; standing on one foot, tearing with beak and claw. Later she flew Diligence in the same way; then—with relief, for her arm was growing tired—the smaller, gentler Prudence.

They are ugly birds, I suppose. But they are beautiful in their own way; strength, power, keen sight . . . and the world would be a fouler place without birds like this, to clear away what is dead and rotting. She was amazed at the way in which the birds had found, even on lines like the lure-lines, their own food, small carcasses in the grass, which she herself had not seen or even smelled. How had the men managed to ignore their real needs, when it was so clear to her what they wanted and needed?

I suppose that is what it means to have laran, Romilly thought, suddenly humbled. A gift which had been born in her family, for which she could claim no credit because it was inborn, she had done nothing to deserve it. Yet even *Dom* Carlo, who had the precious *laran* too—everything about the man spoke of easy, accustomed power—could not communicate with the birds, though he seemed able to know anything about men. *The gift of a MacAran.* Oh, but her father was so wrong, then, so wrong, and she had been right, to insist on this precious and wonderful Gift with which she had been dowered; to ignore it, to misuse it, to play at it, untrained—oh, that was wrong, wrong!

And her brother Ruyven had been right, to leave Falconsward and insist on the training of his natural Gifts. In the Tower he had found his proper place, *laranzu* for the handling of sentry-birds. One day that would be her place too. . . .

Prudence's scream of anger roused Romilly from her daydream and she realized that the sentry-bird had finished feeding and was tugging again at the lure-line. Romilly let her fly in circles on the line for a few moments, then made contact with the bird and urged her gently back to the ground; she hooded her, lifted her (grateful for the glove Orain had given her, for even through the glove she could feel the fierce grip of the huge talons) and set her back on the block.

As she made ready to ride, she thought soberly of the distance still ahead of them. She would keep as close to Orain as she could; if Alaric should find her alone. . . . and she thought, with terror, of the vast and empty chasms over which they had come the day before. A false step there, a slight nudge, and she would have followed that stone down over the cliff, rebounding again and again, broken long before she reached the final impact at the bottom. She felt faint nausea rising in her throat. Would his malice carry him so far as *that*? She had done him no harm. . . .

She had betrayed his incompetence before *Dom* Carlo, whom he evidently held in the highest respect. Remembering Rory, Romilly wondered if there were any men anywhere, alive, who were motivated by anything other than malice and lust and hatred. She had thought, in boy's clothing, she would be safe at least from lust; but even here, among men, she found its ugly face. Her father? Her brothers? Alderic? Well, her father would have sold her to *Dom* Garris for his own convenience. Alderic and her brothers? She really did not know them at all, for they would not have shown their real face to a girl whom they considered a child. No doubt they too were all evil within. Setting her teeth grimly, Romilly put the saddle on her horse, and went about saddling the other horses for Orain and *Dom* Carlo. Her prescribed duties demanded only that she care for the birds, but as things were now, she preferred the company of horses to the company of humankind!

Dom Carlo's kindly voice interrupted her reverie.

"So you have saddled Longlegs for me? Thank you, my lad."

"She is a beautiful animal," Romilly said, giving the mare a pat.

"You have an eye for horses, I can see; not surprising, if you are of MacAran blood. This one is from the high plateaus around Armida; they breed finer horses there than anywhere in the mountains, though I think sometimes they have not quite the stamina of the mountain-bred. Perhaps it does her no kindness, to take Longlegs on these trails; I have often thought I should return her to her native country and get myself a mountain-bred horse, or even a *chervine* for this wild hill country. Yet—" his hand lingered on the glossy mane, "I flatter myself that she would miss me; and as an exile, I have not so many friends that I would be willing to part with one, even if she is a dumb beast. Tell me, my boy; you know horses, do you think this climate is too hard on her?"

"I would not think so," Romilly said after a minute, "Not if she is well fed and well cared for; and you might consider wrapping her legs for extra support on these steep paths."

"A good thought," *Dom* Carlo agreed, and beckoned to Orain; they set about bandaging the legs of their lowlands-bred horses. Romilly's own horse was bred for the Hellers, shaggy-coated and shaggy-legged, with great tufts of coarse hair around the fetlocks, and for the first time since she had fled from Falconsward, she was glad that she had left her own horse. This one, stranger as he was, had at least borne her faithfully.

After a time they set off, winding downward into the valley, which they reached in time for the midday meal, and then along the gradually broadening, well-travelled road which led into Nevarsin, the City of the Snows.

One more night they camped before they came to the city, and this time, noting what Romilly had done the day before, Orain gave orders to the men that they should groom and properly care for their riding-*chervines*. They obeyed sullenly, but they obeyed; Romilly heard one of them grumble, "While we have that damned hawk-boy with us, why can't *he* care for the beasts? Ought to be *his* work, not ours!"

135

"Not likely, when Orain's already made the brat his own pet," Alaric grumbled. "Birds be damned—the wretch is with us for Orain's convenience, not the birds! You think the Lord Carlo will deny his paxman and friend anything he wants?"

"Hush your mouth," said a third, "You've no call to go talking like that about your betters. *Dom* Carlo's a good lord to us all, and a faithful man to Carolin, and as for Orain, he was the king's own foster-brother. Haven't you noticed? He talks all rough and country, but when he wishes, or when he forgets, he can talk as fine and educated as *Dom* Carlo himself, or any of the great Hastur-lords themselves! As for his private tastes, I care not whether he wants women or boys or rabbithorns, so long as he doesn't come after *my* wife."

Romilly, her face burning, moved away out of earshot. Reared in a *cristoforo* family, she had never heard such talk, and it confirmed her opinion that she liked the company of men even less than the company of women. She was too shy, after what she had heard, to join Orain and *Dom* Carlo where they spread their blankets, and spent that night shivering, crouched among the drowsing stag-ponies for their warmth. By morning she was blue with cold, and huddled as long as she dared near the fire kindled for breakfast, surreptitiously trying to warm her hands against the sides of the porridge-pot. The hot food warmed her a little, but she was still shivering as she exercised and fed the birds—Alaric, still grumbling, had snared a couple of rabbithorns, and they were beginning to smell high; she had to overcome surges of nausea as she cut them up, and afterward she found herself sneezing repeatedly. *Dom* Carlo cast her a concerned glance as they saddled and climbed on their horses for the last stage of the ride.

"I hope you have not taken cold, my boy."

Romilly muttered, eyes averted, that the *vai dom* should not concern himself.

"Let us have one thing clearly understood," *Dom* Carlo said, frowning, "The welfare of any of my followers is as important to me as that of the birds to you—my men are in my charge as the birds are in yours, and I neglect no man who follows me! Come here," he said, and laid a concerned hand against her forehead. "You have fever; can you ride? I would not ask it of you, but tonight you shall be warm in the monastery guest-house, and if you are sick, the good brothers there will see to you."

"I am all right," Romilly protested, genuinely alarmed now. She dared not be sick! If she was taken to the monks'

136

infirmary, certainly, in caring for her sickness they would discover that she was a girl!

"Have you warm clothing enough? Orain, you are nearer his size than I—find the lad something warm," said *Dom* Carlo, and then, as he stood still touching her forehead, his face changed; he looked down at Romilly sharply, and for a moment she was sure—she did not know how; *laran?*—that he *knew*. She froze with dread, shivering; but he moved away and said quietly, "Orain has brought you a warm vest and stockings—I saw your blistered feet in your boots. Put them on at once; if you are too proud to take them, we shall have it from your wages, but I'll have no—no one riding with me who is not warm and dry and comfortable. Go round the fire and change into them, this minute."

Romilly bowed her head in acquiescence, went behind the line of horses and stag-beasts, and pulled on the warm stockings—heavenly relief to her sore feet—and the heavy undervest. They were somewhat too big, but all the warmer for that. She sneezed again, and Orain gestured to the pot still hanging over the fire, not yet emptied. He dipped up a ladleful of the hot brew and took some leaves from his pouch.

"An old wives' remedy for the cough that's better than any healer's brew. Drink it," he said, and watched while she gulped at the foul-tasting stuff. "Aye, it's bitter as lost love, but it drives out the fever."

Romilly grimaced at the acrid, musty-tasting stuff; it made her flush with inner heat, and left her mouth puckered with its intense astringency, but, later that morning, she realized that she had not sneezed again, and that the dripping of her nose had abated. Riding briefly at his side, she said, "That remedy would make you a fortune in the cities, Master Orain."

He laughed. "My mother was a *leronis* and studied healing," he said, "and went among the country-folk to learn their knowledge of herbs. But the healers in the cities laugh at these country remedies."

And, she thought, he had been the king's own foster-brother; and now served the king's man in exile, Carlo of Blue Lake. What the men had said was true, though she had not noticed it before; talking to the men, he spoke the dialect of the countryside, while, speaking to *Dom* Carlo, and, increasingly, to her, his accents were those of an educated man. Contrasted to the other men, she felt as safe and comfortable near him as if she were in the presence of her own brothers or her father.

After a time she asked him, "The king—Carolin—he awaits us in Nevarsin? I thought the monks were sworn to take no part in the strife of wordly men? How is it that they take King Carolin's side in this war? I—I know so little about what is going on in the lowlands." She remembered what Darren and Alderic had said; it only whetted her appetite to know more.

Orain said, "The brothers of Nevarsin care nothing for the throne of the Hasturs; nor should they. They give shelter to Carolin because, as they say, he has harmed none, and his cousin—the great bastard, Rakhal, who sits on the throne—would kill him for his own ambition. They will not join in his cause, but they will not surrender him to his enemies while he shelters there, either."

"If Carolin's claim to the throne is so just," Romilly asked, "Why has Rakhal won so much support?"

Orain shrugged. "Greed, no doubt. My lands are now in the hands of the chief of Rakhal's councillors. Men support the man who enriches them, and right has little to do with it. All these men—" he gestured behind them at the followers, "are small-holders whose lands should have been inviolate; they had done nothing but hold loyal to their king, and they should not have been involved in the struggles of the high-born and powerful. Alaric is bitter, aye—know you what was his crime? The crime for which he lost his lands, and was flung into Rakhal's prison under sentence of losing a hand and his tongue?"

Romilly shuddered. "For such a sentence it must have been a great crime indeed!"

"Only before that *cagavrezu* Rakhal," said Orain grimly, "His crime? His children shouted 'Long live King Carolin!' as one of Rakhal's greatest scoundrels passed by their village. They meant no harm—I do not think the poor brats knew one king from the other! So the great scoundrel, Lyondri Hastur, said that he must have taught his little children treason—he took the children from Alaric's house, saying they should be reared by a loyal man, and sent them to serve in his Great House, and flung Alaric into prison. One of the children died, and Alaric's wife was so distraught with what had befallen her man and her babies that she threw herself from a high window and died. Aye, Alaric is bitter, and thinks good of no one, lad; it is not you he hates, but life itself."

Romilly looked down toward her saddle, with a deep breath. She knew why Orain had told her this, and it raised still further her admiration of the man; he had tolerance and sympathy even for the man who had spoken such ugly things of him. She said quietly, "I will try not to think half so evil of him as he thinks of me, then, Uncle."

But still she felt confused. Alderic had spoken of the Hastur-kin as descended from Gods, great and noble men, and Orain spoke as if the very word "Hastur" were an insult.

"Are all the Hastur-kin evil men, then?"

"By no means," Orain said vehemently, "A better man than Carolin never trod this earth; his only fault is that he thought no evil toward those of his kin who were scoundrels, and was all too kind and forgiving toward—" his mouth stretched in what should have been a smile, "bastards with ambition."

And then he fell silent, and Romilly, watching the lines in his face, knew his thoughts were a thousand leagues away from her, or his men, or *Dom* Carlo. It seemed that she could see in his mind pictures of a beautiful city built between two mountain passes, but lying low, in a green valley, on the shores of a lake whose waves were like mist rolling up from the depths. A white tower rose near the shores, and men and women passed through the gateways, tall and elegant as if wrapped in a silken glamour, too beautiful to be real . . . and she could sense the great sorrow in him, the sorrow of the exile, the homeless man. . . .

I too am homeless, I have cast away all my kin . . . but it may be that my brother Ruyven awaits me in Tramontana Tower. And Orain, too, is alone and without kin. . . .

They rode through the great, frowning gates of Nevarsin just as dusk was falling and the swift night of this time of year had begun to blur the sky with rain. *Dom* Carlo rode at their head, his cowled hood drawn over his head concealing his features; along the old cobbled streets of the city, and upward along steep paths and narrow winding lanes toward the snow-covered paths that led to the monastery. Romilly thought she had never felt such intense chill; the monastery was situated among the glacier ice, carved from the solid rock of the mountain, and when they paused before the inner gates, under the great statue of the Bearer of Burdens bowed beneath the world's weight, and the smaller, but still larger-than-life image of Saint-Valentine-of-the-Snows, she was shivering again in spite of the extra warm clothing.

A tall dignified man in the bulky brown robe and cowl of

a monk gestured them inside. Romilly hesitated; she had been brought up a *cristoforo* and knew that no woman might enter into the monastery, even in the guest-house. But she had chosen this disguise and now could not repudiate it. She whispered a prayer—"Blessed Bearer of Burdens, Holy Saint Valentine, forgive me, I mean no intrusion into this world of men, and I swear I will do nothing to disgrace you here."

It would create a greater scandal if she now revealed her real sex. And she wondered why women were so strongly prohibited. Did the monks fear that if women were there they could not keep to their vows of renunciation? What good were their vows, if they could not resist women unless they never saw any? And why did they think women would care to tempt them anyhow? Looking at the lumpy little monk in the cowl, she thought, with something perilously near a giggle, that it would take more charity than even a saint, to overlook his ugliness long enough to try and tempt *him!*

There were comfortable stables for all their riding-animals, and an enclosed stone room where Romilly found blocks and perches for her birds.

"You can go into the city and buy food for them," Orain said, and handed her some copper rings, "But be back in good time for supper in the guest-house; and if you will, you may attend the night prayers—you might like to hear the choir singing."

Romilly nodded obediently, inwardly delighted; Darren had spoken once of the fine singing of the Nevarsin choir, which he had not, in his days as a student, been musical enough to join; but her father, too, had spoken of one of the high points of his life, when he had attended a solemn service in the monastery and heard the singing of the monks. She hurried out into the city, excited and a little scared by the strange place; but she found a bird-seller, and when she made her wants known to him, he knew at once the proper food for the sentry-birds; she had half expected to have to carry a stinking, half-rotted carcass back through the city, but instead the seller said that he would be pleased to deliver the food to the guest-house stables. "You'll be lodged in the monastery, young man? If it is your will, I can have proper food delivered every day for your birds."

"I shall ask my master," she said, "I do not know how long they propose to stay." And she thought this was a fine thing, that such services should be provided; but when he told her the price she was a little troubled. Still, there was no way she could go outside the walls and hunt for food for them herself; so she arranged for the day and for tomorrow, and paid the man what he asked.

Returning through the city streets, grey and old, with ancient houses leaning over the streets and the walls closing around her, she felt a little frightened. She realized that she had lost contact with Preciosa before they entered the gates of Nevarsin; the climate here was too cold for a hawk . . . had Preciosa turned back to a more welcoming climate? The hawk could find no food in the city . . . there was carrion enough in the streets, she supposed from the smell, but no fresh living food for a hawk. She hoped Preciosa was safe. . . .

But for now her charge was the sentry-birds; she saw to their feeding, and there was a large cobbled court where she could exercise them and let them fly. At the edge of the court while she was flying them in circles on the long lines—they screamed less, now, and she realized they were becoming accustomed to her touch and her voice—she saw, crowded into the edges of the court, an assembly of small boys. They all wore the bulky cowled robes of the monastery. But surely, Romilly thought, they were too young for monks; they must be students, sent as Ruyven, then Darren, had been sent. One day, perhaps, her brother Rael would be among them. *How I miss Rael!*

They were watching the birds with excited interest. One, bolder than the rest, called out, "How do you handle the birds without getting hurt?" He came to Romilly, leaving the clustered children, and stretched out his hand to Temperance; Romilly gestured him quickly back.

"These birds are fierce, and can peck hard; if she went for your eyes, she could hurt you badly!"

"They don't hurt *you*," the child protested.

"That is because I am trained to handle them, and they know me," Romilly said, Obediently, the boy moved out of reach. He was not much older than Rael, she thought; ten or twelve. In the courtyard a bell rang, and the children went, pushing and jostling, down the hallway; but the boy who was watching the birds remained.

"Should you not answer that bell with your fellows?"

"I have no lesson at this hour," the boy said, "Not until the bell rings for choir; then I must go and sing, and afterward, I must go to arms-practice."

"In a monastery?"

"I am not to be a monk," the boy said, "and so an arms-master from the village comes every other day to give lessons

141

to me and a few of the others. But I have no duties now, and I would like to watch the birds, if you do not mind. Are you a leronis, *vai domna,* that you know their ways so well?"

Romilly stared at him in shock. At last she asked, "Why do you call me *domna?*"

"But I can see what you are, certainly," the boy answered, "even though you wear boy's clothes." Romilly looked so dismayed that he lowered his voice and said in a conspiratorial whisper, "Don't worry, I won't tell anyone. The Father Master would be very cross, and I do not think you are harming anyone. But why would you want to wear boy's clothes? Don't you like being a girl?"

Would anyone? Romilly wondered, and then asked herself why the clear eyes of this child had seen what no one else could see. He answered the unspoken thought.

"I am trained to that as you are trained to handle hawks and other birds: So that, one day, I may serve my people in a Tower as a *laranzu.*"

"A child like you?" Romilly asked.

"I am twelve years old," he said with dignity, "and in only three years more I shall be a man. My father is Lyondri Hastur, who is a Councillor to the king; the Gods have given me noble blood and therefore I must be ready to serve the people over whom I shall one day be placed to rule."

Lyondri Hastur's son! She remembered the story Orain had told her, of Alaric and the deaths of his family. She pretended to be fussing over the bird's line; she had never had to conceal her thoughts before, and knew only one way to do it—with quick random speech.

"Would you like to hold Prudence for a little while? She is the lightest of the birds and will not be too heavy for your arm. I will keep her quiet for you, if you like." He looked excited and pleased. Carefully hooding Prudence, and sending out soothing thoughts—*this little one is a friend, he will not harm you, be still*—she slipped the glove over the boy's arm with her free hand, set the bird on it. He held her, struggling to keep his small arm from trembling, and she handed him a feather.

"Stroke her breast with this. Never touch a bird with your hand; even if your hands are clean, it will damage the set of their feathers," she said, and he stroked the bird's smooth breast with the feather, crooning to it softly.

"I have never been so close to a sentry-bird before," he murmured, delighted. "I heard they were fierce and not to be tamed—I suppose it is *laran* which keeps her so calm, *domna*?"

"You must not call me *domna here*," she said, keeping her voice low and calm so as not to disturb the bird, "The name I use is Rumal."

"Is it *laran*, then, Rumal? Do you think I could learn to handle a bird like this?"

"If you were trained to it, certainly," said Romilly, "but you should begin with a small hawk, a ladybird or sparrow hawk so that your arm will not tire and your fatigue trouble the bird. I had better take Prudence now," she added, for the small arm was trembling with tension. She set the bird on a perch. "And *laran* can do nothing but help you to make your mind in tune with the bird's mind. But the climate here is too cold for ordinary hawks; for that you must wait till you return to the lowlands, I think."

The boy sighed, looking regretfully at the bird on the perch. "These are hardier than hawks, are they not? Are they akin to *kyorebni*?"

"They are not dissimilar in form," Romilly agreed, "though they are more intelligent than *kyorebni*, or than any hawk." It seemed disloyal to Preciosa to admit it, but after the few days rapport with the sentry-birds, she knew these were superior in intelligence.

"May I help you, *dom*—Rumal?"

"I have mostly finished," Romilly said, "but if you wish, you can mix this green stuff and gravel with their food. But if you touch the carrion, your hands will stink when you go to choir."

"I can wash my hands at the well before I go to the choir, for Father Cantor is very fat and always late to practice," said the boy solemnly, and Romilly smiled as he began portioning the gamy-smelling meat, sprinkling it with the herbs and gravel. The smile slid off quickly; this child was a telepath and the son of Lyondri Hastur, he could endanger them all.

"What is your name?" she asked.

"I am called Caryl," the boy said. "I was named for the man who was king when I was born, only Father says that *Carolin* is not a good name to have now. Carolin was king, but he abused his power, they said, and was a bad king, so his cousin Rakhal had to take the throne. But he was kind to me."

Romilly told herself; the child was only repeating what he

had heard his father say. Caryl finished with the bird-food, and asked if he might give it to one of the birds.

"Give that dish to Prudence," said Romilly, "She is the gentlest, and already, I can see, you have made friends."

He carried the dish to the bird, stood watching as she tore greedily into it, while Romilly fed the other two. A bell rang in the outer court of the monastery, muted softly by the intervening walls, and the boy started.

"I must go to choir," he said, "and then I must have my lesson. May I come tonight and help you feed the birds,—Rumal?"

She hesitated, but he said earnestly, "I'll keep your secret, I promise."

At last she nodded. "Certainly, come whenever you like," she said, and the boy ran away. She noticed that he wiped his hands on the seat of his breeches, like any active youngster, quite forgetting his promise to wash at the well.

But when he was out of sight, she sighed and stood motionless, ignoring the birds for the moment.

Lyondri Hastur's own son, here in the monastery—and it was here that *Dom* Carlo was to meet with King Carolin, with his gift of valuable sentry-birds, and to raise an army in the city. It was not impossible, she supposed, that he might know the king by sight, so if Carolin was in the city in disguise and came near the monastery, he might recognize him, and then. . . .

What do I care which rogue keeps the throne? Her father's words echoed in her mind. But Alderic, who seemed quite the best young man she had ever known beside her own brothers, was Carolin's sworn man, perhaps even his son. Carlo and Orain, too, were loyal to the exiled king. And his councillor, Lyondri Hastur, whatever his son might say, seemed to be one of the worst tyrants she had ever heard about—or so the story of what he had done to Alaric's children seemed to indicate.

And she was *Dom* Carlo's man, at least while she took money in his service. He should know of the danger to the man he called his rightful king. Perhaps he could warn Carolin not to come near the monastery, while there was a child there who would recognize him and penetrate whatever disguise he might wear. Sharp indeed were the boy's eyes and his *laran* . . . he had seen that Romilly was a woman.

Though I cannot tell Dom *Carlo, nor his friend, how I know the child has* laran. . . .

She went to the stables attached to the monastery, finding

144

the horses in good hands; spoke briefly to the stablemen about care for their horses, and tipped them, as was proper, with the generous amount of silver and copper Orain had given her for their expenses. After the encounter with young Caryl, she was on her guard, but none of the stablefolk paid any attention to her; one and all they accepted her as what she was, just another apprentice in the train of the young nobleman staying in the monastery. Then she went in search of *Dom* Carlo, to deliver her warning. In the rooms assigned to them in the guest-house, however, she found only Orain, mending his crudely-sewn boots.

He looked up as she came in.

"Is anything gone wrong with birds or beasts, then, lad?"

"No, they are all doing well," Romilly said, "Forgive me for intruding in your leisure, but I must see *Dom* Carlo—"

"You can't see him now, or for some time," said Orain, "for he's closeted with Father Abbot, and I don't think he's confessin' his sins—he's no *cristoforo*. Can I do anything for ye', boy? There's no great urgency to work, now the birds are cared for and in good health—take time to see some of the city, and if ye need an excuse, I'll send you out on an errand; you can take these boots to be mended." He held them out to her, saying with a droll grin, "They're beyond my skill."

"I will do your errand gladly," Romilly said, "but indeed I have an important message for *Dom* Carlo. He—you—you are Carolin's men, and I have just heard that—that someone who knows the king by sight, and might also know some of his Councillors, is here in the monastery. Lyondri Hastur's son, Caryl."

Orain's face changed and his lips pursed in a soundless whistle. "Truly? The whelp of that wolf is here, poisoning their minds against my lord?"

"The boy is but twelve," protested Romilly, "and seems a nice child; he spoke well of the king, and said he had always been kind—but he might know him—"

"Aye," said Orain grimly, "No doubt; a new-hatched serpent can sting like an old snake. Still, I know no evil of the child; but I'll not let Alaric know he is here, or he might let son pay for son—if he saw the Hastur-Lord's son, I doubt he could keep his hands from his throat, and I know well how he feels. My lord must know of this, and quickly—"

"Would Caryl recognize *Dom* Carlo, too? Was he around the court so much? *Dom* Carlo is—" she hesitated, "Is he not one of Carolin's kin?"

"He's of the Hastur-kin," said Orain, nodding. He sighed.

145

"Well, I'll keep an eye out for the child, and put a word in *Dom* Carlo's ear. It was thoughtful of you to warn me, Rumal, lad; I owe you one for that." As if dismissing the thought deliberately, he bent and picked up the much-patched boots. "Take these into the city—and lest you get lost, I'll come along and show you the way."

He linked his arm carelessly through Romilly's as they went out of the monastery guest-house and down through the streets of the old town. The mountain air was biting and cold, and Romilly drew her cloak tighter about her, but Orain, though he wore only a light jacket, seemed comfortable and at ease.

"I like the mountain air," he said, "I was born in the shadow of High Kimbi, though I was fostered on the shores of Hali; and still I think myself a mountain man. What of you?"

"I was born in the Kilghard Hills, but north of the Kadarin," Romilly said.

"The country around Storn? Aye, I know it well," Orain said, "No wonder you have hawks in your blood; so have I." He laughed, ruefully. "Though you're my master at that; I had never held a sentry-bird before, nor will I think myself ill-used if I never set hand on one again." They turned into the doorway of a shop, smelling strongly of leather and tan-bark and rosin. The bootmaker raised supercilious eyebrows at the patched old boots in Orain's hand, but quickly changed his tone when Orain took out his pocket and laid down silver and even copper.

"When would the *vai dom* be wanting these back?"

"I think they're past mending," Orain said, "But they fit well; make me a pair to the measure of these, for I may be going high into snow country. Have you boots for the far Hellers, Rumal? Ye'll be riding with us to Tramontana, I doubt not—"

Why not, after all? Romilly thought. *I have nowhere else to go, and if Ruyven is there, or I can get news of him there, Tramontana is my best path.*

"Those boots the young sir is wearing, they will not hold up on the paths across the glaciers," said the shoemaker, with an obsequious look at Orain, "I can make your son a stout fine pair for two silver bits."

Only now did Romilly realize how generously *Dom* Carlo had arranged to pay her for her care and knowledge of hawks and birds. She said quickly "I have—"

"Hush, boy, *Dom* Carlo told me to see you had what you

needed for the journey, as I do for all his men," Orain said, "Let you sit there, now, and let him measure your foot . . . son," he added, grinning.

Romilly did as she was told, thrusting out her slender foot in its shabby too-large stocking. The bootmaker hummed, whistling a little tune, as he measured, scrawling down cryptic notes and numbers with a stump of chalk on the board by his bench. "When d'you want these ready?"

"Yesterday," growled Orain, "We may have to leave the city at a moment's notice."

The bootmaker protested; Orain haggled a few minutes, then they agreed on a price and the day after tomorrow.

"Should be tomorrow," Orain said scowling as they left the shop, "but these workmen have no more pride in their craft these days. Humph!" He snorted as Romilly turned. "In a hurry to get back to the monastery, Rumal lad, and dine on cold boiled lentils and smallbeer? After all these days on the road, living on porridge-powder and journey-cake not much better than dogbread, I'm for a roast fowl and some good wine in a cookshop. What reason have ye to get back? The birds won't fly away, now, will they? The horses are warm in their stable, and the monks will give them some hay if we don't get back. Let's walk through the town, then."

Romilly shrugged and acquiesced. She had never been in a city the size of Nevarsin before, and she was afraid she would be lost if she explored alone, but with Orain, she might learn her way about the confusing streets. In any case she could hardly fail to find the way back to the monastery, she need only follow any street straight up the mountain—the monastery was high above the town.

The short winter day brightened, then faded again as they walked through the city, mostly in a companionable silence; Orain did not seem inclined to talk much, but he pointed out various landmarks, the ancient shrine of Saint-Valentine-of-the-Snows, the cave high on the mountain where the saint was said to have lived and died, a forge which, he said, did the best horse-shoeing north of Armida, a sweetshop where, he said with a grin, the students at the monastery chose to spend their pocketmoney on holidays. It was as if she was one of her own brothers, here and free, unconstrained by any of the laws which governed the behavior of women; she felt as easy with Orain as if she had known him all her life. He had quite forgotten the country accent, and talked in a pleasant, well-bred voice, with only the faintest trace, like Alderic's, of a lowland accent.

147

She could not guess his age. He was certainly not a young man, but she did not think he was as old as her father. His hands were rough and calloused like a swordsman's, but the nails were clean and well-cared-for, not grimy or broken like the other men who followed *Dom* Carlo.

He must be well-born enough, anyhow, if he had been foster-brother to the exiled Carolin. Her father, she knew, would have welcomed him and treated him with honor as a noble, and though *Dom* Carlo did not quite treat him as an equal, he showed him affection and respect and sought his advice in everything.

As the twilight gathered, Orain found a cookshop and commanded a meal. Romilly felt inclined to protest.

"You should not—I can pay my share—"

Orain shrugged. "I hate to dine alone. And *Dom* Carlo made it clear he has other fish to fry this night. . . ."

She bent her head, accepting graciously. She had never been in a public tavern or cookshop before, and she noted there were no women present except for the bustling fat waitress who came and slapped crockery in front of them and fussed away again. If Orain had known her true sex he would never have brought her here; if a lady, unimaginably, came in here, there would have been all sorts of deferential fuss made, they would never have taken her quite simply for granted. Far less would she be able to lounge here at ease, her feet propped on the bench across from her, sipping from a tankard of cider, while the good smell of cooking gradually filled the room.

No, it was better to remain a boy. She had respectable work, three silver bits for a tenday; no cook-woman or dairymaid could hope to command such pay for any work she could do, and she remembered that Rory's grandmother, telling of her lost affluence, had spoken of the fact that when her husband did not seek her bed, he was sent, quite without worrying about what the dairymaid thought about it, to sleep with the dairymaid as a matter of course. Better to spend all her life in breeches and boots than have that added to the regular duties of a dairymaid's work!

She found herself wondering if Luciella made such routine demands of her women. Well, he must at some times—there was Nelda's son. It made Romilly uncomfortable to think of her father that way, and she reminded herself that he was a *cristoforo* . . . but would that make such a difference? In the world where she had been brought up it was taken for granted that a nobleman would have bastards and *nedestro* sons and daughters. Romilly had never really thought about their mothers.

She shifted uneasily in her seat, and Orain said with a grin, "Getting hungry? Something smells good in the kitchen yonder." Half a dozen men were flinging darts at a board hung at the back of the tavern, a few others playing dice. "Shall we have a game of darts, lad?"

Romilly shook her head, protesting that she did not know the game. "But don't let me stop you."

"You'll never learn younger, then," Orain said, and Romilly found herself standing, urged to fling the darts.

"Hold it this way," Orain instructed, "and just let it go—you don't have to push it."

"That's the way," said one of the men standing behind her in the crowd, "Just imagine the circle painted on the wall is the head of King Carolin and you have a chance at the fifty copper *reis* offered for his head!"

"Rather," said a bitter voice somewhere behind the first speaker, "that the head is of that bloodthirsty wolf Rakhal—or his chief jackal Lyondri, the Hastur-Lord!"

"Treason," said another voice and the speaker was quickly hushed, "That kind o' talk's not safe even here beyond the Kadarin—who knows what kind of spies Lyondri Hastur may be sending into the city?"

"I say, may Zandru plague'em both with boils and the bald fever," said another, "What matters it to free mountain men which great rogue plants his backside on the throne or what greater rogue tries to pry his arse loose from the seat? I say Zandru take'em both off to his hells and I wish 'im joy of their company, so that they stay souht o' the river and leave honest men to go about their business in peace!"

"Carolin must ha' done something or they'd never o' kicked him off the throne," someone said, "Down there, the *Hali'imyn* think the Hastur are kin to their filthy Gods—I've heard some tales when I travel down there, I could tell you—"

The darts had been forgotten; no one came to take a turn from Romilly. She whispered to Orain, "Are you going to let them talk that way about King Carolin?

Orain did not answer. He said, "Our meat's on the table, Rumal. Neighbors, maybe we'll have another round later, but the dinner's getting cold while we stand here gabbing," and gestured to Romilly to put down the darts and go to their seat. When the food arrived, and Orain was cutting the meat into portions, he muttered under his breath, "We're here to serve Carolin, lad, not defend him to fools in taverns. Eat your dinner, boy." And after a moment, he added, still in a half-whisper, "Part of my reason for walking about town is to hear how the folk think—see how much support there is here for the king. If we're to raise men for him here, it's urgent there must be popular support so no one will betray us—a lot of things can be done in secret, but you can't raise an army that way!"

Romilly put her fork into the roast meat, and ate in silence. She noted that when he spoke to her, Orain had, without thinking, dropped the rough up-country accent and spoken again like an educated man. Well, if he was the king's foster-brother, as she had heard, that was not surprising. Carlo too must have been high in those councils and one of his loyal men—no doubt he too had lost lands and possessions when Carolin was deposed and fled to the hills. Which reminded her again—

I do not know if Carolin has enemies in the city, but he certainly has at least one in the monastery. I do not think a child like Caryl would do him any great harm, he said the king had shown him kindness; but if Carlo and Orain are expecting to meet the king within monastery walls, there is at least one pair of eyes who would recognize him. They must prevent him from coming there. And Romilly wondered why it should matter to her what happened to the exiled king. As her father had said so often, what did it matter what great rogue sat on the throne, or what worse rogue tried to unseat him?

Orain and Carlo could not follow an evil master. Whichever king they follow, he is my king too! And the story she had heard of the evil Hastur-lord Lyondri had filled her with revulsion. She thought, wryly, that without knowing it, she had somehow become a partisan of Carolin.

"Take that last cutlet, lad; you're a growing boy, you need your food," Orain said, grinning, and called to the serving-woman for more wine. Romilly reached for another cup, but Orain slapped her hand away.

"No, no, you've had enough—bring the boy some cider, woman, he's too young for your rotgut here! I don't want to have to carry you home," he added, good-naturedly, "and lads your age have no head for this kind of thing."

Her face burning, exasperated, Romilly took the huge mug of cider the woman set before her. Sipping it, she acknowledged to herself that she liked it better than the strong wine, which burned her mouth and her stomach and made her head swim. She muttered, "Thank you, Orain."

He nodded and said, "Think nothing of it. I wish I'd had a friend to knock my head out of the winepot when I was your age! Too late now," he added with a grin, and lifting his tankard, drank deep.

Romilly sat listening, full and sleepy, as Orain went back to the dart board; when asked to join him, she shook her head, feeling drowsy, listening to the talk around the bar.

"Well thrown! Whang in the eye of whichever king you don't favor!"

"I heard Carolin's in the Hellers because the *Hali'imyn* are too soft to search for him up here—they might freeze their dainty tailbones!"

"Whether Carolin's here or no, there are enough supporters for his rule—he's a good man!"

"Whatever Carolin's like, I'll join anything which gets that bastard Lyondri the rope's end he deserves! Did ye' hear what he did to old Lord di Asturien? Burned over his head, poor old man, and him and the old lady by the side of the road in their night-gear and bedslippers, if one of their woodsmen hadn't taken 'em in and given 'em a place to lie down in. . . ."

After a time Romilly fell into a doze, in which Carolin and the usurper Rakhal wandered in dreams with the faces of great mountain cats, slinking through the woods and tearing at one another, and the shrill cry of hawks, as if she were soaring far above and watching the battle. She flew over a white Tower, and Ruyven was waving to her from the summit, and then he somehow took wing and was flying beside her, telling her gravely that Father would not approve of it. He said solemnly, "The Bearer of Burdens said that it is forbidden for man to fly and that is why I have no wings." and saying it, he fell like a stone; Romilly started awake, to feel Orain lightly shaking her.

"Come, lad, it's late, they're closing the doors—we must go back to the monastery!"

His breath was heavy with wine, his speech slurred; she wondered if he was able to walk. However, she laid his cloak over his shoulders, and they went out into the crisp, frosty darkness. It was very late; most of the houses were dark. Somewhere, a dog barked in a frenzy, but there was no other sound, and little light in the street; only the pale and frosty light of blue Kyrrdis, low on the rooftops of the city. Orain's steps were unsteady; he walked with one hand on the nearest house-wall, steadying himself, but when the narrow streets opened into a stair, he tripped on the cobbles and went flailing down full-length on the stone, howling with drunken surprise. Romilly helped him up, saying in amusement, "You had better hold on to my arm." Had he made certain his companion would stay sober, so that he would have someone to guide him back to the monastery? Romilly was fairly good at finding a path she had once travelled; she managed to direct their steps upward into the shadow of the monastery.

"Do you know if Carolin is truly in the city, Orain?" she asked at last in a low voice, but he peered with drunken suspicion into her face and demanded, "Why d'ye' ask?" and she shrugged and let it go. When he was sober she would talk to him about that; but at least the wine he had drunk would not unseal his mouth and he would not babble of his mission or plans. As they climbed the last steep street, which led into the courtyard of the monastery guest-house, he held tightly to her arm, sometimes putting a drunken arm around her shoulders; but Romilly edged away—if he held her too close he might, as Rory had done, discover that she was a woman beneath the heavy clothes she wore.

I like Orain, I would rather respect him, and if he knew I were a woman he would be like all the others. . . .

As they climbed he leaned on her arm more and more heavily. Once he turned aside from her, and, unbuttoning his trousers, relieved himself against a house wall; Romilly was, not for the first time, grateful for her farm upbringing which had made this something she could accept unblushing—if she had been a housebred woman like Luciella or her younger sister, she would have been outraged a dozen times a day. But then, if she had been a housebred woman, she would probably never have thought to protest the marriage her father had arranged, and she would certainly never have been able to travel with so many men without somehow revealing herself.

At the monastery gates Orain tugged at the bell-pull which announced their presence to the porter at the guest-house. It was very late; for a moment Romilly wondered if they would be admitted at all, but finally the Brother Porter appeared at the gates and, grumbling, let them inside. He frowned and sniffed disapprovingly at the reek of wine which hung around them, but he did let them in, and shook his head when Orain offered him a silver bit.

"I am not allowed, friend. I thank you for the kind

152

thought. Here, your door is this way," he said, and added audibly to Romilly, "Can you get him inside?"

"This way, Orain," said Romilly, shoving him to the door of his room. Inside, Orain looked around, fuzzily, like an owl in daylight. "Whe'—"

"Lie down and go to sleep," Romilly said, pushed him down on the nearer of the two beds and hauled at his heavy boots. He protested incoherently . . . he was drunker than she had realized.

He held her by one wrist. "You're a good boy," he said, "Aye, I like you, Rumal—but you're *cristoforo*. Once I heard you call on the Bearer of Burdens . . . damn . . ."

Gently Romilly freed her hand, pulled his cloak around him, went quietly away, wondering where *Dom* Carlo was. Not, surely, still closeted with the Father Master? Well, it was none of her affair, and she must be up early to care for the animals and the sentry-birds. She shrank from sharing the sleeping quarters of the men who attended on Carlo and Orain, so she had chosen to sleep on the hay in the stables— it was warm and she was unobserved; she need not be quite so careful against some accidental revealing of her body. She had not realized, until she was alone again, quite what a strain it was to be always on guard against some momentary inadvertent word or gesture which might betray her. She pulled off her boots, glad of the thick stockings under them, rolled herself into a bundle in the hay and tried to sleep again.

But she found herself unexpectedly wakeful. She could hear the stirring of the birds on their perches, the soft shifting hooves of horses and chervines; far away inside the depths of the monastery she heard a small bell and a faraway shuffle of feet as the monks went their way to the Night Offices, when all the world around them slept. Had Orain some feud with the *cristoforos* that he would say he liked her, *but* she was *cristoforo*? Was he bigoted about religion? Romilly had never really thought much about it, she was *cristoforo* because her family was, and because, all her life, she had heard tales of the good teachings of the Bearer of Burdens, whose teachings had been, so the *cristoforos* said, brought from beyond the stars in days before any living man could remember or tell. At last, hearing the muffled chanting, far away, she fell into a restless sleep, burrowing herself into the hay. For a time she dreamed of flying, soaring on hawk-wings, or on the wings of a sentry-bird; not over her own mountains, but over a lowland country, green and beautiful, with lakes and broad fields, and a white tower rose above a great lake. Then she came half awake as a bell rang somewhere in the monastery. She thought, a little ruefully, that if she had had supper within the monastery she would have heard the choir singing—perhaps the only woman who would ever do so.

Well, they would be there for days, it seemed; there would be other nights, other services to hear. How lucky Darren was no longer here at the monastery—even from his seat within the choir, he would have seen and recognized her.

If King Carolin comes to the monastery, young Caryl will recognize him—Dom Carlo must warn him. . . .

And then she slept again, to dream confused dreams of kings and children, and someone at her side who spoke to her in Orain's voice and drowsily caressed her. At last she slept, deep and dreamlessly, waking at first light to the screams of the sentry-birds.

Life in the monastery quickly fell into routine. Up at early light to tend the animals, breakfast in the guest-house, occasionally an errand to be done for *Dom* Carlo or Orain. Two days later she had her new boots, made to her own measure, and with the pay they gave her—for now she had been in their service ten days—she found a stall where warm clothing was sold, and bought warm stockings so that she could wash and change the ones she had been wearing since Orain had given them to her. In the afternoon she wandered alone around the city of Nevarsin, enjoying a freedom she had never had in the days when she was still the ladylike daughter of The MacAran; in the evenings, when the birds had been tended and exercised again, after a frugal supper in the guesthouse, she would slip into the chapel and listen to the choir of men and little boys. There was one soprano among the boys, with a sweet, flutelike voice; she strained her eyes to see the singer and realized at last that it was small Caryl, the son of Lyondri Hastur.

He wished King Carolin no ill. Romilly hoped that Orain had passed along his message to *Dom* Carlo and that he, somehow, had gotten word to the king, that Carolin had not come to the city.

Once or twice during the tenday that followed, she went again with Orain to the tavern, or to another, though never again did he drink more than a mug or two of the local wine, and seemed not even a little befuddled by it. *Dom* Carlo she had not seen again; she supposed he was about whatever business for King Carolin had brought him to this city. For all she knew to the contrary, he had left Nevarsin and gone to warn Carolin not to come here—there was one who would recognize him. She did not think the child would betray Carolin—he had said the king had been kind to him—but his loyalties, naturally, would be to his own father. She did not question Orain. It was none of her business, and she was content to have it that way.

Shyly, she began to wonder; if her father had chosen to marry her to one like Orain, would she have refused him? She thought not. But that was conflict too.

For then would I have stayed at home and been married, and never known this wonderful freedom of city and tavern, woods and fields, never have worked free and had money in my pockets, never really known that I had never been free, never flown a sentry-bird.

She was growing fond of the huge ugly birds; now they came to her hand for their food as readily as any sparrow-hawk or child's cagebird. Either her arm grew stronger or she was more used to it, for now she could hold them for a considerable time and not mind the weight. Their docility and the sweetness she felt when she went into rapport with them, made her think with regret of Preciosa; would see ever see the hawk again?

She seldom saw the other men; she slept apart from them, and encountered them only morning and night, when they all came together for meals in the monastery guest-house. She was quite content that it should be so; she was still a little afraid of Alaric, and the others seemed strange and alien too. It seemed sometimes that the only person to whom she spoke these days, aside from the man who delivered the bird-food and fodder for horses and *chervines,* was young Caryl, who came whenever he could escape for a few minutes from his lessons, to look at the birds, hold them, croon lovingly to them. With Caryl she was always a little troubled, lest he should forget and thoughtlessly address her again as *vai domna*—it was a heavy weight of secrets for a child to bear. Once Orain came to the chapel to hear the singing; he took a seat far back and in the shadows, and she was sure that the little boy, in the lighted choir, could not see the face of a solitary man in the darkest part of the chapel, but she remembered that the child knew Carolin and would certainly recognize one of the king's men; she was so agitated that she rose quietly and went out, afraid that the telepathic child would sense her agitation and know its cause.

155

Midwinter-night was approaching; stalls of spicebread trimmed with copper foil, and gaily painted toys, began to appear in the marketplace, and sweet-sellers filled their displays with stars cut from spicebread or nut-paste. Romilly, homesick at the smell of baking spicebread—Luciella always baked it herself, saying that the servants should not be given extra work at this season—almost regretted leaving her home; but then she remembered that in any case she would not have spent this holiday at her home, but at Scathfell as the wife of *Dom* Garris—and by now, no doubt, she would have been like Darissa, swollen and ugly with her first child! No, she was better here; but she wished she could send a gift to Rael, or that he could see these bright displays with her.

On the morning before the Festival, she woke to snow blowing into the cracks of the room where she slept, though she was warm in the deep-piled hay. A midwinter storm had blown down, wailing, from the Wall Around the World, and the monastery courtyard was knee-deep in fresh powdery snow. She put on both pairs of warm stockings when she dressed, and her extra tunic, and even so she shivered as she went out into the yard to wash at the well; but the little novices and students were running about barefoot in the snow, and she wondered how they could do it, laughing and gossiping and tossing snowballs at one another. They looked rosy and warm, whereas her own hands were blue with cold!

She went in to care for the riding-animals, and stopped in dismay; *Dom* Carlo's horse was not in the stable! Had it been stolen? Or had *Dom* Carlo gone out, into this bitter storm? It was still snowing, a few flakes drifting down now and again from the overburdened sky. As she was lifting forkfuls of fragrant hay to the beasts, Orain came in, and she turned to him in distress.

"*Dom* Carlo's horse—"

"Hush, lad," he said in a low tone, "Not even before the men. His life could be in your hands; not a word!"

Romilly nodded, and he said, "Good boy. After mid-day, walk to the town with me; perhaps, who knows, I shall have a Midwinter gift for you, away as you are from home and family—"

It seemed as if he must be reading her mind, and she turned away. "I expect no gifts, sir," she said stiffly. Did he know, had he guessed? But he only grinned and said, "Midday, remember." and went away.

At mid-day Romilly was trying, in the deep snow, to get the sentry-birds to fly a little—they got little enough exercise, in this weather—before they were fed. They screamed rebelliously as she snapped them on lure-lines and tried to encourage them to fly—they were temperamental and did not like the still-falling snow. The snow in the cobbled court, too, was so deep that it came over her boot-tops and trickled down inside, and her feet were cold and her fingers stiff. She was chilled and cross, and even little Caryl's cheerful face could not lighten her mood. She thought, *it might, in this weather, be just as well to be a lady by the fire, with nothing to do but make embroidery stitches and bake spicebread!* Caryl was wearing only a thin tunic, his arms bare, and his feet were bare in the snow, and she asked crossly, "Aren't you freezing?"

He shook his head, laughing. "It is the first thing the monks teach us," he said, "How to warm ourselves from within, by breathing; some of the older monks can bathe in the water of the well and then dry their clothes by their body heat when they put them on, but that seems a little more than I would want to try. I was cold for the first tenday before I learned it, but I have never suffered from the cold since then. Poor Rumal, you look so cold, I wish I could teach it to you!" He held out his arm to take Prudence, saying seriously, "Come, birdie, you must fly, I know you do not like the snow, but it is not good for you to sit all the time on your perch, you must keep your wings strong."

Prudence flapped away and circled at the end of the line, while Caryl cast out the lure, watching her swoop down. "See, she likes to play with it, even in the snow! Look at her!"

"You are happy," Romilly said sourly, "Do you like the storm as much as that?"

"No, I would like to go out, but in this weather I have to stay indoors, and the arms-master cannot come, so I will miss my lesson at sword-play," said the boy, "but I am happy because tomorrow is a holiday, and my father will come here to visit me. I miss my father and my brothers, and father is sure to bring me a fine gift—I am twelve years old and he promised me a fine sword, perhaps he will give it to me for a Midwinter-gift. And he always takes me walking in the town, so that I can buy spicebread and sweets, and my mother always sends me a new cloak at Midwinter. I have been working very hard at all my lessons, because I want him to be pleased with me."

Lyondri Hastur? Here in the monastery? Her first thought was of Orain and *Dom* Carlo; the second of their king. Quieting her thoughts carefully, she asked, "Is your father here now?"

"No, but he will come for the holiday, unless this weather should keep him housebound a day's journey away," the boy said, "and Father is never afraid of storms! He has some of the old Delleray Gift, he can work a little on the weather; you'll see, Father will make it stop snowing before it is night."

"That is a *laran* of which I have not heard," Romilly said, keeping her voice steady, "Do you have it?"

"I don't think so," the child said, "I have never tried to use it. Here, let me fly Temperance while you take Diligence, will you?"

She handed the lure-line to the child, trying to conceal her agitation. Alaric, too, should be warned—or would he try to take vengeance on his enemy, whom he regarded as murderer of his wife and child? She could hardly make conversation with the little boy. And halfway through feeding the birds, she saw the door from the stables open and Orain came into the court. She tried to motion to him to withdraw, but he came into the courtyard, saying, "Not finished with the birds yet, my boy? Make haste, I want your company for an errand in the town," and Caryl turned and saw him. His eyes widened a little.

"My lord," he said, with a courtly little bow, "What are you doing here?"

Orain flinched, and for a moment did not answer. Then he said, "I have come here for sanctuary, lad, since I am no longer welcome at the court where your father rules the king. Will you give the alarm, then?"

"Certainly not," said the boy with dignity, "Under the roof of Saint Valentine, even a condemned man must be safe, sir. All men are brothers who shelter here—this much the *cristoforos* have told me, Master Rumal, if you wish to go with your master, I will put the birds on their perches for you."

"Thank you, but I can manage them," said Romilly, and took Temperance on her fist; Caryl trailed her with the other bird on his two hands. He said in a whisper, "Did you know he was one of Carolin's men? They are really not safe here."

Romilly pretended gruffness and said, "I don't ask questions about my betters. And you should run along to choir, Caryl."

He bit his lip, flushing, and turned away, dashing barefoot through the snow. Romilly drew a long breath; she would have turned and spoken to Orain, but his hand closed with an iron grip on her shoulder.

"Not here," he said. "Outside these walls; I am not sure, now, that they have not ears, and the ears are those of a certain lord."

Silent, Romilly finished her work with the sentry-birds and followed Orain through the gates of the monastery. The street was white and silent, muffled with the thick snow. At last Orain said, "The Hastur-whelp?"

She nodded. After a moment she said in an undertone, pitching her voice so that Orain had to lean close to listen, "That's not the worst of it. His father—Lyondri Hastur—is outside the city and will be visiting him for the holiday."

Orain's clenched fist drove into his other hand. "Damnnation! And Zandru knows, *he's* not one to observe sanctuary-law! If he sets eyes—" Orain fell silent. "Why did *Dom* Carlo have to go away at *this* time of all times—" he said at last. "Ill-luck dogs us! I'll try and get a message to him—"

Silence; even their footsteps were silent in the snow-muffled street. At last Orain said, dismissing it, "Let's go down to the tavern. With such news as this I need a drink, and they have spiced cider in honor of the holiday, so you may drink too."

Romilly said soberly, "Shouldn't Alaric and the others be warned to watch themselves, if the Hastur-Lord is likely to be about?"

"I'll pass a word to them," Orain said, "But for now, no more talk—"

In the tavern where Orain had taught her, some days ago, to play at darts, he commanded wine, and hot cider for Romilly; it smelled sweet with spices, and she drank it gratefully and accepted his offer of a second mug. He said, "I have a gift for you—that filthy cloak you wear is hardly worthy of a stable-man's son. I found this in a stall—it's old and worn but suits you, I think." He beckoned to the serving-woman, said "Bring me the bundle I left here yesterday."

He tossed it across the table at her. "A good Midwinter-night to you, and Avarra guard you, son."

Romilly untied the strings; took out a green cloak, spun of rabbithorn-wool, finely embroidered and trimmed with clasps of good leather. It must have been very old, for it had sleeves cut in one with the cape, in a fashion she had seen in portraits of her great-grandsire in the Great Hall at Falconsward; but it was richly lined and comfortable. She flung aside the shabby old cloak she had taken when she fled from Rory's house in the woods, and put on the new one, saying after a moment, embarrassed, "I have no gift for you, Master Orain."

He put his arm round her shoulders. "I want nothing from you, son; but give me the hug and kiss you'd give your father if he were here today."

Blushing, Romilly embraced him, and touched her lips gingerly to his cheek. "You are very good to me, sir. Thank you."

"Not at all—now you are dressed as befits your red hair and the manner you have of a nobleman's son," he said. There was just enough irony in the words that Romilly wondered; did he *know* she was a woman? She had been sure, at one time, that *Dom* Carlo knew.

"That old thing, you can make into a horse-blanket," said Orain, motioning the tapster's boy to make it up into a bundle. Romilly would rather have thrown it away where she need never touch it again, but in this weather horses could not go un-blanketed, and the horse-blanket she had, had been meant for warmer climates. Her horse would be grateful for the extra warmth, with this midwinter storm.

There were but few patrons in the tavern this evening; the approaching storm, and the morrow's holiday, contrived to keep most of the men at home, Romilly supposed, by their own hearths.

Orain asked, when she had finished her meal, "Will we have a game of darts, then?"

"I am not a good enough player to make it worth your trouble," she said, and Orain laughed. "Who cares? Come along, then."

They stood, alternately flinging the darts and sipping from their tankards, as the evening passed. Suddenly Orain stiffened, went silent.

"Your turn," Romilly said.

"You throw—I'll be back in a moment," Orain said, his speech slurred, and Romilly thought, *he cannot possibly be drunk so early*. Yet as he walked away he reeled drunkenly, and one of the sparse patrons of the tavern yelled jovially, "Drunk so early on midwinter-night? You'll not hold your wine on the holiday, then, man!"

She wondered; *is he sick? Should I go and help him?* One of the things Romilly had carefully avoided, during her weeks in the town, was going inside the common latrine behind any of the taverns—it was the one place where she might possibly be discovered. Yet Orain had been good to her, if he was in trouble, surely he deserved help—

A small voice in her mind said; *No. Stay where you are. Act as if everything were normal.* Since Romilly was not yet accustomed to the use of her own *laran*—and it was rare for her to be so much in touch with the feelings of any human, though she now took rapport with her birds for granted—she was not sure whether this were actually a message reaching her, or her own projected feelings; but she obeyed it. She called out, recklessly drawing attention to herself, "Who'd like a game, then, since my friend's overcome with drink?" And when two townsmen came up to her, she challenged them, and played so badly that she soon lost and had to pay the forfeit of buying them a round of drinks. It seemed that at the very edge of the room she could see movement in the shadows—had Orain not left the room after all, but only withdrawn? Who was he talking to? She kept the game going, and by a great effort did not turn to try and see the other figure, tall and graceful, a hood shrouding face and head, moving softly near Orain. But as if she had eyes in the back of her head, it seemed that she could see it, hear whispers . . . her spine prickled and at every moment she thought she would hear an outcry, voices, shouts. *Holy Bearer of Burdens, whose day this is, tell me, how did I become entangled in this intrigue, as if it mattered to me which king sat on the throne of the Hali'imyr? Damn them both, outcast king and usurper king. Why should a good man like Orain risk a noose for his neck because one king or another holds the throne of the Hasturs?*

If any harm comes to my friend, I will . . . and she stopped there. What could she do? Unlike her brothers, she had no knowledge of arms, she was defenseless. *If I escape this night's intrigue,* she thought, *I will ask Orain to teach me something of the arts of fighting* . . . but she laughed and shouted, "Well thrown, whang in the cat's eye," and flung her own dart almost at random, surprised when it landed anywhere near the target.

"Drink up, young'un," said the man who had lost, setting a mug of wine before her, and Romilly drank recklessly. Her head felt fuzzy, and she stopped halfway through the mugful, but they were all looking at her, and against her better judgment, she finished the drink.

"You'll have another game? My turn to win," said one of the men, and she shrugged and gave up the dart. Her neck felt that cold, vulnerable prickle that she knew meant she was being watched, somewhere undercover. *What is going on in that room? Damn these intrigues!*

Then Orain was at her side again, clapping her on the shoulder. "Aye, now you have the way of it, but you can't yet teach an old dog how to gnaw a bone—gi'me the darts, lad." He took the feathered darts, poised them, called for wine all around; she saw the excited glitter of his eyes. When the next pair took the darts, he muttered next her ear, "Next round we must get away; I've a message—"

She nodded to let him know she understood. The next moment Orain shouted, "What in nine hells do you there, man, your big feet halfway over the line—I won't play darts with a cheating bastard like that, not even at Midwinter—gifts I will make but not be cheated out of a drink or a silver bit!" and shoved angrily against the man who was throwing. The man whirled drunkenly and swung at him.

"Here, you lowland bugger, who do you call cheat? You'll swallow those words with your next drink or I'll ram them down your throat—" He connected with Orain's chin, and Orain's head went back with a crack; he staggered against the wall, came out swinging furiously. Romilly flung her dart, and it landed in the man's hand as he swung again at Orain; the attacker turned, howling, and barged toward her, hands out as if to strangle her. She moved away, tripped on a barrel and went sprawling in the sawdust. Orain's hand grabbed her, pulled her upright.

"Here, here—" the barman came over, scowling, separating them with rough hands. "No brawling, friends! Drink up!"

"The rotten little bastard threw a dart at me," growled the man, shoving up his sleeve to reveal a red mark.

"You're a baby to bawl at a bee-sting?" demanded Orain, and the barman shoved them apart.

"Sit down! Both of you! The penalty for fighting is a drink for the house, from each of you!"

With a show of reluctance, Orain pulled out his purse, flung down a copper piece. "Drink up and be damned to you, and I hope you all choke on it! We'll be off to a quieter place for drinking!" he snarled, grabbed Romilly's elbow and steered a drunken path toward the door. Outside he straightened up and demanded in a low, quick voice, "Are you hurt?"

"No, but—"

"That's all right, then. Let's make tracks!" He set a pace up the hill that Romilly could hardly follow. She knew she

had had too much to drink and wondered, as she staggered
dizzily after him, if she was going to throw it up. After a moment he turned and said, gently, "Sorry—here, lad, take my
arm," and supported her. "You shouldn't have drunk that last
cup."

"I couldn't think of anything else to do," she confessed.

"And you saved my neck by it," he said in a whisper.
"Come, perhaps you can get a bit of rest at the monastery
before—look," he gestured at the clearing sky, "The snow's
stopped. We'll be expected to show at the Midwinter-eve service, any guest at the monastery who's not abed with a broken
leg is expected to be there for their damned hymn-singing!
And with the weather cleared, that rat Lyondri—" he
clenched his fists. "He may well be there, large as life and
twice as filthy, sitting smug in the choir and singing hymns
like a better man."

Romilly asked, troubled, "Would he recognize you, then,
Uncle?"

"That he would," said Orain grimly, "and others than me."

She wondered; *can it be that Carolin himself is somewhere
in the monastery?* Or did he speak of Alaric, whose family
had been condemned to death by the Hastur-lord? Or of
Carlo, who was certainly an exiled man and high in Carolin's
confidence? Orain's hand was beneath her arm.

"Here, lean on me, lad—I'd pretend to be sick and hide in
the guest-house, but then they'd hale me off to the infirmary,
and find out soon there's nothing wrong with me but a cup
too many of their wine."

She looked at the settled snow, cringing in the keen wind
that came as the snow had quieted. "Is there truly a *laran*
which can work sorcery on the weather?"

"So I have heard," Orain muttered, subsiding into gloom
again. "Would that you had some trace of it, son!"

CHAPTER FOUR

The Midwinter-night service in St. Valentine-of-the-Snows was famous throughout the Hellers; people came from all through Nevarsin, and from the countryside round, to hear the singing. Romilly had heard some of the music before this, but never sung so well, and she would have enjoyed the service, had she not been so troubled by Orain's obvious worried state. He insisted that they should sit at the back, and when she asked where *Dom* Carlo was, and why he had not come to the service, scowled and refused to answer. He had cautioned Alaric, too, not to enter the chapel at all. But toward the end of the service, when there was a moment's lull, he whispered "No sign yet of Lyondri Hastur. We may be lucky." His face twisted and he muttered, "We'd be luckiest if he fell off a cliff somewhere and never made it to Nevarsin at all!"

And, as Caryl said, some weather magic has been done. I did not think the weather would clear so quickly.

She saw Caryl, scrubbed and shining, in the front row of the choir, his mouth opening like a bird as he sang; it seemed to Romilly that his voice soared out over all the choir. It was as well, perhaps, that *Dom* Carlo was not here, except for Orain's dread; it seemed that the big gaunt man could hardly sit still, and no sooner was the service ended than he was up and out of his seat, pushing for the back of the chapel. He walked with her to the stable, and busied his hands checking on the sentry-birds, so that Romilly would have been annoyed—did he think she could not care for them properly,

164

then? Later she knew what he had been looking for, why he had arranged everything close together so that they could be snatched up and ready to ride at a moment's notice, but at the moment she was only exasperated and wondered if he was still drunk, or believed *she* was too drunk to handle them properly. He checked on the *chervines* and horses too, turning up each hoof, arranging saddle-blankets and saddles, until she thought she would scream with nervousness at his fiddling. Or was he lingering so that he would see it, if Lyondri Hastur actually arrived at the monastery?

But at last he sighed and turned away. He said, "A good Festival to you, lad," and gave Romilly a rough hug. "If it's too cold here in the stable, you can sleep in *Dom* Carlo's bed, no one will know the difference—"

"I think I should stay near the birds," Romilly said, avoiding his gaze. It was not that she did not trust him, exactly; she had lived in camp among them, and if her real sex had not yet been discovered, he was unlikely to discover it now, even should they share a sleeping room. And if he should— she discovered that she felt shaky and weak when she thought about that—Orain was not a *cristoforo* and would not be bound by their Creed of Chastity—she had heard stories all her life, of how licentious were the lowlanders and the *Hali'imyn*—but somehow she could not imagine that he would attempt to force himself upon her. Still, she was uncomfortable at his touch, and pulled away as quickly as she could, remembering the dream she had had . . . in the dream he had held and caressed her as if she was the woman he did not know her to be. . . .

She burrowed into the hay, still a little dizzied with the wine she had drunk, and after a time she slept. She dreamed, as she had dreamed before, that she was flying on the wings of hawk or sentry-bird, that there was someone flying at her side, who spoke to her in Orain's voice, and drowsily caressed her . . . she sank into the dream, never thinking to resist. . . .

She came abruptly awake in the half-light, hearing the clamor of bells—was it some observance of the *cristoforo* monks for the Festival? She sat up to see Orain, white as death, standing at the door of the little chamber.

"Rumal, lad! Is *Dom* Carlo with you? This is no time for modesty—"

"*Dom* Carlo? I have not seen him in days! What do you mean, Orain?"

"There was a time—no, I see you know not even what I

mean. Damnation!" He staggered, reeled against the wall. "I hoped against hope—it cannot be that he has been taken! Aldones grant he has already been warned and made his escape—listen!" He gestured and again she heard the alarm-bell ringing. "We have been betrayed, someone has recognized him, or recognized me—I knew he should not have ventured down there today!" He swore, striking the wall with his fist. "Quick, up, boy, search the guest-house! They know that where I appear, Carolin—or his men—cannot be far away! And while the Father Master might not violate sanctuary, I would not trust the Hastur-lord to keep it, not if the Lord of Light appeared before his nose and bade him—"

Orain was dead sober now; he looked ill and haggard, his gaunt face sunken, but his eyes blazing with anger.

"That child of Lyondri's—did he babble, do you think, to his playfellows? Lyondri's son—like dog, like pup! I'd run the boy through with my skean and think the world a safer place lest the whelp grow up like his abominable father!"

Romilly shrank back and Orain scowled. "No, I'd not harm a child, not even Lyondri's, I suppose—get your boots on, boy! We must make haste out of here, out of the city—if we are caught here, none of our lives are worth a feather's weight! Go and call—no, I will rouse Alaric and the others! You make the horses ready—"

It seemed suddenly as if *Dom* Carlo's face swam in the air before her—but he was not there! Still it seemed she could hear him saying to her, *Bring the birds, go through the monastery to the highest gate, to the secret pass above the hidden cells on the glacier.*

"Move, lad!" Orain snarled, "What are you staring at?"

Her voice shaking, Romilly repeated *Dom* Carlo's words. "He was here, I heard him; his very voice—"

"Dreams," Orain said, jerking his head impatiently, and it seemed that Carlo's voice said in Romilly's mind, *Bid him remember a certain belt of red leather over which we fought and bloodied both our noses.*

Romilly caught at Orain's sleeve as he turned to go. "I swear, Orain, I heard *Dom* Carlo—something of a red leather belt over which you both bloodied your noses."

Orain blinked. He made a quick, superstitious gesture. Then he said, "You have *laran;* no? I thought as much. Aye, that belt was a jest between us for a hand-span of years. I will go rouse the men. Make ready, as quick as you can."

Romilly found that her hands were steady as she got the saddles on the animals, wrapped herself in the cloak that had been Orain's Midwinter-gift—grateful for the fur lining—and stuffed a couple of saddlebags with grain and fodder for the riding-beasts and another with the smelly food for the sentry-birds. She hooded them—it would have been impossible to handle them in the middle of the night this way without rousing the whole monastery, but hooded they would at least be quiet—and fastened their blocks to her own saddle and to Orain's, and gave the third to Alaric's *chervine*.

After a bit she looked up and found Alaric working at her side. "Some bastard betrayed us," he said shakily, listening to the distant clamor of bells—it was growing nearer and nearer now, "They're searching the city house to house, when the time comes they reach the monastery, they'll search every cranny, the monk's cells, the very chapel! What is it, lad, you know Orain's counsel—are we to ride them down at the gates?"

"I am not in their counsels," Romilly said, "But something of a secret gate at the highest part—"

"And while we waste time looking for the secret paths, Lyondri's men find us and I dance on a rope's end?" demanded Alaric. Romilly said steadily, "I do not think *Dom* Carlo will abandon us like that. Trust him."

"Aye; but the *vai dom* is Hastur, when all's done, and blood's thicker than wine, they say. . . ." Alaric grumbled.

"Alaric!" she turned round to him, shocked beyond speech. After a moment she found her voice and said, "Surely you can't believe Carlo would side with the Hastur-lord against—well, against us, and Orain—"

"Well, not against Orain," he said, "Get that saddle on, boy, if there's a chance—but how do I know? Likely ye're of the gentlefolk yourself. . . ." his voice trailed away, uncertain.

"Finish with the saddling, and don't talk nonsense," she said sharply. "Will you lift that grain-bag to the saddle? I can't lift it alone—"

He helped her to hoist the heavy pack to the back of the chervine, and led the beast out of the stable. A hand seized her wrist in a hard grip and she started to cry out before, not knowing how, she recognized Orain's grip, even in the darkness.

"This way," he whispered, and, knowing his voice even in the silenced whisper, she relaxed and let him lead them into the dark passageway. She heard the other men, trying to move silently, only small creaks and rustles; someone bashed a toe against a rock wall and cursed softly. Then, she heard a soft childish voice.

"My lord Orain—"

"Ah—it's you, ye devil's pup—"

Caryl cried out, a muffled squeak. "I won't hurt you," he said, gasping—Romilly could not see in the dark, but sensed, from the pain in the small voice, that Orain had grabbed him harshly. "No, I only—I meant to guide you on the secret path—I *don't* want my father to find—find the *vai dom*—he will be angry, but—"

"Let him go, Orain," Romilly muttered, "he's telling the truth!"

"Ah—I'll trust your *laran*, boy," said Orain, and she heard a little whimper of relief as, evidently, he loosed his punishing grip on the child. "A path you know? Lead us. But if you play us false—" he added through clenched teeth, "Child or no, I'll run my skean into you—"

They followed through the narrow passage, crowding together, bumping, the sentry-birds making uneasy squealing noises in the darkness. Someone cursed in an undertone and Romilly saw the flash of flint on steel, but Orain commanded harshly, "Put that out!" and the light subsided, with someone grumbling and swearing.

"Silence," Alaric commanded harshly, and there was no sound except the uneasy sounds of animals crowded in the narrow stone passages. There was a place where they had to go single file in the dark and one of the loaded chervines stuck between the stone walls. Alaric and one of the other men had to off-load the beast, hastily, swearing in whispers, while they hauled and shoved. Later they came to a place where the air was bad, coming up as if from the sulphurous center of the earth, and even Romilly could not stifle her coughing. Caryl murmured, "I am sorry—this is only a little bit, but watch your steps here, there are cracks and fissures, someone might break a leg."

Romilly groped her way along in the dark, scuffling her feet slowly against the possibility of an unseen crack underfoot. At last they were all through, and there was a breath of icy air from the glacier, a little riffling wind, and they stood out of doors in chilly starlight. The pallid face of a single moon, the tiny pearl-colored Mormallor, hung just above the hill, hardly bright enough to lighten the darkness at all; and underfoot was pale slippery ice.

"No one travels this path," whispered Caryl, "except for a few of the brothers who practice their mastery of the ordeals

168

by living here, naked, and even if they knew you were here, they would not know or care who you were, they think only of the things of the heavenly realms, not of kings and wars. But oh, go carefully, my lords—there are dangers—"

"What dangers?" demanded Alaric, grabbing his throat. Caryl squeaked softly, but did not cry out.

"No dangers of man; banshee-birds live here, though our Brothers have a pact with them, as they say the holy Saint Valentine-of-the-Snows had a pact when he preached to them and called them God's little brothers—"

"You led us into a nest of banshee-birds, ye devil's pup?" Alaric demanded, but Orain said, "Let him go, damn you, man; touch the boy again and I'll give you something you'll remember! The banshees are not of his calling, he thought to warn us, which is more than even the Father Master thought to do!"

"Take your hands from the boy, Alaric! Are you mad?" demanded a new voice, and *Dom* Carlo stood among them. Romilly did not see from whence he had come; he was simply there. Later she realized he must have come through another secret tunnel or path, but at the moment it was as if he jumped up among them like magic. Caryl gave a little startled cry; Romilly's eyes were adjusting to the darkness now, and she could see the child's face. He held out his arms to *Dom* Carlo for a kinsman's embrace, saying simply, "Uncle. I am glad you are safe."

"It makes my heart glad to know you are not my enemy," said Carlo, not as if he spoke to a child, but as if he spoke to another noble, his equal in rank and age. He kissed the boy on either cheek. "Walk in the Light, lad, till we meet again."

"*Vai dom*—" Caryl's young high voice suddenly wavered, "I am your friend, not your enemy. But—I beg you—if my father is in your hands—spare him for my sake—"

Dom Carlo held Caryl's shoulders gently between his hands. He said, "I wish I could promise you that, son. I do swear this, by the Lord of Light, whom I serve as you the Bearer of Burdens; I will make no quarrel with Lyondri while he makes none with me. For the rest, I will hope with all my heart that Lyondri stays afar from me; I wish him far less ill than he wishes me. He was once my friend, and the quarrel was none of my making." He kissed Caryl again, and released him. "Now get you back to your bed, child, before your father hears that you have been abroad this night, or Father Master seeks to punish you, May the Gods walk with you, *chiyu*."

"And with you, my lord." Caryl turned and started back into the dark mouth of the passage. Then Alaric grabbed him around the waist. He struggled, but one quick blow from Alaric sent him sagging softly, with a little sigh, into the man's arms.

"Are you mad, *vai dom'yn*?" he demanded, "Lyondri's own son in our hands for hostage, and you'd let him free? With this whelp in our hands, we could bargain our way out of Rakhal's very clutches, to say nothing of being secure against Lyondri Hastur!"

"And you would reward him like this for guiding us to safety?" Romilly cried in outrage, but Alaric's face was hard and set.

"You're a fool, boy. And you too, under favor, my lords," he said to Orain and *Dom* Carlo. "The boy may have led us honestly—who'd seek to distrust a little one with angel face like this? But his elders have *laran*—even if *he* means us no harm, how do we know *they* haven't trailed us through the boy's *laran*? I won't hurt the least hair on his head, but he stays with us till we're safe from glacier and Lyondri's men! We can leave him in Caer Donn, or some such place!"

"If you've hurt him—" *Dom* Carlo said with soft menace, and Romilly hoped his wrath would never be turned on *her*. He felt the boy's forehead. "I wouldn't reward the child's loyalty like this! But we can't leave him here unconscious, to die of the cold," he added. "Bring him with you, then, if you must; we dare not delay for him to recover. But you'll hear of this after, Alaric," he said angrily, and turned his back on the man. "Set the boy on one of the horses, and you, young Rumal," he added, beckoning to Romilly, "Ride behind him, for he cannot keep his saddle as he is now, and I am reluctant to tie him as if he were a prisoner. Now come, make haste!"

The limp unconscious form of Caryl was lifted into the saddle and Romilly, mounting behind him, had all she could do to hold the child from falling on the uneven, icy path. They went upward and upward in silence, with no sound but the small, uneasy cries of the hooded sentry-birds. Riding in the dark, holding Caryl, small and limp, in her arms, Romilly thought of Rael, sleeping against her shoulder; missed him, sharply and with bitterness. Would she ever see her little brother again?

The narrow path was steep, so steep that Romilly had to lean forward in the saddle as they climbed; it was narrow, and icy underfoot, and it was all she could do to hold Caryl's unconscious weight against her so that he would not fall from the saddle. But the men, too, had all they could do to manage the nervous chervines and the sentry-birds, who were uneasy, and, even hooded, kept making little squealing sounds and trying to flap their wings and hop around restlessly on their blocks. This made horses and chervines even more nervous; she wondered what their sharper senses saw, and would have tried rapport to find out, but it was all she could do, on the steep path, to hold herself and the unconscious child in the saddle without falling.

Once there sounded a high screaming wail, a paralyzing sound that seemed to turn Romilly's blood to ice. Her horse started and snorted nervously under her, and she fought to control it. The sentry-birds fidgeted on their blocks, flapping their wings in panic. Romilly had never heard such a cry before, but she needed no one to tell her what it was; the cry of a banshee, the huge flightless birds who lived above the snow-line; all but blind, but sensing the body warmth of anything that lived, and their powerful claws that could disembowel horse or man with a single stroke. And it was night, when they actually could see a little, blind as they were in the light of the red sun. Their terrible cries, she had heard, were in-tended to paralyze prey with fright; hearing it now in the distance, she hoped she would never actually *see* one.

At the sound Caryl made a small pained noise and stirred, his hands going up to feel the lump on his head. The move-ment made the horse startle; his hooves all but slipped on the icy path. Romilly bent forward and whispered urgently, "It's all right, but you must be quiet; the road is dangerous just here, and if you frighten the horse, he may fall—and so would we. Be still, Caryl."

"Mistress Romilly?" he whispered, and she said crossly "*Hush!*" He subsided, looking up at her. Her eyes had adjust-ed now to the darkness so that she could see his small frightened face. Still gingerly feeling the lump at his temple, he blinked and she hoped he would not cry.

He whispered, "How did I get here? What happened?" And then, remembering, "Someone *hit* me!" He sounded more surprised than angry. She supposed that he, a pampered lowland child, had never been struck before, that no one had spoken to him other than gently. She held him tight in her arms.

"Don't be afraid," she whispered, "I won't let them hurt you." She knew, as she said it, that if Alaric offered any fur-ther violence to the child she would set herself between them.

He wriggled himself into a more comfortable position on the saddle; now that he could sit upright, and was no longer a dead weight who must be held to keep him from falling, it was easier to control her horse.

"Where are we?" he whispered.

"On the road to which you guided us; *Dom* Carlo brought you with us because he could not leave you lying unconscious to die of the cold, but he means you no harm. Alaric wanted you as a hostage; but Orain won't let him hurt you again."

"Lord Orain has always been kind to me," said Caryl after a moment, "even when I was very small. I wish my father had not quarreled with him. And Father Master will be very angry with me."

"It wasn't your fault."

"Father Master says whatever happens to us is always our fault, one way or another," said the child, keeping his voice low, "If we have not deserved it in this life, we have certainly done so in another. If it is good we have earned it and may enjoy it, but if it is bad, we must also believe that somehow we have deserved the bad too, and it is not always easy to know which is which. I am not sure what that means," he added naively, "but he said I would understand when I was older."

"Then I must be very young too," said Romilly, unable to keep back a laugh—talking elevated *cristoforo* philosophy on this dangerous road, with the king's men, for all they knew, hard at their heels! "For I confess I do not understand it at all."

Orain heard the laugh; he pulled his horse aside and waited for them to come up with him, where the path widened just a fraction. "Are you awake, young Caryl?"

"I wasn't asleep," the boy protested, scowling, "Somebody hit me!"

"True," said Orain seriously, "And he has heard about it, believe me, from *Dom* Carlo. But now, I fear, you must ride with us to Caer Donn; you cannot possibly return alone over this road. I would have trusted you not to betray us willfully, but I know from old that Lyondri has *laran* and might read in your thoughts which way we had gone. I give you my word, which, unlike your father, I have never broken, that when we reach Caer Donn you will be sent back to him under a flag of truce. He—" with an eloquent shrug of his caped shoulder, he indicated *Dom* Carlo, riding ahead, "wishes you no ill. But in this company I should warn you to guard your tongue."

"My lord—" Caryl began, but Orain gave a slight, warning shake of his head, and said quickly, "If you would be more comfortable riding behind me, you may, when we have gotten through this path; this is no place to stop and change horses. Or if you will give me the word of a Hastur that you will not try to flee from us, I will arrange it that one of the pack-animals can carry you, and you may ride alone."

"Thank you," the boy said, "but I would rather stay with—" he paused and swallowed and said, "with Rumal." She was astonished at his presence of mind; no other youngster, she was sure, could have remembered, even in this extremity, not to blurt out her secret.

"Ride carefully, then," Orain said, "and guard him well, Rumal." He turned back to his own riding, and Romilly, settling Caryl as comfortably as she could in front of her—it would indeed be easier if he could sit behind her and hang on, but there was no way to stop and change now—reflected that he had protected her even when he had nothing to gain by keeping her secret, and when he might have made trouble among his captors. An unusual youngster indeed, and cleverer than Rael, disloyal as she felt to her own little brother to think so.

He knew she was a woman. Though, she had thought sometimes that *Dom* Carlo knew and kept his counsel for his own reasons, whatever they were. And then, for the first time—so swiftly had affairs moved since she was awakened—she remembered Orain's exact words when he came seeking her. *Is Carlo with you? This is no time for modesty!* Had Carlo, then, confided to Orain—or been told by him, perhaps?—that he knew her a woman, and, knowing that, did he think her such a woman as might be free of her favors, so that he might have found Carlo in her bed? Even in the bitter cold, Romilly felt the hot flush of shame on her cheeks. Well, riding with them in men's clothes, what sort of woman *could* he think her?

Well, if he knew, he knew, and if he thought *that* of her, he must think what he liked. At least he had been gentleman enough not to spread it among these roughnecks. But she had begun to like Orain so much!

Again from the crags above them came the eerie scream of a banshee; it was closer now, and Romilly felt the throbbing, eldritch wail going all through her, as if her very bones were shuddering at the sound. She knew how the natural prey of the bird must feel; it seemed to stop her in her tracks, to wipe out the world around so that there was nothing except

173

that dreadful vibration, which seemed to make her eyes blur and the world go dark around her. Caryl moaned and dug his hands over his ears with an agonized shiver, and she could see the men ahead of them fighting to control their terrified horses while the sentry-birds flapped, and the chervines made their odd bawling cry and stepped around, almost prancing with terror, on the icy path. One of them stumbled and went down and the rider fell, sliding some way before he could dig his heels into the ice and stand up, scrambling to catch his riding-animal; another beast piled into him and there was a clumsy sprawling collision. Swearing, they fought with the reins. The screaming of the hooded sentry-birds, their bating wings, added to the dismay, and again the eerie terror-filled banshee scream shuddered out from the crags above, and was answered by yet another.

Romilly gave Caryl a little shake. "Stop that!" she demanded furiously. "Help me, help me quiet the birds!" Her own breath was coming ragged, she could see it steaming in the icy air, but she put her mind swiftly to reaching out with that special sense of hers, and sending thoughts of calm, peace, food, affection. She could reach them still; as she felt Caryl's thoughts join with hers, one after another the great birds quieted, were still on their blocks on the saddles, and Carlo and his men could get the riding-animals under control again. Carlo gestured to them to gather close—the path widened here just enough that three or four of the animals could stand abreast, and they gathered in a little bunch.

The crags above them were beginning to stand out stark against the paling sky; pink and purple clouds outlined the blackness of the rocks of the pass. Dawn was near. The trail above them narrowed and led across the glacier; and even as they looked, a clumsy shadow moved on the face of the rocks, and again there came the terrible wailing scream, answered by another from higher up. Orain compressed his narrow lips and said wryly, "Just what we needed; two of the damned things! And daylight still a good hour away—and even when the sun comes up, we might not escape them. And we can't wait anyway; if there's pursuit we should be away and across the path before full daylight, and well to the other side where the woods will conceal our traces! A blind man would be able to read our tracks on ice, and Lyondri's sure to have half a dozen of his damned *leroni* with him!"

"We're in the very mouth of the trap," Carlo muttered, his face going silent and distant. He said at last, into the silence, "No pursuit, at least not yet—I need no *leronis* to tell me so much. You were a damned fool to bring the boy, Alaric—with him to follow, Lyondri will follow us though the track led through all nine of Zandru's hells! Now he has a second and personal grudge!"

"If the boy's with us," Alaric said, his teeth set tight, "we can buy our lives, at least!"

Caryl drew himself upright on the saddle and said angrily, "My father would not compromise his honor for his son's life, and I would not want him to!"

"Lyondri's honor?" growled one of the men, "The sweet breath of the banshee, the welcoming climate of Zandru's ninth hell!"

"I will not hear you say—" Caryl began, but Romilly caught him around the waist before he could physically climb down the saddle and attack the speaker, and Carlo said quietly, "Enough, Caryl. A sentiment seemly for Lyondri's son, lad, but we have no time for babble. Somehow we must get across the path, and though I have no will to hurt you, if you can't keep your tongue behind your teeth, I fear you must be gagged; my men are in no mood to hear a defense of one who has set a price on our heads. And you, Garan, and you, Alaric, you shut your faces too; it's not well done to mock a child about his father's honor, and there's harder work ahead of us than quarreling with a little boy!" He looked up again as the shrilling shriek of the banshee drowned their voices, and Romilly saw his whole body tense in the effort to conquer the purely physical fear that screaming cry created in their minds. Romilly hugged Caryl tight, not sure whether it was to comfort the child or to still her own fears, whispering, "Help me quiet the animals." It was well to give him something to think about except his own terror.

Again the soothing vibration spread out, and she knew her own talent, *laran* or whatever they called it, enhanced by the already-powerful gift of the young Hastur child. As it died into silence, Alaric said, his hand on his dagger, "I have hunted banshees before this, *vai dom*, and slain them too."

"I doubt not your courage, man," said Carlo, "but your wit, if you think we can face two banshees in a narrow pass, without losing man or horse. We have no deaf-hounds, nor nets and ropes. Perhaps, if we keep between the horses and chervines, we may manage to escape with a horse for each, but then would we be afoot in the worst country in the Hellers! And if we stand here, we will be taken in the jaws of the trap."

"Better the beak of the banshee than the tender mercies of

Lyondri's men," said one of the riders, edging uneasily away from his place at the head of the little cavalcade. "I'll face what you face, my lord."

"Too bad your skill with birds extends not to such creatures as *those*," said Orain, looking at Romilly with a wry grin, "Could you but calm *those* birds as you worked with hawk and sentry-bird, then should we be as well off as any Hastur-lord with his pet *leronis!*"

Romilly shuddered at the thought . . . to enter into the minds of those cruel carnivores, prowling the heights? She said weakly "I hope you are joking, *vai dom*."

"Why should that *laran* not be as workable against banshee as against sentry-bird, or for that matter, barnyard fowl?" asked Caryl, sitting upright on the saddle, "They are all creatures of Nature, and if Rom—Rumal's Gift can quiet the sentry-birds, with my own *laran* to help, why, perhaps we can reach the banshees too, and perhaps convince them that we are not destined for their breakfast."

Romilly felt again a perceptible shudder run through her. But before young Caryl's eager eyes, she was ashamed to confess her fear.

Carlo said quietly, "I am reluctant to leave our safety in the hands of two children, when grown men are helpless. Yet if you can help us—there seems no other way, and if we delay here, we are dead men, all of us. Your father would not harm you, my young Carolin, but I fear the rest of us would die, and not too quickly or easily."

Caryl was blinking hard. He said, "I do not want any harm to come to you, sir. I do not think my father understands that you are a good man; perhaps *Dom* Rakhal has poisoned his mind against you. If I can do anything to help, so that he may have time to think more sensibly about all this quarrel, I will be very glad to do what I can." But Romilly noticed that he too looked a little frightened. And as they moved slowly forward he whispered, "I am afraid, Rumal—they look so fierce it is hard to remember that they too are the creations of God. But I will try to remember that the blessed Valentine-of-the-Snows had a pact of friendship with them and called them little brothers."

I do not think I truly wish to be brother to the banshee, Romilly thought, urging her horse forward with a little cluck and the pressure of her knee, trying to throw out soothing thoughts to calm the animal's fear. But she must not think that way. She must remember that the same Force which created the dogs and horses she loved, and the beloved

176

hawks, had created the banshee for its own purposes, even if she did not know what they were. And the sentry-birds, who looked so fierce, were gentle and loving as cagebirds, when she had gotten to know them; she truly loved Prudence, and even for Temperance and Diligence she felt a genuine affection.

If the banshee is my brother . . . and for a moment she felt an amusement bubbling up that she recognized as all but hysterical. Her gentle brother Ruyven, timid Darren, dear little Rael, in the same breath with the screaming horrors on the crag?

She heard Caryl whispering to himself; the only words she caught were, *Bearer of Burdens* and *Blessed Valentine* . . . and she knew the child was praying. She caught him tight against her, burying her face against his caped shoulder, closing her eyes. Was this true goodness, or a mad presumption, to think that somehow their minds could reach the mind of a banshee—*if the banshees have any mind*, she thought, and again forced the rising hysteria down. No one knew she was a girl, she could not cry and scream with terror! She thought, grimly, that both Orain and *Dom* Carlo looked frightened too; where they were afraid, she had no need to feel shame for her fear!

She shut her eyes again and tried to form a prayer, but could not remember any. *Bearer of Burdens, you know what I want to pray, and now I have to try and do what I can to save us all*, she said in a half-voiced whisper, then sighed and said, "We will try, Caryl. Come, link with me—"

Her mind reached out, just aware enough of her body to keep it upright in the saddle, moving with the horse's uneasy step. Reached out—she was aware of the horses, shuddering inwardly yet moving on, step by slow step, out of loyalty to their riders; of the sentry-birds, frightened at the noise, but calm because she and Caryl, whose mental voices they trusted, had bidden them be calm. She reached farther, felt something cold and terrifying, felt again the shrilling scream, shuddering through all creation, but, her hands clasped tightly in Caryl's, she stayed with it, moved into the alien mind.

At first she was conscious only of tremendous pressures, a hunger so fierce that it cramped her belly, a restless cold driving toward warmth, that seemed like light and home and satisfaction, the touch of warmth driving inward and flooding her whole body with a hunger almost sexual, and she knew, with a tiny fragment that was still Romilly, that she had reached the mind of the banshee. *Poor hungry, cold thing*

. . . it is only seeking warmth and food, like the whole of Creation. . . . Her eyes blotted out, she could not see, only feel, she *was* the banshee and for a moment she fought a raging battle, her whole mind alive with the need to fling herself upon the warmth, to rend and tear and feel the exquisitely delicious feel of warm blood bursting . . . she felt her own hands tighten on Caryl's warmth, and then with a leftover part of herself she knew she was human, a woman, with a child to protect, and others dependent on her skill. . . .

Linked tightly to Caryl, she felt his soothing mental touch, like a soft murmur, *Brother banshee, you are one with all life and one with me. The Gods created you to rend and tear at your prey, I praise and love you as the Gods made you, but there are beasts in this wilderness who know not fear because the Gods have given them no consciousness. Search for your prey among them, my little brothers, and let me pass. . . . In the name of the blessed Valentine, I bid you, bear your own burdens and seek not to end my life before the time appointed. Blessed is he who preys and blessed is he who gives life to another. . . .*

I mean you no harm, Romilly added her quiet mental appeal to the child's, *seek elsewhere for your food.*

And for a moment, in the great flooding awareness that she, and the horse she rode, and the child's soft body in her arms, and the banshee's wild hunger and seeking for warmth, were all one, a transcendent wave of joy spread through her; the red streaks of the rising sun filled her with heat and wonderful flooding happiness, Caryl's warmth against her breast was an overflow of tenderness and love, and for a dangerous moment she thought, *even if the banshee takes me for its prey, I shall be even more one with its wonderful life-force. But I too want to live and rejoice in the sunlight.* She had never known such happiness. She knew that there were tears on his face, but it did not matter, she was part of everything that lived and had breath, part of the sun and the rocks, even the cold of the glacier was somehow wonderful because it heightened her awareness of the heat of the rising sun.

Then somehow the magical link shattered and was gone. They were on the downward side of the pass, and high above them, the lumbering form of a banshee was shambling toward a cavemouth in the rocks, without paying them the slightest heed. Caryl was crying in her arms, hugging her tight. "Oh, it was hungry and we cheated it out of its breakfast."

178

She patted him, too shaken to speak, still caught up in the experience. Carlo said huskily, "Thank you, lads. I don't really want to be the banshee's breakfast, even if the poor thing was hungry, it can take its breakfast elsewhere."

The men were looking at them in awe. Orain said shakily, trying to break the spell, "Ah, you're too big and tough a boy for a banshee's delicate appetite—it would rather have a tender young ice-rabbit, I'm sure," and they all guffawed. Romilly felt weak, still under the spell of the wide-ranging enchantment they had woven with their *laran*.

Dom Carlo rummaged in his saddle-bags. He said roughly, "I can't say what I owe you two. I remember the *leroni* were starving after they did such work—here." He thrust dried meat, dried fruit, wafers of journey-bread at them. Romilly began to sink her teeth into the meat, and then somehow her gorge rose.

Once this was living, breathing flesh, how can I make it my prey? Or I am no better than the banshee. Once this dried flesh was the living breath of all my brothers. She gagged, thrust the meat from her and thrust a dried fruit into her mouth.

This too is of the life of all things, but it had no breath and it does not sicken me with the consciousness of what once it was. The Bearer of Burdens created some life with no purpose but to give up its life that others might feed . . . and as she felt the sweetness of the fruit between her teeth, briefly, the ecstasy returned, that this fruit should give up its sweetness so that she might no longer hunger. . . .

Caryl, too, was chewing ravenously at a hunk of the hard bread, but she noted that he, too, had put the meat away, though a piece had small sharp toothmarks in it. So he had shared her experience. Distantly, like something she might have dreamed a long time ago, she wondered how she could ever again eat meat.

Even when they made brief camp, with the sun high in the sky, to give grain to the horses and meat to the sentry-birds, she ate none of the dried meat, but only fruit and bread, and stirred some water into the dried porridge-powder, eating a bowlful. Yet, to her own surprise, it did not trouble her when the sentry-birds tore greedily at the somewhat gamy meat they carried for them; it was their nature, and they were as they were meant to be.

She noticed that the men still kept a wary distance. She was not surprised. If she had seen two other people quiet an attacking banshee, she would have been silent in awe, too. She still could not believe she had done it.

As they finished their meal and resaddled the horses, she looked at *Dom* Carlo, standing straight and tall at the edge of the clearing, with his face distant and listening. She was now skilled enough in the use of *laran* to know that he was extending his mental awareness along the trail behind them, toward the pass.

"So far we are not pursued," he said at last, "And the paths are so many, unless Lyondri has a horde of *leroni* with him, I do not truly think he will be able to pick up our trail. We must keep ordinary caution; but I think we can ride for Caer Donn in safety now." He held out his arms to Caryl.

"Will you ride behind my saddle, kinsman?" he asked, as if he spoke to a grown man and his equal, "There are things I would say to you."

Caryl glanced at Romilly, then collected himself and said courteously, "As you wish, kinsman." He scrambled up into the saddle. As they rode away, she could see that they were talking together in low tones, and Romilly found that she missed the child's warm weight in front of her. Once she saw Caryl shaking his head, seriously, and a word or two reached her ears.

". . . oh, no, kinsman, I give you my word of that. . . ."

Suddenly jealous of this closeness, Romilly wished she could hear what they were saying. So near, now, was her *laran* to the surface, that it occurred to her;

Perhaps I need only reach out and know.

And then she was shocked at herself. What was she thinking, she who had been reared in a Great House and taught proper courtesy toward both equals and inferiors? Why, that would be no worse than eavesdropping at doors, snooping like a nasty child, that would be completely unworthy of her.

Having the power of *laran*, certainly, did not mean that she had a right to know what did not concern her! And then, frowning as she fell into line—she had taken the sentrybird Prudence on her own saddle, so that *Dom* Carlo could carry Caryl behind him—she found herself pondering the proper manners associated with *laran*. She had the power, and perhaps the right, to force her will on the hawks she trained, on the horses she rode, even, to save her life, on the wild banshee of the crags. But how far did this power go? How far was it right to use it? She could urge her horse to bear saddle and bridle, because he loved her and willingly learned what would bring him closer to his master. She had felt Preciosa's deep love, so that the hawk returned of her free will when Romilly had set her free.

(*And that was pain. Would she ever see Preciosa again?*)

But there were limits to this power. It was right, perhaps, to quiet the dogs who loved her, so they would not awaken the household to her going.

But there was trouble, too, and a deep conflict. She could urge the prey into the beak of the hawk she hunted, she could perhaps force the young and stupid ice-rabbit into the waiting mouth of the dogs . . . surely that was not intended, that was not part of nature, that was a distinctly unfair advantage to have in hunting!

Her eyes stinging, she bent her head, and for the first time in her life found herself sincerely praying.

Bearer of Burdens! I did not ask this power. Please, please, help me use it, not for wrong purposes, but only to try and be one with life. . . . Confusedly, she added, *As I was, for a little while, this morning, when I knew that I was one with all that lived. As you must be, Holy one. Help me decide how to use this power wisely.* And after a moment she added, in a whisper, *For now I know I am a part of life . . . but such a small part!*

CHAPTER FIVE

All the long road to Caer Donn, it continued to trouble her. When she hunted meat for the sentry-birds, she thought of her *laran* and feared to use the power for evil, so that sometimes she let game escape them and was roundly scolded by the men. She did use her awareness to seek out dead things in hill and forest which she could use to feed the birds—they had no further use for their bodies, surely it could not be wrong to use a dead creature to feed a living one. She felt as if she wanted to close up her new skill where it would never be touched again, though she had to use it in handling the birds—surely it could not be wrong to show her fondness for them? Or was it, since she used it to keep them quiet for her own convenience?

There were times when she tried to handle them without calling on the MacAran Gift which she now knew to be *laran*, and when they screamed and rebelled, *Dom* Carlo demanded, "What's gotten into you, youngster? Do the work you're paid to do, and keep those birds quiet!" She had to use her *laran* then, and again suffer the conflicts as to whether she did right or wrong.

She wished she could talk to *Dom* Carlo; he had *laran* and had perhaps suffered some of these same worries when he was her age and learning to use it. Was this what Ruyven had had to overcome? No wonder he fled from a horse-training ranch and took refuge behind Tower walls! She found herself envying Darren, who had none of the MacAran Gift and though he feared and hated hawks and horses, at least he was not tempted to meddle with their minds in order to show his power over them! She could not talk to Caryl, he was only a child, and used his power with pleasure, as she had always used it since she found out she had special skill with horses and used it in training them. And whenever she tried to eat fresh-killed game, it seemed that she could feel the life and the blood of the dead animal pounding through her mind, and she would gag and refuse to eat; she made her meals of porridge and fruit and bread, and was fiercely hungry in the bitter, aching cold of the mountain trails, but even when *Dom* Carlo commanded her to eat, she could not, and once when he stood over her until she reluctantly swallowed part of a haunch of the wild chervine they had killed for their meal, she felt such terrible revulsion that she went away and vomited it up again.

Orain saw her coming back from the thicket, white and shaking, and came over to where she was, with fumbling hands, trying to cut up offal and remainder of the chervine for the sentry-birds. It was hard to find gravel in this snowy country, and so she had to mix skin and slivers of bone with the meat, or they would have further trouble in digesting. He said, "Here, give me that," and carried the mess over to the birds where they were fastened on their blocks,

182

safely above the snow. He came back leaving them to tear into it, and said, "What's the matter, lad? Off your feed, are you? Carlo means well, you know, he just was worried that you weren't eating enough for this rotten climate."

"I know that," she said, not looking at him.

"What's ailing you, youngster? Anything I can do to help?"

She shook her head. She did not think anyone could help. Unless she could somehow talk to her father, who must somehow have fought this battle himself in his youth, or how could he have come to terms with his own Gift? He might hate the very word *laran* and forbid anyone to use it in his hearing, but he possessed the thing, whatever he chose to call it or not to call it. With a sudden, homesick force, she remembered Falconsward, the face of her father, loving and kindly, and then his contorted, wrathful face as he beat her. . . . She put her face in her hands, trying desperately to stifle a fit of sobs which must surely reveal her as a girl. But she was so tired, so tired, she could hardly keep back her tears. . . .

Orain's hand was gentle on her shoulder. "There, there, son, never mind—I'm not one to think tears all that unmanly. You're ill and tired, that's all. Bawl if you want to, I'll not be telling on you." He gave her a final reassuring pat, and moved back to the fire. "Here; drink this, it'll settle your stomach," he said; sifting a few of his cherished herbs into a cup of hot water, and shoving the mug into her hand. The drink was aromatic, with a pleasant faint bitterness, and indeed made her feel better. "If you can't eat meat just now, I'll bring you some bread and fruit, but you can't go hungry in this cold." He gave her a chunk of hard bread, liberally spread with the fat of the *chervine*; Romilly was so hungry that she gulped it down, chewed on the handful of fruits he gave her as they were settling the horses for the night. He spread their blanket rolls side by side; Caryl had none, so he had been sleeping in Romilly's cloak, tucked in her arms. As she was pulling off her boots to sleep, she felt an ominous dull pain in the pit of her belly, and began secretly to count on her fingers; yes, it had been forty days since she had escaped from Rory's cabin, she must once again conceal this periodic nuisance! Damn this business of being a woman! Lying awake between Caryl and Orain, still shivering, she wondered grimly how she could manage to conceal it in this climate. Fortunately it was cold enough that nobody undressed at all in the camp, and even to sleep piled on all the clothes and blankets they had. Romilly had been sleeping, not only in the fur-lined cloak Orain had given her, but in the rough old one she had taken from Rory's cabin, rolling herself up in them both, with Caryl in her arms.

She must think. She had no spare rags, or garments which could be made into them. There was a kind of thick moss, which grew liberally all through the higher elevations, here as well as at Falconsward; she had seen it, but paid no attention—though she knew the poorer women, who had no rags to spare, used this moss for babies' diapers, packing them in it, as well as for their monthly sanitary needs. Romilly's fastidious soul felt a certain disgust, but it would be easier to bury moss in the snow than to wash out rags in this climate. Tomorrow she would find some of it; here in snow country it would, at least, not be covered with mud or dirt and need not be washed. What a nuisance it was, to be a woman!

It was so bitterly cold that they all rolled close together, like dogs sleeping in heaps; when the camp was awakening in the morning, Alaric jeered, as Orain unrolled himself from Caryl and Romilly, "Hey, man, are you running a nursery for the children?" But Orain's presence was comforting to her, and, she felt, to Caryl as well; he was gentle and fatherly, and she was not afraid of him. In fact, if it came to necessity, she did not doubt she could confide in Orain without real danger; he might be shocked at finding she was a girl in this rough country and climate, but he would not make that kind of trouble for her, any more than her own father or brothers. Somehow she *knew*, beyond all doubt, that he was not the kind of man ever to ravish or offer any offense to any woman.

She went away to attend to her personal needs in private—she had been jeered at, a bit, for this, they said she was as squeamish as a woman, but she knew they only thought it was because she was a *cristoforo*; they were known to be prudish and modest about such things. She was sure none of them suspected, and Caryl, who knew—and *Dom* Carlo, who, she felt, knew perfectly well—chose to say nothing.

But she could keep her secret as long as she could. When she came to Caer Donn, it might not be so easy as in Nevarsin to find work as hawk-keeper or horse-trainer, but certainly it could be done, and certainly Orain, or *Dom* Carlo himself, could give her a good reference as a willing and skilled worker.

She still felt a certain revulsion against eating meat, though she knew it was foolish—it was in the way of nature that some animals were prey to others, but though she knew the intense immediacy of her revulsion was beginning to fade a little, she still preferred porridge and bread to the meat, and Carlo, (she wondered if Orain had spoken to him about it?) no longer urged her to eat it, but simply gave her a somewhat larger ration of porridge and fruit. Alaric jeered at her once, and *Dom* Carlo curtly bade him be silent.

"The less there is of meat for him, the more for the rest of us, man. Let him have such food as he likes best, and you do the same! If all men were alike, you would long since have been meat for the banshee; we owe it to him to let him have his way."

They had been, she thought, nine days on the road from Nevarsin when, circling high above them, they saw a bird winging from the range of hills. Romilly was feeding the sentry-birds, and they strained at their jesses as the small bird flew down into their camp; then she saw *Dom* Carlo standing motionless, his arms extended, his face the blank, silent stare of *laran*-focused thoughts. The bird darted down; alighted and stood quivering on his hand.

"A message from our folk in Caer Donn," Carlo said, sought for the capsule under the wing and tore it open, scanning the finely-written lines. Romilly stared—she knew of message-birds who could fly back to their own loft across trackless wilds, but never of one which could seek out a particular man whose whereabouts were unknown to the sender!

Carlo raised his head, smiling broadly.

"We must make haste to Caer Donn, men," he cried out, "A tenday hence we will gather beneath Aldaran, and Carolin will be at the head of the great army which is massing there, to march on the lowlands. Now let Rakhal look to himself, my faithful fellows!"

They cheered, and Romilly cheered too. Only Caryl was silent, lowering his head and biting his lip. Romilly started to ask what was wrong, then held her tongue. He could hardly rejoice at an army massed against his father, who was Rakhal's chief advisor. It would be unfair to expect it. Yet she had seen that he loved *Dom* Carlo as a kinsman—in fact, she was sure they were kinsmen, though perhaps distant; she had heard that all of the lowland Hasturs were kin, and she was sure now, recalling Carlo's red hair, the look he had which reminded her of Alderic, that he was one of the Hastur-kin-folk, and higher in rank than any of his men knew. If Orain, who was the king's foster-brother, treated him with such deference, he must be noble indeed.

They rode into Caer Donn late in the evening, and *Dom* Carlo turned, just inside the gates of the city, to Orain.

"Take the men and the birds to a good inn," he said, "and command all my faithful people the best dinner money can buy; they have had a hard journey and paid dearly for their following of the exiles. You know where I must be going—"

"Aye, I know," said Orain, and Carlo smiled faintly and gripped his hand. He said, "A day will come—"

"All the Gods grant it," said Orain, and Carlo rode away through the streets of the city.

If she had never seen Nevarsin, Romilly might have thought Caer Donn a big city. High on the side of the mountain above the town, a castle rose, and Orain said as they rode, "The home of Aldaran of Aldaran. The Aldarans are Hastur-kin from old days, but they have no part in lowland strife. Yet blood-ties are strong."

"Is the king there?" asked Romilly, and Orain smiled and drew a deep breath of relief. "Aye, we are back in country where that beast Rakhal is not admired, and Carolin is still true king of these lands," he said. "And the birds we've brought will be in the hands of the king's *leroni* in a few days. Pity you've not the training of a *laranzu*, lad, you have the touch. You've done Carolin's men a service, believe me, and the king will not be ungrateful when he comes to his throne."

He looked down the streets. "Now, if memory fails me not, I recall an inn near the city wall, where our birds may be housed and our beasts fed, and that good meal Carlo commanded may be found," he said, "Let's go and find it."

As they rode through the narrow street, Caryl pushed close to his side.

"Lord Orain, you—the *vai dom* pledged me I should be sent back to my father under a truce-flag. Will he honor that pledge? My father—" his voice broke, "My father must be wild with fear for me."

"Good enough!" Alaric said harshly, "Let him feel some o'what I feel, with my son and his mother dead—at your father's hands—"

Caryl stared at him with his eyes wide. Finally he said, "I did not recognize you, Master Alaric; now I recall you. You wrong my father, sir; he did not kill your son, he died of the bald fever; my own brother died that same summer, and the king's healer-women tended them both as carefully. It was sad that your son died away from his father and mother, but on my honor, Alaric, my father had no hand in your son's death."

"And what of my poor wife, who flung herself from the window to death when she heard her son had died far away from her—"

"I did not know that," Caryl said, and there were tears in his eyes, "My own mother was beside herself with grief; when my brother died. I was afraid to be out of my mother's sight for fear she would do herself some harm in her grief. I am sorry—oh, I am sorry, Master Alaric," he said, and flung his arms around the man, "If my father had known this, I am sure he would not pursue you, nor blame you for your quarrel with him!"

Alaric swallowed; he stood without moving in the boy's embrace and said, "God grant my own son would have defended me like to that. I canna' fault you for your loyalty to your father, my boy. I'll help Lord Orain see ye get back safe to him."

Orain heaved a great sigh of relief. He said, "We'll not send you into danger in the lowlands without an army behind you, Alaric; ye'll stay here with the army. But here in this city is a hostel of the Sisterhood of the Sword; my cousin is one of the swordswomen, and we can hire two or three of these women to go south to Thendara and take the lad safe there. I'll speak to *Dom* Carlo about it, Caryl, and perhaps you can leave day after tomorrow. And perhaps a message-bird could be sent to your father at Hali, to tell him you are well and safe, and to be escorted safe back to him."

"You are kind to me, Lord Orain," said Caryl simply. "I have enjoyed this trip, but I do not like to think of my father's grief, or my mother's if she knows I am not safe in Nevarsin where she thought me."

"I'll see to it, soon as we reach the inn," said Orain, and led the way toward a long, low building, with stables at the back, and a sign with a crudely-painted hawk. "Here at the Sign of the Hawk we can dine well and rest after that miserable trip through the snows. And how many of you would like to order a bath, as well? There are hot springs in the city and a bath-house not ten doors away."

That roused another cheer, but Romilly thought, a little glumly, that it did her no good; she certainly could not risk a man's bath-house, though she felt grubby and longed to be clear! Well, there was no help for it. She saw the horses and chervines properly stabled, cared for the sentry-birds, and after washing her face and hands as well as she could, went in for the good meal Orain had commanded in the inn. He had ordered rooms for them all to sleep, saying that he had taken the best room the inn offered for young Caryl, as his rank demanded.

"And you are yourself welcome to share my own quarters, Rumal, lad."

"It is kind of you," Romilly said warily, "but I will stay in the stable with my charges, lest the sentry-birds be restless in a strange place."

Orain shrugged. "As you will," he said. "But another thing I would ask you over dinner."

"What you wish, sir."

They went in to the dining-room; there was fresh-baked bread and baked roots, plump and golden, as well as some roasted birds and a stew of vegetables; everyone ate hugely after the long spartan fare of the travelling, and Orain had commanded plenty of wine and beer as well. But he refused Caryl wine, in a kind and fatherly way, and frowned at Romilly when she would have taken her second mug of it.

"You know very well you've no head for it," he scolded, "Waiter! Bring the boys some cider with spiceroot in it."

"Aw," Alaric teased good-naturedly, for once, "Old Mammy Orain, will ye put them to bed and sing 'em a lullabye, while the rest of us are all off to soak out our long travel in the bath-house?"

"Nay," said Orain, "I'm for the baths with the rest of you."

"And for a house of women soon after that," called out one of the man, taking a great spoonful of the stewed fruits that had finished the meal, "I haven't looked at a woman for Zandru knows how long!"

"Aye, and I mean to do more than look," called another one, and Orain said, "Do what you like, but this is no talk before the children."

"I hope for a bath too," said Caryl, but Orain shook his head.

"The bath-house here in the city is not like the one in the monastery, my boy, but a place of resort for whores and such like as well; I can take care of myself, but it's no place for a respectable lad of your years. I'll order you a tub of water in your own room, where you may wash and soak and then to bed and rest well. You too," he said, scowling faintly at Romilly, "You're young for the rough folk at the bath-house; see you that the lad here washes his feet well, and then call for a bath for yourself; you'd be too easy prey for the low-life folk who hang about such places, as much so as if you were a young and respectable maiden."

"Why coddle the boy?" demanded Alaric, "Let him see something of life, as no doubt you did when you were of his years, Lord Orain!"

Orain scowled. "What I may have done is not to the point; the boy's in my charge, and so is Lyondri's son here, and it's not fit a Hastur should go without service. You stay here, Rumal, and look after the lad, see him into his bed. You'll get a bath to yourself then."

"Stand up to him for your rights, lad, you don't have to be treated like a child," said one of the men, who had drunk more than enough wine, "You're no servant to the Hastur-pup!"

Romilly said, relieved at this solution, "Indeed I would as soon stay here; I am a *cristoforo* and have no taste for such adventures."

"Oh ah, a *cristoforo* bound to the Creed of Chastity," jeered Alaric, "Well, I did my best for ye, boy, if ye'd rather be a little boy hiding behind the skirts of the holy Bearer of Burdens, that's for you to say! Come along! Who's for the bath-house, men?"

One after another, they rose and went, not too steadily, into the street. Romilly took Caryl upstairs and sent for the promised bath; when the serving-woman brought it, she would have bathed him as she had done with Rael, but he turned on her, his face pink.

"I won't say anything before the men," he said, "but I know you're a girl, and I'm too big for my mother or my sister, even, to wash me, and I can bathe myself! Go away, mistress Romilly. I'll have them send you a bath too, shall I? Lord Orain is away and doubtless he'll be at the baths half the night, he may be looking for a woman too—see, I'm old enough to know about such things. So you can bathe in his room and go to your own bed afterward."

Romilly could not help but laugh. She said "As you will, my lord."

"And don't make fun of me!"

"I wouldn't dream of it," Romilly said, trying to keep her face straight. "But Lord Orain charged me with the task of seeing that you wash your feet well."

"I have been bathing myself in the monastery for more than a year," said Caryl, exasperated, "Go away, mistress Romilly, before my bath water gets cold, and I will have them send a bathtub to you in Lord Orain's room."

Romilly was grateful for this solution—indeed she had longed for a hot bath, and went to the stable for her saddlebags while the bath-women were hauling the wooden tub into the room and pouring out steaming water into it, laying out great fluffy towels and a wooden cask of soapweed. One of the bath-women lingered, widening her eyes at Romilly and saying in a suggestive voice, "Would you like me to stay and help you, young sir? Indeed, it would be a pleasure to wash your feet and scrub your back, and for half a silver bit I will stay as long as you like, and share your bed as well."

Romilly had to struggle again to hide a smile; this was embarrassing. Was she such a handsome young man as that, or was the woman only looking for her silver bit? She shook her head and said, "I am tired with riding; I want to wash and sleep."

"Shall I send you a masseur, then, young sir?"

"No, no, nothing—go away and leave me to bathe," Romilly said sternly, but she gave the woman a small coin and thanked her for her trouble. "You can come and take the tub away in an hour."

Assured at last of privacy, she stripped and climbed into the tub, scrubbing herself vigorously with soapweed, lying back in the hot water with a sigh of luxurious content. She had last washed herself all over in the old woman's cabin, when she was pretending she would be married to Rory. At Nevarsin she had washed as best she could, but had not, of course, dared to use the bath-house in the monastery, nor had she dared to try and find a woman's bath-house in Nevarsin, though there must have been some of them, lest she be seen coming from the place.

What a splendid thing a bath was! She lay in the hot water, soaking and enjoying it, till the water finally cooled and she got out, dried her hair carefully, and put on her cleanest underclothing. She looked longingly at Orain's bed, spread up for him by the maids; no doubt he was finished at the bathhouse and had found a woman somewhere for the night, and this good bed would be wasted, while he slept in some street-woman's bed. She realized that she felt a twinge of jealousy—she remembered her dream, where Orain had caressed her, sleeping, and she had been happy that he should touch her—did she really envy the unknown woman in whose bed he was spending this night?

Well, she should ring for the bath-woman to take away the tub and go to her own quarters in the stables; there was plenty of hay to keep her warm, and blankets, and she could even command hot bricks and more blankets if she wished. She pulled on her breeches and rang for the bath-woman, and went, knocking softly at Caryl's door. He was in bed and already half asleep, but he sat up in bed to hug her as if she were his own sister, wishing her a good night, and slid down, asleep already in the big bed. It *was* a big bed, big enough for three or four, she was tempted to lie down and sleep beside the child, they had slept curled up together often enough on the road. But she realized that he would be embarrassed if he found her there in the morning—he was just old enough to be aware that she was a woman. It would not matter so much, she thought, yawning and reluctant to go out to the stable, if she lay down to sleep a little—no doubt Orain would not return home before morning, and if he did he would be so drunk that he would not notice her there, nor care whether she was a boy or a dog; he would never know she was a woman, if he had travelled with her all this time and not known, and he had none of the inconvenient *laran* which had betrayed her to Caryl and perhaps to *Dom* Carlo.

She would sleep here a little, at least—she could wake and be away to the stable if she heard Orain coming up the stairs. The bed looked so good, after all this time on the road. The bath-woman, when she took the tub away, had warmed the sheets with a pan of hot coals, and they smelled fresh and inviting. Romilly hesitated no more, but lay down in her tunic and drawers, pulling up the covers and drowsing. At the edge of her mind, wary, she thought, I must not entirely go to sleep, I should go out to the stable, Orain may be coming back before I expect him . . . and then she was asleep.

The door creaked, and Orain, stepping quietly, was in the room, throwing off his clothes and yawning, sitting on the edge of the bed. Romilly sat up, shocked and startled that she had slept so long. He grinned at her.

"Ah, stay where you are, boy," he said drowsily, "Bed's big enough for two." He had been drinking, she could tell, but he was not drunk. He reached out and ran his hand lightly across her hair. "So soft, you must ha' had a nice bath too."

"I will go now—"

He shook his head. "The outside door o' the inn's locked; ye couldna' get out." His voice was again overlaid with the soft low-country accent. "Stay here, lad—I'm half asleep a'ready." He drew off his boots and outer garments; Romilly, rolling to the far edge of the bed, tucked her head down under the blanket and fell asleep.

191

She never knew what waked her, but she thought it was a cry: Orain tossed, turned over, cried out, and sat bolt upright. "Ah—Carolin, they will have ye'—" he cried, staring into the empty room, his voice so full of terror that Romilly knew he dreamed. She tugged at his arm and said, "Wake up! It's only a nightmare!"

"Ah—" he drew a long breath and sanity came into his face again. "I saw my brother, my friend, in the hands of Rakhal, Zandru send him scorpion whips—" His face was still troubled, but he lay back down, and Romilly, curling her feet up, sought to go back to sleep. After a time, however, she was aware that Orain's arm was around her, that he was gently drawing her to him.

She pulled away, frightened. He said in his gentlest voice, "Ah, lad, don't you know how I feel? You're so like Carolin, when we were boys together—red hair—and so timid and shy, but so brave when there's need—"

Romilly thought, shaking, *but there's no need for this, I am a woman—he does not know, but it's all right, I will tell him it's all right—* She was trembling with embarrassment, shy, but still the very real warmth and kindness she felt for Orain made her feel, this was not at all as it had been when *Dom* Garris sought to paw her, nor when Rory sought to force himself on her—

She sat upright and put her arms around him, laying her head on his shoulder. "It's all right, all right, Orain," she whispered, close to his cheek, "You knew all the time, didn't you? I—I—" she couldn't say it. She took his hand and put it inside her tunic, against her breast.

He sat upright, jerking away, his face flaming.

"Hell's fire," he whispered, in incredulous embarrassment, shock, and, Romilly realized with horror, real dismay, "Hell's fire, you're a girl!" And he actually leaped out of bed and stood staring at her, pulling his nightshirt together over his body with shock and modestly looking away from her.

"Mistress—*damisela*, a thousand pardons, I most humbly beg your pardon—never, never, I did not guess for a moment—Avarra's mercy, mistress, I cannot believe it! Who are you?"

She said, shaking with cold and her whole body trembling with the shock of the rejection, "Romilly MacAran," and burst into tears.

"Oh, blessed Gods," Orain implored, bending to wrap the blanket round her, "I—don't cry, someone will hear you, I wouldna' hurt you for the world, lady——" and he gulped and stood back, shaking his head in dismay.

"What an unholy mess this is, and what a damnable fool I've made of myself! Forgive me, lady, I wouldn't lay a finger on you——" Romilly cried harder than ever, and he bent, urgently hushing her.

"Ah, don't cry, little lady, there's nothing to cry about—look, hush, we're friends anyway, aren't we, I don't care if ye're a girl, you must have some reasons——" and as she sought to stifle her weeping, he wiped her nose gently with the sheet and sat down beside her. "There now, there now, that's a good girl, don't cry—sweeting, I think you'd better tell me all about it, hadn't you?"

Book Three:

SWORDSWOMAN

CHAPTER ONE

———•——•◆•——•———

Snow had fallen toward morning, and the streets of Caer Donn were piled high with trackless white. All the same, there was a softness in the air which told the country-bred Romilly that the spring thaw was nearing and this was the last blow of the winter.

Father always said that only the mad or the desperate travel in the winter; now I have crossed the worst of the Hellers after Midwinter-night. Why am I thinking of that now?

Orain patted her shoulder with the same clumsy deference he had shown since last night. It made her want to weep for the old, lost, easy companionship. She should have known he would not have liked her half so well as a woman; it was, when she really took thought, written clear all over him and must have been evident to everyone in the company except herself.

"Here we are, *damisela*," he said, and Romilly snapped, raw-edged, "My name is Romilly, Orain, and I have not changed so much as all *that*."

His eyes, she thought, looked like a dog's that had been kicked. He said, "Here is the hostel of the Sisterhood," and went up the steps, leaving her to follow.

Once he knew—certainly he could not allow her to face the dangers of life in camp and trail. He would always be aware, now, of her unwelcome womanhood. This was, after all, the best answer.

A hard-faced woman, with heavy hands which would have seemed more appropriate holding a hayfork, welcomed them to the front hall—or, Romilly thought, welcome was not quite the right word, but she did let them in. Orain said, "Kindly inform Mistress Jandria that her cousin has come to visit her." His voice was again the impeccably courteous, well-bred voice of the courtier, with the last trace of the soft country accent carefully hidden. The woman stared suspiciously, and said, "Sit there," pointing to a bench as if they were a pair of street urchins come a-begging. She went away down the hall and Romilly heard women's voices at the far end of the building. Somewhere there was the noise of a hammer on an anvil—at least that was what it sounded like—and the small, familiar, friendly, chink-chink-chinking sound made Romilly a little less rigid with apprehension. All the doors along the hallway were closed, but as they sat there, two young women, wearing crimson tunics, their hair all tucked under red caps, went through the hallway arm in arm. They were obviously not what Romilly's stepmother would have called ladies; one of them had great red hands like a milkmaid's, and were wearing loose long trousers and boots.

At the back of the hall another woman appeared. She was slender and pretty, and, Romilly thought, about Orain's own age, forty or more, though her dark, close-cropped hair had faded, with streaks of grey at the temples.

"Well, kinsman," she said, "What's that ye've got wi' ye'?" She had the country accent Orain had learned to conceal. "And what brings ye' into this country in winter? King's business, I hear—and how's himself?" She came and gave him a quick, breezy embrace and a haphazard kiss somewhere on the side of his face.

"The king is well, Aldones be praised," said Orain quietly, "and with the Aldarans at the moment. But I have two charges for you, Janni."

"Two?" Her salt-and-pepper eyebrows went up in a comical grimace. "First of all, what's this, boy or girl or hasn't he or she made up its mind?"

Romilly, with a scalding blush, bent her eyes on the floor; the woman's good-natured mockery seemed to take her in and sort her out and discard her as useless.

"Her name is Romilly MacAran," said Orain quietly, "Don't mock her, Janni, she travelled with us through the

195

worst climate and country in the Hellers and not one of us, not even myself, knew her for a girl. She did her full share and cared for our sentry-birds, which I'd never known a woman could do. She brought them through alive and in good condition, and the horses too. I thought she was a capable lad, but it's even more extraordinary than I thought. So I brought her to you—"

"Having no use for her, once ye' found she wasna' one of your lads," said Jandria, with an ironical grin. Then she looked straight at Romilly.

"Can't you speak for yourself, girl? What led you into the mountains in men's clothes? If it was the better to seek a man, take yerself off again, for we want no girls among us to give us the name of harlots in disguise! We travel with the armies, but we are not camp-followers, be that understood! Why did ye' leave home?"

Her sharp tone put Romilly on the defensive. She said, "I left my home because my father took the hawk I trained myself, with my own hands, and gave it to my brother; and I thought that not fair. Also, I had no will to marry the Heir to Scathfell, who would have wanted me to sit indoors and embroider cushions and bear his ugly children!"

Jandria's eyes were sharp on her. "Afraid of the marriage-bed and childbirth, hey?"

"No, that's not it," Romilly said sharply, "but I like horses and hounds and hawks and if I should ever marry—" she did not know she was going to say this until she said it, "I would want to marry a man who wants me as I am, not a pretty painted doll he can call wife without ever thinking what or who she is! And I would rather marry a man who does not think his manhood threatened if his wife can sit in a saddle and carry a hawk! But I would rather not marry at all, or not now. I want to travel, and to see the world, and to do things—" she broke off. She was saying this very badly. She sounded like a discontented and disobedient daughter, no more. Well, so she was and no otherwise, and if Mistress Jandria did not like her, well, she had lived as a man before in secret and could do so again if she must! "I am not asking charity of you, Mistress Jandria, and Orain knows me better than that!"

Jandria laughed. "My name is Janni, Romilly. And Orain does not know anything about women."

"He liked me well enough till he found out I was a woman," Romilly said, prickled again by that thought, and Janni laughed again and said, "That is what I mean. Now

196

that he knows, he will never see anything about you except that you should be wearing skirts and sending out signs, so that he will not be led unwitting into trusting you. He let down his guard before you, I doubt not, thinking it safe, and now he will never forgive you for it—isn't that it?"

"You are too hard on me, Janni," said Orain uneasily, "But sure you must see that Mistress MacAran cannot travel with men and live rough in a camp with hard men such as I command!"

"In spite of the fact that she has done so for a span of ten-days," said Jandria, with that flicker of a wry grin. "Well, you are right, this is the place for her, and if she is good with horses and birds, we can always make use of her, if she is willing to live by our rule."

"How do I know until I know what that is?" demanded Romilly, and Jandria laughed. "I like her, cousin. You can go and leave her to me, I won't bite her. But wait, you said you had another charge for me—"

"Yes," Orain said, "Lyondri Hastur's son; Carolin. He was a student in Nevarsin monastery, and he came into our hands as a hostage—never mind how, it's better if you don't know. But I have given my word I will have the boy sent back to Thendara under truce-flag when the passes are open, and un-harmed. I cannot go myself—"

"No," Jandria said, "You certainly cannot; for all your head's stuffed with old rubbish and ugly as sin, it adorns your shoulders better than it would adorn a pike outside Lyondri's den! Yes, we'll take the lad to Thendara for you; I may even go myself. Lyondri has certainly not seen my face since we danced together at children's parties and would not remember it without long curls and bows in my hair." She chuckled as at a secret joke. "How old is young Carolin now? He must be eight or nine—"

"Twelve, I think," Orain said, "and a nice child; it's pity he got himself mixed up in this, but he saved my neck and my men's and Carolin has cause to be grateful to his godson, so guard him well, Janni."

She nodded. "I'll take him south as soon as the passes are open, then; you can send him to me here." She chuckled and gave Orain another of her quick, offhand hugs. "And now you must go, kinsman—what of my reputation, if it is known I entertain a man here? Worse, what of yours, if it is found out you can speak civilly to a woman?"

"Oh, come, Janni—" protested Orain, but he rose to take

his leave. He looked, embarrassed, at Romilly, and stuck out his hand. "I wish you well, *damisela*."

This time she did not bother to correct him. If he could not see that she was the same whether in boy's clothes or the name of a Great House, well, so much the worse for him; he did not sound like her friend Orain at all, and she could have cried again, but she did not, for Janni was staring appraisingly at her.

After the door closed behind Orain, she said, "Well, and what happened? Did he try and lure ye' to bed, and recoil in unholy horror when he found out you were a woman?"

"That's not quite how it happened," said Romilly, moved to defend Orain without knowing why, "It was—he had been kind to me, and I thought he knew I was a woman, and wanted me so—I am not a wanton," she defended herself, "Once I came near to killing a man who would have had me against my will." She shivered and shut her eyes; she had thought she was free of the nagging horror of Rory's attempted rape, but she was not. "But Orain was good, and I—I liked him well, and I only thought to be kind to him, if it was what he wanted so much."

Janni smiled, and Romilly wondered, defensively, what was funny. But the older woman only said, quite kindly, "And you are a maiden still, I doubt not."

"I am not ashamed of it," Romilly flared.

"How prickly you are! Well, will you live by our rule?"

"If you will tell me what it is, I will answer you," she said, and Janni smiled again.

"Well then; will you be sister to all of us, whatever rank we may bear? For we leave rank behind us when we come into the Sisterhood; you will not be *My Lady* or *damisela* here, and no one will know or care that you were born in a Great House. You must do your share of whatever work falls to us, and never ask quarter or special consideration because you are a woman. And if you have love affairs with men, you must conduct them in decent privacy, so that no man can ever call the Sisterhood a company of camp-followers. Most of us are sworn to live celibate while we follow the armies and the sword, though we do not force it upon anyone."

It sounded exactly like what Romilly would have wished for. She said so.

"But will you swear it?"

"Gladly," Romilly said.

"You must swear, as well, that your sword will always be ready to defend any of your sisters, in peace or war, should any man lay a hand on one who does not wish for it," said Jandria.

"I would be glad to swear to that," Romilly said, "but I do not think my sword would be any good to them; I know nothing about swordplay."

Now Janni smiled and hugged her. She said, "We will teach you that. Come, bring your things into the inner room. Did that dolt Orain remember to give you breakfast, or was he in so much of a hurry to hustle you away from the camp that he forgot that women get hungry too?"

Romilly, still sore with rejection and pain, did not want to join Janni in making fun of Orain, but it sounded so much like what had actually happened, that she could not help but laugh. "I am hungry, yes," she confessed, and Janni hoisted one of her bundles.

"I have a horse in the stable of the inn," Romilly said, and Janni nodded. "I will send one of the sisters for it, in your name. Come into the kitchen—breakfast is long over, but we can always find some bread and honey—and then we will pierce your ears so that you can wear our sign and other women will know that you are one of us. Tonight you may take the oath. Only for a year at first," she warned, "and then, if you like the life, for three; and when you have lived among us for four years, you may decide if you wish to pledge for a lifetime, or if you wish to go on your own, or to return to your family and marry."

"Never!" Romilly said fervently.

"Well, we will fly that hawk when her pinions are grown," said Janni, "but for now you may take the sword with us, and if you have some skill with hawks and horses, we will welcome you all the more; our old horse-trainer, Mhari, died of the lung-fever this winter, and the women who worked with her are all away with the armies to the south. None of the girls in the hostel now are even much good at riding, let alone for breaking them to the saddle—can you do that? We have four colts ready to be saddle-broken, and more at our big hostel near Thendara."

"I was raised to it at Falconsward," Romilly said, but Janni raised a hand in caution.

"None of us have any family or past beyond our names; I warned you, you are not *my lady* or *Mistress MacAran* among us," she said, and, rebuked, Romilly was silent.

Yet, whatever I call myself, I am Romilly MacAran of Falconsward. I was not boasting of my lineage, only telling her how I came to be so trained—I would hardly have

199

learned it at some croft in the hills! But if she chooses to think I was boasting, nothing I would say can change it, and she must think what she likes. Romilly felt as if she were old and cynical and worldly-wise, having arrived at this much wisdom. She followed Janni silently along the corridor, and through the large double doors at the end of the hall.

Her lineage too must be good, for all her refusal to speak of it, since she spoke of dancing with Lyondri Hastur at children's parties. Maybe she too has been warned against speaking of her past.

It was a long and busy day. She ate bread and cheese and honey in the kitchen, was sent to practice some form of unarmed combat among a group of young girls, all of whom were more adept than she—she did not understand a single movement of the ones they were trying to teach her, and felt clumsy and foolish—and later in the day, a hard-faced woman in her sixties gave her a wooden sword like the ones she and Ruyven had played with when they were children, and tried to teach her the basic defensive moves, but she felt completely hopeless at that too. There were so many women—or it seemed like many, though she found out at dinner-time that there were only nineteen women in the hostel—that she could not even remember their names. Later she was allowed to make friends with the horses in the stable, where her own was brought—she found it easier to remember *their* names—and there were a few *chervines* too. Then Janni pierced her ears and put small gold rings into them. "Only while they are healing," she said, "Later you shall have the ensign of the Sisterhood, but for now you must keep twisting the rings so that the holes will heal cleanly, and bathe them three times a day in hot water and thornleaf." Then, in front of the assembled women, only a blur of faces to Romilly's tired eyes, she prompted her through the oath to the Sisterhood, and it was done. Until spring-thaw of the next year, Romilly was oath-bound to the Sisterhood of the Sword. That finished, they crowded around and asked her questions, which she was hesitant to answer in the face of Janni's prohibition that she must not speak of her past life, and then they found her a much-patched, much-worn nightgown, and sent her to sleep in a long room lined with half-a-dozen beds, tenanted by girls her own age or younger. It seemed that she had hardly fallen asleep before she was wakened by the sound of a bell, and she was washing her face and dressing in a room full of half a dozen young women, all running around half-dressed and squabbling over the washbasins.

For the first few days it seemed to Romilly that she was always gasping behind a group of girls who were running somewhere just ahead of her and she must somehow keep up. The lessons in unarmed combat frightened and confused her—and the woman who taught them was so harsh and angry of voice. Although, one afternoon, when she had been sent to help in the kitchens, where she felt more at home, the woman, whose name was Merinna, came in and asked her for some tea, and when Romilly brought it, chatted with her so amiably that Romilly began to suspect that her harshness in class was assumed to force them all to pay strict attention to what they were doing. The lessons in swordplay were easier, for she had sometimes been allowed to watch Ruyven's lessons, and had sometimes practiced with him— when she had been eight or nine, her father had been amused by her handling of a sword, though later, when she was older, he forbade her even to watch, or to touch even a toy sword. Gradually those early lessons came back to her, and she began to feel fairly confident at least with the wooden batons which served in practice.

Among the horses in the stable, she felt completely at home. This work she had done since she was old enough to rub soapweed on a saddle and polish it with oil.

She was hard at work polishing saddle-tack one day when she heard a noise in the street outside, and one of the youngest girls in the house ran in to call her.

"Oh, Romy, come—the king's army is passing by at the end of the street, and Merinna has given us leave to run out and see! Carolin will march southward as soon as the passes are open—"

Romilly dropped the oily rag and ran out into the street with Lillia and Marga. They crowded into an angle of the doors and watched; the street was filled with horses and men, and people were lining the streets and cheering for Carolin.

"Look, look, there he goes under the fir-tree banner, blue and silver—Carolin, the king," called someone, and Romilly craned her neck to see, but she could catch only a glimpse of a tall man, with a strong ascetic profile not unlike Carlo's, in the instant before his cloak blew up and she could see only his russet hair flying.

"Who is the tall skinny man riding behind him?" someone asked, and Romilly, who would have known him even in darkness with his face hidden, said, "His name is Orain, and I have heard he is one of Carolin's foster-brothers."

"I know him," said one of the girls, "he came to visit Jandria, someone told me that he was one of her kin, though I don't know whether to believe it or not."

Romilly watched the horses, men, banners moving by, with detachment and regret. She might still have been riding with them, had she gone to her own bed in the stable that night, still at Orain's side, still treated as his friend and equal. But it was too late for that. She turned about sharply and said, "Let's go inside and finish our work—I have seen horses enough before this and a king is a man like other men, Hastur or no."

The armies, she heard, were being moved to a great plain outside Caer Donn. A few days later, she was summoned to Janni, and when she went out into the main room where she had met Janni first, she saw Orain again, with Caryl at his side.

Orain greeted her with some constraint, but Caryl rushed at once into her arms.

"Oh, Romilly, I have missed you! Why, you are dressed like a woman, that is good, now I will not have to remember to speak to you as if you were a boy," he said.

"*Dom* Carolin," Janni said formally, and he turned his attention respectfully to her.

"I listen, *mestra*," he said, using the politest of terms for a female inferior in rank.

"The Lord Orain has commissioned me to escort you to Hali and return you, under safe-conduct, to your father," she said, "and there are two choices before you; I am prepared to treat you as a man of honor, and to ask your preference, instead of making the decision for you. Are you old enough to listen to me seriously, and to answer sensibly and keep your word?"

His small face was as serious as when he had sung in the chapel at Nevarsin. "I am, *mestra* Jandria."

"Well, then, it is simple. Shall I treat you as a prisoner and have you guarded—and, make no mistake, we are women, but we shall not be careless with you and allow you to escape."

"I know that, *mestra*," he said politely, "I had a governess once who was much harsher with me than any of the masters and brothers in the monastery."

"Well, then," said Janni, "Will you be our prisoner, or will you give us your parole, not to attempt to escape our hands, so that you may ride beside us and take such pleasure in the trip as you can? It will not be an easy journey, and it will be simpler if we can allow you to ride without watching you every moment of the night and day, nor have you tied up at night. I will have no hesitation in taking the word of a Hastur, if you give me your parole of honor."

He did not answer at once. He asked, "Are you my father's enemies?"

"Not particularly," said Janni, "Of your father, my lad, I know only what I have been told; but I am Rakhal's enemy, and your father is his friend, so I trust him not. But then, I have not asked for his word of honor, either. I am dealing with you, *Dom* Carolin, not with him."

He said, "Is Romilly coming with us?"

"I thought to put you in her charge, since she has travelled with you before, if that is agreeable to you, young sir."

He smiled then, and said, "I would like to travel with Romilly. And I will gladly give you my word of honor not to try and escape. I could not travel through the Hellers alone, whatever happened. I promise you, then, *mestra*, to be at your orders until I am returned to my father's hands."

"Very well," Janni said, "I accept your word, as you may accept mine, that I will treat you as I would one of my own sisters, and offer you no indignity. Will you give me your hand on it, *Dom* Carolin?"

He held out his hand and took hers. Then he said, "You need not call me *Dom* Carolin, *mestra*. That is the name of the former king, who is my father's enemy, though he is not really mine. I am called Caryl."

"Then you shall call me Janni, Caryl," she said, smiling at last, "and you shall be our guest, not our prisoner. Romy, take him to the guest-room and make him comfortable. Orain—" she raised her eyes to her cousin, "we shall set out tomorrow, if the weather allows."

"I thank you, cousin. And you," he added, turning to Romilly, bending ceremoniously—like a courtier, she thought—over her hand. She thought, heart-sore, that a few days before, he would have taken leave of her with a rough hug. She hoped, suddenly and passionately, that she and Orain would never meet again.

They rode out of Caer Donn very early in the morning, and had been more than an hour on the road before the red sun rose, huge and dripping with mist. Caryl rode on the pony Jandria had found for him, side by side with Romilly's horse; behind them were six women of the Sisterhood, leading, on long pack-reins, a dozen good horses which, they said, were for the armies in the South. They did not say *which* armies, and Romilly carefully did not ask.

It was good to be riding free again in the sunlight, without the cold and storms of her earlier journey through the Hellers. They stopped at noon to feed the horses and rest them for a little, then rode on. In late afternoon they made camp, and at Jandria's command, one of the pack-horses was offloaded, and as two women sat about making fire, Janni called to Romilly.

"Come here and help me, Romy, with this tent——"

Romilly had no notion of how to set up a tent, but she obediently hauled ropes and drove in pegs where Janni ordered, and within a minute or two a large and roomy shelter of waterproof canvas was ready for them. Blanket-rolls were spread out within it, and under its hanging flap the evening drizzle could not dampen their fire or their supper. Very soon porridge was cooked, hot and savory with sliced onions frizzled in the fat of a roast fowl, and the women sat crosslegged on their bed-rolls, eating their food out of wooden bowls which had come out of the same pack.

"This is nice," said Caryl admiringly, "Men never make a camp as comfortable as this."

Janni chuckled. "There is no reason they should not," she said, "They are as good at cookery and hunting as we women are, and they would tell you so if you asked them; but maybe they think it unmanly to seek for comfort in the fields, and enjoy hard living because it makes them feel tough and strong. As for me, I have no love for sleeping in the rain, and I am not ashamed to admit I like to be comfortable."

"So do I," said Caryl, gnawing on the ends of his bone, "This is good, Janni. Thank you."

One of the women, not one that Romilly knew well, whose name was Lauria, took a small hand-harp from her pack and began to play a tune. They sat around the fire, singing mountain ballards, for half an hour or so. Caryl listened, bright-eyed, but after a time he fell back, drowsily, half asleep.

Janni signed to Romilly, and said, "Take off his boots, will you, and get him into his sleeping-roll?"

"Of course," Romilly said, and began to pull off Caryl's boots. He sat up and protested sleepily. Lauria said, grumbling, "Let the boy wait on himself, Romy! Janni, why should one of our sisters wait on this young man, who is our prisoner? We're no subjects or servants to the Hastur-kind!"

"He's only a boy," Janni said, placatingly, "and we're being well-paid to care for him."

"Still, the Sisterhood are no slaves to one of these men," grumbled Lauria, "I wonder at you, Janni, that for money you'd take a commission to escort some boy-child through the mountains—"

"Boy child or girl, the boy cannot travel alone," said Janni, "and needs not be drawn into the quarrels of his elders! And Romilly is willing to care for him—"

"I doubt not," said one of the strange women with a sneer, "One of those women who still think her duty in life is to wait on some man, hand and foot—she would disgrace her earring—"

"I look after him because he is sleepy, too sleepy to wait on himself," Romilly flared, "and because he is about the age of my own little brothers! Didn't you look after your own little brother if you had one, or did you think yourself too good to look after anyone but yourself? If the Holy Bearer of Burdens could carry the World-child on his shoulders across the River of Life, shall I not care for any child who comes into my hands?"

"Oh, a *cristoforo*," sneered one of the younger women, "Do you recite the Creed of Chastity before you sleep, then, Romy?"

Romilly started to fling back an angry retort—she made no rude remarks about the Gods of others, they could keep their mouths off her own religion—but then she saw Janni's frown and said, mildly, "I can think of worse things I might be saying." She turned her back on the angry girl, and went to spread out Caryl's blanket beside her own.

"Are we to have a male in our tent to sleep with us?" the girl who had protested asked angrily, "This is a tent for women."

"Oh, hush, Mhari, the boy can hardly sleep out in the rain with the horses," Janni said crossly. "The rule of the Sisterhood is intended for common sense, and the boy's no more than a baby! Are you fool enough to think he'll come into our blankets and ravish one of us?"

"It is a matter of principle," said Mhari sullenly, "Because the brat is a Hastur, are we to let him intrude into a place of the Sisterhood? I would feel the same if he were no more than two years old!"

"Then I hope you will never have the bad taste to bear a son instead of a daughter," said Janni lightly, "or will you, out of principle, refuse to feed a male at your breast? Go to sleep, Mhari; the child can sleep between me and Romilly, and we'll guard your virtue."

Caryl opened his mouth; Romilly poked him in the ribs, and he subsided without speaking. She saw that he was trying not to giggle aloud. It seemed a little silly to her, but she supposed they had their rules and principles, just as the brothers of Nevarsin did. She lay down beside Caryl, and slept.

She found herself dreaming, clear vivid dreams, as if she flew, linked in mind with Preciosa, over the green, rolling hills of her own country. She woke with a lump in her throat, remembering the view of the long valley from the cliffs of Falconsward. Would she ever see her home again, or her sister or brothers? What had they to do with a wandering swordswoman? Her ears ached where they had been pierced. She missed Orain and Carlo and even the rough-tongued Alaric. As yet she had made no friends among these strange women. But she was pledged to them for a year, at least, and there was no help for it. She listened to Caryl, sleeping quietly at her side; to the breathing of the strange women in the tent. She had never felt so alone in her life, not even when she fled from Rory's mountain cabin.

Five days they rode southward, and came to the Kadarin river, traditional barrier between the lowland Domains and the foothills of the Hellers. It seemed to Romilly that they should make more of it, going into strange country, but to Janni it was just another river to be forded, and they crossed with dispatch, at a low-water ford where they hardly wetted their horses' knees. The hills here were not so high, and soon they came to a broad rolling plateau. Caryl was beaming; all the trip he had been in good spirits, and now he was ebullient. She supposed he was glad to be coming home, and glad of the long holiday that had interrupted his studies.

Yet Romilly felt uneasy without mountains surrounding her; it seemed as if she rode on the flat land, under the high skies, like some small, exposed thing, fearfully surveying the skies here as if some bird of prey would swoop down on them and carry her away with strong talons. She knew it was ridiculous, but she kept uneasily surveying the high pale skies, filled with rolling violet cloud, as if something there was watching her. At last Caryl, riding at her side, picked it up with his sensitive *laran*.

"What's the matter, Romy? Why do you keep looking at the sky that way?"

She really had no answer for him and tried to pass it off.

"I am uneasy without mountains around me—I have always lived in the hills and I feel bare and exposed here. . . ." she tried hard to laugh, looking up into the unfamiliar skies.

High, high, a speck hovered, at the edge of her vision. Trying to ignore it, she bent her eyes on the rough-coated grass, only lightly frosted, at her feet.

"What sort of hawking is there on these plains, do you know?"

"My father and his friends keep *verrin* hawks," he said, "Do you know anything of them? Do they have them across the river, or only those great ugly sentry-birds?"

"I fly a *verrin* hawk," Romilly said, "Once I trained one—" and she looked uneasily around again, her skin prickling.

"Did you? A girl?"

The innocent question rubbed an old wound; she snapped at him, "Why should I not? You sound like my father, as if because I was born to wear skirts about my knees I had neither sense nor spirit!"

"I did not mean to offend you, Romy," said Caryl, with a gentleness which made him seem much older than his years. "It is only that I have not known many girls, except my own sister, and she would be terrified to touch a hawk. But if you can handle a sentry-bird, and calm a banshee as we did together, then surely it would take no more trouble to train a hawk." He turned his face to her, watching with his head tilted a little to one side, something like a bird himself with his bright inquisitive eyes. "What are you afraid of, Romy?"

"Not afraid," she said, uneasy under his gaze, then, "Only—as if someone was watching me," she blurted out, not knowing she was going to say it until she heard her own words. Realizing how foolish they were, she said defensively, "Perhaps that is only because—the land is so flat—I feel—all exposed—" and again her eyes sought the sky, dazzled by the sun, where, wavering at the very edge between seen and unseen, a speck still hovered . . . *I am being watched!*

"It is not uncommon, that," said Janni, coming up beside them, "When first I rode into the mountains, I felt as if they were closing in, as if, while I slept, they might move in and jostle my very skirts. Now I am used to them, but still, when I ride down into the plains, I feel as if a great weight has been lifted and I can breathe more easily. I think *that*, more than all kings or customs, divides hillman from lowlander; and I have heard Orain say as much, that whenever he was away from his mountains, he felt naked and afraid under the open sky. . . ."

She could almost hear him say it, in that gentle, half-teasing tone. She still missed Orain, his easy companionship, it seemed she was like a fish in a tree among all these woman! Their very voices grated on her, and it seemed to her sometimes that in spite of their skill with sword and horsemanship, they were far too much like her sister Mallina, silly and narrow-minded. Only Janni seemed free of the pettiness she had always found in women. But was that only because Janni was like Orain, and so less like a woman? She did not know and felt too sore to think much about it.

Yet, she thought with annoyance at herself, forty days ago I was thinking that I liked the company of men even less than that of women. Am I content nowhere? Why can't I be satisfied with what I have? If I am going to be always discontented, I might as well have stayed home and married *Dom* Garris and been discontented in comfort among familiar things!

She felt the gentle, inquiring touch of the boy's *laran* on her mind; as if he asked her what was the matter. She sighed and smiled at him, and asked, "Shall we race across this meadow? Our horses are well-matched, so it will only be a matter of which is the better horseman," and they set off side by side, so rapidly that it took all her attention not to tumble off headlong, and she had to stop thinking about what troubled her. She reached the appointed goal a full length ahead of him, but Janni, coming up more slowly, scolded them both impartially—they did not know the terrain, they might have lamed their horses on some unseen rock or small animal's burrow in the grass!

But that night, as they were making camp—the days were lengthening now perceptibly, it was still light when they had eaten supper—she had again the sharp sense that she was being watched, as if she were some small animal, prey huddling before the sharp eyes of a hovering hawk—she scanned the darkening sky, but could see nothing. Then, incredulous, a familiar sense of wildness, flight, contact, rapport—hardly knowing what she did, Romilly thrust up her hand, felt the familiar rush of wings, the grip of talons.

"Preciosa!" she sobbed aloud, feeling the claws close on her bare wrist. She opened her eyes to look at the bluish-black sheen of wings, the sharp eyes, and the old sense of closeness enveloped her. Against all hope, beyond belief, Preciosa had somehow marked her when she came out of the glacier country, had trailed her even through these unfamiliar hills and plains.

She was in good condition, sleek and trim and well-fed. Of course. There was better hunting on these plains than even in the Kilghard Hills where she was fledged. Wordless satisfaction flowed between them for a long space as she sat motionless, the hawk on her hand.

"Well, will you look at that!" the voice of one of the girls broke through the mutual absorption, "Where did the hawk come from? She is bewitched!"

Romilly drew a long breath. She said to Caryl, who was watching silently, rapt, "It is my hawk. Somehow she has followed me here, so far from home, so far——" and broke off because she was crying too hard to speak. Troubled by the emotion, Preciosa bated, trying to balance on Romilly's fist; flapped her wings and flew to the branches of a nearby tree, where she sat looking down at them without any sign of fear.

Mhari demanded, "Is it your own hawk—the one you trained?" and Janni said in a quiet voice, "You told me your father took her from you, and gave her to your brother——"

With an effort, Romilly controlled her voice. She said, "I think Darren found out that Preciosa was not my father's to give." She looked up through her tears to the tree branch where Preciosa sat, motionless as a painted hawk on a painted tree, and again the thread of rapport touched her mind. Here, among strange women in a strange country, with all she had ever known behind her and past the border of a strange river, as she looked at the hawk and felt the familiar touch on her mind, she knew that she was no longer alone.

CHAPTER TWO

Three days more they rode, and came into a warm country, green, rolling hills and the air soft, without the faintest breath of frost. To the end of her life Romilly remembered that first ride across the Plains of Valeron—for so Caryl told her they were called—green and fertile, with crops blooming in the field and trees without even snow-pods for their night-blossoms. Along the roadside, flowers bloomed, red and blue and silver-golden, and the red sun, warm and huge in these southern skies, cast purple shadows along the road. The very air seemed sweet, euphoric.

Caryl was ecstatic, pointing out landmarks as he rode beside Romilly. "I had not expected to be home before mid-summer-after-this! Oh, I am so glad to be coming home—"

"And your father sent you from this warm and welcoming country into the snows of Nevarsin? He must indeed be a good *cristoforo*."

Caryl shook his head, and in that moment his face looked distant, closed-in, almost adult. He said quietly, "I serve the Lord of Light, as fits a Hastur best."

Then why—Romilly almost burst out with the question, but she had learned not to speak any question of his father to the boy. But he picked up the question in her mind.

"The *cristoforos* at Nevarsin are learned men, and good men," he said at last. "Since the Hundred Kingdoms were made, there has been war and chaos in the lowlands, and such learning as can be gotten is small indeed; my father wished me to learn in peace, away from the wars and safe

210

from the feuds that beset the Hastur-kinfolk. He does not share the worship of the Brotherhood, but respected their religion and the knowledge that they are men of peace."

He fell silent, and Romilly, respecting that silence—what scenes of war and pillage had that child seen, far from the sheltering hills which kept men safe in their own fortressed homes?—rode on, thoughtfully. She had heard tales of war, far away in her own peaceful mountains. She called to mind the battles by which this green and peaceful country had been laid waste. It now seemed, to her hypersensitive consciousness, bestrewn with the black of blood under the crimson sun, all dark, the very ground crying out with the slaughter of innocents and the horrors of armies treading the crops into the soil from which they sprung. She shuddered, and abruptly the whole scene winked out and Romilly knew she had been sharing the child's consciousness.

Indeed his father did well to send his son to safety among the cold and untroubled crags of the City of Snows; a time of rest, a time to heal the wounds of a child with laran, sensitive and aware of all the horrors of war. With sudden passionate homesickness, Romilly was grateful for her childhood of peace and for the stubbornness that had kept The MacAran his own man, taking no part in the factions that swept the land with their lust to conquer. What was his watchword? *To their own God Zandru's deepest forges with both their households. . . .*

Oh, Father, will I ever see you again?

She looked up at Caryl but he rode silent beside her, unseeing, and she knew he rode enclosed in his own pain, unable to see hers, or at least blinded with the effort to block it away from himself. *Have I come to this, then, that I would turn to a child of twelve, a baby no older than my little brother, for comfort when I cannot suffer my own lot, which I chose for myself?* She rode among strangers, and wondered for a moment if each of the women around her rode like this, each closed in with her own weary weight, each bearing her share of the burdens laid upon mankind. *Is this why men call upon the Bearer of Burdens as if he were not only a great teacher of wisdom, but also a God—that we may have Gods to bear our burdens because otherwise they are too heavy for mankind to bear?*

She could not endure the sorrow in Caryl's small face. She at least was a woman grown and could bear her own burden, but he was a child and should not have to. She broke in upon him, gently, asking, "Shall I call Preciosa from the sky to ride

211

with you? I think she is lonely—" and as she whistled to the hawk, and set her upon Caryl's saddle she was rewarded by seeing the unchildlike weight disappear from the childish face, so that he was only a boy again, gleefully watching a hawk fly to his hand.

"When this war is over, Romy, and the land is at peace again, shall I have you for my hawkmaster, and will you teach me all about training hawks? Or no, a girl cannot be a hawk*master*, can you? You will then be hawkmistress to me, one day?"

She said gently, "I do not know where any of us will be when this war is over, Caryl. It would be a pleasure to teach you what I know about hawks. But remember that much of what I know cannot be taught. You must find it somewhere within you, your heart and your *laran*—" and at the edge of her consciousness she realized that now she felt quite comfortable with that alien word—"to know the birds and to love them and to be aware of their ways."

And she found it easy to believe that this small wise boy, with his sensitive awareness of men and beasts, the gravity of the monks among whom he had been reared and the charm of the Hastur-kin, would perhaps one day be king. It seemed for a moment that she could see the luminous glimmer of a corona about his reddish curls—and then she shut away the unwanted sight. She was learning fast, she reflected, to handle the Gift given to her, or to shut it away.

Was this how her father had learned to survive, outside a Tower, she wondered, by closing away all the *laran* he could not use in his work of training horses? And could she stand to shut away all this new part of herself? Could she bear to have it—or *not* to have it, now? It was a terrifying gift and bore its own penalties. No wonder, now, that there were old tales in the mountains of men driven mad when their *laran* came upon them. . . .

And how could Caryl be a king? His father was no king but sworn liegeman to *Dom* Rakhal, and whether Rakhal won this war, or Carolin, Lyondri Hastur was no king. Or would he prove false to Rakhal as he had been false to Carolin, in the ambition to form a dynasty of his own blood?

"Romilly—Romy! Are you asleep riding there?" Caryl's merry voice broke in on her thoughts. "May I see if Preciosa will fly for me? We should have some birds for supper—should we not?"

She smiled at the boy.

"If she will fly for you, you shall fly her," she agreed,

"though I cannot promise that she will fly for anyone but me. But you must ask Dame Jandria if we have need of birds for supper; she, not I, is in charge of this company."

"I am sorry," Caryl said, unrepentant, the words mere formality, "But it is hard to remember that she is a noble-woman, and it does not come naturally to me to remember to ask her, while when I am with you I am always aware that you are one of the Hastur-kind."

"But I am not," said Romilly, "and Janni is Lord Orain's own cousin, if you did not know, so her blood is as good as mine."

Suddenly Caryl looked scared. "I wish you had not told me that," he blurted out, "for that makes her one of my father's greatest enemies and I do not want him to hate her. . . ." Romilly berated herself; he looked stricken. She said quickly, "Rank has no meaning among the Sisterhood, and Jandria has renounced the privileges brought with noble birth. And so have I, Caryl." And she realized that he looked relieved, though she was not sure why.

"I will ask Jandria if we have need of game for the pot," she said quickly, "and you shall fly Preciosa if she will fly at your command; surely Jandria could not object if you want to get a bird for your own supper, unless you try to make one of us pluck and cook it for you."

"I can do that myself," Caryl said proudly, then grinned, lowering his eyes. "If you will tell me how," he said in a small voice, and Romilly giggled, Caryl giggling with her.

"I will help you cook the bird for a share of it—is that a bargain, then?"

Three nights later they began to ride along the shore of a lake, lying in the fold of the hills, and Caryl pointed to a great house, not quite a castle, situated at the head of the long valley.

"There lies Hali, and my father's castle."

Romilly thought it looked more like a palace than a fortress, but she said nothing. Caryl said, "I shall be glad to see Father again, and my mother," and Romilly wondered; how glad would his father be, to see a son held hostage by his worst enemy's men, and taken from the safety of Nevarsin whence he had sent him? But she said nothing of this. Only that morning, flying through Preciosa's eyes, she had seen out over the whole vast expanse of the Plains of Valeron, armies massing and moving on the borders. The war would soon be upon the green lowlands again.

And all that day they rode through a country scoured clean by war; farmsteads lay in ruins, great stone towers with not one stone left upon another, only scattered rubble as if some monstrous disruption like an earthquake had shaken them from their very foundations; what army, what dreadful weapon had done that? Once they had to turn aside, for as they came to the top of the rise, they saw in the valley before them a ruined village. A strange silence hung over the land, though houses stood undamaged, serene and peaceful, no smoke rose from the chimneys, no sound of horses stamping, children playing, hammers beating on anvils or the work-songs of women weaving or waulking their cloth. Dread silence lay over the village, and now Romilly could see a faint greenish flickering as if the houses were bathed in some dreadful miasma, an almost tangible fog of doom. They lay, pulsing faintly greenish, and she knew suddenly that when night fell the street and houses would glow with an uncanny luminescence in the dark.

And even as she looked, she saw the lean, starved figure of a predator slinking silently through the streets; and while they looked, it moved more slowly, subsided, lay down in its tracks, still stirring feebly, without a cry.

Jandria said curtly, "Bonewater-dust. Where that stuff's been scattered from the air, the land dies, the very houses die; should we ride through there, we would be in no better case than that woods-cat before many nights. Turn about— best not come too near; this road is closed as if a nest of dragons guarded it; or better, for we might somehow manage to fight even dragons, but against this there's no fighting, and for ten years or more this land will lie accursed and the very beasts of the forests be born awry. Once I saw a mountain-cat with four eyes and a plains chervine with toes for hooves. Uncanny!" She shuddered, pulling her horse around. "Make as wide a circle as we can around this place! I've no wish to see my hair and teeth fall out and my blood turn to whey in my veins!"

The wide detour added two or three days to their ride, and Janni warned Romilly not to fly Preciosa.

"Should she eat of game tainted by that stuff of war, she would die, but not soon enough to save her great suffering; and should we eat of it, we too might lose hair and teeth if no worse. The taint of the foul stuff lingers long in all the country round, and spreads in the bodies of predators and harmless beasts who wander through the blighted countryside.

She can fast for a day or two more safely than she can risk hunting too close to that place."

And so for two days Romilly carried Preciosa on her saddle, and, though she had sworn to herself that she could never again confine her freed bird, she yielded to fear at last and tied jesses about her legs.

I dare not let you fly or you would eat of game which would kill you, she tried miserably to form a picture in her mind which the hawk could clearly see, of the game glowing with that unhealthy and poisonous glow, and although she was not sure she had made contact with the bird's mind, for the hawk sulked and brooded on the saddle, she did not fight the bonds, and rode with her head tucked under her wing; Romilly could feel the fierce hunger pulsing within her, but she seemed willing to ride thus chained for her own protection.

At last it seemed that they were out of danger, though Janni warned all the women that if they should begin to comb out handfuls of hair, or their teeth should loosen, they should tell her at once; she thought they had made a wide enough circle around the tainted land; "But none can be sure with that deadly stuff," she warned, and rode on, her jaw clenched hard. Once she said to Romilly, with a brief glance that made Romilly think of her hawk, closed-in and brooding, her eyes swiftly hooded, "Orain was fostered in that village. And now no man will be able to live in it for a span of years and perhaps more. All the Gods blast Lyondri and his devil weapons!"

Romilly cast a quick glance at Caryl, but either he had not heard, or concealed it. How heavy a weight the boy must carry!

They camped a little early that night, and while the women were setting up the tent, Janni called Romilly away from the camp.

"Come with me, I need to talk to you. No, Caryl, not you," she added, sharply, and the boy fell back like a puppy that had been kicked. Janni led Romilly a little away from the camp, and motioned to her to sit down, lowering herself crosslegged to the rough soft grass.

"Any sign of loosening teeth, falling hair?"

Romilly bared her teeth in a smile, then raised her hand and tugged graphically at her short hair. "Not a bit of it, Janni," she said, and the woman breathed a sigh of relief.

"Evanda be praised," she said, "Who has guarded her maidens. I found some loose hair this morning when I

215

combed my hair, but I am growing old and must look to falling hair as a woman's lot in age. Still I could not help fearing that we had not ridden wide enough round that cursed site. What madman will destroy the very land of his own vassals? Oh, yes, I have ridden to war, I can see burning a croft—though I like it not to kill the humble folk because of the wars of the great and mighty—but a croft, burned, can be rebuilt, and crops trampled down can be grown again when the land is at peace. But to destroy the very land so no crops will grow for a generation? Perhaps I am too squeamish for a warrior," she said, and fell for a moment into silence. At last she asked, "Have you had trouble with your prisoner?"

"No," said Romilly, "he is glad to be coming home, but he has scrupulously minded his parole."

"I thought as much, but I am glad to hear you say it," said Jandria. She loosened the cheap silver buckles on her cloak and flung it back, sighing as the wind ruffled her thick hair. Her face seemed lined and weary. Romilly said with swift sympathy, "You are so tired, Jandria. Let me take your part in the camp work tonight, and go to rest in your tent now. I will bring your evening meal to you in your blanket-roll."

Janni smiled. "It is not weariness which weighs on me, Romilly; I am old and hardened to travel and camp, and I have slept in places far more comfortless than this without a whimper. I am troubled, that is all, for good sense tells me one thing and honor tells me another."

Romilly wondered what trouble lay on Janni, and the woman smiled and reached for her hand. She said, "Young Carolin is in my care, and honor bids that I be the one to convey him to his father. Yet I thought perhaps I would send you to deliver the lad within the walls of Hali city to the hands of the Hastur-lord."

Romilly's first thought was that she would have a chance to see within the walls of the great lowland city; her next, that she would be very sorry to part with Caryl. Only after that did she realize that she would also have to meet with that great rogue Lyondri Hastur.

"Why me, Janni?"

Jandria's heavy sigh was audible. "Something you know of courtly ways and the manners of a Great House," she said. "I feel traitor to the Sisterhood to say as much, having sworn to leave rank behind me forever. Mhari, Reba, Shaya—all of them are good women, but they know no more than the clumsy manners of their fathers' crofts, and I cannot send

216

them on such a mission of diplomacy. More than this, for the safety of all of us." Her strained smile was faint, hardly a grimace. "Whatever I said to Orain, Lyondri Hastur would know me if I wore banshee-feathers and did the dance of a Ya-man in a Ghost Wind! I have no wish to hang from a traitor's gallows. Carolin, and Orain too, were among those Lyondri loved best, and those whom he pursues with the greater fury now. Carolin, Orain, Lyondri and I—we four were fostered together." She hesitated, sighed again and at last said, "Orain does not know this; he never wished to see what befell between man and maiden, and he did not know—hell's fire," she burst out, "Why does it shame me to say that Lyondri and I lay together more than once, before I was even fully a woman. Now I have turned from him to my own kindred, I think it would give him pleasure to hang me, if my death would give pain to Carolin or to Carolin's sworn man! Nor can I bear to meet him—Avarra comfort me, I cannot but love him still, almost as much as I hate!" She swallowed and looked at the ground, holding tight to Romilly's hand. "So now you know why I am too cowardly to meet with him, however sworn he may be with his flag of truce—he might spare me for our old love, I do not know. . . ."

"It is not needful, Janni," said Romilly gently, feeling the woman's pain, "I will gladly go. You must not risk yourself."

"Seeing you—do you understand this, Romilly?—Lyondri and Rakhal see only a stranger, and more than that, one Caryl loves well, someone who has been kind to his son; and they know only that you are an envoy of the Sisterhood, not a rebel or one sworn to Carolin. Be clear, Romilly, I send you into danger—it may be that Lyondri will not honor his pledged word of safety for the courier who brings his son; but you may risk nothing worse than imprisonment. Lyondri *may* kill you; he would certainly lose no chance for revenge against me."

Danger for her, against certain death for herself? Romilly hesitated just a moment, and Janni said wearily, "I cannot command you to this risk, Romilly. I can only beg it of you. For I cannot send Caryl alone into the city; I pledged he should be safely delivered into his father's very hands."

"I thought he had sworn safe-conduct—"

"Oh, and so he has," said Janni, "But I trust that no further than Lyondri sees his advantage, which he saw ever. . . ." and she covered her face with her hands. Romilly felt weak and frightened. But the Sisterhood had taken her in

217

when she was alone, sheltered and fed her, welcomed her with friendliness. She owed them this. And she was a sworn Swordswoman. She said, tightening her hand on Janni's, "I will go, my sister. Trust me."

Before they rode into the city, Caryl washed himself carefully at a stream, begged a comb from one of the women and carefully combed his hair and trimmed his nails. He dug from his saddlebags his somewhat shabby clothes—for the last few days he had been wearing bits and pieces, castoff trousers and tunic of one of the women, so that he could wash his own in one of the streams and have them clean for his return to court, though nothing could make them look like proper attire for a prince.

He said with regret, "Father sent me a new festival costume before Midwinter-night, and I had to leave it in the monastery when I left so suddenly. Well, it can't be helped, this is the best I have."

"I will cut your hair, if you like," Romilly offered, and trimmed his curling hair to an even length, then brushed it till it shone. He laughed and told her he was not a horse to be currycombed, but he looked at himself with satisfaction in the stream.

"At least I look like a gentleman again; I hate to be shabby like a ruffian," he said. "*Mestra* Jandria, will you not come with us? My father could not be angry with anyone who had been so kind to his son."

Jandria shook her head. "There were old quarrels between Lyondri and me before you were hatched or Rakhal sought out Carolin's throne, dear boy; I would rather not come under your father's eye. Romilly will take you."

"I will be glad to ride with Romilly," said Caryl, "and I am sure my father will be grateful to her."

"In the name of all the Gods of the Hasturs, boy, I hope so," said Jandria, and when Caryl bent over her hand in his courtly manner, she pressed it. "*Adelandeyo*," she said after the manner of the hill women, "Ride on with the Gods, my boy, and may They all be with you, and with Romilly."

Only Romilly, seeing the tensing in Janni's jaw, the tremble in her eyes, knew that Janni was thinking, *Gods protect you, girl, and may we see you again safe out of Lyondri Hastur's hands.*

Romilly clambered into her saddle. With a clarity not usual to her unless she was in rapport with her hawk and seeing all

218

things through her *laran* and not her eyes, she saw the clear pale sky, the tent of the Sisterhood; heard thwacks where Mhari and Lauria were practicing with the wooden batons they used for swords, saw two other women slowly working through the careful training moves of unarmed combat, the dancelike ritual which trained their muscles to work without thought in defensive movement. She could still see smoke from the breakfast fire and felt alerted and frightened—smell of smoke when no food was cooking?—before she remembered that they were not now in the forest and there was, in this green meadow, no chance of wildfire.

She had made herself tidy, with her best cloak, the one Orain had bought for her in the Nevarsin market—though now she felt sore and raw-edged about his gift, she had nothing else nearly so good or so warm—and had borrowed the cleanest tunic she could find in the camp from one of the swordswomen. She was conscious of the still-stinging earrings in her ears, mercilessly revealed by her short hair. Well, she told herself defensively, I am what I am, a woman of the Sisterhood of the Sword—even though I am not very good with it yet—and Lyondri Hastur can just accept me as an emissary under safe-conduct; why should I worry about whether I look like a lady? What is Lyondri to me? And yet a little voice that sounded like Luciella's was saying in her mind, with prim reproach, *Romy, for shame, boots and breeches and astride like a man, what would your father say?* Mercilessly she commanded the voice to be quiet.

She clucked briefly to her horse and nodded to Caryl, who drew his horse into an easy trot beside her own.

Hali was an unwalled city, with broad streets which were uncannily smooth under foot; at her puzzled look, Caryl smiled and told her they had been laid down by matrix technology, without the work of human hands. At her skeptical glance he insisted, "It's true, Romy! Father showed me, once, how it can be done, laying the stones with the great matrix lattices under ten or twelve *leroni* or *laranzu'in*. One day I will be a sorcerer as well and work among the relays and screens!"

Romilly was still skeptical, but there was no use at all in challenging what a child's father had told him, so she held her peace.

He directed her through the streets, and it was all she could do to keep from staring about her as if she were the freshest of country bumpkins, hardly away from the farmyard; Nevarsin was a fine city, and Caer Donn as well, but Hali was wholly different. In place of steep, cobbled streets and stone houses crowded together as if huddling under the great crags of the Hellers or of Castle Aldaran, there were broad streets and low open dwellings—she had never seen a house which was not built like a fortress to be defended, and wondered how the citizens could sleep secure in their beds at night; not even the city was walled.

And the people who walked in these streets seemed a different race than the mountain people—who were strongly built, clad in furs and leather against the bitter chill, and seemed hard and fierce; here in this pleasant lowland city, finely dressed men and women strolled the broad streets, wearing colorful clothing, embroidered tunics and brightly dyed skirts and veils for the women, colorful long coats and trousers for the men, and thin cloaks of brilliant colors, more for adornment than for use.

One or two of the people in the streets paused to stare at the blazing red head of the boy, and the slender, trousered, earringed young woman who rode at his side in the scarlet of the Sisterhood and the old-fashioned mountain-cut cloak of fur and homespun. Caryl said under his breath, "They recognize me. And they think you, too, one of the Hastur-kind because of your red hair. Father may think so too. You must be one of our own, Romilly, with red hair, and *laran* too. . . ."

"I don't think so," Romilly said, "I think redheads are born into families where they have never appeared before, just as sometimes a bleeder, or an albino, will appear marked from the womb, and yet no such history in their family. The Mac-Arans have been redheads as far back as I can remember—I recall my great-grandmother, though she died before I could ride, and her hair, though it had gone sandy in patches, was redder than mine at the roots."

"Which proves that they must at one time have been kin to the children of Hastur and Cassilda," the boy argued, but Romilly shook her head.

"I think it proves no such thing. I know little of your Hastur-kind—" tactfully she bit back the very words on her tongue, *and what little I know I do not much like.* But she knew that the boy heard the unspoken words as he had heard the spoken ones; he looked down at his saddle and said nothing.

And now, as they rode toward a large and centrally situated Great House, Romilly began to be a little frightened.

Now, after all, she was to meet that beast Lyondri Hastur, the man who had followed the usurper Rakhal and exiled Carolin, killed and made homeless so many of his supporters.

"Don't be frightened," said Caryl, stretching out his hand between their horses, "My father will be grateful to you because you have brought me back. He is a kind man, really, I promise you, Romy. And I heard that he pledged a reward when the courier from the Sisterhood should bring him to me."

I want no reward, Romilly thought, *except to get safe away with a whole skin.* Yet like most young people she could not imagine that within the hour she might be dead.

At the great doors, a guard greeted Caryl with surprise and pleasure.

"*Dom* Caryl . . . I had heard you were to be returned today! So you've seen the war an' all! Good to have you home, youngster!"

"Oh, Harryn, I'm glad to see you," Caryl said with his quick smile. "And this is my friend, Romilly, she brought me back—"

Romilly felt the man's eyes travel up and down across her, from the feather in her knitted cap to the boots on her trousered legs, but all he said was "Your father is waiting for you, young master; I'll have you taken to him at once."

It seemed to Romilly that she sensed a way of escape now. She said, "I shall leave you, then, in the hands of your father's guardsman—"

"Oh, no, Romilly," Caryl exclaimed, "You must come in and meet Father, he will be eager to reward you. . . ."

I can just imagine, Romilly thought; but Janni had been right. There was no real reason for Lyondri Hastur to violate his pledged word and imprison a nameless and unknown Swordswoman against whom he had no personal grudge. She dismounted, saw her horse led away, and followed Caryl into the Great House.

Inside, some kind of soft-voiced functionary—so elegantly clothed, so smooth, that calling him a *servant* seemed unlikely to Romilly—told Caryl that his father was awaiting him in the music room, and Caryl darted through a doorway, leaving Romilly to follow at leisure.

So this is the Hastur-lord, the cruel beast of whom Orain spoke. I must not think that, like Caryl himself he must have laran, *he could read it in my mind.*

A tall, slightly-built man rose from the depths of an armchair, where he had been holding a small harp on his knee;

set it down, bending forward, then turned to Caryl and took both his hands.

"Well, Carolin, you are back?" He drew the boy against him and kissed his cheek; it seemed that he had to stoop down a long way to do it. "Are you well, my son? You look healthy enough; at least the Sisterhood has not starved you."

"Oh, no," said Caryl, "They fed me well, and they were quite kind to me; when we passed through a town, one of them even bought me cakes and sweets, and one of them lent me a hawk so I could catch fresh birds if I wanted them for my supper. This is the one with the hawk," he added, loosing his father's hands and grabbing Romilly to draw her forth. "She is my friend. Her name is Romilly."

And so at last Romilly was face to face with the Hasturlord; a slight man, with composed features which, it seemed, never relaxed for a second. His jaw was set in tight lines; his eyes, grey under pale lashes, seemed hooded like a hawk's.

"I am grateful to you for being good to my son," said Lyondri Hastur. His voice was composed, neutral, indifferent. "At Nevarsin I thought him beyond the reach of the war, but Carolin's men, I have no doubt, thought having him as hostage was a fine idea."

"It wasn't Romilly's idea, father," said Caryl, and Romilly knew that he had thought about, and rejected, telling his father that Orain had been angry about it; it was no time to bring Orain's name up at all. And Romilly knew, too, from the almost-imperceptible added clenching of the Hastur-lord's jaw, that he heard perfectly well what his son had not said, and it seemed that a shadow of his voice, faraway and eerie, said almost aloud in Romilly's mind, *Another score against Orain, who was my sworn man before he was Carolin's.*

I should keep this woman hostage; she may know something of Orain's whereabouts, and where Orain is, Carolin cannot be far.

But by now the boy could read the unspoken thought, and he looked up at his father in real horror. He said in a whisper, "You pledged your word. The word of a Hastur," and she could almost see his shining image of his father crack and topple before his eyes. Lyondri Hastur looked from his son to the woman. He said, in a sharp dry voice, "Swordswoman, know you where Orain rides at this moment?"

She knew that with his harsh eyes on her she could not lie, he would have the truth from her in moments. With a flood of relief she knew that she need not lie to him at all. She said, "I saw Orain last in Caer Donn, when he brought

222

Caryl—*Dom* Carolin—to the hostel of the Sisterhood. And that was more than a tenday ago. I suppose by now he is with the Army." And, though she tried, she could not keep from her mind the picture of the army passing at the end of the street, the banner of the Hasturs, blue and silver, and Orain riding at the side of the unseen king. Lyondri would not consider him king but usurper. . . .

I have made promises I could not keep . . . I knew not what manner of man I served, that I have become Rakhal's hangman and hard hand . . . and with shock, Romilly realized that she was actually receiving this thin trickle of thoughts from the man before her; or was this true at all, was she simply reading him as she read animals, in the infinitesimal movements of eyes and body, and somehow co-ordinating them with his thoughts? She was acutely uncomfortable with the contact and relieved when it stopped abruptly, as if Lyondri Hastur had realized what was happening and closed it down.

I have read thoughts, more or less, much of my life, why should it disturb and confuse me now?

The Hastur-lord said with quiet formality, "I owe you a reward for your care of my son. I will grant anything save for weapons which might be used against me in this unjust war. State what you wish for his ransom, with that one exception."

Jandria had prepared her for this. She said firmly, "I was to ask for three sacks filled with medical supplies for the hostels of the sisterhood; bandage-linen, the jelly which helps the clotting of blood, and *karalla* powder."

"I suppose I could call those weapons, since no doubt they will be used to aid those wounded in rebellion against their king," Lyondri Hastur mused aloud, then shrugged. "You shall have them," he said, "I will give my steward the orders, and a pack-animal to take them back to your camp."

Romilly drew a soft sigh of relief. She was not to be imprisoned, then, or held hostage.

"Did you believe that of me?" asked Lyondri Hastur aloud, dryly, then gave a short, sharp laugh. She saw it in his mind again, two telepaths could not lie to one another. She was fortunate that he did not wish his son disillusioned about his honor.

Romilly found herself suddenly very grateful that she had not encountered Lyondri Hastur when Caryl was not by, and when he did not wish to keep his son's admiration.

"But, father," Caryl said, "This is the woman with the hawk, who let me fly her—can I have a hawk of my own?

And one day, I wish Mistress Romilly to be my hawkmistress—"

Lyondri Hastur smiled; it was a dry, distant smile, but nevertheless, a smile, and even more frightening than his laugh. He said, "Well, Swordswoman, my son has taken a fancy to you. There are members of the Sisterhood in my employment. If you would care to stay here and instruct Carolin in the art of falconry—"

She wanted nothing more than to get away. Much as she liked Caryl, she had never met anyone who so terrified her as this dry, harsh man with the cold laughter and hooded eyes. Grasping for an honorable excuse, she said, "I am—I am pledged elsewhere, *vai dom*."

He bowed slightly, acknowledging the excuse. He knew it was an excuse, he knew what she thought him, and he knew she knew. He said, "As you wish, *mestra*. Carolin, say goodbye to your friend and go to greet your mother."

He came and gave her his hand in the most formal way. Then, impulsively, he hugged her. He said, looking up to her with earnest eyes, "Maybe when this war is over I will see you again, Romilly—and your hawk. Give Preciosa my greetings." Then he bowed as if to a lady at court, and left the room quickly, but she had seen the first traces of tears in his eyes. He did not want to cry in front of his father; she knew it.

Lyondri Hastur coughed. He said, "Your pack-animal and the medical supplies will be brought to you at the side door, near the stable. The steward will show you the way," and she knew that the audience with the Hastur-lord was over. He gestured to the functionary, who came and said softly, "This way, *mestra*."

Romilly bowed and said, "Thank you, sir."

She turned, but as she was about to follow the steward, Lyondri Hastur coughed again.

"Mistress Romilly—?"

"*Vai dom?*"

"Tell Jandrai I am not quite the monster she fears. Not quite. That will be all."

And as she left the room, Romilly wondered, shaking to her very toenails, *what else does this man know?*

CHAPTER THREE

When Romilly delivered the message from Lyondri Hastur to Janni—"Tell her I am not the monster she thinks me, not quite," Jandria said nothing for a long time. Romilly sensed, from her stillness, (although she made a deliberate effort, her first, not to use her *laran* at all) that Jandria had several things she would have said; but not to Romilly. Then, at last, she said, "And he gave you the medical supplies?"

"He did; and a pack animal to carry them."

Janni went and looked them over, saying at last, tight-lipped, "He was generous. Whatever Lyondri Hastur's faults, niggardliness was never one of them. I should return the pack animal—I want no favors from Lyondri—but the sober truth is that we need it. And it is less to him than buying his son a packet of sweets in the market; I need suffer no qualms of conscience about that." She sent for three of the women to look over the medical supplies, and told Romilly she might return to her horses. As an afterthought, as Romilly was going out the door, she called her back for a moment and said, "Thank you, *chiya*. I sent you on a difficult and dangerous mission, where I had no right at all to send you, and you carried it off as well as any diplomatic courier could have done. Perhaps I should find work better suited to you than working with the dumb beasts."

Romilly thought; I would rather work with horses than go on diplomatic missions, any day! After a minute or two she said so, and Jandria, smiling, said, "Then I will not keep you from the work I know you love. Go back to the horses, my dear. But you have my thanks."

Freed, Romilly went back to the paddock and led out the horse she was beginning to break to the saddle. But she had not been at the work very long when Mhari came out to her.

"Romy," she said, "saddle your own horse and two pack animals, at once, and Jandria's riding-horse. She is leaving the hostel tonight, and says you must go with her."

Romilly stared, with one hand absent-mindedly quieting the nervous horse, who did not at all like the blanket strapped to his back. "To leave tonight? Why?"

"As for that, you must ask Janni herself," said Mhari, a little sullenly, "I would be glad to go wherever she would take me, but she has chosen you instead, and she bade me make up a packet of your clothes, and four days journey-rations too."

Romilly frowned with irritation; she was just beginning to make some progress in gentling this horse, and must she interrupt the work already? She was sworn to the Sisterhood, but must that put her at the mercy of some woman's whim? Nevertheless she liked Jandria very much, and was not inclined to argue with her decisions. She shrugged, changed the long lunge-line for a short leading-rope and took the horse back into the stable.

She had finished saddling Jandria's horse, and was just putting a saddle-blanket on her own, when Jandria, cloaked and booted for riding, came into the stable. Romilly noticed, with shock, that her eyes were reddened as if she had been crying; but she only asked "Where are we going, Janni? And why?"

Jandria said, "What Lyondri said to you, Romy, was a message; he knows that I am here; no doubt he had you followed to see where the Sisterhood's hostel was located outside the walls of Hali. Simply by being here, I endanger the Sisterhood, who have taken no part in this war; but I am kin to Orain and he might somehow think to trace Orain through me, might think I know more of Orain's plans—or Carolin's—than I really do. I must leave here at once, so that if Rakhal's men under Lyondri come here to seek me, they can say truthfully, and maintain, even if they should be questioned by a *leronis* who can read their thoughts, that they have no knowledge of where I have gone, or where Carolin's men, or Orain, may be gathered. And I am taking you with me, for fear Lyondri might try to lay hands on you, too. These other women—he knows nothing of them and cares less; but you have come under his eyes, and I would just as soon you were out of his field of notice . . . I would rather not have you at the very gates of Hali. Besides—" her smile was very faint, "Did you not know? A woman of the Sisterhood does not travel alone, but must be companioned by one, at least, of her sisters."

Romilly had not thought of that—Jandria was Orain's kin, and Lyondri Hastur could use her for hostage, too, even if he did not, as Jandria had feared, mean to put her to death. She said formally, *"A ves ordres, mestra,"* and finished saddling her horse.

"Go into the hostel and get yourself some bread and cheese," Jandria said, "We can eat as we ride. But be quick, little sister."

Is there need for such haste as that, or is Jandria afraid without reason? But Romilly did not question her; she did as she was told, returning with a loaf of bread and a great hunk of coarse white new cheese, which she stowed in her saddlebag—she was not hungry now, Jandria's message had effectively destroyed her appetite, but she knew she would be glad of it later. She had a bag of apples, too, which the cook had given her.

She did ask, as they led out their horses to mount, "Where are we going, Janni?"

"I think it would be safer if you did not know that, not just yet," said Jandria, and Romilly saw real fear in her eyes. "Come, little sister, let us ride."

Romilly marked that they rode northward from the city, but the trail soon curved, and Jandria took a small, little-travelled road, hardly more than the track left by mountain *chervines*, which wound upward and upward into the hills. Before long Romilly had lost all sense of direction, but Jandria seemed never to hesitate, as if she knew precisely where she was going.

Before long they began to ride under the cover of heavy forested slopes, and Jandria seemed to relax a little; after an hour or so she asked for some of the bread and cheese, and ate it with a good appetite. Romilly, chewing on the coarse crust, began to wonder again, but did not ask.

At last Jandria said, mounting again and taking the lead-rope of the pack animal, "Even a sentry-bird cannot spy us out here. I know not if Lyondri has such birds trained to his use—they are not really all that common—but I thought it better to keep under cover till the trail was well and truly lost; all Gods forbid I should lead him straight to Carolin's armies."

"Is *that* where we are going?"

"The Sisterhood has a cohort of soldiers there," said Jandria, "and your skills may be needed to train horses for the army. And I doubt not that the Sisterhood with Carolin's army can make use of me, somehow or other. If Lyondri knew I was in the hostel—as he must have known or he would not have sent that message—then he might think, or Rakhal might think for him, that if he kept watch on me, I might lead him straight to Carolin's rendezvous; even if he could not tear the knowledge of that rendezvous straight from my mind without even a *leronis* to aid him. So I hastened to get out of there, and into the cover of the forest, so that he could not set watch on the hostel and give orders to have me followed. I may possibly have moved faster than he, for once; and it may be that we are already safe." But she glanced apprehensively down the trail where they had come, and then, even more apprehensively, at the sky, as if even now Lyondri's sentry-birds could be hovering there to spy them out. And her fear made Romilly frightened too.

That night they camped still within the shelter of the forest, and Jandria even forbade a cooking-fire; they ate the cold bread and cheese, and tethered the animals under a great tree. They spread their blankets beneath another, doubled for warmth (although the mountain-bred Romilly found it reasonably warm) and Romilly slept quickly, tired from riding. But she woke once in the night to hear soft sounds as if Jandria was crying. She wished, wretchedly, that she could say something to comfort the other woman, but it was a trouble far beyond her comprehension. At last she slept again, but woke early to find Jandria already up and saddling the horses. Her eyes were dry and tearless, her face barricaded, but the eyelids were red and swollen.

"Do you think we can risk a fire this morning? I would like some hot food, and if we are not pursued by now, surely we must have gotten away," Romilly said, and Jandria shrugged.

"I suppose it makes no difference. If Lyondri truly wishes to find me, I am sure he would not need trackers, seeing that he read my thoughts of him so far away. It would not be Lyondri who pursued us, but Rakhal, in any case." She was silent, sighing. "Build us a fire, and I will cook some hot porridge, little sister. I have no right to make this trip harder for you with my causeless fears and dreads; you have travelled so long and hard already, Romy, and already I have you off again when you thought you had found a place of repose."

"It's all right," Romilly said, not knowing what to say. She would rather travel with Jandria than remain in the hostel with the strange women among whom she had made no friends as yet. She knelt to kindle a fire. But when they were eating hot porridge, and their horses munching at ease in the grass, Romilly asked, hesitantly, "Do you grieve for—for Lyondri?" What she was wondering, was this; Lyondri had been her lover, was she still bound to him? Jandria seemed to know what she meant, and sighed, with a small sad smile.

"My grief, I suppose, is for myself," she said at last. "And for the man I thought Lyondri was—the man he might have been, if Rakhal had not seduced him with the thought of power. That man, the man I loved, is dead—so long dead that even the Gods could not recall him from whatever place our dead hopes go. He still wants my good opinion—so much the message, or warning, meant—but that could be no more than vanity, which was always strong in him. I do not think he is—is all evil," she said, and stumbled a little over it, "The fault is Rakhal's. But by now he must know what Rakhal is, and still follows after him. So I cannot hold him guiltless of all the atrocities done in Rakhal's name."

Romilly asked, shyly, "Did you know them both—Carolin and Rakhal? How did Rakhal come to seize his throne?"

But Jandria shook her head. "I do not know. I left court when Rakhal still professed to be Carolin's most loyal follower, accepting all the favors Carolin showered on him as his dearest cousin who had been fostered with him."

"Carolin must be a good man," said Romilly at last, "to inspire such devotion in Orain. And—" she hesitated, "in you."

She said, "But surely when you were with Orain, you met with Carolin?"

Romilly shook her head. "I understood the king was at Nevarsin; but I did not meet with him."

Jandria raised her eyebrows, but all she said was, "Finish your porridge, child, and rinse the dish in the stream, and we shall ride again."

Silently, Romilly went about her work, saddling the horses, loading what was left of their food. But as they mounted, Jandria said, so long after that Romilly had almost forgotten what she asked, "Carolin is a good man. His only fault is that he trusts the honor of the Hasturs without reason; and he made the mistake of trusting Rakhal. Even Orain could not tell him what Rakhal was, nor could I; he thought Orain was only jealous. Jealous—Orain!"

"What is Rakhal like?" asked Romilly, but Jandria only shook her head.

"I cannot speak of him fairly; my hate blinds me. But where Carolin loves honor above all things, and then he loves learning, and he loves his people, Rakhal loves only the taste of power. He is like a mountain-cat that has had a taste of blood." She climbed into her saddle, and said, "Today you will take the pack-animal's leading-rope, and I will ride ahead, since I know where we are going."

When they had come out from under the cover of the forest, Romilly had again the faint far sense of being watched; that trickle of awareness in her mind that told her Preciosa was watching her; the hawk did not descend to her hand, but once or twice Romilly caught a glimpse of the bird hovering high in the sky, and knew she was not alone. The thought warmed her so deeply that she was no longer aware of fear or apprehension.

She and I are one; she has joined her life to mine. Romilly was dimly aware that this must be something like marriage, indissoluble, a tie which went deep into the other's body and spirit. She had no such tie for instance with her present horse, though he had carried her faithfully and she wished him well and thought often of his welfare.

The horse is my friend. Preciosa is something else, something like a lover.

And that made her think, shyly and almost for the first time, what it might be like to have a lover, to have a bond with someone as close to her as the hawk, tied in mind and heart and even in body, but someone with whom she could communicate, not as the MacArans did with their horses and hounds and hawks, across the vast gulf that lay between man and horse, women and hawk, child and dog, but with the close bonding of species. *Dom* Garris had wanted her, but his lecherous glances had roused nothing in her but revulsion; revulsion doubled when it was Rory, who would as soon have cut her throat for her horse and cloak and a few coppers, but had wished to bed her as well.

Orain had wanted her—at least while he still believed her to be a boy. And . . . deliberately facing something she had not even clearly understood at the time . . . she had wanted him. Although, when it was happening, she had not realized what her own strange feelings meant. Even so, she would rather have had Orain as a friend than a lover; she had been willing to accept him as a lover, when she thought he knew

230

her a woman and wanted her, in order to keep him as a friend. But had she never seriously thought of any man in that way? Certainly none of the boys she had grown up knowing, her brothers' friends—she could no more envision them as lovers than as husbands, and a husband was the last thing she would have wanted.

I think I could have married one like Alderic. He spoke to me as a human being, not only as his friend Darren's silly little sister. Nor was he the kind of man who would feel he must control me every moment, fearing I would fly away like an untamed hawk if he let go of the jesses for a moment.

Not that I wanted him as a husband, so much. But perhaps I could make up my mind to marry if the husband had first been my friend.

All during that day and the next, whenever she took her eyes from the trail, she could see, at the furthest range of her vision, that Preciosa still hovered there, and feel the precarious thread of communication from the hawk, strange divided sight, seeing the trail under her feet, aware of her own body in the saddle, and yet some indefinable part of her flying free with the hawk, far above the land and hillside slopes. Jandria had told her that they were travelling now in what was called the Kilghard Hills.

They were not like her home mountains—bleak and bare with great rock cliffs and poor soil of which every arable scrap must be carefully reclaimed and put under cultivation for food; and even less were they like the broad and fertile Plains of Valeron which they had crossed enroute to Hali. These were hills, high and steep and with great deserted tracts of wild country set with virgin forest and sometimes overgrown in thick brush-tangles so that they must cut their way through or, sometimes, retrace their steps tediously and go round. But there was no lack of hunting. Sometimes, before sunset, drowsing in her saddle, Romilly would feel something of her fly free with the hawk, stoop down and feel, sharing with Preciosa, the startle of the victim, the quick killing stroke and the burst of fresh blood in her own veins. . . . Yet every time it came freshly to her as a new experience, uniquely satisfying.

Once, she thought it was the sixth day of their journey, she was flying in mind with the hawk when her horse stepped into a mudrabbit-burrow and stumbled, fell; lay thrashing and screaming, and Romilly, thrown clear of the stirrups, lay gasping, bruised and jarred to the bone. By the time she was conscious enough to sit up, Jandria had dismounted and was helping her to rise.

"In the name of Zandru's frozen hells, where was your mind, you who are so good a horseman, not to see that burrow?" she demanded crossly. Romilly, shocked by the horse's screams, went to kneel by his side. His eyes were red, his mouth flecked with the foam of agony, and, quickly sliding into rapport with him, she felt the tearing pain in her own leg, and saw the bare, white, shattered bone protruding through the skin. There was nothing to be done; weeping with horror and grief, she fumbled at her belt for her knife and swiftly found where the great artery was under the flesh; she thrust with one fast, deep stroke. A final, convulsive struggle, a moment of deathly pain and fear—then it was quiet, all around her stunned and quiet, and the horse, with his fear, was simply gone, gone from her, leaving her empty and cold.

Stunned, fumbling, Romilly wiped her knife on a clump of grass and put it again into its sheath. She could not look up and meet Jandria's eyes. Her damned *laran* had cost the horse his life, for had she been attending to her riding, she would surely have seen the burrow. . . .

Jandria said, at last, "Was it necessary?"

"Yes." Romilly did not elaborate. Jandria did not have *laran* enough to understand, and there was no reason to burden her with all Romilly's own feelings of guilt, the rage at her own Gift which had tempted her to forget the horse beneath her in straining for the hawk above. Swallowing hard against the tears still rising and making a lump in her throat, she cursed the Gift. "I am sorry, Janni. I—I should have been more careful—"

Jandria sighed. "I was not reproaching you, *chiya*; it is ill fortune, that is all. For here we are shy of a horse in the deepest part of the hills, and I had hoped we could reach Serrais by tomorrow's nightfall."

"Is that where we are going? And why?"

"I did not tell you, in case we were followed; what you did not know, you could not tell—"

So Jandria does not trust me. Well enough; it seems I am not trustworthy . . . certainly my poor horse did not find me so. . . . yet she protested. "I would not betray you—"

Gently, Jandria said, "I never thought of that, love. I meant only—what you did not know could not be wrung from you by torture, or ravished from your mind by a *leronis* armed with one of their starstones. They could find out

232

quickly that you knew nothing. But now you would know in a day or two, anyhow."

She knelt beside Romilly and began to tug at the saddle straps. "You can ride one of the pack chervines; they cannot travel at the speed of your horse, but we can put both the packs on the back of the other. We will travel less swiftly by chervine-pace than we would with two good horses, but it can't be helped."

She began to off-load the nearer of the chervines, saw Romilly standing stone-still and snapped, "Come and help me with this."

Romilly was staring at the dead horse. Insects were already beginning to move in the clotted blood around the smashed leg. "Can't we bury him?"

Jandria shook her head. "No time, no tools. Leave him to feed the wild things." At Romilly's look of shock she said gently, "Dear child, I know what your horse meant to you—"

No you don't, Romilly thought fiercely, *you never could.*

"Do you think it matters even a little to him whether his body is left to feed the other wild things, or whether he has a funeral fit for a Hastur-lord? He is not *in* his body any more."

Romilly swallowed hard. "I know it—it makes sense when you say it like that, but—" she broke off, gulping. Jandria laid a gentle hand on her arm.

"There are beasts in this forest who depend on the bodies of the dead things for their food. Must they go hungry, Romy? This is only sentiment. You feel no pain when your hawk kills for her food—"

To Romilly's sore senses it seemed that Jandria was taunting her with her inattention, that she was away somewhere sharing the kill with her hawk and thus leading her horse to its death. She wrenched her arm free of Jandria's and said bitterly, "I don't have any choice, do I? *A ves ordres, mestra,*" and began wrenching at the pack-loads of the other chervine. In her mind, aching, accusing, was the memory of the sentry-birds for whom she had spied out carrion. Now her horse would fall prey to the *kyorebni,* and perhaps that was as it should be, but she felt she could not bear to see it, knowing her own carelessness had cost the faithful creature his life.

As if for comfort she looked into the sky, but Preciosa was nowhere in sight.

Perhaps she too has left me. . . .

* * *

233

Toward nightfall the land changed; the green fields gave way to sandy plateaus, and the roads were hard-baked clay. The chervines were forest and hill creatures, and walked laggingly, little rivulets of sweat tracing vertical lines down their thick coats. Romilly wiped her forehead with her sleeve and took off her thick cloak and tied it in a bundle on her saddle. The sun was stronger here, it seemed, and blazed with cloudless intensity from a clear, pale sky. Twilight was beginning to fall when Jandria pointed.

"There lies Serrais," she said, "and the hostel of the Sisterhood where we shall sleep tonight, and perhaps for a span of tendays. I shall be glad to sleep in a proper bed again—won't you?"

Romilly agreed, but secretly she was sorry that the long journey was coming to an end. She had grown fond of Jandria, and the thought of living in a houseful of strange women really frightened her. Furthermore, she supposed, now she was in a regular dwelling-place of the Sisterhood, she would be required to go back to the frightening lessons in swordplay and unarmed combat, and she dreaded it.

Well, she had chosen to swear to the Sisterhood, she must do her best in that place in life to which she had been guided by providence. *Bearer of Burdens, help me to bear mine then as you bear the world's weight!* And then she felt surprised at herself. She could not remember, before this, thinking much about prayer, and now it seemed that she was forever turning to such little prayers. *I wonder, is this what the Book of Burdens calls Dhe shaya, a grace of God, or is it only a kind of weakness, a sense born of loneliness, that I have nowhere else to turn?* Jandria was her friend, she thought, but she would not share her fears, Janni enjoyed the life of the Sisterhood and was not terrified at the very thought of wars and battles; such things as the village blighted with bonewater-dust enraged and horrified her, but they did not fill her with that kind of terror; Janni seemed quite free of that kind of personal fear!

They rode into the city when dusk had already fallen, and made their way through the strange wide street, the old houses of bleached stone that shone with pallid luminescence in the moonlight. Romilly was almost asleep in her saddle, trusting the path to the steady plodding pace of her chervine. She roused up a little when Jandria stopped before a great arched gate with a rope and bell hanging from it, and pulled on it. Far away inside, she heard the sound, and after a time a drowsy voice inquired, "Who is it?"

234

"Two women of the Sisterhood come from Hali," Janni called, "Jandria, Swordswoman, and Romilly, apprentice Swordswoman, oathbound and seeking shelter here."

The door creaked open, and a woman peered out into the street.

"Come in, Sisters," she said. "Lead the beasts into the stable there, you can throw them some fodder if you wish. We are all at supper." She pointed to a stable inside the enclosure, and they dismounted, leading the tired animals into the barn. Romilly blinked when she saw the place by the faint lanternlight; it was not large, but in a couple of loose-boxes at the back she saw crowded horses, some of the finest horses she had ever seen. What was this place, and why did they crowd so many horses into so small a stable? She felt full of questions, but was too shy to speak any of them. She put her chervine into one of the smaller stalls, led Jandria's horse into another, then shouldered her pack and followed the strange woman into the house.

There was a good smell of fresh-baked bread, and the spicy, unfamiliar smells of some kind of cooking food. In a long room just off the hall where they left their packs, at a couple of long tables, what looked like four or five dozen women were crowded together, eating soup out of wooden bowls, and there was such a noise of rattling bowls and crockery, so much shouting conversation from one table to another and from one end to the other of the long tables that Romilly involuntarily flinched—after the silence of the trails through forest and desert, the noise was almost deafening.

"There are a couple of seats down there," said the woman who had admitted them. "I am Tina; after supper I will take you to the housemother and she can find you beds somewhere, but we are a little crowded, as you can see; they have quartered half the Sisterhood upon us here, it seems, though I must say they're good about sending army rations here to feed them. Otherwise we'd all be living on last year's nuts! You can go and sit down and eat—you must be wanting it after that long ride."

It did not seem that there was any room at all at the table she indicated, but Jandria managed to find a place where the crowding was a little less intense, and by dint of some good-natured pushing and squeezing, they managed to wriggle into seats on the benches, and a woman, making the rounds of the tables with a jug and ladle, poured some soup into their bowls and indicated a couple of cut loaves of bread. Romilly pulled her knife from her belt and sawed off a couple of

235

hunks, and the girl squeezed in next to her—a good-natured smiling woman with freckles and dark hair tied back at her waist—shoved a pot of fruit spread at her. "Butter's short just now, but this goes pretty good on your bread. Leave the spoon in the jar."

The spread tasted like spiced apples, boiled down to a paste. The soup was filled with unidentifiable chunks of meat and strange vegetables, but Romilly was hungry and ate without really caring what it was made of.

As she finished her soup, the woman next to her said, "My name is Ysabet; most people call me Betta. I came here from the Tendara hostel. And you?"

"We were in Hali, and before that, in Caer Donn," Romilly said, and Betta's eyes widened. "Where the king fled? Did you see his army there?"

Romilly nodded, remembering Orain and a banner in a strange street.

"I heard Carolin was camped north of Serrais," Betta said, "and that they will march, before snow falls, on Hali again. The camp is full of rumors, but this one is stronger than most. What is your skill?"

Romilly shook her head. "Nothing special. I train horses and sometimes hawks, and I have handled sentry-birds."

Betta said, "They told us that an expert in horse-training was to come from Hali! Why, you must be the one, then, unless it is your friend there—what is her name?"

"She is Jandria," Romilly said, and Betta's eyes widened.

"Lady Jandria! Why, I have heard of her, if it is the same one, they said she is cousin to Carolin himself—I know we are not supposed to think of rank, but yes, I see she has red hair and a look of the Hasturs—well, they said they would send a Swordswoman from Hali, and a woman adept at horse-training. We will need it—did you see all the horses in the stable? And there are as many more in the paddock, and they were taken as a levy from the Alton country in the Kilghard Hills . . . and now they are to be broken for Carolin's armies, so that the Sisterhood will ride to battle for Carolin, our true king . . ." Then she looked at Romilly suspiciously. "You are for Carolin, are you not?"

"I have ridden from before daylight till after dark, today and for the last seven days," Romilly said, "By now I hardly know my own name, let alone that of the king." It seemed very hot in the room, and she could hardly keep her eyes open. But then, remembering that they had fled from the possibility of being followed by Lyondri Hastur, she added, "Yes; we are for Carolin."

"As I said, half the Sisterhood seems to be quartered on us here," Betta said, "and there are so many rumors in this place. Two nights ago we had women sleeping on the tables in here, and even under them, even though we who live here in the hostel slept two to a bed and gave up the emptied beds to the newcomers."

"I have slept on the ground often enough," Romilly said, "I can sleep somewhere on the floor." At least this was out of the rain, and under a roof.

"Oh, I am sure that for the Lady Jandria they can find a bed somewhere," Betta said. "Are you her lover?"

Romilly was too tired and confused even to know for certain what Betta meant. "No, no, certainly not." Although, she supposed, the question was reasonable. Why would a woman seek the life of a Swordswoman, when she could just as well marry? There had been a time or two, since she had come among the Sisterhood, when she had begun to wonder if her constant rejection of the idea of marriage meant that at heart she was a lover of women. She felt no particular revulsion at the thought, but no particular attraction to it either. Fond as she had grown of Jandria during these days, it would never have occurred to her to seek her out as she had sought Orain. But now her attention had been forcibly drawn to the subject, she wondered again. *Is this why I have never really wanted a man, and even with Orain, it was a matter of liking and kindness, not any real desire?*

I am too tired to think clearly about anything, let alone anything as important as that! But she knew she must consider it some day, especially if her life was to be spent among the Sisterhood.

One by one, or in little groups of three and four, the women of the Sisterhood were leaving the table and going to seek their various beds. Blanket rolls stowed in a corner of the big room were unrolled on the floor, with some good-natured bickering for places near the log-fire; Tina came and found them and led them to a room with three beds, two of which were already occupied.

"You can sleep there," she told them, "And the House-mother wants to see you, Lady Jandria."

Janni said to Romilly, "Go to bed and sleep; I will be along later." Romilly was so tired that, although she told herself it would be difficult to sleep in a room with four other women, some of whom were certain to snore, she was fast asleep even before her head hit the pillow, and did not remember, afterward, at what hour Jandria had come in.

But the next morning, when they were dressing, she said to Jandria, "They seemed to know who you were, and to be expecting us. How could you send a message that would come faster than we did ourselves?"

Jandria looked up, a stocking in her hand. She said, "There is a *leronis* of my acquaintance with Carolin's army; this is why I dared not fall into the hands of Lyondri. I know too much. I sent word, and asked that news be sent to the hostel of the Sisterhood; so that they were ready to admit us. Do you really think they would open their doors after dark in a city full of soldiers, and readying for war?"

It seemed to Romilly that every day she learned something new about Jandria. So she had *laran* too? *Laran* of that curious kind which could link to send messages over the trackless miles? She felt shy and confused again—could Janni read what she was thinking, know all her rebellion, her fears? She kept her mind away from the implications of that.

"If I am to break horses here," she said, "I suppose I should go at once to the stables and begin."

Jandria laughed. "I think there will be time to have breakfast first," she said, "The Housemother told me to sleep as long as I could after the long ride; and I think we have slept long enough that we can find someplace to eat in the dining-room without kicking the sleepers off tables. That was the only reason I did not want to sleep on the floor there—I knew the cooks and servers for this tenday would come in and rouse us at daybreak so they could get to their breakfast kettles!"

And indeed by the time they were dressed, the dining-room was empty, with only a few old women lingering over cups of hot milk and bread soaked in them. They helped themselves to porridge from the kettle and ate, after which Betta came in search of them.

"You are to go to the Housemother, Lady Jandria," she said, "And Mistress Romilly to the stables—"

Jandria chuckled good-naturedly and said, "Just Jandria or Janni. Have you forgotten the rule of the Sisterhood?"

"Janni, then," Betta replied, but she still spoke with residual deference. "Practice in unarmed combat is at noon in the grass-court; swordplay at the fourth hour after. I will see you there."

In the stables and paddock, Romilly found a number of horses; black horses from the Kilghard Hills, the finest she had ever seen. It would be, she thought, a pleasure and a privilege to train these to the saddle.

"They are needed by the Army, in as much haste as possible," said Tina, who had brought her here, "And they must be trained to the saddle, to a steady pace, and to stand against loud noises. I can get you as many helpers as you need, but we have no expert, and Lady Jandria told us that you have the MacAran Gift. So you will be in charge of the work of training them."

Romilly looked at the horses; there were a good two dozen of them. She asked, "Have any of them been trained to pacing on a lunge-line?"

"About a dozen," Tina said, and Romilly nodded.

"Good; then find a dozen women who can try their paces, and take them out in the paddock," she said, "and I will begin getting to know the others."

When the women came she noticed that Betta was among them, and greeted her with a nod and smile. She sent them out to work for a few minutes at running the horses in circles on the lunge-lines, steadying their paces, and went into the stable to choose the horse which she would herself work with.

She decided to give each horse into the charge of the woman who had exercised it today; it was easier if they formed a close tie with the horse.

"For then the animal will trust you," she told them, "and will do things to please you. But it cannot be a one-way connection," she warned, "Even as the horse loves and trusts you, you must love him—or, if it is a mare, love *her*—and be completely trustworthy, so that the horse can read in your mind that you love; you cannot pretend, for he will read a lie in moments. You must be open to the horse's feelings, too. Another thing—" she gestured to the short training-whips which were in their hands, "You can snap the whips if you like, to get their attention. But if you hit any horse enough to mark it, you are no trainer; if I see a whip in serious use, you can go and practice your swordplay instead!"

She sent them to work and listened for a moment to the chattering as they went out.

"Not to use our whips? What are they for, then?"

"I don't understand this woman. Where is she from, the far mountains? Her speech is so strange. . . ."

Romilly would have thought it was *their* speech which was strange, slow and thoughtful, as if they chewed every word a dozen times before speaking; while it seemed to her that she talked naturally. Still, after she had heard a dozen women say they they could not understand her, she tried to slow her own speech and speak with what seemed to her an affected, unnatural slowness.

If they were at Falconsward, everyone would think their speech silly, foreign, affected. I suppose it is a matter of what they are used to.

She turned to the horses with definite relief. At least, with them, she could be herself and they, at any rate, would not be critical of her speech or manners.

The horses, at least, speak my language, she thought with pleasure.

There were so many of them, and of all kinds, from sturdy shaggy mountain ponies like the one she had killed on the way here, to sleek blacks such as her own father bred. She went into the loose-box among them (to the distinct horror of Betta, who seemed as troubled as if she had gone into a cage full of carnivorous mountain-cats) and moved through them, trying to find the right horse to begin with. She must do a splendid job of training, because she knew that there was some grumbling—she looked so young, they said, and they would be quick to spot any mistakes.

I am not so young, and I have been working among horses since I was nine years old. But they do not know that.

As she moved through the box, one horse backed up against the wooden rails and began kicking; Romilly noticed the wide rolling eyes, the lips drawn back over the teeth.

"Come out and away from that one, Romilly, he's a killer—we are thinking of returning him to the Army, who can turn him out to pasture for stud; no one will be able to ride that one—he's too old for breaking to saddle!" Tina called it anxiously, but Romilly, lost and intent, shook her head.

He is frightened almost to death, no more. But he won't hurt me.

"Bring me a lead-rope and bridle, Tina. No, you needn't come into the box if you are afraid, just hand it to me across the rails," she said. Tina handed it through, her face pale with apprehension, but Romilly, rope in hand, had her eyes only on the black horse.

Well, you beauty, you, do you think we can make friends, then?

The horse backed nervously, but he had stopped kicking. *What fool put him into this crowded box, anyhow? Softly,*

softly, Blackie, I won't hurt you; do you want to go out in the sunshine? She formed a clear image of what she meant to do, and the horse, snorting uneasily, let him pull her head down and slip bridle and lead-rope over it. She heard Tina catch her breath, amazed, but she was so deeply entwined now with the horse that she had no thought to spare for the woman.

"Open the gate," she said abstractedly, keeping close contact with the mind of the stallion. "That's wide enough. *Come along now, you beautiful black thing.* . . . See, if you handle them right, no horse is vicious; they are only afraid, and don't know what's expected of them."

"But you have *laran*," said one of the watchers, grudgingly, "We don't; how can we do what you do?"

"*Laran* or no," Romilly said, "if your whole body and every thought in it is stiff with fear, do you expect the horse not to know it, to smell it on you, even? Act as if you trusted the animal, talk to him, make a clear picture in your mind of what you want to do—who knows, they may have some kind of *laran* of their own. And above all, let him know absolutely that you won't hurt him. He will see and feel it in every movement you make, every breath, if you are afraid of him or if you wish him ill."

She turned her attention back to the horse.

"So, now, lovely fellow, we're going into the sunshine in the paddock . . . come along, now . . . no, not that way, silly, you don't want to go back in the stable," she said half aloud, with a little tug on the ropes. In the paddock half a dozen women were running horses in circles on the long lunge-lines, calling to them, and in general keeping the pace smooth. Romilly made a quick check of what was going on—none of them were doing really badly, but then no doubt they had chosen the more docile animals for training first—and found a relatively isolated place of paddock; one or more of the mares might be in season and she did not want him distracted. She backed away on the lunge-line and clucked to him.

He was strong, a big, heavy horse, and for a moment Romilly was almost jerked off her feet as he began to lope, found the line confining him, then explored its limits and began to run in a circle at its limit. She pulled hard and he slowed to a steady walk, around and around. After a little, when she was sure he had the idea, she began to let him move a little faster.

241

His paces are beautiful; a horse fit for Carolin's self. Oh, you glorious thing, you!

She let him run for almost an hour, accustoming him to the feeling of the bridle, then called for a bit. He fought it a little, in surprise—Romilly half sympathized with him; she did not much blame him, she did not think she would care to have a cold metal thing forced into her mouth, either.

But that's the way it is, beauty, you'll get used to it, and then you can ride with your master. . . .

At noon she led him back, suggesting to one of the women they they put her more docile horse into the loose-box and leave her own small stall for the black stallion. Already, it seemed, she could see the nebulous figure of King Carolin riding into Hali on this splendid horse.

From this work, which she found easy—well, not exactly easy, but familiar and pleasant—she was sent to practice unarmed combat. She did not especially mind having to learn to fall without hurting herself—she had, after all, fallen from a horse more times than she could remember while she was learning to ride, and she supposed the skill was similar—but the series of holds, thrusts, jabs and throws seemed endlessly complex, and it seemed that every woman there, including the beginners with whom she was set to practice basic movements, knew more of it than she did. One of the older women, watching her for a moment, finally motioned her away, signalled to the others to go on, and said, "How long have you been pledged to the Sisterhood, my girl?"

Romilly tried to remember. Things had been happening so swiftly in the last few moons that she really had no notion. She shrugged helplessly. "I am not sure. Some tendays—"

"And you do not see much cause for this kind of training, do you?"

She said, carefully trying to be tactful, "I am sure there must be some reason for it, if it is taught in every hostel of the Sisterhood."

"Where were you brought up—what's your name?"

"Romilly. Or I'm called Romy sometimes. And I was brought up in the foothills of the Hellers, near Falconsward."

The woman nodded. "I would have guessed that much from your speech; but you grew up in outland country, then, not near to a big city, where you never met a stranger?"

"That's true."

"Well, then. Suppose you are walking down a city street, one of the more crowded and dirty sections." She beckoned and the girl who had sat next to Romilly at supper last night, Betta, came and joined them.

"You are walking along a dirty street where thieves cluster and men think all women like the doxies of the taverns," the older woman said. Betta shrugged, began to walk along the wall and the older woman suddenly leaped at her with a strangling grip. Romilly gasped as Betta twisted her upper body, jerked the woman forward and flung her to her knees, her arm immobilized behind her back.

"Ow! Betta, you are a little rough, but I think Romy sees what is meant. Now, come at me with a knife—"

Betta took up a small wooden stick, about the size of a clasp-knife, and came at the woman with 'knife' lowered to stab. So rapidly that Romilly could not see what happened, the 'knife' was in the other woman's hands and Betta lying on her back on the floor, where the older woman pretended to kick her.

"Careful, Clea," Betta warned, laughing and moving out of the way, then suddenly jerked at the woman's foot and pulled her down.

Laughing in her turn, Clea scrambled up. She said to Romilly, "Now do you see what good this might be to you? Particularly in a city like this, where we are at the edge of the Drylands, and there are likely to be men who think of women as possessions to be chained and imprisoned? But even in a civilized city like Thendara, you are likely to meet with those who will have neither respect nor courtesy for man or woman. Every women taken into the Sisterhood must learn to protect herself, and—" her laughing face suddenly turned deadly serious, "When you are life-pledged to the Sisterhood, like myself, you will wear this." She laid her hand on the dagger at her throat. "I am pledged to kill rather than let myself be taken by force; to kill the man if I can, myself if I cannot."

A shiver ran down Romilly's back. She did not know whether she would be able to do that or not. She had been prepared to injure Rory seriously, if she must. But to kill him? Would that not make her as bad as he was?

I shall face that if, and when, I am sworn for life to the Sisterhood, should that day ever come. By then, maybe, I will know what I can do and what I cannot.

Clea saw her troubled look and patted her shoulder. "Never mind, you will learn. Now get over there and practice. Betta, take her and show her the first practice moves so she won't be so confused; time enough later to throw her into a group of beginners."

Now that somebody had bothered to inform Romilly what they were doing and why, it went better. She began to realize, then and in the days that followed, that when she faced another woman in these sessions, she could read, by following tiny body and eye movements, precisely what the other was going to do, and take advantage of it. But knowing was not enough; she also had to learn the precise movements and holds, jabs and thrusts and throws, the right force to use without actually damaging anyone.

And yet, in men's clothing, I travelled all through the Hellers. I would rather live in such a way that I need not be prey to any man.

Yet there was pride, too, in knowing that she could defend herself and need never ask for mercy from anyone. Later the lessons in swordplay seemed easier to her, but they brought another fear to the surface of her mind.

It was all very well to practice with wooden batons where the only penalty for a missed stroke was a bad bruise. But could she face sharp weapons without terror, could she actually bring herself to strike with a sharp weapon at anyone? The thought of slicing through human flesh made her feel sick.

I am not a Swordswoman, no matter what they call me. I am a horse trainer, a bird handler . . . fighting is not my business.

The days passed, filled with lessons and hard work. When she had been there for forty days, she realized that Midsummer was approaching. Soon she would have been absent from her home for a whole year. No doubt her father and stepmother thought her long dead, and Darren was being forced to take his place as Heir to Falconsward. Poor Darren, how he would hate that! She hoped for her father's sake that little Rael was able to take her place, to learn some of the MacAran gifts,—if Rael was what her father would have called "true MacAran", perhaps Darren would be allowed to return to the monastery. Or perhaps he would go as she had done, without leave.

A year ago her father had betrothed her to *Dom* Garris. What changes there had been in a year! Romilly knew she had grown taller—she had had to put all the clothes she had worn when she came here, into the box of castoffs, and find others which came nearer to fitting her. Her shoulders were broader, and because of the continuous practice at swordplay and her work with the horses, her muscles in upper arms and legs were hard and bulging. How Mallina would jeer at her, how her stepmother would deplore it—*You do not look like a lady, Romilly*. Well, Romilly silently answered her stepmother's imagined voice, I am not a lady but a Swordswoman.

But all her troubles disappeared every day when she was working with the horses, and especially for the hour every day when she worked with the black stallion. No hand but hers ever touched him; she knew that one day, this would be a mount fit for the king himself. Day followed day, and moon followed moon, and season followed season; winter closed in, and there were days when she could not work even with the black stallion, let alone the other horses. Nevertheless, she directed their care. Time and familiarity had changed the strange faces in the hostel to friends. Midwinter came, with spicebread, and gifts exchanged in the hostel among the Sisterhood. A few women had families and went home to visit them; but when Romilly was asked if she wished for leave to visit her home, she said steadily that she had no kin. It was simpler that way. But she wondered; how would her father receive her, if she came home for a visit, asking nothing, a professional Swordswoman in her tunic of crimson, and the ensign of the Sisterhood in her pierced ear? Would he drive her forth, say that she was no daughter of his, that no daughter of his could be one of those unsexed women of the Sisterhood? Or would he welcome her with pride, smile with welcome and even approve of her independence and the strength she had shown in making a life for herself away from Falconsward?

She did not know. She could not even guess. Perhaps one day, years from now, she would risk trying to find out. But in any case she could not travel into the depths of the Hellers at the midwinter-season; most of the women who took leave for family visits lived no further away than Thendara or Hali, which was, perhaps, seven days ride.

In this desert country there were few signs of spring. One day it was cold, icy winds blowing and rain sweeping across the plains, and the next day, it seemed, the sun shone hot and Romilly knew that far away in the Hellers the roads were flooding with the spring-thaw. When she could work the horses, she took off her cloak and worked in a shabby, patched tunic and breeches.

With the spring came rumors of armies on the road, of a battle far away between Carolin's forces and the armies of

Lyondri Hastur. Later they heard that Carolin had made peace with the Great House of Serrais, and that his armies were gathering again on the plains. Romilly paid little heed. All her days were taken up with the new group of horses brought in to them early in the spring—they had put up a shelter for them and rented a new paddock outside the walls of the hostel, where Romilly went with the women she was training, every afternoon. Her world had shrunk to stables and paddock, and to the plain outside the city where they went, two or three days in every ten, to work and exercise the horses. One afternoon when they left the city and went out through the gates, leading the horses, Romilly saw tents and men and horses, a bewildering crowd.

"What is it?" she asked, and one of the women, who went out every morning to shop for fresh milk and fresh fruits, told her, "It is the advance guard of Carolin's army; they will establish their camp here, and from here they will move down again across the Plains of Valeron, to give battle to King Rakhal—" her face twisted with dislike, and she spat.

"You are a partisan of Carolin, then?" Romilly asked.

"A partisan of Carolin? I am," the woman said vehemently, "Rakhal drove my father from his small-holding in the Venza Hills and gave his lands to a paxman of that greedy devil Lyondri Hastur! Mother died soon after we left our lands, and Father is with Carolin's army—I shall ride out tomorrow, if Clea will give me leave, and try to find my father, and ask if he has word of my brothers, who fled when we were driven from our lands. I am here with the Sisterhood because my brothers were with the armies and could no longer make a home for me; they would have found a man for me to marry, but the man they chose was one Lyondri and his master Rakhal had left in peace, and I would not marry any man who sat snug in his home while my father was exiled!"

"No one could blame you, Marelie," said Romilly. She thought of her travels in the Hellers with Orain and Carlo and the other exiled men; Alaric, who had suffered even more from Lyondri Hastur than Marelie's family. "I too am a follower of Carolin, even though I know nothing about him, except that men whose judgment I trust, call him a good man and a good king."

She wondered if Orain and *Dom* Carlo were in the camp. She might go with Merelie, when she went to seek her father in the camp. Orain had been her friend, even though she was

246

a woman, and she hoped he had come safe through the winter of war.

"Look," said Clea, pointing, "There is the Hastur banner in blue with the silver fir-tree. King Carolin is in the camp—the king himself."

And where Orain is, Carolin is not far away, Romilly remembered. That night in the tavern, when he had wanted her to make a diversion—had that shadowy figure to whom he spoke, been Carolin himself?

Would he welcome a visit from her? Or would he only find it an embarrassment? She decided that when next Jandria visited the hostel—she had been coming and going all year, on courier duty between Serrais and the cities to the south, Dalereuth and Temora—she would ask what Jandria thought.

She should have remembered that when a telepath's mind was drawn unexpectedly to someone she had not seen for a time, it was not likely to be coincidence. It was the next day, when she had finished working with the black stallion, and finally led him back into the stable—after a year of work, he was perfectly trained, and docile as a child, and she had spoken to the housemother of the hostel about, perhaps, presenting him to the king's own self—she saw Jandria at the door of his stall.

"Romy! I was sure I would find you here! He has come a long way from that first day when I saw you bridle him, and we were all sure he would kill you!"

Jandria was dressed as if she had just come from a long journey; dusty boots, dust-mask such as the Drylanders used for travel hanging unfastened at the side of her face. Romilly ran to embrace her.

"Janni! I didn't know you were back!"

"I have not been here long, little sister," Jandria said, returning her hug with enthusiasm. Romilly smoothed back her flying hair with grubby hands, and said, "Let me unsaddle him, and then we will have some time to talk before supper. Isn't he wonderful? I have named him Sunstar—that is how he thinks of himself, he told me."

Jandria said, "He is beautiful indeed. But you should not give the horses such elaborate names, nor treat them with such care—they are to go to soldiers and they should have simple names, easy to remember. And above all you should not grow so fond of them, since they are to be taken from you very soon—they are for the army, though some of them will be ridden by the women of the Sisterhood if they go with Carolin's men when they break camp. You have seen the camp? You know the time is at hand when all these horses are to go to the army. You should not involve yourself so deeply with them."

"I can't help growing fond of them," Romilly said, "It is how I train them; I win their love and trust and they do my will."

Jandria sighed. "We must have that *laran* of yours, and yet I hate to use you like this, child," she said, stroking Romilly's soft hair. "Orain told me, when first he brought you to us, that you have knowledge of sentry-birds. I am to take you to Carolin's camp, so you can show a new handler how to treat them. Go and dress yourself for riding, my dear."

"Dress for riding? What do you think I have been doing all morning?" Romilly demanded.

"But not outside the hostel," Jandria said severely, and suddenly Romilly saw herself through Janni's eyes, her hair tangled and with bits of straw in it, her loose tunic unfastened because it was hot and sweaty, showing the curve of her breasts. She had put on a patched and too-tight pair of old breeches she had found in the box of castoffs which the Sisterhood kept for working about the house. She flushed and giggled.

"Let me go and change, then, I'll only be a minute or so."

She washed herself quickly at the pump, ran into the room she shared now with Clea and Betta, and combed her tousled hair. Then she got swiftly into her own breeches and a clean under-tunic. Over her head she slipped the crimson tunic of the Sisterhood and belted it with her dagger. Now she looked, she knew, not like a woman in men's clothes, nor yet like a boy, or a street urchin, but like a member of the Sisterhood; a professional Swordswoman, a soldier for Carolin's armies. She could not quite believe it was herself in that formal costume. Yet this was what she was.

Jandria smiled with approval when she came back; Janni too wore the formal Swordswoman tunic of crimson, a sword in her belt, a dagger at her throat, her small ensign gleaming in her left ear. Side by side, the two swordswomen left the gates of the hostel and rode toward the city wall of Serrais.

CHAPTER FOUR

Now Romilly had a closer look at the encampment of Carolin's men, the silver and blue fir-tree banner of the Hasturs flying above the central tent which, Romilly imagined, must be either the king's personal quarters or the headquarters of his staff. They rode toward the encampment, past orderly stable-lines, a cookhouse where army cooks were boiling something that smelled savory, and a field roped off, where a Swordswoman Romilly knew only slightly was giving a group of unshaven recruits a lesson in unarmed combat; some of them looked cross and disgruntled and Romilly suspected that they did not like being schooled by a woman; others, rubbing bumps and bruises where she had tossed them handily on the ground, were watching with serious attention.

A guard was posted near the central part of the camp, and he challenged them. Jandria gave him a formal salute.

"Swordswoman Jandria and Apprentice Romilly," she said, "and I seek the Lord Orain, who has sent for me."

Romilly tried to make herself small, supposing that the guard would say something sneering or discourteous, but he merely returned her salute and called a messenger, a boy about Romilly's age, to request Lord Orain's attention.

She would have recognized the tall, gaunt figure, the lean hatchet-jaw, anywhere; but now he was dressed in the elegant Hastur colors and wore a jewelled pendant and a fine sword, and Romilly knew that if she had met him first like this, she would have been too much in awe of him to speak. He bowed formally to the women, and his voice was the schooled accent of a nobleman, with no trace of the rough-country dialect.

"*Mastra'in*, it is courteous of you to come so quickly at my summons," he said, and Jandria replied, just as formally, that it was her pleasure and duty to serve the king's presence.

A little less formally, Orain went on "I remembered that Romilly was schooled in the training, not only of hawks but of sentry-birds. We have a *laranzu* come with us from Tramontana, but he has had no experience with sentry-birds, and these are known to you, *damisela*. Will it please you to introduce the skills of handling them to our *laranzu?*"

"I'd be glad to do it, Lord Orain," she said, then burst out, "but only if you stop calling me *damisela* in that tone!"

A ragged flush spread over Orain's long face. He did not meet her eyes. "I am sorry—Romilly. Will you come this way?"

She trailed Jandria and Orain, who walked arm in arm. Jandria asked, "How's Himself, then?"

Orain shrugged. "All the better for the news you sent ahead, love. But did you see Lyondri face to face?"

Romilly saw the negative motion of the older woman's head. "At the last I was too cowardly; I sent Romilly in my place. If I had met him then—" she broke off. "I do not know if you saw those villages last year, along the old North road. Still blighted, all of them . . ." she shuddered; even at this distance, Romilly could see. "I am glad I am an honest Swordswoman, not a *leronis!* If I had had to have a part in the blighting of the good land, I know not how I could ever again have raised my eyes to the clean day!"

Was this, Romilly wondered, the reason why The MacAran had quarreled with the Towers, why Ruyven had had to run away, and he had driven the *leronis* from his home without giving her leave to test Romilly and Mallina for *laran*? *Laran* warfare, even the little she had seen of it, was terrifying.

Orain said soberly, "Carolin has said he will not fight that kind of war unless it is used against him. But if Rakhal has *laranzu'in* to bring against his armies, then he must do what he must; you know that as well as I, Janni." He sighed. "You had better come and tell him what you learned in Hali, though the news will make him sorrowful. As for Romilly—" he turned and considered her for a moment, "The bird-handlers' quarters are yonder," he said, pointing. "The bird-master and his apprentice have that tent there, and no doubt you will find them both around behind it. This way, Janni."

Jandria and Orain went off arm-in-arm toward the central tent where the banner flew, and Romilly went on in the indicated direction, feeling shy and afraid. How was she to talk to a strange *laranzu*? Then she straightened her back and drew herself up proudly. She was a MacAran, a Swordswoman, and a hawkmistress; she need not be afraid of anyone. They had summoned her to their aid, not the other way round. Behind the tent she saw a roughly dressed lad of thirteen or so, carrying a great basket, and if she had not seen him she could have smelled him, for it stank of carrion. On heavy perches she saw three familiar, beautiful-ugly forms, and hurried to them, laughing.

"Diligence! Prudence, love!" She held out her hands and the birds made a little dipping of their heads; they knew her again, and the old, familiar rapport reached out, clung. "And where is Temperance? Ah, there you are, you beauty!"

"Don't get too close to them," a somehow-familiar voice said behind her, "Those creatures can peck out your eyes; the apprentice there lost a finger-nail to one of them yesterday!"

She turned and saw a slight, bearded man, in the dark robes not unlike those of a monk at Nevarsin, scowling down at her; then it seemed as if the strange bearded face dissolved, for she knew the voice, and she cried out, incredulous.

"Ruyven! Oh, I should have known, when they said it was a *laranzu* from Tramontana—Ruyven, don't you know me?"

She was laughing and crying at once, and Ruyven stared down at her, his mouth open.

"Romy," he said at last. "Sister, you are the last person in the world I would have expected to see *here!* But—in this garb—" he looked her up and down, blushing behind the strangeness of the beard. "What are you doing? How came you—"

"I was sent to handle the birds, silly," she said, "I bore them all the way from the foothills of the Hellers into Nevarsin, and from Nevarsin to Caer Donn. See, they know me." She gestured, and they made little clucking noises of pleasure and acknowledgement. "But what are you doing here, then?"

"The same as you," he said. "The Lord Orain's son and I are *bredin*; he sent word to me, and I came to join Carolin's army. But you—" he looked at the dress of the Sisterhood with surprise and distaste, "Does Father know you are here? How did you win his consent?"

"The same way you won consent from him to train your

251

laran within the walls of Tramontana Tower," she said, grimacing, and he sighed.

"Poor father. He has lost both of us now, and Darren—" he sighed. "Ah, well. Done is done. So you wear the earring of the Sisterhood, and I the robes of the Tower, and both of us follow Carolin—have you seen the king?"

She shook her head. "No, but I travelled for a time with his followers, Orain and *Dom* Carlo of Blue Lake."

"Carlo I know not. But you handle sentry-birds? I remember you had always a deft hand with horses and hounds, and I suppose hawks as well, so the MacAran Gift should fit you to handle these. Have you had *laran* training then, Sister?"

"None; I developed it by working with the beasts and the birds," she said, and he shook his head, distressed.

"*Laran* untrained is a dangerous thing, Romy. When this is ended, I will find a place for you in a Tower. Do you realize, you have not yet greeted me properly." He hugged her and kissed her cheek. "So: you know these birds? So far I have seen none but Lord Orain who could handle them. . . ."

"I taught him what he knows of sentry-birds," Romilly said, and went to the perches, holding out her hand; with her free hand she jerked the knot loose, and Prudence made a quick little hop to sit on her wrist. She should have brought a proper glove. Well, somewhere in Carolin's camp there must be a proper falconer's glove.

And that made her think, with sudden pain, of Preciosa. She had had no sight of the hawk since they came into this drylands country. But then, Preciosa had left her before they came to the glaciers, and rejoined her again when she had returned to the green hills. It might be that Preciosa would return to her, some day . . .

. . . and if not, she is free . . . a free wild thing, belonging to the winds of the sky and to herself. . . .

"Can you get me a glove?" she asked, "I can, if I must, handle Prudence with my bare hands, because she is small and gentle, but the others are heavier and have not such a delicate touch—"

"That creature, delicate?" Ruyven said, laughing, then the smile slid off as he saw how serious she was. "Prudence, you call her? Yes, I will send my helper for a glove for you, and then you must tell me their names and how you tell them apart."

The morning passed quickly, but they spoke only of the birds; not touching at all on their shared past, or on Falconsward. At midday a bell was rung, and Ruyven, saying that it was dinnertime in the army mess, told her to come along.

"There are others of the Sisterhood in the camp," he said, "They sleep in their hostel in the city—but I dare say you know more about them than I. You can eat at their table, if you will—and I suppose it would be better, since they do not mix with the regular soldiers except when they must, and you cannot explain to the whole army that you are my sister."

She joined the long lines of the army mess, taking her bread and stew to the separate table with the seven or eight women of the Sisterhood who were employed with the army—mostly as couriers, or as trainers of horses or instructors in unarmed combat—one, in fact, as an instructor in swordplay. Some of the women she had met in the hostel and none of them seemed even slightly surprised to see her there. Jandria did not appear. Romilly supposed that she had been kept with Lord Orain and the higher officers, who evidently had their mess apart.

"What are you doing?" one asked her, and she replied briefly that she had been sent for to work with sentry-birds.

"I thought that was work for *leronyn*," one of the women remarked, "But then you have red hair, are you too *laran*-gifted?"

"I have a knack for working with animals," Romilly said, "I do not know if it is *laran* or something else." She did not want to be treated with the distant awe with which they regarded the *leroni*. When she had finished her meal she rejoined Ruyven at the bird-handlers' quarters, and by the end of the day he was handling the birds as freely as she did herself.

Dusk was falling, and they were settling the birds on their perches, to be carried in under the tent-roof, when Ruyven looked up.

"King Carolin's right-hand man," he said briefly, "We see Carolin's self but seldom; word comes always through Lord Orain. You know him, I understand."

"I travelled with him for months; but they thought me a boy," Romilly said, without explaining. Orain came to them and said to Ruyven, ignoring Romilly, "How soon will the birds be ready for use?"

"A tenday, perhaps."

"And Derek has not yet arrived," said Orain, scowling. "Do you think you could persuade the *leronis* . . ."

Ruyven said curtly, "The battlefield is no place for the Lady Maura. Add to that, Lyondri is of her kin; she said she

253

would handle the birds but she made me promise to her that she would not be asked to fight against him. I blame her not; this war that sets brother against brother, father against son, is no place for a woman."

Orain said, with his dry smile, "Nor for a man; yet the world will go as it will, and not as you or I would have it. This war was not of my making, nor of Carolin's. Nevertheless, I respect the sentiments of the Lady Maura, so we must have another to fly the sentry-birds. Romilly——" he looked down at her, and for a moment there was a trace of the old warmth in his voice, "Will you fly them for Carolin, then, my girl?"

So when he wants something from me, he can be halfway civil, even to a woman? Anger made her voice cold. She said, "As for that, *vai dom,* you must ask my superiors in the Sisterhood; I am apprentice, and my will does not rule what I may do."

"Oh, I think Jandria will not make trouble about that," Orain said, smiling. "The Sisterhood will lend you to us, I have no doubt at all."

Romilly bowed without answering. But she thought, *not if I have anything to say about it.*

They rode back to the hostel in the light of the setting sun, the sky clear and cloudless; Romilly had never ceased to miss the evening rain or sleet in the hills. It still seemed to her that the country here was dry, parched, inhospitable. Jandria tried to talk a little of the army, of the countryside, to point out to Romilly the Great House of Serrais, perched on the low hillside, where the Hastur-kind had established their seat, as at Thendara and Hali and Aldaran and Carcosa in the hills; but Romilly was silent, hardly speaking, lost in thought.

Ruyven is no longer the brother I knew; we can be friendly now but the old closeness is gone forever. I had hoped he would understand me, the conflicts that drove me from Falconsward—they are like his own. Once he could see me simply as Romilly, not as his little sister. Now—now all he sees is that I have become a Swordswoman, hawkmistress . . . no more than that.

Even when I lost Falconsward, father, mother, home—I thought that when I again met with Ruyven we would be as we were when we were children. Now Ruyven too is forever gone from me.

I have nothing now; a hawk and my skills with the sword and with the beasts. They reached the hostel, where supper was long over, but one of the women found them something in the kitchens. They went to their beds in silence; Jandria, too, was wrapped in thoughts which, Romilly thought, must be as bitter as her own.

Damn this warfare! Yes, that is what Ruyven said, and Orain too. It may be that father was right . . . what does it matter which great rogue sits on the throne or which greater rogue seeks to wrest it from him?

Every day, Romilly worked first with the other horses, who were simpler to handle because they were less intelligent; they seemed to have less initiative. Sunstar she saved as a reward for herself at the end of a long morning of working with the other horses, directing her assistants in exercising them and personally supervising their gaits and the speed with which they had been broken to saddle and riding gear. She knew that she was only one of the army horsetrainers in Serrais who had been engaged by Carolin to produce the cavalry for his armies—she saw some of the others, sometimes, come out from the city of Serrais and working on the plains. But she would have been a fool not to know that her horses were trained fastest and best.

Now, at the near end of a long morning, she walked around her little domain, with a pat and a touch on the nose and a long, blissful moment of emotional rapport with each of her horses. She loved every one, she felt the bittersweet knowledge that soon she would have to part with them; but every one of them would carry some of herself wherever Carolin's armies might ride. Touch after touch, a hug around a sleek neck or a stroking of a velvety nose, and each moment of rapport building her awareness higher, higher yet, till she was dizzied with it, with the sense of racing in the sun, the awareness of running at full stretch on four legs, not two, the mastery of the burden of the rider with its own delight, and somewhere at the back of her mind Romilly felt as if each of these beasts bearing its rider knew something of the inward rightness of the Bearer of Burdens who, said in the writings of the sainted Valentine, bore alone the weight of the world. She *was* each horse in turn, knowing its rebellions, its discipline and submission, the sense of working in perfect unity with what was allotted to it.

Blurrily, she thought, *perhaps only horses know what true faith may be as they share with the Bearer of Burdens . . . and yet I, only human, have been chosen to share and to know this. . . .* it was easier to be carried away in union and rapport with the horses than with hawks or even the more brilliant sentry-birds, because, she thought, horses had a keener intelligence. The birds, sensitive as they were, blissful as it was to share the ecstasy of flight, still had only limited awareness, mostly focused in their keener eyesight. The sensual awareness was greater in the horses because they were more organized, more intelligent, a human *style* of awareness and yet not quite human.

And now at the end of her morning, when the other horses had been led away, she brought out Sunstar from his place. He worked so closely with her now that a bare word summoned him, and a part of her flooded out in love, she *was* the horse, she felt the saddle slipped over her own back as she caressed the leather straps of it, she was in a strange doubled consciousness.

She did not know whether she climbed into the saddle or accepted the grateful weight on her own back. Part of her was sunk joyously into her own body awareness, but that was all swallowed up in the larger consciousness of striding free, racing with the wind . . . so balanced, so fused into the horse that for a long time she was hardly aware of which was herself, which Sunstar. Yet for all the blurring she felt she had never been so precisely and wholly herself, flooded with a kind of reality she had never known. The heat of the sun, sweat streaming down her flanks, her exquisite leaning to balance from above the weight she felt from below, from *within*. Time seemed divided into infinitesimal fragments, to each of which she gave its true weight, with no thought of past or future, all gathered up into the absolute present.

And, then, regretfully, she came back and separated herself from Sunstar, sliding down at the paddock rail, falling against him and flinging her arms around his glossy neck in an absolute ecstasy of love, wholly giving, wholly aware. It needed no words. She was his; he was hers; even if they never again knew this ecstasy of consummation, this delicious flooding delight, if she never mounted him again nor he raced with her toward an endless plain of oblivious pleasure, they would always, in some part of their being, be fused together; this moment was eternal and would go on happening forever.

And then, with faint regret—but only faint, for in her exalted state she knew that all things had their proper moment and this one could not be prolonged too far—she let herself slide down another level of awareness and she was Romilly again, giving the horse's silken shoulders a final pat of love and leading him, separate now but never far, to his own paddock. She could hardly feel her feet beneath her as she walked back toward the hostel, but she felt distinct annoyance at Clea's friendly voice.

"How beautiful he is—is that is the black stallion they told me about? Is he too fierce, will they have to turn him out to stud again?" Then alerted by something in Romilly's face, she asked, "You—you've been riding him?"

"He is gentle as a child," said Romilly absently. "He loves me, but a child could ride him now." Absurdly, she wished she could give this beautiful creature over to Caryl, who would surely love him as she did, for he had more than a trace of her own kind of *laran*. Since she could not keep this imperial creature herself, it would be finest if he could go to that sensitive boy. Who was, she reminded herself with a sharp coming-down-to-earth, the son of Lyondri Hastur and her sworn enemy. "What did you want, Clea?"

"I was coming to speak to you about your unarmed-combat lesson," the other woman said, "but on the way I met with Jandria, who says that you have been sent for again to the king's camp; you are to work with sentry-birds, I hear. You are to take all your things; you will not be coming back here, I understand."

Not coming back? Then she must say farewell to Sunstar even sooner than she had believed. But in her aware state she knew it really did not matter. They would always be part of one another. For now she was to be mistress of hawks to Carolin's armies—she did not stop to think how she knew that—and she, like Sunstar, must carry her appointed share of the world's weight. She said, "Thank you, Clea. And thank you for everything, all you have taught me—"

"Romy, how your eyes shine! It has been a pleasure to teach you; it is always a pleasure to teach anyone who is so apt and quick to learn," Clea said, and hugged her with spontaneous warmth. "I am sorry to lose you. I hope you come back to our hostel some day, but if not, we will meet at another. Swordswomen are always travelling and we are sure to come across one another somewhere on the roads of the Hundred Kingdoms."

Romilly kissed her with real warmth and went into the hostel to pack her few possessions.

By the time she was finished, she found Jandria in the hallway ready to ride, she too bearing a rolled pack with all her possessions.

"I had Sunstar brought out," Jandria said, "The other horses are being brought along later in the day; but you have spent so much time, and so much love, on this one, that I thought you should have the privilege of handing him over yourself to King Carolin."

So it has come quicker than I thought. But after this morning, Sunstar and I will always be one.

He did not take kindly to the leading rein; Romilly wished that she could ride him herself, but that was not suitable for a horse to be presented to the king. She soothed him in soft words with her voice, and even more, with the outreaching of contact, so that, guided by her soothing flood of tenderness and reassurance, he came along, docile, feeling her concern and her touch guiding him.

You are to be a king's mount, did you know that, my beauty?

The contact between them needed no words; it meant nothing to Sunstar, who knew nothing of kings, and Romilly knew that while he might, and probably would, come to love and trust Carolin, no other would ever ride Sunstar with that same sense of close oneness with the horse. Suddenly she felt sorry for Carolin. The beautiful black stallion might be his. But she, Romilly, would always own him in both their hearts.

CHAPTER FIVE

There was a subtly different feel to the army camp today. The great central tent where the Hastur banner had flown was being pulled down by what looked like a horde of workmen, there was confusion coming and going through the length and breadth of the camp. Leaving Sunstar with Jandria and the others who had come to help her with the stallion, Romilly hurried off to the bird-handlers quarters. She found Ruyven there, fussing with the perches installed for the sentry-birds atop pack-animals. The chervines, disliking the carrion smell that clung to the birds, were stamping restlessly and moving around with little, troubled snorts and pawings.

"I imagine," Romilly said, "that this all means that the army is about to move southward and I am to go with you."

He nodded. "I cannot handle or fly three birds alone," he said, "and there is not another qualified handler for these sentry-birds within a hundred leagues, except, God help us, for the ones who may be among Rakhal's scouts or advance guard. We have had intelligence from Hali that Rakhal is massing his own armies under Lyondri Hastur, and if he moves as we think—and that will depend to some degree upon how well you and I use the eyes of our birds—we will meet him near Neskaya in the Kilghard Hills. In fact, Lord Orain has asked if we can fly the birds out today and see what we can spy out."

"And, of course, when Orain speaks, all the army jumps to attention," said Romilly dryly. Ruyven stared at her.

"What is the matter with you, Romy? Lord Orain is a good and kindly man, and Carolin's chief adviser and friend! Do you dislike him? And with what reason?"

That recalled Romilly to herself. It was only wounded vanity; while he thought her a boy, Orain had admired her and trusted her, and when he knew her a woman, all that went into discard and she was just another nonentity, another woman, perhaps a danger to him. But that was Orain's problem and not hers; she had done nothing to deserve being ruthlessly cast out of his affections like that.

And he is the loser by it. Not I.

She said steadily, "I value Orain's gifts better than you know; I travelled with him and worked close to him for many moons. I do not think he should look down on me simply because I am a woman; I have shown I can do my work as well and skillfully as any man."

"No one doubts that, Romy," said Ruyven, in a note so conciliating that Romilly wondered how much of her hidden anger had actually shown in her face, "But Orain loves not women, and he has not had Tower teachings—we know in Tramontana that women's strengths and men's are not so different, after all. We are the first Tower who experimented with a woman for Keeper in one of our circles, and she is as skillful with the work as any man, even a Hastur. I think you, too, could benefit by such training."

"I used to think so," said Romilly, "But now I know what my *laran* is and my Gift. Father too must have some of this Gift, or he could not train horses as he does, and now I know how well I have inherited it."

"I would not be too quick to decide against Tower training," said Ruyven, "I too thought I had mastered my *laran* even in Nevarsin, but I discovered that while I kept all at bay on the front lines of the war with self, I had left undefended fortresses at my back, and through these I was almost conquered."

Romilly made an impatient gesture; the symbolism of the warrior struck her as far-fetched and unnecessary. "If we are to take the birds out and fly them, let us be about it, then. After all, if Lord Orain has given orders, Carolin's chief adviser cannot be kept waiting."

Ruyven seemed about to protest the sarcasm, but he sighed and was still. In his black robe he looked very much like a monk, and his narrow face had the detached, impassive look she associated with the Nevarsin brothers. "They will come for us when they want us. Will you make sure that Temperance's jesses are not too tight? I was afraid they were tearing an old scar on her leg, and Orain said that before you came to them, she had suffered some damage. I think your eyes are keener than mine."

Romilly went to examine the bird's leg, soothing Temperance with her ready thoughts. She found no serious trouble, but she did shift the location of the jesses around the bird's leg; the old scar did indeed look red and raw. She sponged it with a solution of *karalla* powder as a precaution, then turned the three hoods inside out and dusted them lightly inside with the same powder as a preventive against any dampness or infection, or the tiny parasites which sometimes got on birds and caused trouble at molting.

Ruyven said at last, "I am sorry to use my talents this way, at war, when I would rather stay peacefully in the Tower and work for our own people in the hills. But otherwise, all the Kingdoms may fall, one by one, to the tyranny of Lyondri Hastur and that wretch Rakhal, who has neither honor nor *laran* nor any sense of justice, but only a vicious will to power. Carolin, at least, is an honorable man."

"You say so and Orain says so. I have never seen him."

"Well, you shall see him now," said Orain, standing at the back of the enclosure; he had evidently heard the exchange. "Jandria told me of your hostel's gift to the king, and she

260

thought it only right, Mistress Romilly, that you should present it with your own hands, so come with me."

Romilly glanced at Ruyven, who said, "I will come to," and, replacing his glove, came after them.

Why is Ruyven the king's hawkmaster and I regarded only as his helper? I am a professional Swordswoman and it is I who have the greater skill. Ruyven would rather be in his Tower, and this work is life to me. He says himself that in the Tower women are allowed to hold high offices, yet it never seems to occur to him that I, his little sister, should be treated with that kind of fairness. Carolin's armies, then, are ruled by the old notion that a man must always do any work better than the most skilled of women?

But her rebellious thoughts were interrupted by the sight of Jandria, who stood holding Sunstar by the reins. He was saddled and bridled, and as he raised his silken nose and whickered softly in recognition of Romilly, she reached out again to touch the horse's mind in greeting and love.

Jandria said, "It is an honor to the Sisterhood that we can make this splendid gift to the king, and for their sake I thank you."

"I am the one who is honored," Romilly answered in a low voice, "It has been a pleasure to work with Sunstar."

"There he is, with Lord Orain," said Jandria, and Romilly saw Orain, dressed for riding, next to a hooded and cloaked man who was walking toward them. She gripped Sunstar's reins in excitement.

"High-lord, you lend us grace," Jandria began with a deep bow. "The Sisterhood of the Sword is honored and pleased to present you with this magnificent horse, trained by our finest horse-woman. Romilly?"

She did not raise her eyes to the king's, though she was conscious of Orain's glance. She said, looking only at the horse's sleek nose, "His name is Sunstar, Your Majesty, and he is trained to all paces and gaits. He will carry you for love; he has never felt whip or spur."

"If you had his training, Mistress Romilly, I know he is well trained," said a familiar voice, and she looked up at the hooded form of the king, to look into the eyes of *Dom* Carlo of Blue Lake. He smiled at her surprise. "I am sorry to have the advantage of you, Mistress MacAran; I knew who you were long ago. . . ." and she remembered the moment when she had felt the touch of his *laran*.

"I wish you had told *me*, *vai dom*," said Orain, "I had no notion she was a girl and I made a precious fool of myself!"

Dom Carlo—*no*, Romilly reminded herself, *King Carolin, Hastur of Hastur, Lord of Thendara and Hali*—looked at Orain with open, warm affection. He said, "You see only what you want to see, *bredu*," and patted Orain's shoulder. He said to Romilly, "I thank you, and the Sisterhood, for this magnificent gift, and for your loyalty to me. Both are precious to me, believe me. And I have heard, too, that you are to continue with your handling of the sentry-birds whose lives you saved when we met with you on the trail to Nevarsin. I shall not forget, my—" he hesitated a moment, smiled and said, "Swordswoman. Thank you—thank you all."

Romilly touched Sunstar again, a loving and final gesture of leave-taking. "Serve him well," she whispered, "Carry him faithfully, love him as I—as I love you." She moved away from the animal, watching as the king gathered up the reins and mounted.

He has some touch of that gift. I remember well. Sunstar, then, does not go to a brutal or insensitive man, but to one who will reckon him at his true worth.

Still she was troubled. *Dom* Carlo had known she was a girl and had not betrayed her among the men; but he might have spared her humiliation at Orain's hands, too, by warning his friend. But then, remembering to be fair, she told herself that he might have had no notion of her feelings for Orain, and he certainly could never have guessed that she would throw herself at Orain's head—or into his bed—in that way.

Well, it did not matter; done was done. Ruyven came toward her and she presented him to Jandria.

"My brother Ruyven; the Lady Jandria."

"Swordswoman Jandria," corrected the older woman, laughing. "I have told you; rank we leave behind us when we take the sword. And your brother is—"

"Ruyven MacAran," he told her, "Fourth in Tramontana, Second Circle. Have you finished with my sister, *domna?*" Romilly noted that, as if automatically, he called Jandria by the formal title given an equal or superior, *domna*—Lady—rather than the simpler *mestra* which he would have used to a social inferior.

"She is free to go," Jandria said, and Romilly, frowning, followed Ruyven.

She had hoped that some time that day it would seem natural to speak to Ruyven of her departure from Falconsward. She had intended, then—how long ago it seemed!—to seek the Tower where he had taken refuge. Somehow she had expected that he would welcome her there. But this quiet, monkish stranger seemed to bear no relation whatever to the brother who had been so close to her in childhood. She could not imagine confiding in him. She felt closer now to Jandria, or even to Orain, stranger that he had now become!

She looked back briefly at Sunstar, pacing along at a stately gait with *Dom* Carlo—no, she must remember, King Carolin—in the saddle. A brief mental touch renewed the old communication, and she felt herself smile.

I am closer to that horse than to anything human; closer than I have ever been to anything human.

When they had done for the day, Jandria came for her.

"At the edge of the camp, there is a tent where the Swordswomen who follow Carolin are to sleep," she said. "Come with me, Romilly, and I will show you."

"I should sleep here with the birds," Romilly said with a shrug, "No hawkmaster goes out of earshot of his trained birds—I will roll myself in my cloak, I need no tent."

"But you cannot sleep among the men," said Jandria, "it is not even to be thought of."

"The king's hawkmaster is my own brother born," said Romilly, impatient now, "Are you saying that he is likely to be any damage to my virtue? Surely the presence of my older brother is protection enough!"

Jandria said with a touch of sharpness, "You know the rules for Swordswomen outside their hostels! We cannot tell everyone in the army that he is your brother, and if it becomes known that an oath-bound Swordswoman has slept alone in the tent with a man—"

"Their minds must be like the sewers of Thendara," said Romilly angrily. "I am to leave my birds because of the dirty minds of some soldiers I do not even know?"

"I am sorry, I did not make the rules and I cannot unmake them," said Jandria, "but you are sworn to obey them."

Fuming with wrath, Romilly went along with Jandria to supper and to bed in the tent allotted to the dozen women of the Sisterhood who were assigned to Carolin's army. She found Clea there, along with a strange woman from another hostel; the two were to train Carolin's men in close-quarters unarmed combat. The others were not well known to Romilly; they were among the women who had been quartered in the hostel but did not really belong to it. They were horse-handlers, quartermasters and supply clerks, and one, a short, sturdy, dark woman who spoke with the familiar mountain accent of the Hellers, was a blacksmith, with arms like whipcord, and great swelling muscles across back and shoulders that made her look almost like a man.

I cannot believe that one's virtue would be in danger if she slept naked among a hundred strange soldiers—she looks as if she could protect herself, as the Hali'imyn here say, against all the smiths in Zandru's forges!

And then she thought, resentfully, that she had been more free when she travelled in men's clothes through the Hellers with Orain and Carlo—*Carolin*—and their little band of exiles. She had worked along with the men, had walked alone in the city, drunk in taverns. Now her movements were restrained to what the rules of the Sisterhood thought suitable to avoid trouble or gossip. Even as a free Swordswoman, she was not free.

Still grumbling a little, she made ready for bed. It struck her again; even these free women, how petty their lives seemed! Jandria she loved, and she could speak freely with Jandria without stopping to censor her thoughts; but even Jandria was trammeled by the question of, what would the men in the army think, if the Swordswomen were not bound by their rules to be as proper and ladylike as any marriageable maiden in the Hellers? Clea, too, she respected and genuinely liked, but still she had few friends in the Sisterhood. *Yet when I came among them, I though I had found, at last, freedom to be myself and still let it be known that I was a woman, not the pretense of male disguise.*

I do not want to be a man among men, and hide what I am. But I do not care much for the society of women—not even Swordswomen—either. Why can I never be contented, wherever I am?

Nevertheless, at last she was doing work for which she was fitted, and if any man offered her any insult she need not fear him as she had feared Rory. And the king himself had complimented her work with horses. Before she climbed into her bedroll, she reached out drowsily, as she had done every night of her year in the hostel, and sought for Sunstar's touch. Yes, he was there, and content. King Carolin would be good to him, certainly, would appreciate his intelligence, his wondrous speed, his beauty. She reached out again, a little further, seeking for the sentry-birds on their perches. Yes, all was well with them, too, and if it was not, Ruyven at least slept near them as a proper hawkmaster should. Sighing, Romilly slept.

She had returned to the bird-handlers's tent the next morning, and with Ruyven's young apprentice, a boy of fourteen or so called Garen, they set about feeding the birds. As she was examining the bandaged spot on Temperance's leg, she sensed a stranger's presence, and in the next moment, confirming it, the birds set up the high shrilling sound they had to indicate uneasiness in the presence of a stranger.

It was a young officer, in a green-gold cape; his hair was a light strawberry-blonde, his face narrow and sensitive.

"You are the hawkmaster?"

"Do I look like it?" Romilly snapped, "Swordswoman Romilly, *para servitre*. Carolin's hawkmistress."

"Forgive me, *mestra*, I meant no insult. I am Ranald Ridenow, and I came to give orders from His Majesty; I am to lead the detachment which will move ahead of the main army this morning." His voice was crisp, but without arrogance, and he smiled a little nervously. "I was also to seek my kinswoman, *Domna* Maura Elhalyn." He had to raise his voice over the shrilling noise the sentry-birds were making.

"As you can see, the lady is not in my pocket," said Romilly tartly, "Nor, as far as I know, abed with my brother, but you can ask him. Now, *Dom* Ranald, if you would kindly move away from the birds, since they will keep up this godforgotten noise until you are out of their sight. . . ."

He did not move. "Your brother, *mestra*? Where will I find him?" He managed to sound anxious even while he was yelling to make himself heard over the noise of the nervous birds, and Romilly came and physically shoved him out of range. The sound slowly quieted to soft churring noises, then silence.

She said, "Now that we can hear ourselves think, I know nothing about your kinswoman, though my brother, the hawkmaster, spoke of a Lady Maura, now I come to think of it. I will go and—no, I need not, for here he is."

"Romy? I heard the birds—is someone bothering them?" Ruyven suddenly sighted the Ridenow officer.

"*Su serva, Dom* . . . may I help you?"

"Lady Maura—"

"The lady sleeps in that tent yonder," said Ruyven, indicating a small pavilion nearby.

"Alone? Among the soldiers?" Ranald Ridenow's nostrils narrowed in distaste, and Ruyven smiled.

"Sir, the lady is better chaperoned by these birds than by a whole school of lady-companions and governesses," he said, "for you yourself have heard that any stranger coming near will rouse them, and if I hear them aroused, I would come to her aid, and could rouse the camp if there was danger."

Ranald Ridenow looked at the young man in the ascetic dark robe, and nodded with approval. "Are you a *cristoforo* monk?"

"I have not that grace, sir. I am Ruyven MacAran, Fourth in Tramontana, Second circle," he said, and the young officer in the green and gold cloak acknowledged him with another nod.

"Then my cousin is safe in your hands, *laranzu*. Forgive my question. Do you know if the lady is yet awake?"

"I was about to awaken her, sir, as she asked, or better, send my sister to do so," said Ruyven. "Romy, will you tell Lady Maura that a kinsman seeks her?"

"It is not urgent, not at this moment," said the Ridenow lord, "But if you could awaken her, Carolin has sent orders that we are to ride as soon as possible. I have orders—"

"I will need no more than thirty minutes to be ready," said Ruyven, "Romy, you are ready for riding? Awaken the Lady Maura, and tell her—"

His offhand assumption of authority nettled Romilly; so, for this arrogant lowland lordlet, she was to become errand-girl to some plains lady? "It's not that easy," she snapped, "the birds must be fed, and I'm nae servant to the lady; if ye' want her fetched and carried for, me lord, ye' can even do it yerself." She realized with horror that her strong mountain accent was back in her speech when her year in the plains had almost smoothed it away. Well, she was a mountain girl, let him make of it what he wanted. She was a swords-woman and no lowlander to bow and scrape before the *Hali'imyn!* Ruyven looked scandalized, but before he could speak a soft voice said;

"Well spoken, Swordswoman; I, even as you, am servant to Carolin and to his birds." A young woman stood at the door of the small tent, covered from neck to ankle in a thick night-gown, her flame-red hair loose and curling halfway to her waist. "I did not have the pleasure of meeting you yester-day, Swordswoman; so you are our bird-handler?" She bowed slightly to Ranald. "I thank you for your concern, cousin, but I need nothing, unless Carolin has summoned me—no? Then, unless you wish to lace up my gown for me as you used to do when you were nine years old, you may tell Carolin that we will be ready to ride within the hour, as soon as the birds are properly fed and tended. I will meet you in good time, kinsman." She nodded in dismissal, and as he turned away, she laughed gaily.

"So you are Romy?" she said, "Ruyven spoke to me of you on the way here, but we had no idea you would be our handler. Perhaps while we are on the road, you can get leave from your Swordswoman company to share my tent, so that we can both be near the birds at night? I am Maura Elhalyn, *leronis*, monitor in Tramontana to the Third Circle, and my mother was a Ridenow, so that I have some of the Serrais Gift . . . do you know that *laran?*"

Romilly said, "I do not. I know little of *laran*—"

"Yet you must have it, if you can handle sentry-birds," Lady Maura said, "for they can be handled only with *laran*; they are almost impossible to work with otherwise. You have the old MacAran Gift, then? In which Tower were you trained, *mestra*? And who is your Keeper?"

Romilly shook her head silently. She said, "I have never been in a Tower, *domna*."

She looked surprised, but her manners were too good to show it. She said, "If you will excuse me for five minutes, I will go and put on my gown—I was only teasing my cousin Ranald, I can perfectly well dress myself—and I will do my part in tending the birds, as I should do; I had no intention of leaving all their care to you, Swordswoman."

She went quickly to the tent, her fingers already busy at the fastenings of her night-gown, and pushed it shut behind her. Romilly went to examine the bandages of Temperance's leg, seeing with approval that the sore spot was smooth and not at all festered. While Ruyven went to tend Diligence she said, with a frown, "Are we to have this lady to rule over us, then?"

Ruyven said, "The *leronis* knows better than that, Romilly. She is not familiar with sentry-birds, so she told me; yet you noted that they did not scream at her approach either. She helped to care for them on the trip from the mountains— surely you did not think I handled three birds alone?"

"Why not?" Romilly asked, "I did." Yet Maura's frank friendliness had disarmed her. "What is this Serrais *laran* of which she spoke?"

"I know very little about it," said Ruyven, "even in the Towers it is not common. The folk of Serrais were noted, in the days of the breeding-program among the Great Houses of the Hastur kinfolk, because they had bred for a *laran* which could communicate with those who are not human . . . with the trailfolk, perhaps, or the catmen, or . . . others beyond them, summoned from other dimensions by their starstones. If they can do that, communicating with sentry-birds should be no such trouble. She said to me once that it was akin to the MacAran Gift, perhaps had been bred from it."

"You knew her well in the Tower?" Romilly asked with a trace of jealousy, but he shook his head.

"I am a *cristoforo*. And she is a pledged virgin. Only such a one would come among soldiers with no more fuss or awareness than that."

He might have said more, but Lady Maura came from her tent, dressed in a simple gown, her sleeves rolled back. Without a moment's hesitation she took the smelly basket of bird-food and took a handful, without any sign of distaste, holding it out to Prudence, crooning to the bird.

"There you are, pretty, there is your breakfast—speaking of which, Romilly, have you breakfasted? No, you have not, like a good handler, you see to your beasts first, do you not? We need not exercise them, they will have exercise enough and more today. Ruyven, if you will send an orderly to the mess, we should have breakfast brought to us here, if we are to ride as soon as all that." As she spoke, she was feeding the bird tidbits of carrion, smiling to it as if they were fragrant flowers, and Prudence churred with pleasure.

Well, she is not squeamish, she does not mind getting her hands dirty.

Ruyven picked up the thought and said in an undertone, "I told you so. In Tramontana she flies a *verrin* hawk and trained it herself. To the great dismay, I might add, of Lady Liriel Hastur, who is highest in rank there, and of her Keeper, Lord Doran; who both love hawking but would rather leave their training to the professional falconer."

"So she is not some soft-handed lady who wishes to be waited on hand and foot," Romilly said, grudgingly approving. Then she went to finish her work with Temperance, and when she had done, an orderly had brought food and small-beer from the mess, and they sat on the ground and breakfasted, Lady Maura, with no fuss, tucking her skirt under her and eating with her fingers as they did.

When they had finished, Ranald Ridenow appeared with half a dozen men, and the three of them loaded the sentry-birds on to blocks on their horses; the little detachment moved through the just-wakening camp, and took the road east across the desert lands toward the Plains of Valeron.

The Ridenow lord set a hard pace, though Romilly and Ruyven and the soldiers had no trouble keeping up with them. Lady Maura was riding on a lady's saddle, but she did not complain and managed to keep up. Although she did say to Romilly, at one stop to breathe the horses, "I wish I could wear breeches as you do, Swordswoman. But I have already scandalized my friends and my own Keeper, and I should probably not give them more cause for talk."

"Ruyven told me you trained a *verrin* hawk," Romilly said.

"So I did; how angry everyone was," Maura said, laughing, "but now, knowing you, Swordswoman, I know I am not the first nor yet the last woman to do so. And I would rather have her trained to my own hand than to a strange falconer's and then try to transfer her loyalty to me. Sometimes I have actually felt that I *am* flying with the bird; though perhaps it is my imagination—"

"And perhaps not," Romilly said, "for I have had that experience." Suddenly, and with poignant grief, she remembered Preciosa. It had been more than a year that she had dwelt in that damned desert town, and Preciosa had no doubt gone back to the wilds to live, and forgotten her.

Yet, even if I see her no more in life, the moments of closeness we have known are part of me now as then, and there is no such thing as future or past. . . . For a moment her head swam, and she confused the moment of ecstasy with Preciosa's flight with that all-consuming moment in which she had ridden Sunstar, joined absolutely with the horse, she flew, she raced, she was one with sky and earth and stars. . . .

"Swordswoman—?" Lady Maura was looking at her, troubled, and Romilly swiftly jerked her awareness back to the moment. She said the first thing that came into her head.

"My name is Romilly, and if we are to work together you need not say *Swordswoman*, so formally, every time . . ."

"Romilly," Maura said with a smile, "and I am Maura; in the Tower we do not think of rank separating friends, and if you are a friend to these birds I am your friend too."

Then the Towers have something in common with the Sisterhood, she thought, but then Ranald called the men together and they rose to ride again. She wondered why they were going so far ahead of the main army.

All day they rode, and at night made camp; the men and Ruyven slept under the stars, but there was a little tent for Lady Maura, and she insisted that Romilly must share it. They were tired from riding at a hard pace all day, but before they slept, Lady Maura asked quietly, "Why did you never go to a Tower for training, Romilly? Surely you have *laran* enough—"

"If you know Ruyven, and how he had to come there," said Romilly, "then you will know already why I did not."

"Yet you left your home, and quarreled with your kin," said Maura, quietly insistent, "After that, I should think you would have come at once—"

And so I had intended, Romilly thought. *But I made my way on my own, and now have no need of the training the* leronis *told me I must have. I know more of my own* laran *than any stranger.* She fell into a stubborn silence, and Lady Maura forbore to question her further.

Two days they rode, and they came out of the desert land and into green country; Romilly breathed a sigh of relief when they were able to see hills in the distance, and the evening breath of cool rain. It was high summer, but at this season frost lay on the ground at morning, and she was glad of her fur cloak at night. On the third day, as the road led over a high hill which commanded a view for many leagues around, Ranald Ridenow drew them to a halt.

"This will be the right place," he said, "Are you ready with the birds?"

Maura evidently knew what was wanted, for she nodded, and asked, "Who will you link with? Orain?"

"Carolin himself," said the Ridenow lord quietly. "Orain is not head-blind, but has not *laran* enough for this. And they are his troops."

Maura was blinking rapidly and looked as if she was about to cry. She said in an undertone, more to herself than Romilly, "I like this not at all, spying upon Rakhal's movements. I—I swore not to fight against him. But Lyondri has brought all this upon himself, for he too is oath-forsworn! After what he has done . . . kinsman or no . . ." and she broke off, pressing her lips tight together and saying, "Romy, will you fly first?"

"But I know not what to do," Romilly said.

"Yet you are hawkmistress . . ."

"I know the sentry-birds, habits, diet and health," said Romilly, "I have not been schooled to their use in warfare. I do not know—"

Maura looked startled, but quickly covered it, and Romilly was amazed; *she is being polite to me?* She said quietly, "You need only fly the bird and remain in rapport with her, seeing what she sees through her eyes. Ranald will make the link with you and so relay what you have seen to Carolin, so that he can spy out the land ahead and know what are Rakhal's movements in the land."

The name *sentry-birds* suddenly made sense to her; she had never really thought about it before. She took Prudence from the block, loosing with one hand the knots which secured her jesses, and lifted her free; watched her soar high into the sky. She arranged her body carefully in the saddle, leaving a part of her consciousness . . . a very small part . . . to make certain she did not fall from the saddle, and then. . . .

. . . high into the sky, on long, strong winds, rising higher and higher. . . .

All of the land lay spread out below her, like a map. She could see the curve of water below, and was dimly aware of a presence within her mind, seeing what she saw through her link with the bird. Through this mind, which she recognized as Carolin's, she began to make sense out of what she saw, although this was very distant and almost unconscious . . . most of her was soaring with the bird, seeing with keen sharpness everything which lay below.

. . . There the shores of Mirin Lake, and beyond that, Neskaya to the north, at the edge of the Kilghard Hills. And there . . . ah, Gods, another circle of blackness, not the scar of forest-fire, but where Rakhal's men have rained clingfire from the sky from their infernal flying machines! My people and they burn and die beneath Rakhal's fires when it was given to me and I swore with my hand in the fires of Hali that I would protect them against all pillage and rapine while they were loyal to me, and for that loyalty they burn . . .

. . . Rakhal, as Aldones lives, I shall burn that hand from you with which you have sown disaster and death on my people . . . and Lyondri I shall hang like a common criminal for he has forfeited the right to a noble death; the life he now lives as Rakhal's sower of death and suffering is more ignoble than death at the hands of the common hangman. . . .

Over the Kilghard Hills now, where the hills lie green with summer, and the resin-trees blaze in the sun . . . there again a Tower rises . . . quickly, fly to the North, little bird, away from the spying eyes of Lyondri's own forsworn laranzu'in. . . .

And there they lie, Rakhal's armies, where I can march to the East and take them unawares, unless they can spy with eyes like mine . . . and I think there are no sentry-birds now except in the far Hellers. . . .

Romilly heard the shrill crying of the bird as if from her own throat; the contact melted and for a moment she sat on her horse again, Carolin gone from her mind, Ranald Ridenow suddenly jolted out of contact, staring at her. She

271

lurched in the saddle, swayed, and Maura said quietly, "Enough. Ruyven, your turn, I think. . . ."

Romilly had not noticed; Ruyven had loosed Temperance at the same time as Prudence. Diligence, too, was gone from Maura's saddle. She saw Ruyven slump . . . *as she had done?* . . . and for an instant she was part of Ruyven/Ranald/Carolin flying in rapport with the bird, swooping low over the armies, something inside her *counting* . . .

Horsemen and foot soldiers, so many . . . wagons of supplies, and archers, and . . . ah Gods . . . Evanda guard us, that smell I know, somewhere within their ranks they are again making clingfire . . .

By sheer force of will Romilly tore herself, exhausted, from the rapport. She was not interested in the details of Rakhal's armies. She would rather not know; the horror she had felt in Ruyven's mind, or was it Carolin's, made her feel dizzy and sick. Spent, she collapsed in her saddle, almost asleep where she sat, weak, light-headed. She noticed at the edge of her consciousness that the sun was substantially lowered, almost at the edge of the horizon, and the light was dimming enough so that the great violet disk of Liriel could be seen rising from the eastern horizon, a few nights before its full. Her mouth was dry, and her head ached and throbbed as if a dozen tiny smiths were beating on their forge-anvils inside it.

Darkness descended so swiftly that Romilly wondered if she had been asleep in her saddle; it seemed to her that one moment she looked on sunset and the next, on violet moonlight, with Liriel floating in the sky. As she came aware, she realized Ruyven was looking at her anxiously.

"You're back?"

"For some time," he said, surprised. "Here, the soldiers have food ready for you," He gestured, and she slid from her horse, aching in every muscle, her head throbbing. She did not see Maura at all. Ranald Ridenow came and said, "Lean on me, if you wish, Swordswoman," but she straightened herself proudly.

"Thank you, I can walk," she said, and Ruyven came and motioned her to sit beside them on the grass. She protested "The birds—"

"Have been seen to; Maura did it when she saw the state you were in," he said. "Eat."

"I'm not hungry," she said, shrugging it off, and rose swiftly to her feet. "I had better see to Prudence—"

"I tell you, Maura has the birds and they are perfectly all

right," Ruyven said impatiently, and thrust a block of sticky dried fruit into her hand. "Eat this."

She took a bite of it and put it aside with a grimace. She knew that if she swallowed it she would be sick. From somewhere her little tent had been put up, the one she shared with Maura, and she shoved into it, aware from somewhere of Ranald Ridenow's face, white and staring, troubled. Why should he care? She flung herself down on her pallet in the tent and fell over the edge of a dark cliff of sleep.

She knew she had not really wakened, because she could somehow see through the walls of the tent to where her sleeping body lay, all thin like gauze so that she could see through it to beating heart and pulsing veins. She waved a hand and the heart speeded up its beat slightly and the veins began to go in swirling circles. Then she flew away and left it behind her, rising over plains and hills, flying far away on long, strong wings toward the Hellers. Ice cliffs rose before her, and beyond them she could see the walls of a city, and a woman standing on a high battlement, beckoning to her.

Welcome home, dear sister, come here to us, come home . . .

But she turned her back on them too, and flew onward, higher and higher, mountain peaks dropping away far below, as she flew past the violet disk . . . no, it was a round ball, a sphere, a little world of its own, she had never thought of the moon as a world. Then a green one lay beneath her, and the peacock crescent of Kyrrdis, dark, lighted only at the rim by the red sun, which somehow was still shining at midnight. She flew on and on, until she left the blazing sun behind and it was only a star among other stars, and she was looking down from somewhere on the world with four moons like a jeweled necklace, and someone said in her mind, *Hali is the constellation of Taurus, and Hali the ancient Terran word for necklace in the Arabic tongue,* but the words and the worlds were all meaningless to her; she dropped down, down slowly, and the great ship lay smashed against the lower peaks of the Kilghard Hills, and a Ghost wind blew across the peaks . . . and a little prim voice in her mind remarked, *racial memory has never been proven, for there are parts of the brain still inaccessible to science* . . . and then she began to fly along the rim of the Hellers. But the glaciers were breathing their icy breath at her, and her wings were beginning to freeze, the dreadful cold was squeezing her heart, slowing the wing-strokes, and then one wing, hard like ice, broke and splintered, with a dreadful shock of pain in her head and

273

heart, and the other wing, white and frozen and stiff, would no longer beat, and she sank and sank, screaming. . . .

"Romilly! Romilly!" Lady Maura was softly slapping her cheeks. "Wake up! Wake up!"

Romilly opened her eyes; there was a soft lantern-glow in the tent, but through it she was still freezing among the glaciers, and her wings were broken . . . she could feel the sharp jagged edges near her heart where they had shattered in the cold and splintered away. . . .

Maura gripped her hands with her own warm ones, and Romilly, confused, came back to her own body's awareness. She felt the unfamiliar, intrusive touch . . . somehow Maura was *within* her body, touching it with mental fingers, checking heart and breathing . . . she made a gesture of refusal, and Maura said gently, "Lie still, let me monitor you. Have you had many attacks of this kind of threshold sickness?"

Romilly pushed her away. "I don't know what you're talking about; I had a bad dream, that is all. I must have been tired. I've never done that before with the birds, and it was exhausting. I suppose the *leroni* are accustomed to it."

"I wish you would let me monitor you and be sure—"

"No, no. I'm all right." Romilly turned her back to the other woman and lay still, and after a moment Maura sighed and put out the lantern, and Romilly picked up a fragment of her thought, *stubborn, but I should not intrude, she is no child, perhaps her brother* . . . before she slept again, without dreams this time.

In the morning she still had a headache, and the smell of the carrion for bird-food made her as queasy—she told herself impatiently—as if she were four months pregnant! Well, whatever ailed her, it was not that, for she was as virgin as any pledged *leronis*. Perhaps it was her woman's cycles coming on her—she had lost track, with the army coming and her intense work with Sunstar. Or perhaps she had eaten something that did not agree with her; certainly she had no mind for breakfast. After caring for the birds, she got into her saddle without enthusiasm; for the first time in her life she thought it might be rather pleasant to sit inside a house and sew or weave or even embroider.

"But you have eaten nothing, Romilly," Ruyven protested.

She shook her head. "I think I caught a chill yesterday, sitting so still after sunset in my saddle," she said. "I don't want anything."

He surveyed her, she thought, as if she were Rael's age,

274

and said, "Don't you know what it means when you cannot eat? Has Lady Maura monitored you?"

It was not worth arguing about. She said sharply, "I will eat some bread in my saddle as we ride," and took the hunk of bread, smeared with honey, that he handed her. She ate a few bites and surreptitiously discarded it.

Ranald was riding with the blank look Romilly knew enough, now, to associate with a telepath whose mind was elsewhere. At last he came out of it and said, "I should know how far it is to the main branch of the armies; Carolin will join with us sometime today, though they are some way behind us. Romilly, will you take your bird and see if you can spy out Carolin's armies, and see how far they are behind us?"

She felt some qualms after her last experience with the flight with birds. Yet when she flung the bird in the air and followed it with her linked mind, she found that there was none of the disquieting disorientation; to her intense relief, it was only like flying Preciosa; she could see with a strange doubled sight, but that was all. The bird's sight, keener than her own a hundred times, told her that Carolin's armies lay half a day's ride behind where she rode with their little advance party, and she could sense, but with no sense of intrusion, that Ranald had picked up their position and relayed it to Carolin himself.

"We will camp here and wait for them," Maura said with authority, "We are all weary, and our hawkmistress needs rest."

I should not let them pamper me. I do not want Ruyven, nor Orain, nor Carolin himself, to think that because I am a woman I must be favored. Orain will respect me if I am as competent as a man. . . .

Lord Ranald yawned. He said, "I too feel as if I had been dragged backward over a waterfall, after these days of hard riding. I shall be glad of the rest. And the birds need not be moved more." He gestured to the soldiers to set up the camp.

CHAPTER SIX

Romilly knew the main army was approaching, not from what she heard—though, when she listened quietly, where she lay inside the tent she shared with *Domna* Maura, she could hear a soft distant sound in the very earth which she knew to be the noise of the great column of men on the march. But what really told her of Carolin's approach was a growing awareness within her mind, a sense of oneness, an approaching that she knew. . . .

Sunstar. Her mind was within and surrounded by the black stallion, it seemed that it was not on his but her back that the king rode, surrounded by his men, and for a moment her mind strayed to touch his too, to see Orain for a moment through his eyes, with love and warmth. Once she had seen them together, unguarded, wishing somehow that she had such a friend. Now she shared, for a moment, the quick unconscious touch between the king and his sworn man, something not sexual but deeper than that, a closeness which went back through their lives, mind and heart and somehow encompassed even a picture of their first meeting as young children, not yet in their fourth year . . . all three dimensions of time as somehow she was aware of Sunstar as a colt running in the hills of his native country. . . .

She jerked herself away from the extended contact and back into her own body, shocked and startled. She did not know what was happening, but she supposed it was some new dimension of her *laran*, opening of itself—what did she need, after all, of a Tower?

But the first person who came to her, when she was working around the birds, picking up little tags and fringes of the sight-awareness she had known yesterday when she flew them, was Jandria. After the two Swordswomen had greeted one another with a hug, Jandria said, "We had your message through the birds; it was Himself who told me." Romilly remembered that this was always how she spoke of King Carolin when he was not actually present. "You are doing well, Romy. And I have permission from the Swordswomen here for you to go on sharing Lady Maura's tent, if you will. I will go and speak to her; we were girls together."

Romilly held her peace—she had long known that Jandria was of higher rank than she had ever realized, though she had left it behind her when she took the oath of the Sisterhood. She turned her attention to the birds, though she could hear, with a tiny pang she recognized as jealousy, the two women talking behind her somewhere.

And I have no friend, no lover, I am alone, alone as any monk in his solitary cell in the ice caves of Nevarsin . . . and wondered what she was thinking about, for even now her mind was filled with the awareness of the great stallion racing in the sun, and Carolin with him, riding. . . .

She made her reverence before she ever looked up at the king's face and then was not really sure whether she had bowed to Carolin or to Sunstar, his black mane disordered with the hill-country wind. Carolin slid from his back and greeted her graciously.

"Swordswoman Romilly, I came myself to bring you my thanks for your message; you and your companions with the sentry-birds. We are to march tomorrow on Rakhal's armies and you and the *laranzu* must do this, for I have pledged to my kinswoman Maura that she need not take part in any battle against her kinsman." He smiled at her. "Come, child, you were not so tongue-tied when you rode with me to Nevarsin. You called me 'Uncle' then."

Romilly blurted, "I did it in ignorance, sir. I meant no disrespect, I thought you were only Carlo of Blue Lake—"

"And so I am," said Carolin gently, "Carlo was my childhood nickname, as my little cousin is called Caryl. And my mother gave me the country estate called Blue Lake when I was a boy of fifteen. And if I was not what you thought me, why, neither were you, for I thought you a stable boy, some MacAran's bastard, and not a *leronis*, and now I find you."

She remembered that he had seen her in boy's clothes, and she sensed that he had known her a girl quite soon, and for his own reasons had kept silent. That silence had allowed Orain to befriend her, and for that she was grateful. She said, "Your Majesty—"

He waved that aside. "I stand on no ceremony with friends, Romilly, and I have not forgotten that if it had not been for you, I would have been the banshee's breakfast. So; you will fly the sentry-birds to keep my advisers ahead of Rakhal's—or Lyondri's—movements into battle?"

She said, "I shall be honored, sir."

"Good. Now I must speak with my kinswoman and relieve her fears," he said. "Dame Jandira, too, I think, still has enough love for Lyondri—"

"For what he was," said Jandria quietly, standing in the door of Maura's tent, "not for what he is, Carlo. It goes against me to raise my own hand to him, but I will not lift a single hand to hold back his fate. If I had *laran* enough, I would be among your *leroni* today, to hold back what he has become. If he still holds enough of what he was to know what he is now, he would pray for clean death."

Maura's eyes were wet with tears. She said, "Carlo, I swore I would never raise hand or *laran* against my Hastur kin. I am Elhalyn, and they are blood of my blood. But like Jandria, I will not hinder you from what you must do, either." She went to the perch where Temperance sat and bent her head before the bird, and Romilly knew it was because she was crying.

This war that sets brother against sister and father against son . . . what matters it which rogue sits on the throne or which greater rogue seeks to wrest it from him . . . ? she was not sure whether it was Ruyven's thought she heard, or whether her father spoke in her memory, for it seemed that time had no more existence. . . .

Carolin said, looking at them sadly, "Still, I swore to protect my people, even if I must protect them from the Hastur kin who are unmindful of that oath. I wish you could know how little I want Rakhal's throne, or how gladly would I cede it to him if only he would treat my people as a king must, respecting them and protecting them. . . ." But it seemed he spoke to himself, and afterward Romilly was not sure whether he had spoken aloud or if she had imagined it all. Her *laran*, it seemed, was playing strange tricks on her, it seemed as if her mind was too small to enclose everything that wanted to crowd into it, and she felt somehow stretched, violated, crammed with strangenesses, as if her head were bursting with it. She said to Carolin, "May I greet my good friend, your horse, my lord?"

"Indeed, I think he is missing you," Carolin said, and she went to Sunstar, where Carolin had flung his reins around a rail when he dismounted, and flung her arms around the horse.

You are a king's mount but still are you mine, she said, not in words, and felt Sunstar in her mind, reaching out, *mine, love, together, sunlight/sunstar/always together in the world. . . .*

She discovered that she was clinging to the rail alone; Sunstar was gone and Ruyven was touching her hesitantly. "What ails you, Romy? Are you sick?"

She said brusquely, "No," and went to the birds. Again, somehow, it seemed, she had lost track of time. Could this be some new property of her *laran* that she did not understand? Maybe she should ask Maura about it. She was a *leronis* and would certainly be willing to help. But she could hear Maura in her mind now, weeping for Rakhal who had once sought her hand, so that afterward Maura had become *leronis* and a pledged virgin . . . mourned for Rakhal as Jandria mourned for Lyondri . . . and she for Orain's old comradeship . . . no, that was gone, what was *wrong* with her mind these days?

There was no need of the sentry-birds this day, and Romilly, still weak and confused after yesterday's fierce efforts and the evil dreams of the night, was glad of it. Yet as she rode, in the favored place near Carolin and his advisers, she was not really conscious of herself or of her own horse, so much was she riding with Sunstar at the head of the troops. Orain was riding near them, and she heard him talking easily and as equals with Lady Maura and Lord Ranald.

"You have the Serrais *laran,* Ranald, it would be no trouble to you, I dare say, to learn to handle the birds; it is near enough the MacAran Gift, which I saw in Mistress Romilly all those weeks when we travelled together." From her distance Romilly could sense the memory of how Orain had watched her, with tenderness not unmixed with something else, something akin to love. She knew now why Orain avoided her, because he could not see Romilly now without the painful memory of the boy Rumal who he had thought he knew, and he felt like a fool, layers of awareness overlapping and blurring.

Ranald said, "I am willing to try. And perhaps Mistress Romilly would be willing to school me. Though like all Swordswomen she is arrogant and harsh of tongue—" and

Maura's merry laughter, saying that he was not used to women who did not regard him, a Ridenow lord, as a special creation for their delight.

"Oh, come, Maura, I am not all that much of a womanizer, but if women were made by the Goddess Evanda for the delight of men, why should I refuse the Lady of Light her due by failing to worship Her in her creation, the loveliness of women?" he laughed. "No doubt She will punish *you*, one day, Orain, that you deny her due." And Orain's good-natured laughter, and Romilly knew that she was listening to a conversation not meant for her ears. She tried to shove it away but she did not know how, except by turning her attention elsewhere, and then she was riding again with Sunstar and too aware of Carolin. It was not a comfortable day, and when that evening Ranald came and asked if he could assist her to dismount, and said that he wished to learn the ways of the birds, so that he could fly one while Lady Maura was oath-bound not to do so, she was short with him.

"It is not so simple as all that. But you may try to approach them; however, do not complain to me if you should lose a fingernail or even an eye!"

She did not like the way he looked at her. It reminded her all too much of *Dom* Garris, or even Rory, as if he had physically fingered her young breasts with rude hands; she was painfully aware of his look—*I have never felt this way before*—and of the open desire in it. But he had done nothing, said nothing, how could she make any objection to it? She drew her cloak about her as if she was cold, and gestured him toward the birds.

He lowered his eyes and she knew he had picked up some sense of her unease. He said quietly, "Forgive me, *mestra*, I meant no offense." No more than Carolin could he seek to force any attentions on a woman unwilling, since he would share the victim's shock and distress, her sense of violation even at a rude look. But he was not used to women who were not of his own Hastur-kind who would be aware of this sensitivity.

Yet a woman who has not laran—*it is like coupling with a dumb beast, hardly alive* . . . she saw the scalding crimson on his turned-away neck and wished she knew how to tell him that it was all right. He approached the birds; she sensed the way in which he reached out to them, trying to echo the sense of harmlessness; to extend his senses toward the birds with nothing but the friendliest feelings. For a moment Romilly waited . . . then Temperance lowered her head and

280

rubbed it against the scratching-stick in the Ridenow lord's hand.

So he will be flying them, and he will be one with us, as Maura was . . . she did not know why the thought troubled her.

Maura must be still with the army, Romilly thought, they could not have left her behind, with the country alive with war; but Romilly had not seen her that day. When they rode out ahead with the birds, it was Lord Ranald who came with them, Temperance on his saddle; Romilly had yielded her own favorite, Prudence, to Ruyven, so that she could take Diligence, who was the most difficult of the birds to handle, on her own saddle. Diligence fussed and shrilled restlessly, but quieted when Romilly touched her mind.

Yes, you're a beauty too, Romilly told the bird, and saw nothing incongruous in so addressing the huge, ugly creature.

But there was no call for their services that day, and Romilly was glad, for it would give Lord Ranald extra time to be completely familiar with the bird, to create close rapport with her. After an hour or so, when Romilly felt sure there would be no trouble and no need for her service, Romilly let her mind drift again into close contact with Sunstar, where he rode with Carolin at the head of the army.

Now it seemed that the countryside was deserted, with great open tracts of deserted lands, and now and again a quiet farmstead lying empty, wells broken, houses burnt or fallen away with time. Romilly, riding with Sunstar, was really not aware that she was eavesdropping on Carolin and Orain, riding together with Lady Maura close to them. Maura was wrapped in her cloak and spoke little, but Carolin said, looking at the deserted country, "When I was a child I rode through here and this was all settled land with farmers and crops. Now it is a wasteland."

"The war?" Maura asked.

"War in my father's time, before I was old enough to hold a sword—still I remember how green and fertile was this country. And now the settled lands are nearer to the edge of the hills; in the aftermath of war there are always bandits, men made homeless by war and conscienceless by the horrors they have seen; they ravaged this country, what the war had left of it, until the folk settled nearer to the protection of the forts and soldiers near Neskaya."

But Romilly, her mind submerged in Sunstar, thought only, how green and fertile were the fields, how lovely the pastures. They camped that night by a watercourse, a narrow brook which rolled and tumbled down a cascade of old piled rocks, then flowed smooth and lovely across a fertile meadow starred with little blue and golden flowers.

"It will be a perfect night in High Summer," said Carolin lazily, "Before the night is past, three of the moons will appear in the sky, and two of them near the full."

"What a pity we will not have Midsummer-Festival here," Maura laughed, and Carolin said, suddenly sober, "I vow to you, Maura—and to you, *bredu*," he added, turning to Orain with a smile of deep warmth, "that we shall hold our Midsummer-Festival within the walls of Hali, at home. What say you to that, cousins?"

"Evanda grant it," Maura said seriously, "I am homesick—"

"What, none of the young men in that faraway tower beyond the mountains—" lightly, Carolin punned on the name of Tramontana—"have shaken your resolve to remain maiden for the Sight, Maura?"

Maura laughed, though the sound was strained.

"On the day when you invite me to be queen at your side, Carolin, I shall not send you away disappointed."

Sunstar jigged sidewise, restlessly, as Carolin leaned from his saddle to touch Maura's cheek lightly with his lips. He said, "If the Council will have it so, Maura, so be it. I had feared your heart was dead when Rakhal turned away from you—"

"Only my pride was wounded," she said quietly. "I loved him, yes, as cousin, as foster-brother; but his cruelty slew my heart. He thought he could come to me over the bodies of my kinfolk, and I would forgive him all when I saw the crown he offered, like a child forgetting a bruise when she is given a sweetnut. I would not have it said that I turned from Rakhal to you because I would have the one who could bring me the crown—" her voice faltered, and Sunstar tossed his head indignantly at the jerk on the reins which brought him to a halt so that Carolin could lean again toward Maura's saddle; but this time he felt it as his rider lifted the slight from of the *leronis* bodily from her saddle to his own, and held her there. There were no more words, but Sunstar, and Romilly with him, sensed an outflow, an outpouring of emotion that made him restless, made him prance until Carolin chided him with a tug on the reins, and in Romilly's mind were flooding images of sleek flanks and satiny bodies, of swift running in moonlight, which made her rub her head as if she were feverish, with unfamiliar sensations flooding her whole body, so that she retreated abruptly into herself, away from the great stallion's unfamiliar emotions and touch.

What has come over me, that I am so filled with emotion, that I laugh and cry without a word spoken or a touch?

Carolin said in her mind, and she was not conscious that he was not at her elbow, *We can leave the horses for tonight in this field; you are a* leronis, *can you keep them there without fencing, which we have no time to set up?* And Romilly was about to answer when she heard Maura's voice as clear as if spoken aloud, *I have not Romilly's gift, but if you will summon her to help me, I will do what I can.*

Romilly tugged the reins a little and pulled her own horse to a stop. Ruyven turned startled eyes on her, but she said, "We are to stop here for the night and I am summoned to the king and the *leronis*."

It was Orain who brought her the word, riding through the mass of men and horses and equipment flowing along the road, calling out, "Where are you off to, Romilly? The *vai dom* has requested you to attend him!"

"I know," said Romilly, and went on toward the king, leaving Orain staring and surprised behind her.

Carolin extended his arm toward the broad field. He said, "We are to make camp here for the night. Can you help Maura to set pastures here for the horses so that they will not stray?"

"Certainly," she said, and the men set about making camp, turning the best horses into the field, Sunstar among them.

Maura said, when they were done, "Now we shall set a chasm across which they will see, though we cannot; horses are afraid of heights, so we need only make them see it."

Romilly linked minds with the young *leronis*, and together they wove an illusion; a great chasm between horses and men, surrounding the pasture . . . Romilly, still partly linked in mind with Sunstar and her senses extending to her own horse and to the others in the field . . . and aware with them of the great black stallion—saw it and physically flinched, great spaces down which she might fall, shrinking back. . . .

"Romilly," said Maura seriously, breaking away from the link, "You are what we call a wild telepath, are you not?"

She turned, filled with a prickly awareness of the critical sound in Maura's voice. "I don't know what you mean," she said stiffly.

"I mean, you are one whose *laran* has been developed of itself, without the discipline of a Tower," Maura said. "Do you know that it can be dangerous? I wish you would let me

283

monitor you, and make certain that you are under control. *Laran* is no simple thing—"

She said, even more stiffly, "The people of MacAran have been animal trainers, working with birds and horses and dogs, since time unknown; and not all of them have been supervised by the Towers either." A trace of the mountain accent crept back in her speech, as if the echo of her father's voice, saying, "The *Hali'imyn* would have it that a man's own mind must be ruled over by their *leronyn* and their Towers!"

Maura said placatingly, "I have no wish to rule over you, Romilly, but you look feverish, and you are still of an age where you might be subject to—to some of the dangers of *laran* improperly supervised and developed. If you cannot allow me to monitor you and see what has happened to you, your brother—"

Still less, Romilly thought, could she allow her stern and ascetic brother, so like a *cristoforo* monk, to read the thoughts she hardly dared acknowledge to herself. She twisted away impatiently, fumbling at a barrier against Maura. "It is generous of you, *vai domna*, but truly you need not concern yourself about me."

Maura frowned a little, and Romilly sensed that she was weighing the ethics of a Tower-trained telepath, never to intrude, against a very real concern for the girl. It annoyed Romilly—Maura was not *so* much older than she was herself, why did she think she was needed to straighten out Romilly's *laran*?

I was left on my own with it, and now when I need it no longer they are eager to offer help! I was not offered help when my father would have sold me to Dom Garris, and there was none to help me when I would have been raped by Rory, or when I made an idiot of myself forcing my way into Orain's bed. I have won these battles alone and unhelped, what makes them think I need their damned condescension now?

Maura still looked at her uneasily, but at last, to Romilly's relief, she sighed and turned away.

"Look," Carolin said, and pointed, "Are you sure that your illusion has worked?"

Romilly looked up, her breath almost stopping; Sunstar was rushing toward them, his head flung up, his legs seeming hardly to touch the ground as he bolted. Maura lifted her hand. "Wait," she said, and as Sunstar reached the corner of the meadow he stopped short, placing all four feet together as if truly on the edge of a cliff, his head lowered, foam dripping from his teeth as if in mortal terror. He shuddered with fear, then snorted, backed away, tossed his head and raced away in the other direction.

"The illusion will hold them tonight, at least," Maura said.

"But he is so frightened," Romilly protested; she was dripping with the stallion's sweat of fear.

"Neither memory nor imagination," said Maura quietly. "You have both, Romy, but look at him now." And, indeed, Sunstar was quietly cropping grass; he stopped, sniffed the wind and began to move closer to a group of mares silently grazing in the meadow.

"He will improve the quality of your royal stables," said Orain jocularly, "and any mare he covers tonight will have a foal worthy of those same stables, I doubt not."

Carolin chuckled. "He is welcome to his sport, old friend. We who are responsible for this war—" he touched Maura gently, only on the shoulder, but the look that passed between them made Romilly blush, "must wait for a while for our satisfactions; but they will be all the dearer for that, will they not, my love?"

She only smiled, but Romilly physically turned her eyes from the intensity of that smile.

That night Jandria came and asked Romilly if she wished to join the Swordswomen's mess again, now that she was not riding ahead of her special detachment with the birds. It was evident from Jandria's voice that she expected Romilly to be overjoyed at being allowed again to join her sisters, but Romilly was too weary and raw-edged for the chatter, the noise and giggling of the young women of the Sisterhood, eager to sleep away from their communal tent. She made the excuse that she was still needed among the birds.

"And you need not fear that I am improperly guarded," she said sourly, "for between the Lady Maura and my monkish brother, I might as well be a priestess of Avarra on her guarded isle where no man may come without the Dark Mother's death-curse!"

She could see that Jandria was still troubled, but the older woman only embraced her. She said, "Rest well, then, little sister. You look so weary; they have demanded much of you in very little time, and you are still young. Be sure to eat a good supper; I have known *leroni* before this, and to replenish their energies after their work, a fragile little girl will eat enough to satisfy three wood-cutters! And sleep long and soundly, my dear."

She went away; Romilly fed the birds, with Ruyven's help,

and even Lord Ranald, she noted with satisfaction, did not shirk his share of the tending. But the smell of their carrion food which the army hunters had brought her, made her feel queasy again, and although Carolin had sent a good haunch of roast *chervine* from his own tables, with his compliments to his bird-handlers, she could hardly eat and only shoved the food around on her plate.

By the time the camp was completely settled for the night, it was well past sunset, but the night was lighted with three full moons, and the fourth was a half-filled crescent.

"Four moons," said Lord Ranald, laughing, "What madness shall we do? They say in Thendara, *What is done under four moons need not be remembered or regretted* ...

Ruyven said with frozen courtesy, "Such nights are sacred, friend; I shall spend much of my night in sacred silence and meditation, if Carolin's soldiers—" he gestured to where, faintly and downwind, he could hear the sound of a *rryl* and loud, untuneful voices all shouting the chorus of a popular drinking song, "will allow me a little peace."

"The king's quartermasters have given the soldiers an extra ration of wine," Lord Ranald said, "but not enough to make them drunk; they will sit round their fires and sing in the moonlight, that is all." He offered Romilly his arm. "Shall we join them at their fires? There are three or four men in my old unit who have fine voices and sing together in taverns; they sing well enough to get all the beer they want, and more. And be assured they will offer a Swordswoman no discourtesy, but be pleased to know you have come to hear their music."

"They sound not like such fine voices," said Romilly, listening to the discordance of the faraway song, and Ranald laughed.

"They are but amusing themselves; it would not be worth the trouble of the Windsong Brothers—for so they call themselves, though they are not brothers but four cousins—to sing before all are assembled and calling for entertainment. We will be in plenty of time to hear them, and the soldiers like it if the gentry come to their fires to hear their amusements."

Put like that, Romilly could not refuse, though she felt dull and headachy and wished she could go quietly to bed. But with the camp filled with song and laughter she knew she would not sleep anyhow; perhaps Ruyven had the discipline for quiet meditation in such a racket, but she did not. She took his offered arm.

The moonlight made it almost as bright as day—well, perhaps a grey and rainy day; she did not think she could have read print, and the colors of Ranald's garish cloak and her own crimson tunic, were indistinct, but there was plenty of light to make out where they were going. A part of Romilly, unawares, was cropping grass in the meadow with Sunstar, and yet she was filled with a strange restlessness. As they neared the fires they could hear the soldiers roaring out a song whose words were far from decorous, about some scandalous goings-on among the nobility.

> "O, my father was the Keeper of the Arilinn Tower,
> He seduced a chieri with a kireseth flower;
> From this union there were three;
> Two were *emmasca* and the other was me . . ."

"That song," said Ranald, "would have them torn to pieces if they sang it anywhere on the Plains of Arilinn. Here it is different, there is an old rivalry between Arilinn and Neskaya Towers . . ."

"Curious goings-on for a Tower," said Romilly, whose picture of a Tower was still colored by what she had seen in Ruyven's disciplined and austere thoughts.

He chuckled. "I spent a few years in a Tower—just enough to learn control of my *laran*. You must know how it is. When it began, when I was thirteen, I sometimes could hardly tell myself from a *cralmac* in rut, or from going into heat with every bitch on the farm! It was very upsetting to my governess—I was still in the schoolroom then. Of course, she was a frozen-faced old viper—I won't insult my favorite dog by calling the lady a bitch! I am sure she often wished she could have had me gelded like the pack chervines, so she could go with my lessons!"

Romilly giggled uneasily. He sensed her unease and said kindly, "I am sorry—I had forgotten you were a *cristoforo* and brought up to their ways. I had thought girls were different, but I had four sisters, and if I had ever entertained any feelings that girls were different and more delicate, I got over them soon enough—and I won't apologize, you are a woman from the mountains and I know from your work with the birds that you have been around animals enough to know what I mean."

Romilly blushed, but the feeling was not unpleasant, and she remembered the high summer in her own hills near Falconsward, the world flowing with life, cattle and horses mating, so that she too had unashamedly shared the flow of

287

nature all round her, even though, with her child's body, it had been an undifferentiated awareness, sensual but never personal. She knew he was teasing her, but she did not really care.

"Listen," said Ranald, "There are the singers."

They were all in the uniform of common soldiers; four men, one tall and burly, another with shaggy, reddish-brown hair and an untrimmed patch of beard, one short and fat with a round, rosy face and a lopsided smile, and the fourth tall and gaunt, with a scrawny face and big red hands; but from his throat came the most exquisite tenor she had ever heard. They hummed a little together to find their pitch, then began to sing a popular drinking song which, Romilly knew was very old.

> "Aldones bless the human elbow.
> May he bless it where it bends;
> If it bent too short, we'd go dry, I fear,
> If it bent too long, we'd be drinking in our ear . . ."

They finished the catch by up-ending their tankards with a flourish to show them empty, and the soldiers roared approval and poured them all brimming mugfulls, which they drank and then began another song.

Their songs were rowdy but not indelicate, mostly concerned with the pleasures of drink and women, and their voices were splendid; with the rest, Romilly cheered and sang along on the choruses till she was hoarse. It made her forget her own strange feelings, and she was grateful to Lord Ranald for suggesting this. At one point someone thrust a mug into her hand—it was the strong, fragrant lowlands beer, and she felt a little tipsy from it; her voice sounded good to herself—usually she had no singing voice to speak of—and she felt pleasantly dizzied and yet not drunk enough to be off her guard. At last, it grew later and the men sought their beds, and the Windsong Brothers, full of wine and yet walking steadily, sang their last song to wild cheers and applause. Romilly had to lean on Ranald as she sought her tent.

He drew her close to him in the bright moonlight. He whispered, "Romy—what is done under the four moons need not be remembered or regretted—"

Half-heartedly she shoved him away. "I am a Swordswoman. I do not want to disgrace my earring. You think me wanton, then, because I am a mountain girl? And Lady Maura shares my tent."

"Maura will not leave Carolin this night," Ranald said seriously, "They cannot marry, till the Council had agreed, and will not while she is needed as his *leronis*, but they will have what they can; do you think she would blame you? Or do you think me selfish enough to make you pregnant, while we are in the middle of this war and your skills are as valuable as mine?" He tried to pull her into his arms again, but she shook her head, wordless, and he let her go.

"I wish—but it would be no pleasure to me if it was none to you," he said, but he pressed a kiss into her palm. "Perhaps—never mind. Sleep well, then, Romilly." He bowed again, and left her; she felt empty and chill, and almost wished she had not sent him away. . . .

I do not know what I want. I do not think it is that.

Even in her tent—and Ranald had been right, Lady Maura was not within, her blanketroll was tossed empty on the floor of the tent—she felt that the moonlight was flooding through her whole body. She crawled into her blankets, pulling off her clothes; usually she left on her undertunic at night, but tonight she felt so heated in the moonlight that she could hardly bear the touch of cloth on her feverish limbs. The music and the beer were still pounding in her head, but in the dark and silence, it seemed that she was outside in the moonlight, that she was somewhere pawing at the grass, a sweet, heady smell arising from the earth and somewhere a frantic restlessness everywhere within her.

Sunstar, too, seemed flooded with the restlessness of the four moons and their light . . . now she was linked deep in rapport with the stallion . . . this was not new to her, she had sensed this before, in bygone summers, but never with the full strength of her awakened laran, her suddenly wakeful body . . . the scent of the grass, the flooding of life through her veins till she was all one great aching tension . . . sweet scents with a tang of what seemed to her shared and doubled senses a tang of musk and summer flowers and something she did not even recognize, so deeply was it part of herself, profoundly sexual, sweeping away barriers of thought and understanding . . . at one and the same time she was one with the great stallion in rut, and she was Romilly, frightened, fighting to break out of the rapport which she had, before this, shared so unthinking, it was too much for her now, she could not contain it, she was bursting with the pressure of the raw, animal sexuality under the stimulating light of the moons. . . . She felt her own body twisting and turning as she fought to escape, hardly knowing what it was she dreaded, but if it should happen she was terrified, she would not bear it she would be drawn in forever and never get back never to her own body what body she had no idea it was too much unendurable . . . PASSION, TERROR, RUT . . . NO, NO. . . .

Blue moonlight flooded the tent as the flap was drawn back . . . but she did not see it, she was beyond seeing, only the moonlight somehow reached her fighting body, tossing head. . . .

She was held gently in gentle arms; a voice was calling her name softly. Gentle hands were touching her.

"Romilly, Romy . . . Romy, come back, come back . . . here, let me hold you like this, poor little one . . . come back to me, come back *here* . . ." and she saw Ranald's face, heard his voice softly calling her; she felt as if she was drowning in the flood of what she was not, came back gratefully to awareness of her own body, held close in Ranald's arms. His lips covered hers and she put up her arms and drew him down wildly to her, anything now, anything to keep her here safely within her own body, shut out the unendurable overload of emotion and physical sensation; Ranald's arms held her, Ranald caressed her, she was herself, she was Romilly again, and she hardly knew whether it was fear, or gratitude, or real desire, that locked her lips to his, flung her into his arms, thrusting away all the unwanted contact with the stallion, reminding her that she was human, human, she was real, and this, this was what she wanted. . . . She could read in his mind that he was startled and delighted, even if a little overcome, by her violent acceptance, and more startled yet to find her virgin, but it did not, in that shared violence of that moment, matter to either of them at all.

"I knew," he whispered afterward, "I knew it would be too much for you. I do not think it was to me you were calling, but I was here, and I knew. . . ."

She kissed him thankfully, astonished and delighted. It had happened so naturally, it now seemed so sweet and right to her. A random thought, as she floated off into sleep, touched her mind at the edge of laughter.

It would never have been like this with Dom Garris! I was perfectly right not to marry him.

CHAPTER SEVEN

Carolin's army remained encamped in the watercourse for three days. On the third day, Romilly went out to fly the sentry-birds again, Ranald at her side. She was quite aware that she must somehow shield her thoughts from Ruyven; he would not understand at all what had happened. He would see only that his young and innocent sister had shared her bed with a Ridenow lord, and to do her justice, Romilly was more worried that this might spoil the ability of the three of them to work together, than she was troubled by any sense of shame or regret for what she had done. Ruyven would be certain to think that Ranald had played the seducer, and it was not like that at all; he had simply pulled her free from something she had found herself quite unable to tolerate. Even now, Romilly did not know why she had found it unendurable.

"Remind me not to look at you and smile like that," Ranald said, picking up her concern lest Ruyven should know, and she smiled back. She felt soothed and happy, able to look into the pasture by the watercourse where Sunstar and the horses were grazing and pick up her old, close communion with the stallion, with no sense of distaste or unease, no break in her warm sense of unity with Sunstar.

Ranald made it so easy for me.

Maura told me, about something else; *horses have neither memory nor imagination.* That is why I can pick up where I left off.

Twice during these days she went and joined the Swords-

291

women's mess, sharing her meal with the women of the Sisterhood. Clea jeered a little at her.

"So you are still one of us, in spite of hob-nobbing with the nobility and all?"

"Be fair," said Jandria, "she has her work to do just as we do, and Lady Maura is as good a chaperon as a whole hostel full of our sisters. One of the handlers is her own brother, too. And if rumor tells true—" but she looked inquisitively at Romilly, "that same Lady Maura will one day be our queen—what do you know of that, Romy?"

Romilly said, "I know no more than you. And King Carolin cannot marry until the Council gives him leave—a noblewoman of Lady Maura's station cannot marry without parental consent, and how much more if the king comes wooing? But certainly, if they have their will, there will be a marriage made."

"And if there is not, the king will get him a bastard to make as much trouble in the kingdom as that *gre'zuin* Rakhal," said Tina scornfully. "Nice behavior for a *leronis*—I know from her waiting-woman that she spent two nights in the king's tent; what sort of chaperon is she for Romy, then?"

Ranald had taught her to shield herself a little; so Romilly managed neither to blush nor turn away her eyes. "Between three ugly birds and my brother, do you truly think I need a chaperone, Tina? As for Maura, I have heard she is kept virgin for the Sight, and I cannot believe she would endanger that, even in a king's bed, while the war still rages; but I am not the keeper of her conscience; she is a grown woman and a *leronis*, and need account to no man."

Clea made a contemptuous sound. "So she might sell her maidenhood for a crown, but not for love? Bravely done, *leronis*!" she made an applauding gesture. "See that you profit by her example, Romy!"

She had thought that among these women, who were free to follow their own wills, she might have been able to speak of this thing that had happened to her; even now, she felt, if she could speak with Jandria alone, she would like to tell her . . . but Jandria was already rising to attend on Carolin's advisers, and there was no other, not even Clea, whom she had thought her friend, to whom she felt she could talk freely. Not after their scornful words. No, she would not speak of Ranald. They would not understand at all.

She knew that she had not disgraced her earring, nor brought the Sisterhood into contempt. Her oath bound her to nothing more; and at least she had not sold herself to that

292

elderly lecher *Dom* Garris in return for riches and the prospering of her father's horse-trade with Scathfell!

So on the third day, when she went out to fly the birds, with Ruyven and Ranald, her spirits were high. The day was grey and drizzly, with little spats and slashes of gusty rain coming across the plains, and even when a rare break came in the clouds, the wind was high. The sentry-birds huddled on their perches, squalling with protest when they were put on their blocks; they did not like this weather, but they needed exercise after two days of full fed rest, and Carolin needed to know where Rakhal's armies moved in the countryside.

"Somehow we must keep them low enough to spy through the mists," Ranald said, and Romilly protested, "They will not like that."

"I am not concerned with their liking or the lack of it," Ranald said curtly, "We are not flying the birds for our own pleasure nor yet theirs—have you forgotten that, Romy?"

She had, for a moment, so close she felt to the great birds. As she tossed Diligence free of her gloved hand, she went into rapport with the winged creature, flying on strong pinions, high over the ranges, then remembered, forced it into flying lower, hovering, guiding the bird eastward to where they had last seen Rakhal's armies.

Even so, and with the bird's extra keen sight, she could not see very far; the drizzle clouded vision, so that she had to fly the bird low enough to see the ground, and the rain, slanting in from the northeast, dimmed sight further. This kind of flight bore no relationship to what she had known last time they flew, soaring in headlong flight, hovering high and letting the picture of the ground be relayed through Ranald to Carolin. Now it was slow, sullen effort, forcing the bird's will against the stubborn wish to turn tail and fly home to huddle on the perch till fine weather, then forcing it down against the instinct to fly high above the clouds.

Sentry-birds; spy-birds. Like all of us I am a tool for Carolin's army to strike. How angry her father would be! Not only the runaway son he had disowned, but the daughter he had thought compensation for one runaway son and one worthless bookish one . . . how was Darren managing, she wondered, had he resigned himself to handling hawks and horses now?

She had lost track of the bird, and a sharp sense of question from Ruyven recalled her to the flying in the rain, chilled and battered by the icy gusts of sleet which buffeted her . . . or Diligence? She must risk flying lower, for they could see nothing through the thick curtain of wet. They were linked three ways, and now she set herself to follow Temperance, flying ahead strongly toward a break in the clouds. Below them the land lay deserted, but low on the horizon she could see smoke which she knew to be Rakhal's army where it waited out the rain. Behind her she could actually feel the displacement in the air where Prudence flew at her tail. At the same time a part of her was Romilly, balanced carefully in her saddle, and a part of her still Carolin, waiting for intelligence through the minds of bird-handlers and birds.

A speck against her sight, swiftly growing larger and larger . . . of course, she should have known that they too would have had spy-birds out in this weather! She—*or was it Diligence?*—shifted course ever so slightly, hoping to miss unseen the oncoming bird. Was it Rakhal himself, or one of his advisers, behind the hovering wings of that bird, poised to intercept. . . .

Would it come to a fight? She could not hope to control the bird if raw instinct took over; there was not much difficulty in controlling the mind of the bird if all was well, but in danger instinct would override the shared consciousness. Temperance was still flying well ahead, and through the link with Ruyven's mind she too could see the outskirts of the enemy camp, and a wagon about which something black and sinister was hovering . . . she was not sure she saw it with her eyes; was she perceiving something through Ruyven's mind or the bird's? Birds—Maura's phrase echoing in her mind, *neither memory nor imagination*—could only see with their physical sight, and could not interpret what they saw unless it concerned them directly, as food or threat.

It was taking all of her strength to hold Diligence on course. The wagon was there, and a curious, acrid smell which seemed to sting her, whether her own nose or the bird's she was not sure; but the blackness was something she must be perceiving through one of the minds linked in rapport with the sentry-birds spying. She was vaguely curious, but so sunk in the bird's consciousness that she was content to leave it to Carolin to interpret.

Something was in the air now . . . danger, danger . . . as if a red-hot wire had seared her brain, she swerved, shrieking and then there was a slicing pain in her heart and Romilly came with a cry out of the rapport, fighting to hold to it . . . *pain . . . fear . . .* somewhere, she knew, Diligence was falling like a stone, *dizzy, consciousness fading out, dy-*

ing. . . . Romilly, seated on her horse, physically clutched at her breast as if the arrow which had slain the sentry-bird had penetrated her body as well. The pain was nightmarish, terrifying, and she stared wildly around her in anguished disorientation. Then she knew what must have happened.

Diligence! She had flown her bird deliberately into the danger of those arrows, over-riding the bird's own sense of caution, its instinct to fly high and away from danger. Guilt and grief fought within her for dominance.

Someone very far away seemed to be calling her name . . . she came up out of grey fog to see Ranald looking at her, with deep trouble in his face. She said, strangled, "Prudence . . . Temperance . . . get them back . . ."

He drew a long breath. "They are away from the soldiers; I sent them high up, out of range . . . I am sorry, Romy; you loved her—"

"And she loved life!" she flung at him wildly, "And died because of you and Carolin—ah, I hate you all, all you men and kings and your damned wars, none of them are worth a feather in her wing-tip—" and she dropped her head in her hands and broke into passionate crying.

Ruyven's head was still flung back, his face glazed with intent effort; he sat unmoving until a dark form dropped from the clouds, sank down to his gloved hand.

"Temperance," Romilly whispered, with relief, "but where is Prudence—"

As if in answer from the clouds came a shrilling cry, answered by another; two dark forms burst through the layers of mist and rain, locked together, falling joined in battle; feathers fell, and the screaming and shrilling died. A small dark limp body dropped at their horses' feet; another sped away, screaming in triumph.

"Don't look! Ranald, hold her—" Ruyven began, but Romilly was off her horse, crying wildly, catching up the small blood-spattered form of Prudence, still limp and warm with recently-departed life. She clutched it against her breast, her face wet and furious. "Prudence! Ah, Prudence, love, not you too—" she cried, and the bird's blood smeared her hands and her tunic. Ranald dismounted, came and gently took it from her.

"No use, Romilly; she is dead," he said quietly, and his arms caught her to him. "Poor little love, don't cry. It can't be helped; that is war."

And that is supposed to be the excuse for all! Romilly felt fury surging within her. *They play with the lives of the wild things and hold themselves harmless, saying it is war . . . I question not their right to kill themselves and one another, but what does an innocent bird know or care of one king over another?*

Ruyven was gentling Temperance on his fist, sliding the hood over her restless head. He said, "Romilly, try to be calm, there is work to do. Ranald—you saw—"

"Aye, I saw," Ranald said shortly, "Somewhere in Rakhal's train there is *clingfire* and I know not where he means to use it, but Carolin must know at once! Time may be short, unless we want to burn beneath the stuff, and I for one want none used against me, or any of the lands hereabout—"

"Nor I. I saw what clingfire can do, in Tramontana," said Ruyven, "Though not in war. Carolin has pledged he will not use it against folk who must live in his lands. But if it is used against us, I know not how he can fight it."

Romilly, still standing silent, demanded, "What is clingfire?"

"The very breath of Zandru's forges," said Ranald, "Fire flung which burns and keeps on burning as long as there is anything to feed it, through skin and bone and into the very stone . . . fire made by wizardry and *laran*."

I doubt it not. Folk who would kill an innocent bird for some king's claim, why should they stop at killing people too?

"You must come with us." Ranald gently urged her into her saddle. "Carolin must know of this and he will need all of his *leronyn*—Maura has sworn not to fight against Rakhal, but I do not think she will hesitate to stop the use of clingfire against her own people, no matter what she may still feel for Rakhal!"

But Romilly rode blind, tears still streaming from her eyes. She knew nor wished to know nothing of the weapons these men and their kings and their *leroni* used. Dimly she knew that Ranald rode away from her, but she reached out blindly for contact with Sunstar, feeling, in the reassuring strength of the great stallion, an endless warmth and closeness. He was in her and she was in him, and drawn into the present, with neither memory nor anticipation, without imagination or emotion save for the immediate stimuli; green grass, the road under foot, the weight of Carolin, already beloved, in the saddle. She rode unseeing because the best part of her was with Sunstar, loss and grief wiped out in the unending present-moment of timelessness.

At last, comforted somewhat, she came out of the submersion in the horse's world, half aware that somewhere they spoke of her.

She was very fond of the sentry-birds, she is very close to them. It was so from the moment we first saw her, we spoke of how ugly they were, and it was she who pointed out to us that they had their own kind of beauty. . . .

. . . her first experience with this kind of loss, she must learn how to keep herself a little separate. . . .

. . . what can you expect, then, of a wild telepath, one who has tried to learn without the discipline of the Towers. . . .

She thought, resentfully, that if what they taught in the Towers would teach her to be complacent about the deaths of innocent beasts who had no part in men and their wars, she was glad she had not had it!

"Please understand," Carolin said, looking at the three bird-handlers, "No blame attaches to any one of you, but we have lost two of our three sentry-birds, and the remaining one must be sent out at once, danger or no. Which of you will fly her?"

"I am willing," said Ruyven, "My sister is new to this work and she is deeply grieved—she has handled these birds since they were young and was very close to them. I do not think she is strong enough to work further now, Sire."

Carolin glanced at Ranald and said, "I shall need all my *leronyn* if we are to destroy the clingfire in Rakhal's hands before he can manage to use it. As for Romilly—" he looked at her, compassionately, but she bristled under his sympathy and said, "None but I shall fly Temperance. I know enough now not to take her into danger—"

"Romilly—" King Carolin dismounted and came toward the girl. He said seriously, "I am sorry, too, about the birds. But can you look at this from my point of view, too? We risk birds, and beasts too, to save the lives of men. I know the birds mean more to you than they can to me, or to any of us, but I must ask you this; would you see me die sooner than the sentry-birds? Would you risk the lives of the birds to save your Swordswomen?"

Romilly's first emotional reaction was, *the birds at least have done Rakhal no harm, why cannot men fight their battles without endangering the innocent?* But she knew that was irrational. She was human; she would sacrifice bird or even horse to save Ranald, or Orain, or Carolin himself, or her brother. . . . She said at last, "Their lives are yours, your

Majesty, to save or spend as you will. But I will not run them heedless into danger for no good reason, either."

She saw, and wondered, that Carolin looked so sad. He said, "Romilly, child . . ." and broke off; finally, after a long pause, he said, "This is what every commander of men and beasts must face, weighing the lives of some against the lives of all. I would like it better if I need never see any of those who have followed me die—" and sighed. "But I owe my life to those I am sworn to rule . . . in truth, sometimes I think I do not rule but serve. Go, send your bird," he added, and after a time Romilly realized, in shock, that only the last four words had been spoken aloud.

I read his thoughts, and he knew I would read them . . . he would not have spoken such things aloud before his armies, but he could not hide his thoughts from anyone with laran. . . .

It was bad enough that such a king must lead his people to war. She should have known that Carolin would waste no life, needless. And if by sending sentry-birds into danger he thus could spare the lives of some of his followers, he would do so, there must be responsible choice; as when she had chosen to let the banshee go hungry, because for it to feed would have meant death for all of them. She was human; her first loyalty must always be to her fellow men and women. She bowed, rode a little away from Carolin with Temperance on her saddle, and raised a gloved fist to send the bird into the rainy sky again.

She was flying, hovering over the field . . . and not far away, she heard the thunder of charging horses, as Rakhal's army swept down over the brow of the hill and the troops charged toward one another. There was a tremendous shock, and Romilly saw through the bird's eyes. . . .

Horses, down and screaming, sliced open by swords and spears . . . men lying on the ground, dying . . . she could not tell whether Carolin's men or Rakhal's, and it did not matter. . . . A picked group of men swept down toward where the blue fir-tree banner flew over Carolin's guard . . . Sunstar! Carry my king to safety . . . and a part of her rode with the great black stallion, thundering away with the king, to form a compact group, awaiting the charge again.

Flames seemed to sear the air; it was filled with the acrid smell of burning flesh, men and horses shrieking, and death, death everywhere. . . .

Yet through it all Romilly kept still, hovering over the field, bringing the bird's-eye picture of the battle to Carolin's eyes so that he could direct his men where they were most needed. Hours, it seemed, dragged by while she swept over the field, sated with horrors, sickened with the smell of burning flesh. . . .

And then Rakhal's men were gone, leaving only the dead and dying on the field, and Romilly, who had been in rapport with the remaining sentry-bird (she knew now that it was Ruyven who had siezed her bridle and led her horse to safety atop a little hill overlooking the field, while she was entranced in rapport with the bird) returned to her own awareness, sick and shocked.

Dying horses. Seven of them she had trained with her own hands in the hostel . . . dead or dying, and Clea, merry Clea who had talked so lightly of death, lying all but dead on the field, her blood invisible on the crimson tunic of the Swordswoman. . . . Clea, dying in Jandria's arms, and an empty place, a vast silence where once had been a living, breathing, human being, beloved and real. . . .

There was no rejoicing on this battlefield; Carolin had felt too many deaths that day. Soberly, men went to bury the dead, to give the last few dying horses the mercy-stroke, Ruyven went with the healers to bind up the wounds of those who had been struck down. Romilly, shocked beyond speech, set up the tent aided only by Ruyven's young apprentice, who had a great burn on his arm from the *clingfire* that had rained down on the army. Three perches were with the baggage, but only one bird perched alone, and Romilly felt sick as she fed her . . . the carrion smell was now all around them. She could not bring herself to sleep in the little tent she had shared with Lady Maura; she searched through the camp at the edge of the battlefield till she found the rest of the Sisterhood, and silently crept in among them. So many dead. Horses, and birds, who had been part of her life, into whom she had put so much time and strength and love in their training . . . the Sisterhood had set her to training these horses, not that they might live and serve, but that they might die in this senseless slaughter. And Clea, whom Jandria had carried dead off the field. Two of the Sisterhood called to Romilly.

"Sister, are you wounded?"

"No," Romilly said numbly. She hardly knew; her body was so battered with the many deaths which had swept over her wide-open mind, which she had felt in her very flesh; but now she realized that she was not hurt at all, that there was not a mark anywhere on her flesh.

"Have you healing skills?" And when Romilly said no, they told her to come and help in the digging of a grave for Clea.

"A Swordswoman cannot lie among the soldiers. As she was in life, so in death she must be buried apart."

Romilly wondered, with a dull pain in her head, what it would matter now to Clea where she lay? She had defended herself well, she had taught so many of her sisters to defend themselves, but the final ravishment of death had caught her unaware, and she lay cold and stiff, looking very surprised, without a mark on her face. Romilly could hardly believe that she would not laugh and jump up, catching them off guard as she had done so many times before. She took the shovel one of the Swordswomen thrust into her hand. The hard physical labor of digging the grave was welcome; otherwise she caught too much pain, too many wounded men, screaming, suffering, in silence or great moans, their pain racking her. She tried to shut it all out, as Ranald had taught her, but there was too much, too much. . . .

Out on the field, dark flapping forms hovered, waiting. Then one swept down to where a dead horse lay, already bloating, and thrust in his beak with a great raucous cry of joy. Another flapped down and another, and then dozens, hundreds . . . feasting, calling out joyously to one another. Romilly picked up a thought from somewhere, she could not tell whether from one of the Swordswomen beside her at the grave, or someone out of sight on the dark campground, *the defeat of men is the joy of the carrion-bird, where men mourn the kyorebni make holiday* . . . and dropped her shovel, sickened. She tried to pick it up, but suddenly doubled over, retching. She had not eaten since morning; nothing came up but a little green bile, but she stayed there, doubled over, sick and exhausted, too sickened even to weep.

Jandria came and led her silently inside the tent. Two Swordswomen were tending the wounds of three others, one woman with a clingfire burn on her hand which was still burning inward, another unconscious from a sword-cut across her head, and still another with a leg broken when her horse fell and rolled on her. One looked up, frowning, as Jandria led Romilly inside and pushed her down on a blanket.

"She is unwounded—she should be helping to bury our dead!"

Jandria said gruffly, "There is more than one kind of wound!" She held Romilly close, rocking her, stroking her hair, soothing her, but the girl was unaware of the touch, lost

300

in a desperate solitude where she sought and sought for the dead. . . .

Romilly wandered in a dark dream, as if on a great grey plain, where she saw Clea before her, laughing, riding on one of the dead horses, and Prudence perched on her fist . . . but they were so far ahead, no matter how she raced, her feet were stuck as if she waded through thick syrup and she could not catch up with them, never, never. . . .

Somewhere Romilly heard a voice, she felt she ought to know the voice but she did not, saying, *She has never learned to shut it out. This time, perhaps, I can give her barriers, but there is really no remedy. She is a wild telepath and she has no protection.*

Romilly only knew that someone . . . *Carolin? Lady Maura?* . . . touched her forehead lightly, and she was back in the tent of the Swordswomen again, and the great desolate grey plain of death was gone. She clung to Jandria, shuddering and weeping.

"Clea's dead. And my horses, all my horses . . . and the birds . . ." she wept.

Jandria held and rocked her. "I know, dear. I know," she whispered, "It's all right, cry for them if you must, cry, we are all here with you." and Romilly thought, in dull amazement, *She is crying too.*

And she did not know why that should seem strange to her.

CHAPTER EIGHT

Romilly woke, on the morning after the battle, to a grey and dismal day of heavy rain. On the field nothing stirred except the omnipresent carrion-birds, undaunted by the downpour, feeding on the bodies of men and horses.

It makes no difference to her now, Romilly thought, but even so she was grateful that Clea lay in the earth, her body guarded from the fierce beaks of the quarreling *kyorebni.* Yet one way or another, her body would return to its native elements, food for the small crawling things in the earth, to feed grasses and trees. She had become part of the great and endless cycle of life, where those who fed on the earth became in turn food for the earth. *Why, then, should I grieve?* Romilly asked herself, but the answer came without thought.

Her death did not come in the full course of time, when she had lived out her days. She died in a quarrel between kings which was none of her making. And yet, troubled, she remembered how she had met with Lyondri Hastur. Lyondri's cruelties were many, while Carolin at least seemed to feel that it was his duty to serve and protect those who lived in the lands he had been born to reign over.

Carolin is like a horse . . . with her love of Sunstar and of the other horses, it never occurred to Romilly that she was being offensive to the king. . . . *While Rakhal and Lyondri are like banshees who prey on living.* Suddenly, for the first time in the year she had been among the Swordswomen, Romilly was glad that Preciosa had abandoned her.

She too preys on the living. It is her nature and I love her but I could not, now, endure to see it, to be a part of it!

She dressed herself, drew the hood of her thickest cloak over her head, and went to tend Temperance. Her first impulse was to leave her to Ruyven: she felt that the sight of the empty perches of Prudence and Diligence would rewaken all the horror and dread of their deaths. But she was sworn to care for them, she was the king's hawkmistress, and Ruyven, though he cared dutifully for the birds, did not love them, as she did.

Temperance sat solitary on her perch, huddled against the chilly dampness; the perches were sheltered but there was no protection against the wind, and Romilly decided to move the bird inside the tent in which neither she nor Maura had slept now for several nights; Temperance was the only remaining sentry-bird with Carolin's armies, and if she took cold in this damp and drizzly weather, she could not fly. Romilly shrank from the memory of her last flight, but she knew that she would, as her duty commanded, fly the bird again, even into danger. Not gladly; that gladness had been a part of innocence and it was gone forever. But she would do it, as duty demanded, because she had seen warfare and known a hint of what would befall the folk of these hills under Lyondri Hastur's harsh rule.

Lyondri did not wish—she knew this from her brief contact with him—to be only Rakhal's executioner. *Tell Jandria,* he had said, *that I am not the monster she thinks me.* Yet he believed that this was his only road to power, and therefore he was as guilty as Rakhal.

He is Carolin's kinsman. How can they be so unlike?

As she was caring for Temperance, there was a step outside the tent, and she turned to see a familiar face.

"*Dom* Alderic," she cried, but before he had more than a moment to stare at her in surprise, Ruyven hurried to greet Alderic with an enthusiastic kinsman's embrace.

"*Bredu*! I should have known you would hurry to find us here—does your father know?"

Alderic Castamir shook his head and smiled at his friend. He said, "I am recently come from Falconsward; your father gave me leave to go, though not willingly; you should know that Darren has returned to the monastery."

Ruyven sighed and shook his head. "I would so willingly have yielded my place as Father's heir to Darren, and hoped, when he was not in my light, that Father would come to see his true worth. . . ."

"His *own* worth," Alderic said quietly. "Darren has small love for horses or hawks, and no trace of the MacAran Gift. He cannot be blamed for what he is not, any more than you for what you are, *bredu.* And I think The MacAran has had to grant that you cannot forge a hammer from featherpod fluff, nor spin spider-silk even from precious copper. Darren's skills are otherwise, and The MacAran has sent him to Nevarsin, to complete his schooling; one day he shall be Rael's steward, while Rael—I have already begun to teach him to work with horses and hawks."

"Little Rael!" marvelled Ruyven, "When I left Falconsward he was still at Luciella's knee, it seemed! Yet I knew he would have the MacAran Gift; I think I was blinded about Darren because I love him and I wanted so much for him to have the Gift, that he might be free. Well, Darren has found his place, as I mine."

Alderic came and bent over Romilly's hand. "Mistress Romilly," he said gently, and Romilly corrected him:

"Swordswoman Romilly—and I know what my father would say to that; he shall have no chance."

"Under favor, Romy," said Alderic, looking directly into her eyes, "Your father loves you and mourns you as dead;

and so does your stepmother. May I beg you as your friend—and theirs, for your father has been more than kind to me—to send them word that you live."

She smiled wryly. "Better not. I am sure my father would rather think of me dead than earning my bread by the sword, or wearing the earring of the Sisterhood."

"I would not be quick to be too sure of that. I think, when you left Falconsward, he changed; it was not long after that, that he bowed his head to the truth and gave Darren leave to return where he was happy. You must have been blind, deaf and dumb, Romilly, if you did not know that you were the favorite of all his children, though he loves you all."

"I know that," Ruyven said, lowering his eyes, and his voice was strangled and harsh, "I never thought he would bend so far. I too have been harsh and stiff-necked. If we come alive from this war—*Bearer of Burdens, grant that!*—" he interjected in that stifled voice, "I shall go to Falconsward and be reconciled to him, and beg him to make his peace with the Towers, so that Rael may have proper training for his *laran* before it is too late. And if I must abase myself to him, so be it. I have been too proud."

"And you, Romilly?" asked Alderic. "He has grieved for you so terribly that he has grown old in this single year."

She blinked tears from her eyes. It tore at her heart to think of her father grown old. But she insisted, "Better he should think me dead, than that a daughter of his should disgrace him by wearing the earring—"

Alderic shook his head. "I cannot persuade you, but would it ease your heart to know that Mallina was married to *Dom* Garris at Midwinter?"

"Mallina? My little sister? To that—that disgusting lecher?" Romilly cried, "and you say my father has changed?"

"Be not too quick to judge," Alderic cautioned, "Garris dotes on her, and she, to all appearances, on him—even before they were wedded, she confided to me that Garris was not so bad at all, when she came to understand him; she said, the poor fellow has been so lonely and unhappy that his wretchedness drove him to all kinds of things, and now he has someone to love him and care about him, he is completely changed! You should see them together!"

"God forbid," Romilly said, shaking her head, "but if he makes Mallina happy, better her than me!" She could not imagine how anyone could tolerate that man, but Mallina had always been something of a fool, perhaps they deserved one another! "Anyhow, Mallina would be the kind of docile and obedient wife that Garris wanted."

Ruyven said, "You are so fond, you say, of my father; but have you yet gone to greet your own?"

"My father can willingly dispense with my company," Alderic frowned stubbornly. "He has never sought it; he sees only my mother in my face."

Romilly remembered what she had guessed before she left Falconsward; Alderic was Carolin's son! And therefore, rightfully heir to all these lands. . . .

She bowed and said, "Let me take you to your father, my prince."

Alderic stared and laughed. "Romilly, Romilly, my young friend, if you have believed me the king's son, better that you know now how you have misjudged me! Carolin's sons are safely in the care of the Hastur of Carcosa, and I have heard rumors that Carolin is courting a certain *leronis* of Tramontana—" he smiled at Ruyven and said, "That was in the air even before you left the Tower, my friend."

"And *Domna* Maura has promised to wed him, if the Council gives leave," said Ruyven, adding grimly, "Providing any of us escape this war. Rakhal fell upon us with *clingfire*-arrows; we managed to fight him away, but he will rally and be upon us again, and the Bearer of Burdens knows alone what devilry of *laran*-work he will fling against us when next he comes! So make haste to greet your father, 'Deric, for this is but the lull before the storm, and by this time tomorrow we may be fighting for our lives! Would you greet your Gods after death with the stain of kin-strife still upon you? For it is most likely you have come only to die at your father's side."

"As bad as that?" Alderic asked, searching Ruyven's face. Ruyven nodded, grimly.

"We are, as I said, at the center of the storm; at peace for a moment, no more. Carolin has need of all the *leronyn* he can summon to his side, 'Deric."

Romilly interrupted, "What is this? If you are not Carolin's son—"

Alderic said quietly, "My father is called Orain, and he is foster-brother and friend of Carolin. I was reared at Carolin's court."

She reached for his hand with sudden confidence. She should have guessed, when he had spoken of the way in which his father could not endure to look on him. Carolin, even in an unwanted dynastic marriage, could have shown courtesy and kindness to a woman; but, as reward for her moment of foolishness, she had seen straight into Orain's heart. She was sorry for Alderic that he had not known a father's love; for now she knew how blessed she had been in that love.

"I am the king's hawkmistress," she said, "and he will have need of my bird soon, if we are to meet Rakhal again on the field of war. And, no doubt, your father is with him."

"I doubt it not at all," Alderic said, "He is never far from the side of his king. When I was younger, I hated him for that, and resented it because he cared more for Carolin's sons, and even Lyondri Hastur's little son, than for me." He shrugged and sighed. "The world will go as it will; love cannot be compelled, even within kin, and to such a man as my father, my very existence must have been a painful reminder of an unhappy time in his life. I owe Orain a son's duty— may I never fail in it—but no more. Kinship, I sometimes think, is a joke the gods play, to bind us to those we do not love, in the hope we can somehow be reconciled to them; but friends are a gift, and your father has been a friend, almost a foster-father to me. When we are free of this war—" he touched her hand lightly. "We need not speak of that now. But I think you know what I would say."

She did not look at him. There had been a time, indeed, when she had thought she would willingly have married this man. But much had happened to her in the year since then. She had desired Orain himself, even though he had not wanted her. And Ranald . . . what had happened with Ranald was not the sort of thing which led to marriage, nor would a Drylands lord be likely to marry a mountain Swordswoman; indeed, she did not think she would marry him if he asked, and there was no reason he should. Their bodies had accepted one another joyfully, but that was under unusual conditions; she would have accepted any man she supposed, who had come to her and offered surcease from what was so tumultuous within her. But apart from that, they knew little of one another. And if Alderic knew she was not the virtuous maiden she had been a Falconsward, would he even want her?

She said, "When this war is done, Lord Alderic—"

"Call me Deric, as your brother does," he interrupted her. "Ruyven and I are *bredin*, and as friend to both your brothers, I owe you always a brother's protection, even if no more."

"I am a Swordswoman—Deric," she said. "I need no man's protection, but I will gladly have your friendship. That, I

306

think, I had, even at Falconsward. As for anything more than friendship, I think—" uncontrollably, her voice was shaking. "We should not even speak of that, until we are free of this accursed war!"

"I am grateful for your honesty, Romilly," he said. "I would not want a woman who would marry me just because I am the son of Carolin's chief counselor and friend. My father married because the old king wished to honor his son's foster-brother by giving him in marriage to a high-born lady; they despised one another, and I have suffered for that; I would not wish my own children torn by hatred between their parents, and I have always sworn that I would marry no woman unless we were, at least, friends." His eyes, levelled and gentle, met hers, and for some reason the kindness in them made her want to cry.

"For anything more we can wait—Swordswoman."

She nodded. But all she said was, "Let us go, then, and greet your father."

But they did not reach Carolin's tent before they met Orain, hurrying toward the place where the birds were kept. He said, "Mistress Romilly, your sentry-bird is wanted—" and stopped, blinking, at the sight of her companion.

"Father," Alderic said, and bowed.

Orain took him, for a moment, in a brief, formal embrace. The sight hurt Romilly; she was so accustomed to Orain's rough affection. She thought, he would have greeted *me* with more kindness than that! He said, "I did not know you had come, my boy. Carolin has need now of any who are skilled at *laran*; perhaps you have heard that he came down on us with clingfire."

"I heard it when I came to camp, Father," Alderic said, "and I was making haste to offer such small skill as I have to Carolin's service; but I came first to greet you, sir."

Orain said, with constraint, "For that I thank you in his name. The king's *leronyn* are gathered there—" and he gestured. "Mistress Romilly, bring your bird; we must know how long we have before Rakhal falls on us again."

"Are we to march out on Rakhal, then?" Alderic asked, and Orain said, with his mouth set in a grim line,

"Only to get free of the bodies here, so that we can maneuver if we must. If Rakhal has clingfire at command, we dare not meet him in the woods, or all this land will be burned over between here and Neskaya!" And as Romilly looked toward Carolin's headquarters she saw the tent struck, and the Hastur banner taken out by his guardsmen. Alderic glanced once at Romilly, but all he said was, "I must join the others, then. Guard yourself well, Romilly," and hurried away.

She went back swiftly to prepare herself for riding, and set Temperance on her saddle, leaving it to Ruyven's young assistant to strike the tent and pack it for moving with the army. Could Rakhal indeed be so thoughtless of the land as to send fire-arrows in forested country, at this season, and risk fire? Well, it was like what she had heard of the man. For that reason, if for no other, somehow they must defeat that unprincipled man who called himself king!

Now that she knew what she was seeking, it proved easier to send up the sentry-bird. Because of the rain, Temperance was reluctant to fly, but this time Romilly did not hesitate to send the bird up, almost to the bottom of the low-lying clouds. She flew her slowly in circles, gradually widening, so that she could see Rakhal's army on the move. As she rode, half of her mind on the bird, she joined Carolin and his array of skilled *leronyn*, men and women; it crossed her mind, briefly, that she was one of them, that perhaps at last, she had found her true place.

I am Swordswoman still. But I am grateful that I need not bear a sword in this combat. If I must, I think I could do so, but I am glad that my skills lead me elsewhere. I do not want to kill . . . and then, grimly, she forced herself to be realistic. She was a part of this killing, as much as if she bore sword or bow into the battlefield; more, perhaps, for her sentry-bird's eyes directed the killing. She took her place, resolutely, between Lady Maura and Ranald. One or both of them would remain in rapport with her, to relay the information to the ears of Carolin and his general.

It cannot be easy for Jandria, to go against Lyondri this way, and know that she will be instrumental in his death— and now there is no help for him but death. She was not sure at that moment whether the thought was hers, or Lady Maura's, or even, perhaps, Lord Orain's. They were all in a tight little group, clustered around Carolin, and Alderic was among them. At the edge of her awareness she saw Alderic greet Jandria kindly, and call her "My lady Aunt." As if it were something she had dreamed a long time ago, it crossed her mind that if she married Alderic, she would be kinswoman to Jandria.

But we are sworn to one another in the Sisterhood, anyway, I need not that to be her kin. Alderic said it so; kinsmen are born, but friendship is a gift of the Gods. . . .

Maura looked at her meaningfully, and Romilly remembered her work; she went swiftly into rapport with Temperance, who was still flying in widening circles over the great plain. At last she spotted, through the keen eyes of the bird, a darkening cloud of dust on the horizon. . . .

Rakhal's army, on the move, and riding swiftly toward the forested cover of the hills. As she saw, and as this information was relayed swiftly to Carolin, she caught the thought of the king, *So he would hide within the cover of the trees, for he knows I am unwilling to use* clingfire, *or even ordinary fire-arrows, where there is danger that the resin-trees may bring on wildfire. Somehow we must overtake him before he reaches the forest, and do battle on ground of my choosing, not his.* And Romilly sensed the touch of his mind on Sunstar's;

Lead my men, then, great horse. . . .

She saw with a strange widening consciousness, linked to Carolin, to Sunstar, to all the men around her. She knew that Ranald had seized her horse's rein and was guiding him, so that she could ride safely even while she was in rapport with the sentry-bird, and spared him a quick thought of gratitude. The rain was slowing, and after a time a strange, low, watery sunlight came through the clouds. She flew Temperance lower, over the armies, trying to fly high enough that she could not be seen, yet dipping in and spying . . .

Rakhal's armies seemed shrunken in size, and off to the north she saw another body of men and horses. Were they coming to Rakhal's aid, now that the first battle had thinned his ranks? No; for they were riding away from Rakhal's main army as swiftly as they could. And Carolin's thoughts were jubilant.

Rakhal's men are deserting him, now they know what he is . . . they have no more stomach than I for this kind of warfare. . . .

But the main body of men was still formidable; they had come to a halt at the brow of a little hill, and Romilly knew, being in communication with the minds of Carolin's men, that Rakhal had seized the most advantageous terrain, and would make a stand there and defend it.

This, then, would be the decisive battle. Under urging from Carolin, she flew the bird down closer, so that through her eyes, Carolin's advisers might take stock of the size of the forces arrayed against them. Rakhal had the advantage, it seemed, in numbers, and in terrain.

Somehow we must lure Rakhal from that hill. . . .

Alderic rode toward his father and spoke to Orain urgently for a few moments, and Romilly, what small part of her mind was not with the bird, heard Orain say to Carolin, "By your leave, my lord. My son has put me in mind of an old trick in the mountains, and we have *leronyn* enough to make it effective. Let me lead a dozen or two of your men, with the *leronyn*, to cast an illusion as if there were four times as many of us, to force Rakhal to charge down upon us; then you can come and take him on the flank."

Carolin considered for a moment. "It might work," he said at last, "But I'll not send your *leronyn* into danger; most of them do not even wear swords."

Ranald Ridenow said, "My *laran* as well as my sword are at your service, my King. Let me lead these men."

"Pick your men, then—and Aldones ride with you, all of you!" Carolin said, "but pick your moment carefully—"

"Mistress MacAran shall do that for us," said Ranald, with his hand on Romilly's bridle.

Orain said, "Would you take a woman into battle?" and Romilly, pulling herself free for a moment of the rapport with the bird-mind, said, "My lord Orain, I am a Swordswoman! Where my brother will go, I shall go with him!"

Ruyven did not speak, but she felt the warmth that said, not in words, *Bravely spoken, sister,* and with it a touch from Alderic. Somehow it reminded her of the day when they had flown hawks at Falconsward, at Midsummer-festival.

When I am free of this war, I shall never again hunt for pleasure, for I know now what it is to be hunted . . . and with amazement, she knew that the mind which held this thought was Orain's.

How near to my own thought! Romilly felt again the bitter regret for the distance that had fallen between Orain and herself. *We were so close in so many ways, so much alike!* But the world would go as it would, and Orain was as he was and not as she would have him. She threw herself back into rapport with the sentry-bird, letting Ranald see through her mind, and relay to Orain and Alderic, what she saw in Rakhal's army.

Horsemen were drawn up at the perimeter of his army, surrounding foot-soldiers and bowmen, and at the center, a number of great wagons, with the acrid smell she knew now to be the chemical smell of *clingfire*. They ringed the brow of the little hill completely while they took their stand there, it would be impossible to breach their defenses.

But that is precisely what we must do, it was Alderic's

thought, and he rode the company of two dozen men, headed by the small band of *leronyn,* breakneck toward the hill; suddenly stopped them.

Now!

And suddenly it seemed to Romilly that a great cloud of dust and fire moved on the hill, with a racing and a pounding of hooves, and cries . . . *what soldiers are these?* And then she knew that she had seen these men, the men who had deserted Rakhal and were riding away . . . it was like a great mirror, as if the image of this separate army were thrown straight at Rakhal's men . . . for a little they held firm, while a cloud of arrows came flying down toward the close-clustered band of soldiers and *leronyn* at the foot of the hill . . . but they were shooting short, at the image of the racing *soldiers* . . .

Join with us! In the name of the Gods, everyone who has laran, *join us to hold this image* . . . on and on the racing cloud of dust, in which Romilly could now see indistinct shapes, horses' heads like great grey skulls, the burning visages of skeletons, glowing with devil-fire inside the hidden cloud of dust and sorcery. . . .

She heard a voice she had never heard before, reverberating within her mind, bellowing; "Stand firm! Stand firm!" But that could not stand against the assault of the ghostly army; Rakhal's men broke and charged down the hill, riding straight into the cloud of magical images, screaming in terror, and their line faltered, broke in a dozen places. Fire struck up through the ground, licking, curling, green and blue flames rising . . . then it was as if a river of blood flowed up the hill, through the horses' feet, and they stopped short, snorting, screaming in terror, stamping. Some of their riders fell, a few men held their ground, crying out, "No smell of blood, no smell of burning, it's a trick, a trick—" but the line was broken; horses stampeded, colliding with one another, trampling their riders, and the officers struggled wildly to rally the broken line, to gather the men into some semblance of order.

"Now! Carolin!"

"A Hastur! A Hastur!" Carolin's men charged, the main body of the army, flowing like water up the hill and into the broken ranks of the horsemen. Right over Rakhal's outer defenses they flowed, and then they were fighting at close quarters, but Ranald and Alderic broke and dashed right through to the center of the armies, where the guarded wagon stood with the *clingfire.* Men were gathered, hastily dipping their arrows in the stuff, but Alderic and Orain and their little band rode right over them and toward the wagon. Swiftly, like a running tide of energy, they linked minds, and a band of blue fire rolled out toward the wagon with the clingfire. It struck, blazed upward, and then a roaring column of fire burst skyward, blazing so fiercely that Rakhal's men scattered and ran for their lives. Burning droplets fell on some of them and they blazed up like living torches and died screaming; the fire ran through Rakhal's own armies, and, panicked, they ran, scattered, and ran right on Carolin's spears and swords.

Although a part of Romilly was still linked with the bird, she knew there was no more need of it. She found herself closely linked in mind with Sunstar, as Carolin urged him forward; she knew the terror of fire, shuddering with the smell of burning grass and burning flesh; even in the rain which had begun to drizzle down again in the fitful sunlight, the *clingfire* burned on. But the great stallion, bravely overcoming that inborn fear, carried his rider forward . . . or was it Romilly herself, bearing the king into the heart of the fleeing enemy.

"See where Rakhal flies with his sorcerers!" cried out Orain, "After them, men! Take them now!"

Romilly let Temperance fly upward out of range of the fire; it was burning inward now, with a ring round it where there was nothing left to burn—so much had the *leronyn* of Carolin's armies accomplished; but she, with Carolin, was away with the stallion Sunstar, forging to the heights, where the last remnant of Rakhal's men, cut off between Carolin and the raging remnant of clingfire, fought with their backs to the fire. Sunstar seemed to fly forward with Carolin's own will to take the height, and Romilly felt that it was she herself who bore him on to the last moment of success. . . .

Then she stumbled—for a moment Romilly was not sure it was not she herself who had stumbled—recovered, and reared high in the air, Carolin's hand guiding him up, then down, to trample the man who had risen, sword in hand, before him. His great hooves were like hammers pounding the man into the ground. Romilly felt the man go down, his head splitting like a ripe fruit beneath her hooves—Sunstar's hooves—felt Carolin fighting for balance in the saddle. And then another man reared up with a lightning-flash of steel, she felt Carolin slip back in the saddle and fall, and in that moment Romilly felt sharp shearing pain as the sword sliced through neck and throat and heart, and blood and life spurted away. . . .

She never felt herself strike the ground.

. . . rain was falling, hard cold rain, pounding down; the ground was awash with it, and even the smell of the *clingfire* had been washed away. The sky was dark; it was near nightfall. Romilly sat up, dazed and stunned, not even now fully aware that it was not she who had been felled by the sword.

Sunstar! She reached out automatically for his mind, found—

Found nothingness! Only a great sense of vacancy, emptiness where he had been. Wildly she looked around and saw, lying not far away, the stallion's body, his head nearly severed, and the man he had killed lying beneath his great bulk. The rain had washed the blood clear so that there was only a great gaping wound in his neck from which the blood had soaked into the ground all around him. *Sunstar, Sunstar—dead, dead, dead!* She reached out, again, dazed, to nothingness. Sunstar, whose life she had shared so long. . . .

And whom she had betrayed by leading him to death in a war between two kings . . . *neither of them is worth a lock of his black mane . . . ah, Sunstar . . . and I died with you* . . . Romilly felt so empty and cold she was not sure that she was still alive. She had heard tales of men who did not know they were dead and kept trying to communicate with the living. Dazed, drained of all emotion except fury and grief, she managed to sit up.

Around her lay the bodies of the dead, Rakhal's men and Carolin's; but of Carolin himself there was no sign. Only the body of Sunstar showed where Carolin had once been. Vaguely, not caring, she wondered if all Carolin's men were dead and Rakhal victor. Or had Orain's party captured or killed Rakhal? What did it matter?

What matters it which great rogue sits on the throne. . . .

She began to get her bearings a little. As before the previous battle, the field was covered with the dark shapes of *kyorebni*, hovering. One lighted, with a harsh scream, on Sunstar's head, and Romilly rushed at it, flapping her arms and crying out. The bird was gone, but it would come back.

Sunstar is dead. And I trained him with my own hands for this war, betrayed him into the hands of the one who would ride him into this slaughter, and the noble horse never faltered, but bore Carolin to this place and to his death. I would have done better to kill him myself when he ran joyously around our green paddock behind the hostel of the Sisterhood. Then he would never have know fire and fear and a sword through his heart.

Dark was falling, but far away at the edge of the battlefield, a lantern bobbed, a little light wandering over the field. Grave-robbers? Mourners seeking the slain? No; intuitively Romilly knew who they were; the women of the Sisterhood, seeking their fallen comrades, who must not lie in the common grave of Carolin's soldiers.

As if it mattered to the dead where they lay. . . .

They would come here soon, thinking her dead—when she had fallen from her horse, stricken down by Sunstar's death, no doubt they had left her for dead. Now they would come to bury her, and find her living, and they would rejoice. . . .

And then Romilly was overcome with rage and grief. They would take her back to themselves, reclaim her as a warrior-woman. She had fled from the company of men, come among the Sisterhood, and what had they done? Set her to training horses, not for their own sake or for the service of men, but to be slaughtered, slaughtered senselessly in this strife of men who could not keep their quarrels to themselves alone but involved the innocent birds and horses in their wars and killings. . . .

And I am to go back to that? No, no, never!

With shaking hands, she tore the earring of the Sisterhood from her ear; the wire caught and tore her ear but she was unconscious of the pain. She flung it on the ground. *An offering for Sunstar, a sacrifice offered to the dead!* She could hardly stand. She looked around, and saw that riderless horses were wandering here and there on the battlefield. It took only the slightest touch of her *laran* to bring one to her, his head bent in submission. It was too dark now to see whether it was mare or gelding, grey or black or roan. She climbed into the saddle, and crouched over the pommel, letting the horse take his own way . . . *where? It matters not. Away from this place of death, away, friend. I will serve no more, not as soldier nor Swordswoman nor leronis. From henceforth I shall serve no man nor woman.* Blindly, her eyes closed against streaming hot tears, Romilly rode alone from the battlefield and into the rain of the night.

All that night, she rode, letting the horse find his own pathway, and never knew where she went or what direction she took. The sun rose and she was still unaware, sitting as if lifeless on the animal's back, swaying now and again but always recovering herself before she quite fell. It did not seem to matter. Sunstar was dead. Carolin and Orain had gone she knew not where, nor did it matter, Orain wanted nothing of her . . . she was a woman. Carolin, like the Sisterhood, sought only to have her use her *laran* to betray other inno-

cent beasts to the slaughter! Ruyven . . . Ruyven cared little
for her, he was like a monk from the accursed Tower where
they learned devilry like *clingfire*. . . .

There is no human who shall mean anything to me now.

She rode on, all day, across a countryside ravaged and
deserted, over which the war had raged. At the edge of the
forest, she slid from her horse, and set him free.

"Go, my brother," she whispered, "and serve no man or
woman, for they will only lead you to death. Live free in the
wild, and go your own way."

The horse stared down at her for a moment; she gave it a
final pat and pushed it away, and, after a moment of motionless surprise, it turned and cantered awkwardly away.
Romilly went quietly into the darkness of the forest. She was
soaked to the skin, but it seemed not to matter, any more
than the horse minded his wet cloak of hair. She found a
little hollow between the roots of a tree, crawled into it, drew
her cloak tightly around her, covering her face; curled herself
into a ball and slept like the dead.

At dawn she woke to hear birds calling, and it seemed,
mixed with their note, she could hear the harsh screams of
the *kyorebni*, still feeding on the waste of the battlefield. She
did not know where she was going; somewhere away from
the sound of those screams. She got numbly to her feet and
walked, not caring in which direction, further into the wood.

She walked most of that day. She was not conscious of
hunger; she moved like a wild thing, silently, avoiding what
was in her path and whenever she heard a noise, freezing
silently in her tracks. Late in the day she nearly stumbled
into a small stream, and cupping her hands, drank deeply of
the clear sweet water, then laid herself down in a patch of
sunlight that came between the leaves and let the sun dry the
remaining damp from her clothes. She was still numb. As
darkness fell, she curled up under a bush and slept. Some
small thing in the grasses brushed against her and she never
thought to turn aside.

The next morning she slept late and woke with the sun's
heat across her back. Before her, a spider had spun its web,
clear and jewelled with the dew; she looked on its marvelous
intricacy and felt the first pleasure she had felt in many days.
The sun was bright on the leaves; a bushjumper suddenly
bolted on long legs, followed by four miniature babies, their
bushy tails standing up like small bluish flags riding high. Romilly heard herself laugh aloud, and they stopped, tails
quivering, dead silent; then, as the silence fell around them,

with a burst of speed all four of the tiny flags popped down a hole in the grass.

How quiet it was within the woods! There could certainly be no human dwelling nearby, or nothing could have been so peaceful, the wild things so untroubled and unafraid.

She uncurled herself from sleep, lazily stretching her limbs. She was thirsty, but there was no stream nearby; she licked the dew from the low leaves of the tree over her head. On a fallen log she found a few old woody mushrooms, and ate them, then found some dried berries hanging to a stem and ate them too. After a little while, as she wandered lazily through the wood, she saw the green flags of a root she knew to be edible, grubbed it up with a stick, rubbed off the dirt on the edge of her tunic, and chewed it slowly. It was stringy and hard, the flavor acrid enough to make her eyes water, but it satisfied her hunger.

She had lost the impetus that had kept her moving restlessly from place to place; she sat in the clearing of the fallen log most of the day, and when night fell again she slept there.

During her sleep she heard someone calling her name; but she did not seem to know the voice. Orain? No, he would not call her; he had wanted her when he thought her a boy, but had no use for the woman she really was. Her father? He was far away, across the Kadarin, safe at home. She thought with pain of the peaceful hills of Falconsward. Yet it was there she had learned that evil art of horse-training by which she had betrayed the beloved to his death. In her dream she seemed to sit on Sunstar's back, to ride like the wind across the grey plain she once had seen, and she woke with her face wet with tears.

A day or two later she realized that she had lost shoes and stockings, she did not remember where, that her feet were already hardening to the dirt and pebbles of the forest floor. She wandered on aimlessly, ever deeper into the forest, eating fruits, grubbing in the earth for roots; now and again she cooled her feet in a mountain stream but she never thought of washing. She ate when she found food; when once for three days together she found nothing edible, she was dimly aware of hunger, but it did not seem important to her. She no longer troubled to rub the dirt from the roots she ate; they seemed just as good to her in their coats of earth. Once she found some pears on an abandoned tree and their taste was so sweet that she felt a rush of ecstasy. She ate as many as she could but it did not occur to her to fill her pockets or to tie them into her skirt.

One night she woke when the purple face of Liriel stood over her in the sky, seeming to look down and chide her, and thought, *I am surely mad, where am I going, what am I going to do? I cannot go on like this forever.* But when she woke she had forgotten it again. Now and again, too, she heard, not with her ears but within her mind, voices that seemed to call, *Romilly, where are you?* She wondered faintly who Romilly was, and why they were calling her.

She came to the end of the woods, the next day, and out into open plains and rolling hills. Waving grasses were covered with seeds . . . all this country must once have been settled and planted to grain, but all around the horizon which stretched wide from west to east, from the wall of the forest behind her to the mountains which rose greyish-pink in the distance, there was no human dwelling. She picked a handful of the seeds, rubbed their coats from them, and chewed them as she walked.

High in the sky, a hawk soared, a single hawk, and as she watched, it dropped down, down, down, falling toward her with folded wings, it alighted on her shoulder. It seemed to speak in her mind, but she did not know what it was saying, yet it seemed that once she had known this hawk, that it had a name, that once she had flown beside it in the sky . . . no, that was not possible, yet the hawk seemed so sure that they knew one another. She reached out to touch it, then stopped, there was some reason she should not touch it with her finger . . . she wished she could remember why. But she looked into the hawk's eyes, and wished she knew where she had seen the hawk before this.

She woke again that night, and again she was aware that she was certainly quite mad, that she could not wander forever like this. But she had no idea where she was, and there was no one to ask. She knew who she was, now, she was Romilly, and the hawk, the hawk which had perched on the low limb of a nearby tree, the hawk was Preciosa, but why had she sought her out here? Did she not know that she, Romilly, set the touch of her mind on bird or horse only to train it to follow humankind meekly to its own death?

It took her five days to cross the plain; she counted them, without thinking, as the face of Liriel grew toward full. When last the moon was full, she had followed Sunstar—she slammed the memory shut; it was too painful. There were plenty of the grainlike seeds to eat, and water to drink. Once the hawk brought a bird down from the sky and lighted on her shoulder, screaming in frustration; she looked at the dead bird, torn by the hawk's beak, and shuddered. It was the hawk's nature, but the sight of the blood made her feel sick, and at last she flung it to the ground and walked on.

That night she came beneath the edges of another patch of forest. She found a tree heavy with last year's nuts, and by now she had sense enough to fill her pockets with them. She was still not certain where she was going, but she had begun to turn northward when there was a choice. She moved noiselessly now through the woods, driven restlessly onward . . . she did not know why.

Overhead, toward evening, she heard the cry of waterfowl, flying toward the south. She looked up, soaring with them in their dizzy flight, seeing from afar where a tall white tower rose, and the glimmer of a lake. Where was she?

The moons were so bright that night, four of them shining down on her, Liriel and Kyrrdis round and full, and the other two shining pale and gibbous, that she could not sleep. It seemed to her that when last she had seen four moons in the sky, something had happened . . . no, she could not remember, but her body ached with desire and hunger unslaked, and she did not know why. After a time, lying in the soft moss, she began to range outward, feeling hungers like her own all round her. . . .

A cat crawled along a branch, and she felt the tug of the light within her, too, the flow of the life of the world, and herself with it. She could see the gleam of the great eyes, followed it with her mind while she prowled around the foot of the tree. There was a sweet, sharp, musky scent in the air now and, in the mind of the cat, she followed it, not knowing whether or not she moved or whether only the cat moved . . . closer and closer she came, and heard herself make a small snarling, purring cry of hunger and need . . . turned with a lashing of the great tail as the cat's mate pounced down the tree trunk, with cries and frisking sounds. Her body ached and hungered and as the cat seized her mate, Romilly twisted on the moss of the ground and dug her hands into the ground, gasping, crying out . . .

Ranald . . . she whispered, in the moment before she was lost in the wild surge of heat. The night seemed filled with the snarling, purring sound of the great cats in their mating, and she lay silent, battered down beneath it, and at last, her senses and *laran* overloaded, she lost consciousness.

The next morning she woke, hardly aware what had happened, feeling sick and exhausted. She did not know why, but her aimless moving through the forest had quickened pace. She must get away, get away . . . a nameless apprehension was on her, and when she heard, above her, the same snarling cry of the great cat, she was too numbed to be afraid. And then there was a dark flash as it slithered to the ground and stood facing her, mouth drawn back in a snarl over sharp fanged teeth. Behind it she sensed the presence of the little balls of brownish fur, hidden in the hollow tree. . . .

The cat was protecting her young! And, she, Romilly, had blundered into the proximity of the cat's protected territory . . . she blundered backward, fighting the temptation to turn and run, run away . . . if she did, she knew the cat would be on her in a moment! Slowly, stealthily, she drew backward, backward, trying to catch the animal's eyes, to press on it with her *laran* . . .

Peace, peace, I mean no harm, not to you, not to your little ones. . . . At some time, she had done this before, something which menaced her, cold, fierce, in the snows. . . .

Silently, silently, step after step, withdraw, withdraw . . . *peace, peace, I mean you no harm, your cubs no harm.* . . .

Then, when she was almost at the edge of the clearing, the cat moved like a streak, with a single long leap, and landed almost at Romilly's feet.

Peace, peace . . . The cat bent her head, almost laid it at Romilly's feet. Then shock struck through her.

No, no! I betrayed Sunstar to death, I swore I would use that laran *no more, never, never . . . no more of the innocent to die* . . .

One paw lashed out like a whip; claws raked Romilly's face, and the weight of the arm stretched her sprawling and gasping with pain; she felt blood break from her cheek and her lip. *Now she has spilled my blood, will she kill me now as sacrifice to her cubs, in expiation for the death of Sunstar.* . . .

The hoarse, soft snarling never stopped. Romilly rolled herself into a ball, to protect her face. Then, as the cat sprung again, a fury of wings lashed down, and the hawk's claws raked at the eyes of the great cat, beating wings flapping around the cat's muzzle.

Preciosa! She has come to fight for me!

Romilly rolled free, springing up and climbing into a nearby tree. Preciosa hovered, just out of reach of the deadly claws, flapping and striking with beak and talons, until the cat, snarling softly, turned her back and vanished into the long grasses where her cubs were hidden. Her breath catching in her throat, Romilly slid down the tree and ran as far as she could in the opposite direction, Preciosa close behind her; she heard the sound of the wings and the little shrilling sound of the hawk. When she was out of range, she stopped, turned, thrust out her fist, in a gesture so familiar that she did not even make it consciously.

Preciosa!" she cried, and as the hawk's talons closed, gently, on her arm, she remembered everything, and began to cry.

"Oh, Preciosa, you came for me!"

She washed in a stream, that night, and shook the leaf-mold and dirt from her cloak. She took off her tunic and trousers, and shook them out to air, and put them on again. She had lost, somewhere, her Swordswoman's earring—she never knew where. With the hawk riding on her shoulder, she tried to orient herself.

She supposed the white Tower nearby must be Neskaya, but she was not certain. A day's walk should bring her there, and perhaps she could send a message somewhere, and know what had befallen Carolin, and what the armies did. She still flinched from the thought of joining them again, but she knew someday she must return to her own kind.

Late that night, as she was looking for a dry place to sleep, and wondering how she had managed all these days alone— she thought she must have been in the woods all of three days, perhaps—it seemed that she heard someone calling her name.

Romilly! Romilly!

Search for her with laran, *only so we can find her, she is hiding . . .*

She cannot be dead. I would know if she was dead. . . .

She recognized, vaguely, some of the voices, though it was still not clear.

If you can find her, bid her come back to us. This was a voice she knew, a voice she loved; Jandria, mourning. And although she had never done it before, somehow Romilly knew how to reach out with her mind.

Where are you? What has happened? I thought the war was over.

It is ended, and Carolin is encamped before the walls of Hali, came the answer. *But it is stalemate, for Lyondri has Orain as hostage somewhere within the city.*

And Romilly did not even stop to remember her grudge, or what it had been.

I will come as swiftly as I can.

CHAPTER NINE

She slept only a little that night, and was awake and walking by daylight, sending out her *laran* to spy out a dwelling of men. Once in the village she sought out a man who had horses for hire.

"I must have a fast horse at once. I am of the Sisterhood of the Sword, and I am on an urgent mission for King Carolin; I am needed at once at Hali."

"And I am His Majesty's chief cook and bottle-washer," jeered the stableman. "Not so fast, *mestra*; what will you pay?" And Romilly saw herself reflected in his eyes, a gaunt scarecrow of a woman in a tattered tunic and breeches, barefoot, her face savagely clawed and bleeding where the mountain-cat had swiped at her, the unkempt hawk riding on her shoulders.

"I have been through the war and worse," she said. She had dwelt among animals so long she had forgotten the need of money. She searched the deep pockets of tunic and breeches and found a few coins forgotten; she spilled them out before him.

"Take these as earnest," she said, not counting them, "I swear I will send the rest when I reach a hostel of the Sisterhood, and twice as many if you will find me a pair of boots and some food."

He hesitated. "I will need thirty silver bits or a copper

royal," he said, "and another as token that you will return the horse here—"

Her eyes glittered with rage. She did not even know why she was in such need of haste, but she was sought for at Hali. "In Carolin's name," she said, "I can take your horse if I must—"

She signalled to the nearest horse; he looked fast, a great rangy roan. A touch of her *laran* and he came swiftly to her, bowed his neck in submission. His owner shouted with anger and came to lay his hand on the horse's lead-rope, but the horse edged nervously away, and lashed out, kicking; circled, and came back to rub Romilly's head with his shoulder.

"*Leronis* . . ." he whispered, his eyes widened, staring.

"That and more," said Romilly tartly.

A young woman stood watching, twisting her long apron. At last she whispered, "My mother's sister is of the Sisterhood, *mestra*. She has told me that the Sisterhood will always pay debts incurred by one of them, for the honor of them all. Let her have the horse, my husband, and—" she ran into the house, brought back a pair of rough boots.

"They were my son's," she said in a whisper, "Rakhal's men came through the village and one of them killed him, cut him down like a dog, when they seized our plow-beast and slaughtered it for their supper, and he asked them for some payment. Carolin's men have done nothing like this."

Romilly slipped the boots on her feet. They were hillmen's boots, fur-lined, soft to her toes. The woman gave her half of a cut loaf of bread. "If you can wait, *mestra*, you shall have hot food, but I have nothing cooked. . . ."

Romilly shook her head. "This is enough," she said. "I cannot wait." In a flash she was on the horse's back, even while the man cried, "No lady can ride that horse—he is my fiercest—"

"I am no lady but a Swordswoman," she said, and suddenly a new facet of her *laran* made itself clear to her; she reached out, as she had done to the mountain cat, and he backed away before her, staring, submissive.

The woman cried, "Do you not want saddle—bridle—let me bind up your wounds, Swordswoman—"

"I have no time for that," Romilly said, "Set me on the road to Hali."

The woman stammered out directions, while the man stood silent, goggling at her. She dug her heels into the horse's back. She had ridden like this, with neither saddle nor bridle, when she was a child at Falconsward, just learning her laran,

322

guiding the horse with her will alone. She felt a brief, poignant regret; *Sunstar!* Sunstar, and the nameless unknown horse she had ridden away from the battle and turned loose to wander in the wild. She had surely been mad.

The horse moved swiftly and steady, his long legs eating up the road. She gnawed at the hard bread; it seemed that no fine meal had ever been quite so delicious. She needed fresh clothes, and a bath, and a comb for her hair, but nightmare urgency drove her on. *Orain, in the hands of Lyondri!* Once she stopped to let the horse graze a little and rest, and wondered, *What do I think I can do about it?*

The Lake at Hali was long and dim, with a Tower rising on the shore, and pale waves lapping like stormclouds at the verge; at the far end Carolin's army encamped before a city whose walls were grey and grim. And now she was sure enough of her *laran* to reach out and feel for the presence of the man she had known as *Dom* Carlo, and to know that he was her friend, king or no. He was still the man who had welcomed her, protected her among his men even when he knew she was a woman, kept her secret even from his dearest friend and foster-brother.

She made her way through the staring army, hearing one of the Swordswomen call her name in amazement. She knew how she must look to them, worn and gaunt, her tunic and breeches filthy, her hair a ragged and uncombed mop, the cat-claw marks still bloody across her face, riding a countryman's horse with neither saddle nor bridle. Was this any way to present herself to a king?

But even as she slid from her horse, Jandria had her in a tight embrace.

"Romilly, Romy, we thought you were dead! Where did you go?"

She shook her head, suddenly too exhausted to speak.

"Anywhere. Everywhere. Nowhere. Does it matter? I came as swiftly as I could. How long since the battle? What is this about Orain being held hostage for Lyondri?"

Alderic and Ruyven came to stare, to clasp her in their arms. "I tried to reach you, with Lady Maura," Alderic said, "but we could not—" and Jandria cried out, "What happened to your face—your earring—?"

"Later," she said, with an exhausted shake of her head, and then Carolin himself was before her; he held out both his hands.

"Child—" he said, and hugged her as her own father might have done. "Orain loved you, too—I thought I had lost both of you, who followed me not as a king but as an outlaw and fugitive! Come in," he said, and led the way into his tent. He gestured, and Jandria poured her a cup of wine, but Romilly shook her head.

"No, no, I have eaten almost nothing, I would be drunk if I drank half a cup now—I would rather have some food," she said. The remnants of a meal were laid around the rough table inside, and Carolin said, "Help yourself." Jandria cut her a slice of meat and bread, but Romilly laid the meat aside—she knew she would never taste it again—and ate the bread, slowly. Jandria took the rejected wine and washed the deep claw-marks on her face.

"Why, how came you to have these? The healer must tend them, a cat's claw-wounds always fester; you could lose the sight of an eye if they spread," she said, but Romilly only shook her head.

"I hardly know. Some day I will tell you all I can remember," she promised, "But Orain—"

"They have him somewhere in the city," Carolin said. He had been pacing the tent but now he dropped wearily into one of the folding camp-chairs. "I dare not even enter to search for him, for they have warned me . . . yet it might give him an easier death than what Lyondri plans for him. Rakhal's army is cut to pieces; most of them have made submission to me, but Rakhal himself, with a few of his men, and Lyondri, took refuge here . . . and they have Orain captive; he has been in their hands since the battle. Now they are using him to parley—" she could see his jaw move as he swallowed and said, "I offered them safe-conduct across the Kadarin, or wherever they wished to go, and both their lives, and to leave Lyondri's son safe in Nevarsin, and have him reared as kinsman at my court, with my own sons. But they—they—" He broke off, and Romilly saw that his hands were trembling.

"Let me tell her, Uncle," Alderic said gently. "I sent word I would surrender myself in exchange for my father, and go with them where they wished across the Kadarin to safety, to whatever place they should appoint for refuge; I also made offer of copper and silver—"

"The long and short of it is," Jandria said, "that precious pair have demanded that Carolin surrender *himself* to them for Orain's life. I, too, offered to exchange myself—I thought Lyondri might agree to that. And Maura said she would give herself up to Rakhal, even go with him into exile if that was what he wished, so that Carolin might have his paxman.

But—" her face was grim, "Let her see what answer they sent us."

Ruyven fumbled with a little package wrapped in yellow silk. His hands shook dreadfully. Carolin took the silk from him and tried to unwrap it. Maura laid her hands over his, stroked them for a moment, then opened the bloodstained cloth.

Inside—Romilly thought that she would retch—was a calloused finger. Clotted blood caked the end where it had been cut from the hand; and the horror was, that one finger bore a copper ring, set with a blue stone, which she had seen on Orain's hand.

Carolin said, "They sent word—they would return Orain to me—a little piece at a time—unless I surrendered myself to them, and made complete submission of my armies." His hands were shaking, too, as he carefully wrapped up the finger again. "They sent this two days ago. Yesterday it was—it was an ear. Today—" he could not go on; he shut his eyes, and she saw the tears squeezing from his eyes.

"For Orain I would give my life and more, and he has always know it," Carolin said, "but I—I have seen what Rakhal has done to my people—how can I give all of them over to him and his butcher Lyondri?"

"Orain would let himself be cut into little pieces for you, and you know that—" Maura said, and Carolin lowered his head and sobbed. "Lyondri knows that, too. Damn him! Damn him waking and sleeping—" His voice rose, almost in hysteria.

"Enough." Maura laid a gentle hand on his, took the horrid silk package from him and set it aside.

Jandria said grimly "I swear, I shall not sleep nor drink wine till Lyondri has been flayed alive—"

"Nor I; but that will not save Orain from his fate," said Carolin. "You come when we have lost hope, and are almost ready to storm the city, so that Orain may have a death that is swift and clean. Yet somehow we must find out where they are keeping him, and he has managed to shield the city against *laran*. But we still have one sentry-bird, and we thought, perhaps—we could fly her; she has not been manageable since the battle, Ruyven could not handle her—"

Maura said, "And Ranald was killed in the final charge, where we thought you too had died. But Ruyven said you were not dead, that he would have felt you die—and the Swordswomen could not find your body. But we knew not where you had gone. Yet perhaps, if we can find out in what part of the city they have kenneled for their filthy work—if we enter the city, they have threatened, they will start to cut him to pieces at that moment, and we may have what is left by the time we have searched long enough to find him." Her face twisted with dread and horror. "So we cannot search at random, and—and somehow his *leronyn* have guarded the city—but perhaps they would not notice a bird—"

"They would see a sentry-bird at once," said Romilly. "Their *leronyn* would be aware of just such a plan—"

"That is what I told them," Ruyven said, "but it seemed a chance—if you can handle Temperance—"

"Better that I should send Preciosa," said Romilly. "She would not come into the army with me, but flew away—but I can call her." Had she ever believed that she would not use her *laran* again? It was, like her body and her life, at Carolin's service. No land could survive with a mountain-cat like Lyondri at its head. No; the cat killed because it was its nature from hunger or fear, but Rakhal and Lyondri for power alone.

"That might do," said Carolin, "They might think her only a wild hawk—the Gods know there are enough of them in the country round Hali, and you might spy out where Orain is being held, so that we can make directly for that place, and they will have to surrender Orain or kill him quick and clean."

Somewhere a horn blew; Carolin started and cringed. "That is their accursed summons," he said weakly, "It was at this hour—just before sunset—that they came on the other two days, and while I sit here trying to summon courage to storm the city, Orain—" his voice failed again. Again the horn sounded, and Carolin went out of his tent. A common soldier came toward him, with insolent bearing. In his hand he bore a little packet of yellow silk. He bowed, and said, "Carolin, pretender to the throne of the Hasturs, I have the honor to return another portion of your faithfully sworn man. You may take pride in his bravery."

He laughed, a jeering, raucous laugh, and Alderic leaped forward.

"Wretch whom I will honor by calling *dog*, I will at least rid you of that laugh—" he shouted, but Jandria flung her arms round him.

"No, Deric, they will only revenge themselves on Orain—"

The soldier said, "Do you not want to see what token they have sent you of your paxman's bravery and devotion?"

Carolin's hands were shaking. Jandria said, "Let me," released Alderic and unwrapped the horrid packet. Inside there was another finger. The soldier said, "This is the message of Lyondri. We weary of this play. Tomorrow it will be an eye; the next day, the other eye; and the day after that, his testicles. Should you hold out beyond that, it will be a yard of skin flayed from his back—"

"Bastards! Sons of bastards!" cursed Carolin, but the soldier turned his back and, to the sound of the trumpet again, walked within the gates of the city.

"Follow him with *laran!*" commanded Carolin, but although Ruyven, Maura and Alderic all sought to do so—Romilly could sense it, tried to follow the man with her special senses—it was as if her body rammed against an impregnable wall of stone; as soon as the man was inside the gates, she could not reach him. Carolin was shaking with horror, unable to even shed tears; Maura held him tightly in her arms.

"My dearest, my dearest, Orain would not have you surrender—"

"Avarra protect me, I know that—but ah, if I could only kill him quickly—"

Inside the tent again he said with implacable fury, "I *cannot* let them blind him, geld him, flay him. If we can think of nothing this night, tomorrow at dawn I storm the city with everything I have to throw at them. I will send word that no citizen will be harmed who does not raise hand against me, but we will search every house till we find him; and at least there will be a swift end to his torment. And then the tormenters will come into *my* hands."

Yet Romilly knew, watching him, that Carolin was a decent man; he would do nothing worse, even to Lyondri Hastur, than to kill him. He might hang him, ignobly, and expose his corpse for a warning, rather than giving him a nobleman's swift death by the sword; yet Lyondri would still be in better case than Orain, should it go on so far. Carolin sent word quietly through the army to make ready to storm the gates at dawn.

"Can your hawk see well enough in the dark to lead us to where Rakhal hides with his torturers? I do not think he did this by himself, alone—" he gestured weakly at the little packet.

"I do not know," said Romilly quietly, but while they spoke, a plan had been maturing in her.

"How many men watch the city walls?"

"I do not know; but they have sentry-birds all along the wall, and fierce dogs, so that if anyone tries to sneak into the

327

city by breaking the side gates—we tried that once—the birds and the dogs set up such a racket that every one of Rakhal's men is wakened and rallies to that spot," he said despondently.

"Good," said Romilly quietly. "That could hardly be better."

"What do you say—"

"Think, my lord. My *laran* is of small use against men. And you say Rakhal's *leronyn* have guarded the city against our *laran*—*laran* such as your men use. But I fear no bird, no dog ever whelped, nothing that goes on four legs or flies on a wing. Let me go into the city alone, before dawn, and search that way, my lord."

"Alone? You, a girl—" Carolin began, then shook his head.

"You have proved again and again that you are more than a girl, Swordswoman," he said quietly. "It is worth a risk. If it fails, at least we will have some notion before dawn where to strike first, so they will have to give him a quick death. But let the night fall first; and you have had a long ride. Find her some proper food, Jandria, and let her go and sleep a little."

"I could not sleep—" Romilly protested.

"At least, then, rest a little," Carolin commanded, and Romilly bent her head.

"As you will."

Jandria took her to the tent of the Swordswomen, then, and found her food and fresh clothing.

"And washing-water and a comb," Romilly begged, so Jandria brought her hot water from the army's mess fires, and Romilly washed, combed out her tangled hair—Jandria, who helped her, finally had to cut it very short—and climbed gratefully into the clean soft underlinen and fresh tunic and breeches. She had no boots except the countrywoman's, but she put clean stockings on her feet under them. What a relief it was, to be clean, dressed, to eat cooked food, to be human. . . .

"And now you must rest," Jandria said, "Carolin commanded it. I promise you, I will have you called at the midnight hour."

Romilly lay down beside Jandria on the blanket roll. The light of the waning moon came into the tent, and Romilly thought, with a great sadness, of Ranald lying beside her when last the moons were full. Now he was dead, and it seemed so bitter, so useless. She had not loved him, but he had been kind to her, and she had first accepted him as a man, and she knew she would remember him and mourn for him a little, forever. Jandria lay silent at her side, but she knew that Jandria, too, mourned; not only because of Orain's peril, but for Lyondri Hastur who had once been to her what Ranald was to Romilly herself, the first to rouse womanhood and desire. And she could not even think of him with the sweet sadness of the dead; he had gone further from her, become a monster—she put her arms around Jandria, and felt the woman shaking with grief.

There has been so much sorrow, all useless. In my pride, I too have brought grief on those who have done me no harm. I will do my uttermost to save Orain from the fate they have measured for him; it looks hopeless, but not all porridge cooked is eaten. But whichever way it goes, if I am alive at dawn I shall send word to Father and Luciella that I live and they must not grieve for me.

Jandria's sorrow is worse than mine. Orain, if he dies, I will mourn, because he was my friend and because he died nobly for Carolin, whom he loves. But who could mourn, or have any feeling except relief, if Lyondri can do no more evil?

She held Jandria's sobbing body in her arms, and at last felt her drop away into sleep.

She had slept for an hour or two, when Jandria shook her shoulder softly.

"Get up, Romilly. It is time."

Romilly splashed her face with cold water, and ate a little more bread, but she refused wine. For this she must be perfectly alert. Carolin was waiting for her in his tent, his face composed and grim. He said, "I hardly need tell you that if you free Orain—or save him any more suffering, even if you must put your own dagger through his heart—you may name your own reward, even if you wish to marry one of my own sons."

She smiled at the thought; why should she wish to do that? She said, speaking as if he were the *Dom* Carlo she had first known, "Uncle, I will do what I can for Orain because he was kind to me beyond all duty when he thought me only a runaway hawkmaster's apprentice. Do you not think a Swordswoman and a MacAran will risk herself as well for honor as from greed?"

"I know it," Carolin said gently, "but I will reward you for my own pleasure, too, Romilly."

She turned to Jandria. "The boots will make too much noise. Find me a pair of soft sandals, if you will." When Jandria had brought a pair of her own—they were too big, but Romilly bound them tightly on her feet—she tied her hair into a dark cloth, so that no stray gleam would give her away, and smeared her face with dirt so that it would not shine in a watchman's lantern. Now she could go noiselessly into the city, and she feared no sentry-bird nor dog. At this hour, certainly, all but a few men would be sleeping.

Alderic said in a tone that brooked no denial, "I will go with you to the side gate."

She nodded. He too had a touch of this *laran*. She held his hand, silently, as they stole on their soft shoes away from Carolin's tent, making a wide circle away from the gates. Somewhere a dog barked; probably, she thought, sending out a questing tendril of awareness, at a mouse in the streets; but she silenced him anyway, sending out thoughts of peace and drowsiness . . .

"The gate will creak if you try to open it, even if you can quiet the sentry-birds," whispered Alderic, and without a word, made a stirrup of his hand as if he helped her to mount a tall horse; she caught at the top of the small side-gate and climbed to the top, looking down on the sleeping city by moonlight.

She sent out her thoughts to the sentry-birds, sending out peace, quiet, silence . . . she could see them on the walls now, great ugly shapes with their handlers, like statues against the sky. A disturbance and they would scream, awakening all of Rakhal's armies. . . .

Peace, Peace, silence . . . through their eyes she looked down at the moon-flooded streets, which lay dark, with only, now and again, a single lighted window . . . one after another she reached out to investigate them. Ordinary *laran* was clouded, but reaching into the minds of animals, she could feel silence . . . behind one lighted window, a woman struggled to give birth to a child and a midwife knelt, holding her hands and whispering encouragement. A mother sat beside a sick child, singing in a voice hoarse with worry and weariness. A man wounded somewhere in the war tossed with the fever in the stump on his leg. . . .

A dog snarled from a side street, and Romilly knew it would burst into a frenzy of barking . . . she reached out, silenced it, felt its bewilderment, where had the disturbing one gone . . . ? She crept silently past.

Now she was far from the walls, the sentry-birds silent. Would they have thought to guard the rest of the city against *laran?* Or had it stretched the few *leronyn* at Rakhal's command, to guard the gates, so that they were open inside the city?

Carefully, ready to retreat at a moment's touch, she reached out. . . . Orain had little *laran*, she knew, but he was not head-blind and she could *feel* him somewhere; he lay wakeful with the pain of his injuries . . . she must not let him feel her presence; he might be monitored by Rakhal's or Lyondri's sorcerers. Yet she moved, softly, nearer to him, block by block of the ancient city, and as she stole quietly through, no dog barked, no mouse in the walls squeaked aloud. *Silence, silence, peace on the city.* Horses drowsed in their stables, cats left off chasing mice and dozed before hearths, restless babies quieted under the powerful spell; from one end to the other of the ancient city of Hali, no living soul felt anything but peace and silence. Even the woman in labor fell into a peaceful sleep, and the midwife dozed at her side.

Peace, calm, silence. . . .

Outside a silent house near the opposite wall—she had traversed the whole city in her entranced spell—Romilly became aware of the two minds she had touched before. Orain; Orain lay within, somnolent under the sleep-spell that she had put on all things, but through it she could feel pain, fear, despair, a hope that perhaps he could somehow manage to die. Carefully, carefully, she thrust out a tendril of thought. . . .

Keep silence, do not move or stir lest someone be alerted when you wake. . . .

The door creaked, but so still was all within that the sleeping man outside Orain's door did not stir. Beyond him, in an inner room, she sensed the stony wall of Lyondri Hastur's thoughts—he too was deeply troubled. *The dreadful thing is that Lyondri is not a cruel man by nature. He will not even watch the torturer who does his beastly work. He does this only for power!*

His thoughts seemed to quest out, seeking an intruder . . . Romilly quickly submerged her own mind in that of a cat, sleeping across the hearth, and after a moment Lyondri Hastur slept . . . the watchman drowsed . . .

*Even if I kill him too swiftly for him to cry out—*Romilly's hands tightened on the dagger in her belt, *his death-cry even in thought will waken Lyondri! But perhaps he would stop at killing Orain with his own hands. . . .*

She must. There was no help for it. Then she realized that the watchmen was more deeply asleep than she, with her soothing consciousness extended throughout the whole city, could have managed; and felt another mind touch hers. Then there was a soft movement behind her, and she whirled, alert, dagger in hand—

"Don't kill me, Romilly," Caryl whispered. He was wearing a white child's night-gown, and his fair hair was tousled as if he had come from his bed. He reached out and gripped her in a great hug . . . *but not for one moment did the spell relax. . . .*

"Oh, Romilly, Romilly—I pleaded with my father, but he would not hear me—I cannot bear it, what they are doing to Orain—it—it hurts me too—have you come to take him away?" His whisper was all but inaudible. If Lyondri Hastur stirred in his sleep, and touched his son's mind, he would think him gripped in nightmare.

And Lyondri Hastur did this where his son could know of it, feel it. . . .

"He said it would harden me to the necessity of being cruel sometimes, when the good of the realm demands it," Caryl whispered, almost inaudibly, "I am—I am sickened—I did not think my father *could* do this—" and he struggled to hold back tears, knowing that would waken his father too . . .

Romilly nodded. She said, "Help me quiet the dogs as I go . . ."

But she could not take Orain sleeping. Silently, she stole past the sleeping watchman.

The torturer. He is worse than any brute; his mind is an animal's mind, otherwise I could not so easily enspell him. . . .

"Orain—" she whispered, and her hand went out to grip his mouth silent against an involuntary cry. *Remember you are dreaming this. . . .*

Orain knew instantly what she meant; if Lyondri wakened or his slumber lightened, he would think he wandered in dreams. . . . Softly, moving as noiselessly as Romilly herself, he drew himself to his feet. One of them was bleeding through a rough bandage. She had not seen the cut-off finger. But she fought to suppress her horror, to keep the sleep-spell strong, as he moved softly across the room, forced his feet, wincing, into his boots.

"I would not leave that man alive—" he whispered, glancing with implacable hate at his jailer, but he sensed, so close they were in rapport, Romilly's reason for not killing him, and contributed a single wry thought:

When Lyondri wakes and finds me escaped while he slept, what he will do to the man will be worse than your dagger

*through his heart; for mercy I should kill the man! But I am
not kind enough for that.*

The smell of the air told Romilly that dawn was nearing;
she would soon have to contend with dogs waking all over
the city, with the sentry-birds on the wall rousing, and if they
did *not* waken at the proper time, that too would alert their
handlers; they must be free of the city before then. She took
Orain's shoulder. His hand, too, was wrapped in rough bandages, and there was a patch over the cut-off ear which had
bled through. But he was not seriously harmed, and came
silently after her. Now they were outside the house, and she
came aware that Caryl was following them on noiseless feet,
in his nightgown.

"Go back!" She whispered, and shook the boy's shoulder.
"I cannot be responsible—"

"I will not return!" His voice was stubborn and set. "He is
no longer my father; I would be worse than he is, to stay
with him." She saw that great silent tears were rolling down
his face, but he insisted, "I can help you quiet the guards."

She nodded and signalled him to steady Orain, who was
limping. Now she must quiet pain, keep the tumult of his
thoughts and emotions under her own, and . . . yes, she must
let the birds wake normally, with ordinary cries, elsewhere in
the city, while keeping those near here safely entranced until
they had somehow made their escape—

They had reached the side gate. Caryl set a hand on the
latch and the lock gave way and swung open. There was a
horrendous creaking from the broken lock, a sound of tor-
tured metal and wood that rent the sky; everywhere, it
seemed, there was an uproar from the walls, but they dropped
all caution and ran, ran hurriedly through the camp and the
forming army, ran toward Carolin's tents . . . and then Carolin caught Orain in his arms, weeping aloud in relief and
joy, and Romilly turned and hugged Caryl tight.

"We're safe, we're safe—oh, Caryl, we could never have
done it without you—"

Carolin turned a little and opened his arms to clasp Romilly and Caryl in the same hug that encircled his friend.

"Listen," Orain said, "The racket—they know I am
gone—"

"Yet our army is here to guard you," said Carolin quietly.
"They shall not touch you again, my brother, if our lives answer for it. But now, I think, they will have to surrender; I
will not burn my people's city over their heads, but I will
spare any man who makes his submission and swears loyalty

to me. I think Rakhal and Lyondri will find few partisans this morning." He felt Orain flinch as the embrace touched the bandage over his ear.

"My brother, let me have your wounds tended—"

He brought him into the tent, and Maura and Jandria hastened to attend Orain. While the hacked fingers and ear were bandaged, Carolin sat blinking back tears in the lamplight.

"How can we reward you, Romilly?"

"There is no need of reward," she said. Now it was over, she was shaking, and glad to feel Alderic's arm supporting her, holding a wine-cup to her lips. "It is enough that now my lord Orain knows—" she did not know what she was going to say until she heard herself saying it, "that even though I am only a girl, I have no less courage or worth than any boy!"

Orain's arms swept out and he hugged her close, knocking the bandage loose and bleeding all over her. "Sweetheart, sweetheart," he whispered, holding her tight and crooning to her like a child, "I did not mean—I could not want you that way, but always I wanted to be your friend . . . only I felt such a fool—"

She knew she was crying too as she hugged him and kissed his cheek. She found herself in his lap like a child, while he stroked her hair. Orain held out his free hand to Alderic and said, "They brought me news that you had offered to exchange yourself for me, my son—what have I done to deserve that? I have never been a father to you—"

"You gave me life, sir," said Alderic quietly. "I owe you that, at least, since you have had nothing else from me of love or respect."

"Perhaps because I have not deserved it," Orain said, and Caryl came to his knees and hugged Orain too, and Romilly who was still in his lap. Carolin said, finding his voice through thickness in his throat, "You are all here and safe. That is enough. Caryl, I swear I shall be a father to you, and you shall be brought up with my own sons. And I will not kill Lyondri if I can help it. He may leave me no choice, and I cannot now trust his oath or his honor; but if I can, I shall let him live out his life in exile."

Caryl said shakily, "I know you will do what is honorable, Uncle."

"And now if you are all done with your love-feast," said Jandria, waspishly, "I would like to bandage this man up again so he will not be bleeding into our breakfast!"

Orain grinned at her and said, "I'm not hurt as badly as

that. The man knew his business as well as any army surgeon. He made it quick, at least. They told me, though—" and suddenly he shuddered, and said, shaking, "You came just in time, Romilly."

He took her hand in his undamaged one. He said gently, "I cannot marry you, child. It is not in my nature. But if Carolin gives leave, I will betrothe you to my son—" and he looked up at Alderic. "I can already see that he is willing."

"And nothing would please me better," said Ruyven, coming to smile at Alderic.

"Then that's settled," Orain said, smiling, but Romilly pulled loose in outrage.

"And am I to have nothing to say about this?" she demanded, and her hand went to her ear where the earring had been torn loose. "I am not free of my vows to the Swordswomen until the year has ended. And then—" she grinned a little nervously at Alderic and Ruyven, "I know now that however good my *laran*, it is still not properly trained, or I could have done better with it. It betrayed me on the battlefield, when Sunstar was killed . . . I came near to dying with him because I did not know how to keep myself clear. If they will have me—" she looked from Ruyven to Alderic, "I will go to a Tower, and learn what I must do to master my *laran* so that it will not master me. And then I must make my peace with my father and stepmother. And then—" she smiled now, waveringly, at Alderic, "Then, perhaps, I will know myself well enough to know if I want to marry you—or anyone else, my lord."

"Spoken like a Swordswoman," Jandria said approvingly, but Romilly hardly heard, Alderic sighed, then took her hand.

"And when that is done," he said quietly, "I shall await your decision, Romilly."

She clasped his fingers, but only for a moment. She was not sure; but she was no longer afraid.

"My lord," she said to Carolin, "Have I leave to take your kinsman to the tent of the Swordswomen and find him some breeches?" She looked at Caryl, who flushed with embarrassment and said, "Please, Uncle. I—I cannot show myself to the army in a night-gown."

Carolin laughed and said, "Do as you wish, hawkmistress. You have been faithful to me, and to those I love. And when you have done your duty to your *laran* and to your parents and to the one who would marry you, I shall expect you to come back to us in Hali." He turned and took Maura's hand, saying, "I pledged to you that we would celebrate our Midsummer-festival in Hali, did I not? And the next moon will see us at Midsummer. If it will please you, Lady—I had thought to make the hawkmistress's marriage at the same time as her Queen's. But we can wait for that." He laughed aloud and said, "I am not so much of a tyrant as that. But one day, Romilly, you will be hawkmistress to the reigning king as you were in exile."

She bowed and said, "I thank you, sir." But her mind, ranging ahead, was already seeking the walls of Tramontana Tower.